For David

who treats me like the princess I always wanted to be

ADDITIONAL INFORMATION FOR THE READER

At the back of this book the reader will find additional information which may be helpful as a reference. There is a list identifying the modern names of the fifth century places on the map. There is also a guide to Celtic pronunciations and a list of characters, including their relationships to each other and their roles in the stories.

Robyn Lamm

1

BLAISE

There was an aura of sadness about the lady who stood before me which went beyond that of the usual parent dropping off a child. She was definitely a lady, defined by the lift of her chin and the fur-trimmed cloak of sky-blue velvet that did not quite hide a gown of matching blue silk.

I dismissed the priest who had brought her in with a hand gesture, rose from my desk, and escorted her to a chair before the fireplace. "May I take your cloak?" I asked, but she shook her head no and clutched at the edges as if she thought I might physically strip her of it. I tried to put her at ease. "May I offer you a glass of wine, my Lady?"

Finally she sat, with a graceful swirl of skirts, declining the wine with a timid voice. I took the chair across from her and smiled. "Let me introduce myself," I said. "I am Master Blaise, the Headmaster. I've been running this school for boys for fifteen years and the school has been in existence since before the Romans left."

She nodded, but did not interrupt.

"We take all boys, regardless of their religious beliefs or their status in society. We teach them how to read and write, the fundamentals of Latin if they don't know it, practical and theoretical mathematics, music including instruction on instruments and voice. We also teach history and the reasons for its importance as well as the basic awareness of nature – animal, plant and star - and how to behave in a civilized manner."

Once again she nodded.

"Most of our students are sent by noble families and returned to their homes by the time they are twelve or thirteen for training in military arts, but we also teach those few with selective talents to become Druids."

She lifted an eyebrow at this, which did not surprise me since her hand flew to a small gold cross at her throat, but she said nothing and gestured for me to continue.

"There is no easy path to become a Druid," I told her. "It takes twenty years of advanced study in all facets of nature, music and law, all laced with a thorough knowledge of ceremony to the one God with all his faces. That is why you will see men here, still dressed in the robes of a novice."

This brought a strong and quick response. "If Druids truly believe in one God, it seems they are not that distant from Christians. Am I wrong?"

A correct answer to this would have taken too much time to fully explain, so I side stepped it. "There is a nearby monastery. Their priests and our priests often study together, and meet for discussion. We have much in common. We respect the teachings of Jesus Christ, and we try to share our beliefs that for every action there is an opposite reaction, and that all living things must be respected and protected."

I waited, but she said nothing.

After a long pause where I actually stood and paced about and she sat staring at her lap, I became abrupt. "Why are you here, my Lady?"

Her eyes – very blue eyes – met mine. She must be truly desperate, I thought, for she was Romanized and Christian and the priests had evidently failed to subdue her offspring – to the point that she was willing to allow him to learn the Old Ways.

"Emrys," she said. "My son." She looked around the room for the first time, and then at me. "I'm sorry. I've been rude. I'm King Maelgwyn's daughter. Of Dementia. Please sit down again."

She waited until I accommodated her, then continued. "Emrys will have no place at court, but he's very bright. He was eight months old when he began talking. Not baby babble, but full sentences, grammatically correct. I have hired the best tutors that I can find, but none of them will stay." She looked down again at the hands she had nestled in her lap again.

I knew she was telling me that her brothers were the heirs and their children after them. In the Romanized world, women did not inherit. She was also telling me that there was something wrong with her son.

"Is it your father?" I asked then realized how rude that sounded. "It's rather common for kings to educate sons who will follow them to the throne, and ignore their other children and grandchildren," I explained.

"No, it's not that. He doesn't really care. It's the tutors themselves, you see. They all leave, sometimes within days, even hours."

"There's a behavior problem?"

She looked horror stricken. "Oh, no, not that. Actually, he seems to know more than they do which embarrasses and infuriates them. You see, he has complete access to his grandfather's library, and he reads all the time."

"His grandfather must have a wonderful library," I said dryly.

Her eyes swept the crowded shelves around us. "Oh, not like this. Yours is much grander."

"I study and write the history of our people," I said proudly, then bit my lip. Why was I trying to impress her? Was it the boy? I'll admit I was intrigued. "Have you a place to stay in the area?"

She nodded.

"All the boys live here and I know we can make room for him. Let us take young Emrys for a week. If we can help him, we'll discuss payment when you return. How old is the child, by the way?"

"He's seven."

"Seven," I repeated thinking how she'd claimed that he knew more than his tutors. A prodigy? Emrys could prove to be very interesting.

I thought of something else. "What of the King? Will your father object to his being here?"

She lifted her chin slightly. "The King of Dementia will not care."

2

BLAISE

I had the boy brought in. Everyone's heard of Merlin now, but when I first met him, he was a skinny child, who stood so close to this mother that he seemed to be wearing her skirts. He wasn't called Merlin then, of course, for that was a title that came much later, when he'd earned it.

Our High Priest or Archdruid became known by the title of Merlin. I suppose the first person who held this title was given it because the merlin – a small falcon, was excellent at catching his prey and this first Merlin was excellent at catching men's souls, an important job for those early Druids who had to train their recruits in secrecy.

Again I will stress that Merlin was a title, not the name of an individual. This has caused historians confusion, for centuries passed and tales of the Merlin all came to be identified with one man, which of course caused difficulties, for one man could hardly have lived for hundreds of years. So it came to be said that since Merlin could not have lived so long nor had so many different stories applied to him, he never lived at all – he was a myth.

The Merlin I am writing about was no myth. He was my student who became my superior and my friend, and it is to him that I owe the following history, for from the time he was a young man until he disappeared from this world, he visited me frequently and wrote voluminous letters to me, describing the doings of soldiers and kings. Even after he was gone, he arranged to keep the information coming through his replacement advisor to the king, Nimue, the Lady of the Lake.

Here in the beginning when we first met, I had no inkling that this scrawny child who would not look me in the eye would change my life – change all our lives, every man and woman in Britannia, for this child would be so famous that our school would become the premier destination for boys, and my humble histories would be read and studied by our leaders.

He would become the greatest of all Merlins – the kingmaker who would crown our three High Kings – Ambrosius Aurelianus, Uther Pendragon and the Arthur who made them all into legends.

"This is my son, Emrys," the princess said. "And this is Master Blaise, Emrys. He is the headmaster here."

There was no response until she nudged him forward, her expression – desperation – easy to read. The boy's was unfathomable. Still, he bowed politely. "Master Blaise."

"There's no need to bow to anyone here," I told him.

He studied me quite openly at that, probably to see what weaknesses I had.

"Has your mother told you that you'll be staying here on Ynys Witrin?"

"Yes, Master. I'm here to learn what you can teach me."

It was seemingly a careful, compliant answer, but the slight raise of his voice at the end, made it not only a question, but a challenge.

It was such a surprise that I nearly laughed out loud. I made myself a little taller and spoke in a stern voice. "Yes, you will learn."

I turned away with a sharp swish of my robes, pausing at the door. "Stay here and bid your mother farewell, lad. Someone will come in shortly and show you to your quarters and then to your classroom." With a slight bow of my head to the princess, I left them alone.

3

BLAISE

Emrys lasted until noon in classes. I had placed him with boys his own age, but the teacher left the students to read Sophocles by themselves and took him to a class with older boys. That teacher, a good and patient man, took me aside before we reached the tables. The initiates were serving. An array of delicious odors passed us in the form of trays heaped with fresh bread, bowls of apples and tureens of savory lamb stew.

"I have nothing to teach him, Master Blaise." He ran his fingers through thinning grey hair and frowned. "I think he could teach me."

"He's seven years old, Orvid," I said.

"Ah, you're discussing the prodigy." Morgwy, a stout man with a heart as big as his belly, joined us. "It didn't take long to see that he didn't belong with my youngsters. You say he's ahead of the older boys too, Orvid?"

"In every subject."

"Every subject?" Caius joined us and cocked his head in that way he had, lips drawn in a half smile. "Is he an expert on Druid ways, too? With a Christian upbringing?"

I smiled back at him, shaking my head no. "Happen the mysteries might bring a challenge to our young one."

"Should I take him in my class after our noon repast?" he asked.

"No. First he'll need some preparation. I'll take him on myself."

4

BLAISE

Reviewing the teachers' comments, I have to admit that I faced Emrys with trepidation, but within the first hour I discovered that not only was I enjoying him, but that he was enjoying me. It seemed we were fated for a long and easy friendship.

It began when I threw out a friendly challenge. "Emrys, what do you know about God?"

"You teach theology, Master? You wear no turned collar."

"I do teach theology. I'm not a Christian priest."

He folded his arms and narrowed his eyes, but he kept his gaze steady, and the expression on his face clearly showed that he wondered what trick I was trying on him.

I sat behind my writing desk, legs crossed, body in a relaxed position, and I waited without moving, my eyes on his, my expression friendly, but firmly waiting for an answer to my question until he finally looked away. I continued waiting.

He looked back. No, I hadn't moved.

"Do you want the answer the priests taught me? I can give it verbatim."

I laughed. "I'm sure you can, but that's not what I'm after. I want your own thoughts on the matter."

He took a moment to rearrange himself, hooking stick legs around the chair, and using his rather large hands to gesture as he talked.

"I'm pretty sure the old Romans didn't have it right. Seems they borrowed their pantheon of gods from the Greeks more as a convenience than out of faith. In fact, it doesn't seem at all a matter of faith with those Romans I've read.

"The Christians and the Jews with their concept of one God may be on the right trail, but something went wrong when the Jews denied their own Messiah. Now that might be because they were too stubborn to accept new ideas from a man who had no formal position in their community, or because of jealousy, or because of politics within their own hierarchy, or because the Christ was truly a fake. I don't know."

Now totally engaged he leaned forward, hands lighting for a moment on his knees.

"I do like the ideas of love and respect that Jesus taught, but I don't care for the way the church was directed by Paul.

"I think Britannia's Pelagius had the right of it in the battle with Germanicus and the Pope. I don't think man was born sinful and I don't think it's necessary for an intermediary/priest to be the only bridge to communicating with a higher power. The church took one serious step away from truth when the Pelagians were excommunicated and another earlier one when Constantine's Nicene Council decided to declare God a triumvirate of three persons in one."

Oh my. He not only knew about Pelagius, who had been recalled to Rome and executed in my lifetime, but about the earlier Council of Nicaea where Emperor Constantine had ordered all the various Christian sects to come together and agree on a common doctrine?

All Druids are trained to control their emotions, so outwardly I showed none, though his words filled me with excitement. Oh, not the specific analysis, but the fact that a child could have taken such knowledge, actually thought about it at age seven, and used it to form a philosophy at all. Already he was Druid by the act of questioning, apparently a natural part of his thinking process.

It struck me that though the scrawny body of a young child sat before me, he was an old and wise soul, returned to teach us all, but, of course, I didn't let my expression change in the slightest degree, nor the tone of my voice. "Why do you think the Pelagian philosophy was native to Britannia?" I asked.

He stared at me, evaluating openly.

"You don't want the simple answer that Pelagius lived in Britannia, do you?"

I shook my head.

"Did it have to do with his background?"

"That's part of it. In the earliest days of Christianity, the followers of Christ spread apart to bring his message to places that had not known him. Joseph of Arimathea, he who had provided Christ's tomb, came to Britannia with his son and a dozen or so followers and built the first Christian church here on our island. They and those of later generations, by the way, have lived next to us and are friendly. We have learned about their religion and they have learned about ours and we live peaceably, sharing our island in harmony."

"I see," he said. "So the descendants of Joseph were not influenced by those who became Roman Catholics."

"That's right, and until recently when they decided that their way is the only way, they left us in Britannia alone. When I was a child, the great Pelagius led the church and many followed his teachings which were based on loving mankind as Jesus taught. The people loved him, but the Roman Catholics called him to Rome and executed him."

"So because we're on an island away from the rest of the Empire we were isolated from influence from the Roman church and now they want us to believe what they do."

It was like talking to an adult. No, not just any adult - an adult educated in the Roman way.

"Correct. Do you still consider us Roman?"

He looked down to think and drew circles on the floor with the toe of his boot, though I don't believe he was aware of it.

"I realize," he said at last, "that it's been some years since the legions withdrew totally, but they'll be back when they've contained the barbarians. My grandfather is sure of that."

This was the first time he had credited a source to any of his statements. It didn't matter to me that it was his grandfather - it could have been a tutor, or a book.

I deliberately challenged his conclusion to see how he would answer. "What if they don't come back?"

A very blank look came over him. Later I was to recognize this as the Merlin in prophecy mode and grab at quill and parchment to take down every word, but this time it was so quick that I didn't at first realize what had happened.

"No," he said. "They won't come back."

"Probably not," I prompted.

"Grandfather's wrong. This time they won't beat the barbarians back."

This was the first time I'd seen it, yet I pride myself in recognizing what was happening to him. If this was just more clever analysis I wondered, why the vacancy in his eyes and why was it so quickly gone?

"You seem very sure. How do you know this?"

He shrugged, looked down while he inwardly debated whether or not to tell me the truth.

I realized he was testing me when he spoke. "I had a nurse once who followed the old ways. She called it a gift."

Again I struggled with excitement, but answered him calmly. "I want to understand this very clearly. You see things that will happen in the future? Somehow you know they are right?"

He nodded, meeting my gaze unflinchingly with eyes that were momentarily a piercing blue.

"And are they? Right?"

He shrugged again, and his mouth twisted.

"Yes," he admitted with just a touch of pride.

I did not let him know how important this was.

"Does your mother know about this ability?"

"I don't usually tell anyone."

His mouth pursed as he admitted, "Sometimes, though, when I'm not careful, it just comes out."

His legs unwound slowly, one foot flat on the floor, the other on the ball as if he were about to spring up and run away, but he was still thinking it through.

"It's usually okay. They think I'm making it up."

"Why don't you just tell everyone?"

"Because - because they don't believe me."

He looked truly miserable. Eyes back on the floor, shoulders rounded in discouragement.

He needed to know that I could be trusted in what he told me. "That's because you've lived with a Christian family," I said.

A puzzled look crossed his face. "Would you believe me?"

"I believe what you said about the Romans."

I let the statement hang, and was rewarded with a dazzling smile - a smile that told me how unusual it was that anyone believed in him.

"It must be very difficult," I continued, "to have such an unusual talent discouraged. We won't do that here. In fact, we encourage it, and we'll help you to develop and control it."

It was his turn to struggle with excitement, but he had not been trained for over twenty years in our ways and I saw it easily, and saw too that most of his previous desires had been dashed with disappointment. He would not let himself hope too much.

"What do you know of the Old Ways?"

He sat up very straight, both feet on the floor, and thought before he spoke. "There seem to be quite a few gods, Master Blaise. There are offerings made to the appropriate god at a time of need. For example, if a man is cutting wood, he thanks the god of the tree first, or if he's traveling, he leaves offerings at the crossroads in hopes that he will be safely kept."

I nodded, encouraging him to go on.

"The gods are honored by festivals - yearly festivals - each god in his season."

I thought him finished, but just as I was about to speak, he added, "I've heard that only the simple folk believe in these things nowadays - that it's what used to be Druid belief dissolving into myth because there are no more Druids. The Romans didn't like the Druids. They killed them. Long ago."

"Yes. It was eighteen years after the Emperor Claudius conquered Albion. The Roman general, Paulinus, sought to rip the soul from our tribes by destroying the Druids," I told him - or, more probably, reminded him.

"Paulinus thought he had succeeded by driving them all to the island of Ynys Mon. After an initial standoff with the men casting spells of magic and the women shrieking curses that seemed to paralyze the soldiers, they were shamed by their Roman leader into attacking. It wasn't a battle, it was a slaughter. After the bodies were thrown into huge stacks and fired, the Romans went after the oak circles and the standing stones, destroying all the sacred places. Why would they do that?" I asked him.

I watched his face and saw that several thoughts were considered and tossed away.

"It obviously wasn't because the Romans were Christian and hated them for believing in many gods, since the Romans weren't Christian then."

"True. It was also true that when the Romans conquered a land,

17

they generally left the local authorities in charge of local affairs and left other religions alone. But not with us. Why?"

"They - they must have been afraid of the Druids."

I could tell this was a new thought to him.

"You're right," I assured him. "They were afraid. Can you guess why?"

His eyes, now seeming more grey than blue, held mine in steady regard. "They must have been very powerful. The kings used them as advisors."

"There's another reason too," I told him, "and this applies to many situations. You must remember this and be able to use it." I saw his eyebrows lift in question and held back no longer.

"People are afraid of things they don't understand. They often don't take the time necessary to try to understand. Instead, they fear, they spread rumors, and fear breeds hatred as a result. It's hard to destroy something you fear and don't understand. It's easy to destroy something you hate."

His answer, "I see," did not say what was in his mind, but I saw that he had experienced hatred that could be explained by fear firsthand.

How could he not have with such incredible intelligence? Other children would have teased and belittled him. The tutors he had surpassed would have resented him, caretakers might have overpowered him with frightful punishments, and any adults with authority would have stifled his ability with whatever method they could.

His mother had probably protected him at times, but gone to her knees with a rosary at others, which might have done her good, but not him.

His grandfather? From what I knew of the king's temperament, I'm sure Emrys infuriated him.

5

BLAISE

"Let's go for a walk," I said, moving toward the door. "I've got something to show you."

This surprised him, but he wasted no time in following me. It was necessary to disavow some of his notions, and it seemed appropriate to begin that task immediately. He expected me to lead him to a new classroom, for he paused at several of the doors we passed, but I didn't slow down. Nor did my pace slacken as we left the building and took a trail leading into the forest, away from the lake he had crossed to reach our island.

We crossed a fast-flowing stream using six well-placed rocks. We stopped to watch a roe gather two fawns for a run away from us and followed them up a steep hillside, but made no move to chase after them when they went down the other side. Instead we edged along the ridge, high enough to see the lake again, until we came to a trail that twisted down to a valley green with trees.

Another trail crossed it and we took the left fork where the trees grew taller, blotting the path with shadows.

Not a word had passed between us all this time, but when we reached a circular clearing fenced with mighty oaks, he held back and I asked why. His narrow shoulders shrugged to indicate the words had no importance. "I - I just had a feeling. Silly."

"I don't think you've ever had a silly feeling in your life," I told him. "What is it?"

"Just that … for a moment … I thought I'd been here before. But I haven't ever been in these woods."

"And?"

He looked all around, observing everything carefully, then moved toward the center of the circle and stopped, his eyes shut, his arms spread wide, as if he were gathering sensations. "This is a place of power," he said seriously, then smiled apologetically, "whatever that means."

There were several large stones back by the trees. I led him to them and we sat. "Not all the Druids are dead," I told him. "I'm a Druid, and so are all the other teachers and many of the students. The word 'Druid' means one who knows. We are caretakers of the earth who study the world around us, so that we can know as much as possible.

"If you stay with us, we will teach you about the physical world and about the spiritual world and how to master the forces of each.

"You will also learn self-mastery, and we will begin now with a key Druid concept: to know, to dare, to keep silent. You must thirst to know all that you can, you must be daring in your search for knowledge, and you must keep silent about what you have learned."

I paused to see what he'd absorbed. He did not disappoint me. His eyes, blue again in the shadow of the great trees, burned with the light of enthusiasm. "Yes, I want to learn everything about every-thing. I can see that sometimes this will take daring." His head was nodding up and down. "I promise. I won't say a word to anyone."

I stopped him before he could spit on his hand or make some

other uncouth gesture of faith. "The work will not be easy. Here no one will force you to absorb a lesson you're not ready for, but also, no one will hold you back."

He was very solemn. "All right."

"Your first lesson is that a great deal of our teaching takes place in threes. Three is a sacred number - we'll learn about that later, but for now what is important is that man is able to remember three similar things when they're grouped together. It's harder to recall a group of four things, or five, and two could have similarities, but that's not enough to be memorable. Have you heard of Triads?" He nodded. "You will learn thousands of them - not just the words, but the meanings within." This had frightened some of my students, but I saw that he was easy with it.

"I would also like to clear up one misconception. Druids do not believe in many gods. We believe that all the gods are One God, but the One God has many faces. When we have a festival honoring the great goddess who shows the three stages of life or the gods of light or darkness, we are really honoring that aspect of the One God."

I stood up and indicated the circle about us. "You were right to feel power here. This is a Druid Circle - a sacred circle - a circle of Oaks, and it is where we conduct our ceremonies. It may have felt familiar to you, because you've been in other oak circles - possibly without noticing."

"The Romans burned the living circles," he said, not noticing that he used a euphemism.

"We've had nearly five hundred years to replenish them." I offered a hand and pulled him up from the stone. "Time to start back, but before we do I have two things to tell you."

"Not three?"

I laughed at his quick wit and he beamed his appreciation. "Always feel free to ask me a question. If you don't understand, ask. If you wonder about something, ask. The only stupid question is one that has never been asked."

"All right."

"The other thing I'd like you to think about is that sometimes when something feels very familiar to you - as the sacred circle did, it's because you've experienced it in a prior life." I looked to see if he would argue the point, but he was silent, deep in thought, and I did not disturb him as we walked back.

6

BLAISE

Thus began the lessons with my most difficult and most reward-
ing student, for he was both. I kept him as my own apprentice for all
of his years with us, occasionally sending him away for a month or
two of lessons with another Master who was more adept than I at a
particular specialty, and as time passed, we grew so close that it
seemed he was my own son. Indeed, he was my spiritual son if not
my natural son.

I tried to teach him the fundamentals of our faith in an orderly
natural progression that would first tease his senses, then lead to
thought provoking questions about the next logical steps, and end
with the mastering of a skill - the way we taught the other students,
but with Merlin, it was like trying to throw a saddle on an untamed
stallion.

The first month we were walking in the woods, and I was
teaching him the names of the plants we passed when we stopped to
share a meal. It was cool with a heavy mist blowing in from the lake,

so he ran off to gather brush and dead wood for a fire.

He returned, laid the sticks while he asked a question about a mathematical problem that had bothered him, and while describing it, he made a simple gesture with his hand. To my shock the wood flamed instantly. He didn't notice my reaction until, having finished his question, he looked up at me.

"Emrys? Where did you learn to start a fire like that?"

He looked puzzled. "I don't know. It's what I always do. Did I do it wrong?"

I didn't answer his question immediately, but he was already used to that and didn't object. "What did you grandfather have to say about your method?"

He pursed his lips, admitting, "He never saw me make a fire."

"Your mother?"

"Nor did she." His chin came up defiantly. "My nurse said I was too young to be playing with fire, but I wasn't playing with it, I was helping her. I tried to tell her that, but she threatened to beat me with a stick if I ever did it again."

"You frightened her."

"It was in the fireplace. It wouldn't have burned the palace down."

"That's not what she feared. What bothered her was the way you made the fire." A thought occurred to me. "Or did she make fire with a hand gesture, too?"

"No, she made sparks with flint then nursed the sparks into flame using straw."

"Have you ever seen anyone make a fire like you just did it?"

"Master Auliss lit the hall holder torches that way. I was walking behind him." He looked suddenly abashed. "I guess that's why I thought it would be all right with you."

"Oh, it's quite all right, Emrys." I smiled, emphasizing my words. "Very much all right. It's the first special skill we teach."

"Special skill? You mean magic?"

"The word 'magic' has a connotation that I don't like. It implies that a skill is really a trick, and when you use that skill, you do so to fool people, while what you're really doing is using a skill that they don't have and don't understand. It's just knowledge, Emrys - there for the taking if one learns and practices."

"That's why they didn't like me - because I knew different things than they did."

"Who's 'they?'"

"The town children." He was silent for a moment.

"Their mothers and fathers."

More silence.

"The servants."

Silence.

"My cousins and my uncles and my aunts."

The longest silence of all.

"My grandfather."

I considered carefully before I answered, remembering the rumors, understanding suddenly how difficult it was for a royal bastard in a royal household.

"Did you sometimes pretend not to know things? So they would like you more."

There was an affirmative flick of his head that sent his straight dark hair flying about his face.

"It did no good. I - I most often tried to ignore them."

He sat balanced on a log, hugging his knees and looking very small.

"It took me a while to figure it out. At first it confused me. When I was three, my grandfather learned that I could read when a scroll fell off his desk. I picked it up and as I handed it to him, I told him I knew it was precious because of what it said. He made me read it to him, then had me read a second scroll and a third. Then he slapped me so hard that I hit the wall across the room. My mother started screaming at him, but he outshouted her, calling me the devil's child.

That was when I figured out that I should hide what I knew."

I swallowed an angry exclamation, forcing myself to speak calmly. "Who taught you to read?"

"I don't think anyone really taught me. Mother read to me often, and when I realized that the stories were always told with the same words and that those words were on the scrolls, I figured out what they said."

"I suppose the stories were more comforting than the people around you," I said.

"Yes. I liked the stories. I didn't like the people. Except Mother. Whenever I could manage it, I hid so I could be by myself."

In his folded position he looked like he would still like to be hidden. "Where did you hide, Emrys?"

"The library when my tutor wasn't there. Guest rooms when there were no guests. A store room for medicines. The woman who took care of it was kind. She let me go there and taught me a little about crushing plants, mixing them, and their uses."

His eyes gleamed with excitement as he let his legs fall to the floor and leaned toward me.

"Can you keep a secret?"

"Of course."

"When I was four, one of my uncle's came home from a war. He decided I should learn to ride, so he saw that one of the groomsmen taught me."

I noticed that he didn't say the uncle taught him.

"By the time I was five I had a small horse allotted for my use, and six months after that he judged me competent to ride on my own, so I'd slip off by myself, usually riding the road by the river which ended at the mill. They had dogs there - sometimes litters of pups, and I liked to visit."

He lowered his voice.

"One day, before I got to the mill, I noticed a trail going up the hill."

His head came closer.

"It was a steep climb. The horse didn't like it much, but I kept him going and eventually we came to a clearing. That's where the spring was. Truly, not much of a spring, but it looked tended - the greens cleared away, and a cup so you could drink, resting close to where the water trickled out of the cliff. I understood what it was," he told me conspiratorially.

"It was Mryddin's spring, so when I drank, I gave the first cup as an offering to the old god."

I nodded, which satisfied him that he had done the proper thing.

"The next time I visited the spring, I followed the trail all the way up."

His eyes sparkled.

"There was a cave there. I threw a rock in, not wanting to be surprised by a wolf or something worse."

He laughed.

"Out came a stream of bats, like a plume of black smoke. Scared me so, that I was on the horse and halfway down the mountain before I realized it was just bats, and went back."

"You were brave," I told him.

"No, curious," he answered. "Mother always said I was too curious, and that I'd get in trouble by it someday, but I couldn't back away without knowing what it was."

Then, too," he gave me the testing look he often adopted - to see if I would reprimand his impetuousness, "I felt like I had to go in - like something was drawing me there."

"What was there?" I prompted.

"Well, nothing really. It was just a cave. The miller called it Myrddin's Cave."

Then, defensively, "It was a very nice cave. The floor was fairly level, and it was light from both the large entrance and from a hole near the ceiling, so that a shaft of light fell on the back wall when the sun was out. There was a series of ledges and niches, and I started storing things there. Some books I'd been given, experiments, plants, drawings I'd made - that sort of thing.

The best part of it, though, was that there was a secret cave inside. You had to climb up on one of the ledges and crawl to the hole, and of course it was dark, so you had to take a torch, but inside it was dry and larger than the outside cave, and you'd never see the entrance unless you knew just where to look, so it was safe. And the bats got used to me being there, but if anyone else came, they'd fly out, so I'd know. Oh, and I made a shelter for the horse so she wouldn't run off, and she'd be under cover if it rained, and I piled greens around it so no one could see it."

"Emrys," I said, wanting to understand it all, "why did you need a 'safe' hiding place? Everyone wants somewhere to be alone at times, but this sounds so much more. Were you in danger?"

"Yes," said quickly.

A shake of the head.

"No, probably not. It was just something I felt I had to do in case … in case something did happen."

"Was someone cruel to you?" I pressed.

"No one ever hit me after that one time. Once I - I thought my grandfather would, but Mother stepped between us and just stood there, staring at him until his fist hit the stone wall instead, and he turned and walked away. She told me he wasn't really angry at me, he was angry at her, but I - I should try to avoid being around him."

He looked down at the ground as if the rocks held the answer.

"She said the same thing about my uncles, but none of them wanted anything to do with me so that wasn't really a problem."

"So they were unkind?"

Both lips pressed together in a taut line.

"They said I couldn't be a knight because I had no father. My cousins were going to be great knights, they said, and go off to war and win battles."

He looked up and smiled.

"I don't really want to be a knight, but when I was very young, I wanted to be like them."

When he was young? He was all of seven and a half. I choked back a laugh. Smiled encouragingly.

"Everyone told me that I had no future at the palace. They were princes and princesses. I was nothing. The most I could hope for was to practice writing, so that I could be a scribe. Mother said I could be a priest, but when I told them that, they laughed and told me the devil's spawn could never be a priest."

"Now where would they get the idea that you were the devil's spawn, Emrys?"

I was pleased that he was sharing his most important secrets with me, and he didn't disappoint now.

"It was because of my mother. She wouldn't tell who my father was - no matter how much they threatened her. Some said I was the child of a slave, but most whispered that it was the devil, himself, come down to impregnate her."

"Why didn't they say it was an angel?"

That seemed a new idea to him. He considered it carefully before he answered.

"They would have had to honor us then, wouldn't they? Easier to hate us than to make us special."

I took him in my arms, for in some ways he was still a small child and needed comforting and I didn't think he'd had much comfort up to then. I was pleased that he came willingly.

"Emrys, you are special to your mother, and you are very, very special to me."

7

MERLIN

I can't believe my good fortune? I've been in Ynys Witrin a week now, and I think – no I hope that I can stay here. It's so different from my home. I'm actually beginning to think of this as my true home. They just can't send me away!

Here I'm encouraged to question what I've learned – not only what I was taught in Dementia, but things I've just learned here. I don't have to be careful to keep my thoughts to myself. The other boys don't tease me. They listen, and sometimes we argue – but in a friendly way. They don't call me names and make fun of me if we disagree. And the adults don't belittle me or hit me or send me away to my room. They actually treat me as if they're delighted to listen to me.

Master Blaise is the best. If I ask a question, he usually doesn't tell me the answer straight away, he asks me more questions until I eventually understand that I've been led to the answer. He's really teaching me to think for myself.

He's the most powerful man I've ever seen. It's not a blustery power, like my grandfather and my uncles. No, it's a power that one feels in his presence. Physically he's just an average man – not particularly comely, not ugly, not tall, not short, not young, not old. But when he enters a room, you feel his presence, and when you look around, you see that all eyes are upon him. He needs no weapon and no crown to make him the authority. He does not shout, but he is always heard. I want to be just like him when I'm grown up.

He's also kind. I can still hardly believe that he gave me this precious scroll for my own, so that I can write down my thoughts – my unformed, unimportant thoughts – and my questions.

Master Blaise is a Druid. I thought all the Druids were gone after the Romans came, but he says that one survived and began teaching others, and that Druids from Gaul helped them by sending them teachers. They were in hiding, of course, but most of the people still believed and helped hide them.

The word 'Druid' means to know, and it seems that all the Druids here want to know about everything – which, come to think of it, is probably why they even pay attention to me, since I'm new to them with different experiences that I can share. At any rate, it seems that by my very real desire to learn about everything, I am a Druid too – not in training, of course, but in attitude. That makes me want to do the training. It's supposed to be very hard – it takes twenty years. You have to learn thousands of Triads and hundreds of ballads, and all the laws. I want to try.

Master Blaise has entrusted me with a second very valuable scroll. It's not the original. He says that one is nearly five hundred years old and so faded that it's barely readable. What I have is the copy that he made from it, and from this copy many others have been made. I'm supposed to make a copy of my own to improve my penmanship, so here goes …

8

GWION

Something pulled him back to Abred. He sat down slowly, trembling, his head reeling with the disorientation of leaving the Otherworld so abruptly. Had he failed the last of his tests? He forced himself to concentrate, staring at a single stone, and when he knew it was clearly in the Realm of Matter, he stood, made the sign of banishment to end the Rite, and turned around slowly, counting the stones in the circle, seeing that all eight were real.

Now he could see beyond the stones. His eyes swept the woods, but the moon was dark and his fire had burned to embers, so he saw only shades of darkness. For a moment he hesitated, not sure what was expected of him. Surely the three days had passed. But where was Bladeludd? Was he supposed to make his own way back to the Cor? No, he remembered other Rites of Passage. Always there was a procession to bring the Acolyte back.

His senses told him he was alone. He took three deep breaths, slow and measured to his heartbeat. Should he rest a little and try the

Rite again?

Then he heard the sounds and froze. Far away they were, and muffled, but they struck him with such terror that he crouched and cowered, hands pressed tightly over his ears to block the screaming.

Slowly, he told himself. Think it out. It may be part of the test.

But his heart told him differently.

Cautiously he stood, straining sounds to see if danger was near.

Making as little noise as possible, he walked counter-sunwise, lifting each stone and placing it in the blue leather bag that hung from his belt. He stamped the dying sparks of his fire to dust and, waiting to regain his night vision, stared until the trees appeared, each distinct from the next.

He began moving, gliding noiselessly, but not toward the sounds, toward the sea.

It wasn't far, for the island was small, but when he poked his head gingerly over the rocks and looked down to the beach, he saw nothing out of place. He followed the coastline, moving in the general direction of the sounds, and at the ninth cove he saw the boats, some still out at sea. More than he had ever seen in one place. Filling the Menai Strait. Roman. What had the Elders said? That they expected a visit from the Romans. No cause for alarm then, yet his breath quickened and his heart pounded. What? What was it?

Then he realized that it was the lack of something. No sounds now - nothing. Just silence.

He sat down on a rock, wondering what he should do. The feeling of disquiet was still upon him, and that part of him led by his heart wanted to run back to the settlement to make sure that all was well, and it warred with the logical part - the part that told him he should return to his silent vigil, and that he should not let anything distract him from his internal preparation. Maybe this was part of his testing - false screams to tear him out of his internal state, a deliberate attempt to mislead him.

He had nearly convinced himself that this was true when he heard someone coming. Many men. Soldiers. He could hear it in the cadence of their march, and in the clanking of shields against breast-plates, and now he could see the flash of metal. More soldiers than he had ever seen before.

He slid off the rock, sinking behind it, not afraid of them, but cautious. Relations were not the best with Romans right now. It was said that in some places on the mainland they had burned the sacred circles of oak. He swallowed the bile that rose with such a thought. What man could take the life force of a tree? Who would rend branches that reached to the stars and trunks that counted centuries? The Roman Conquerors were powerful, some said wise. But how could they be wise if they were not Caretakers of the Earth?

He was near enough to hear the commands to push off from the shore as the soldiers piled into their boats, and he observed that the men were quiet.

Discipline? Exhaustion? It was late. Tired men were usually quiet. No cause for alarm. Dawn was coming, clouds turning red in the east, and showing against them a flock of dark birds was circling to land.

The commander was last off. As the final boat loaded, he bent and wiped the blade of his sword, using the tough marsh grass that bordered the shoreline, then stood and looked back over the trail, his gaze lifting finally to the crimson clouds. On his face was a grim expression. He did not keep his men waiting. He turned quickly, stepping into the boat on the heels of the last of his men, barking an order even before he sat.

The young Druid listened to the oars plying the water until he could no longer hear them then tramped down to the beach. Still thinking he ought to go back to his solitary vigil, he crouched down, peering out into the waves, straining to see the boats until they were gone. Absently he became aware that one hand was damp, and knew it was not from dew. This was sticky.

His head went down, nose sniffing like a hound then he jerked up in alarm. Blood!

He was fifty paces up the path before he realized that the red clouds were not heralding dawn. Fire? Something was burning. Something big.

He ran until his breath was ragged and pain knotted his side, slowing him to a fast walk, and now he could smell the sick odor of burning flesh and he knew that the birds were not feeding on carrion. There was no question in his mind that it was the settlement burning. He knew it from the screams he'd heard and from the location of the smoke. So, it surprised him when he saw the other fire at the top of the hill, trees charred, underbrush billowing thick columns of black smoke to the sky. The bile rose to his throat and he swallowed it down, sick as he watched living oaks die, sick for the defilement of the sacred circle.

He was running again, nearly at the clearing where the settlement should be, when he saw the first body - nearly tripped over it.

Down on his knees he looked for signs of life. Tears blurring his quest, he hugged the man to his chest when he saw the futility of his searching, for it was his friend, Gawydel, just one year behind him in training. Gently, with great care to arrange the limbs properly, he pulled the body to the side of the path so it wouldn't be stepped on. He began running again, skidding to a stop when the path ended and the full devastation was revealed.

Gone. The buildings were gone. The home he'd known for twenty-two years - where he'd learned, and questioned, and studied, and eaten, and slept, and laughed, and cried from exhaustion and loneliness, and eventually built friendships that should last a lifetime - was gone.

Not much remained to show where buildings had stood - a stone fireplace, the section of one wall with a wooden door nearly burned away, the cooking hearth with an iron kettle half filled with water.

He felt a wind come up and ran to stamp out the last embers, fearing that the wind would spread the flames to the whole island. Only then did he become aware of a stench so sickening that the bile rose to his throat. He made his way slowly toward the smell, covering his nose with the sleeve of his robe. Even so his stomach heaved when he realized what he was seeing.

A dark anger came upon him and he scattered the birds that had come to scavenge, shouting at them, running with his robe and cape flapping, much like a giant bird himself.

The fire had died before it had finished its job. There were a few arms, some complete with hands, more than one foot, a whole leg, an almost recognizable head. He checked quickly, methodically, not allowing himself to feel anything. The wind freshened, creating urgency so he worked faster and faster, knowing that up on the mountain where the sacred circle had marked the heart of the island the wind was kicking dying embers back to life.

He found no one alive. There was still hope, though, for they would not have gone to death willingly. He took the high trail this time - the one that came out by the spring just above the oak grove.

There was no sign of fire by the spring. Encouraged he skirted the rocks and plunged into the forest, keeping an eye out for smoke. The first fire was easy to put out and so were the next three, but the fifth and the sixth threatened to eat the leather sandals from his feet, and twice the fire jumped behind him and licked at his robes, so he pulled the smoldered hem up and tied it about his waist, and then it singed the hair on his bare legs.

He had worked into the circle before he saw the man working as he was, using a cloak to beat at the ground around a blackened tree trunk. The trees had long ago dropped their leaves which made a fertile ground for the nibbling monster of flame, so there was an entire forest to check.

Hours passed as he battled running rivulets and smoldering debris and gaping mouths of flame, and when, finally, he found himself passing the same clearing over and over without finding the least sign of flame, he sank to the ground, weary beyond belief.

He slept, physically too exhausted to go on, mentally seeking the replenishment of rest for a mind that refused the horror. When he awoke, with raindrops pelting him roughly, the glade was washed with the last bit of twilight, and he leaped to his feet, still groggy, but inundated with guilt. The fire? Had he really stopped it?

This time his search was slow and methodical, and when he finally gave it up, he was satisfied that none of the brush was smoldering. Only charred fragments remained of the oak circle, but most of the rest of the forest was intact, and the rain would stop anything he might have missed.

His feet dragging, he walked to the center of the sacred circle and said prayers that would speed the recovery of the land. This made him remember his duties to those slain and again he felt remiss at sleeping when he should have been trying to find those who were missing.

Making his way back to the body of Gawydel, he checked once more for signs of life, then carried his friend back to what remained of the other bodies. Again he beat off the birds.

He searched the debris for a shovel but couldn't find one. He used a stick and a bucket that was still hanging in the well, and worked until he had a shallow grave large enough to hold the remnants of what was left of the Holy Order of Druids.

He had nothing but his prayers to speed their souls through the Waters of Annwn, and with these he was generous, sure when he was finally finished that there was nothing more he could say or do for them.

The rain had long since ended and the sun was rising again when he remembered seeing the man beat the underbrush with his cloak. There was an unbroken bowl that he had used several times at the well that long night. He filled it and set off through the trees, trying to move quickly without spilling the water. It was Tiaddych, he thought. His favorite teacher. He called out as he walked, and searched bushes that might conceal a man who was frightened and injured and exhausted. He had collapsed. Might not Tiaddych have done the same?

He had nearly given up when he heard a soft groan. He listened hard.

Nothing.

Called out and listened again.

Nothing.

Where had it come from? Checking likely places, calling out frequently, he circled the spot where he'd heard the sound. Made a wider circle and went round again.

It was on his third rotation that he came across the stream that cut down toward the ocean. Wading across, he thought he heard the sound again - a little upstream. There. A man's hand coming from behind a tree. He ran the last few steps, sank to his knees, propping Tiaddych's head up, tipping the bowl of water to lips that were dry and cracked. He was rewarded when the old man gasped and choked and finally got a little moisture down. Tiaddych's voice wavered and he gripped the tunic of the young man. "Penbard," he said.

The novice shook his head. "No, Master. I'm not the Chief of Bards. It's just me - Gwion ap Gwynedd."

His grip tightened as he pulled the young man closer. "Penbard. The founder. You. All that's left." His fingers loosened and he sank back into the other's arms, but his voice became more intense. "You … must be the Penbard."

The young man began a protest, but with a wave of his fingers Tiaddych silenced him. "Listen." There was a long pause as he fought for breath to speak. "The new Roman, Paulinus … stands against us. All through the land … he has cut the sacred groves and driven our brothers from their shrines. You … are the only one left."

He made the sacred sign above the bowed head of the novice. "Now you are one of us. Now you are equal and the One God has accepted you." He struggled to a sitting position. "It is on you to be the flower who … gives seed. Do not argue. You know everything you need … to teach the next generation."

Urgently he clasped the young man's shoulder. "Do you under-stand, Gwion? You … are the only hope of the Brotherhood. You … must … spread the wisdom." He gasped as a spasm of pain rippled over his thin body.

"Is there no one at Holyhead?" Gwion asked, naming the small and sacred island that nestled to the west of Ynys Mon.

Tiaddych's eyes shut then opened wide as if he were making this small motion with deliberate thought. "All were called here … to … to stop the Romans."

Gwion knew that Ynys Mon had been the last Druid holdout in Britannia, that the Knowing Ones from all over the island had come here for sanctuary, and that there had been many brothers from the continent as usual, but this - what Tiaddych was telling him - was unthinkable. He couldn't be the only one left!

"You … salvation. Cannot … fail."

Gwion ap Gwynedd was stunned at the burden his teacher would lay on his shoulders. "But there must be others?"

"No. Paulinus is … methodical. Those … those from the main-land had come because of persecution in their own lands."

"No. They came because this was the greatest Druidic school, Tiaddych."

"We were … the last."

Gwion knew that all the Druids in Britannia had been on the island. He didn't know that the visiting priests were the last from their lands. The enormity of such a thing finally struck him. "You're saying those on our island were the only Druids left?"

The old man had strength only to blink his agreement.

The enormity of the challenge bent Gwion's head in shame and tears sprang to his eyes. "Will you not stay to help me?"

"Nay, lad. I … am near gone."

Still Gwion could not meet his master's eyes. "I am not worthy."

"You see with your heart. More brightly than any … star shining is your … gift of … understanding. Gwion, you are our … star of hope. Our wisdom will … live … through you."

Gwion could not help but think of the endless hours of frustration. He had feared that never would understanding touch him for always there was more to learn, and never were his responses quite what his teachers were looking for. It seemed that Tiaddych had followed his thought, for he responded, "Yes. That is truly understanding for … only when you realize that one can have only a glimmer of … truth, can one … truly understand his … place in the world." Tiaddych weakened and fell back, heavy in Gwion's arms. His eyes rolled back in his head and his back arched as spasms of coughing wracked his chest. At last he fell quiet.

Many minutes passed and Gwion grew greatly afraid that the end had come. "Master?" he whispered, "Master, hold. Do not leave me." Despair swamped him. "Do not leave me alone!"

"Not … alone. The Goddess who wears the face of the Maiden and is the beginning of all will guide you, and as the Mother will give you comfort when you have need, and as the Crone will give you the wisdom of the aged. The Horned One will give you courage and lead you through darkness, Lleu will lead you through the glare of the sun, and you will never be alone in this, for the One God with many faces is with you."

Gwion's eyes widened in amazement. Had Tiaddych truly spoken these words aloud and with strength, or had they sprung into his mind?

There was no drama as Tiaddych died. He was simply breathing, then not breathing a moment later. Gwion listened for a heartbeat, found none, closed the eyes, and said the prayer for the dead that would speed his soul toward its preparation for its next life.

Gwion laid the old man gently back to the earth then leaped up to pace spiraled circles as he thought. What should he do? He was nothing - the lowliest and not worthy to teach others. He hadn't lived enough years to gain the knowledge that went beyond the ritual. And what if he forgot some vital step and offended the One God? What if he couldn't remember things correctly and taught them wrong? How could he be accepted as a teacher when yesterday he was a student?

His steps had taken him to the edge of a cliff, and he sat down and watched the stream spill down the slope, a froth of white as it struck the rocks and split into four small trickles which were swallowed by waves as they met the beach.

The vision came slowly, taking a long time in the forming. At first he seemed to become the stream then it was his knowledge twined with the running water. It wasn't much of a stream - so narrow that his arm could bridge it, but it gathered strength as it tumbled, and the four rivulets marched to meet the ocean like four soldiers ready to conquer the world.

Then each drop in the stream became a separate soldier and they were all Druids, not an army of trained killers, but an army of trained thinkers and teachers and healers and bards and advisors, becoming one with the waves, indistinguishable from the mass of droplets they had joined.

He came to himself dizzy and knew enough to sit calmly breathing in and out until the dizziness passed, then he hugged his knees and thought how to go about it.

It must be secret, he knew. Knowledge learned and spread and passed on - perhaps for generations, but all in secret to protect them from retribution.

As he walked back to the body of his teacher and hoisted it on to his shoulder, he realized that the desperation had left him. He was excited, eager to begin - would have actually been cheerful if he had not had such a grim task immediately ahead. "Thank you, Lady," he said aloud, knowing that because of her association with water it was the Goddess who had showed him the image.

He buried the body with the proper ritual so that Tiaddych's spirit would be eased through the waters of Annwn. One cry of anguish burst from his lips as he thought of his lost friends and teachers, and the enormous task before him, unqualified as he was, but as he worked, he thought, and by the time he climbed into the small skiff that had been overlooked by the Romans he had worked out a plan. This time he shouted in triumph. Yes, it would be work, but it was work of the One God. How could he fail with such an ally?

9

BLAISE

"Who wrote the story of Gwion?" Emrys asked me. "It's written as if he wrote it."

"We don't really know. I believe it was written by his successor, Gwydion. I have another work by him and the style seems the same." He nodded, but I went on, "Gwydion was his most talented pupil, and they were very close."

"How do you know if someone is talented?" He was wringing his hands. I knew how desperately he wanted to stay with us and I understood that he was really asking how one became talented.

"Let's sit," I said, finding a nice flat rock, and taking a long look at the beautiful valley below us. He was quick to copy me.

I couldn't help but smile … he was so eager. "A person who grasps concepts easily, a person who contributes his own concepts, a person who does not forget a lesson and learns from it and sees easily when that lesson applies, a person who shows great ability in one area – a seer of accuracy, a musician who moves people to tears or to joy, a bard who can create a song so appropriate to the occasion that the people rise to their feet – those are attributes that the teacher can rejoice in. Do you understand?"

"I think so." He looked down at his clenched hands, released them to a comfortable position on his knees, and straightened up, his eyes back on mine. "So it sounds like one should work hard on all his lessons and, perhaps, some spark of creation or inspiration will come."

"That's about all one can do," I said.

"Let me tell you more about Gwion and Gwydion and you can see how talented they both were." I took a deep breath and began, quoting from something I had written about the history of the period.

"When the Romans left the slaughter on the island, they thought they had annihilated the spirit of the tribes, but there was a survivor, mighty Gwion known as the Penbard, who had a warrior's grace and a tongue of quicksilver. He gathered a dozen men of promise from all across Albion, then a dozen more, and each year after that scores and scores. Taking them to secret places which changed frequently - forests of densely packed trees, caverns deep in the bowels of the earth, close-guarded homes of sympathizers - he drilled the knowledge of the ages into them, and they in turn taught others. It took twenty years to become a Druid priest and in spite of the urgent need of the people, this study was not shorted.

"There were times when the Romans were recalled by their Consuls or moved to different locations and left parts of our land on its own. Then the priests worked openly with the people and became their leaders again, advising them on every form of governing, working with the Ladies of the Goddess to heal the sick, celebrating the Wheel of the Seasons with huge festivals and traveling as bards to entertain and to sing the great deeds of the ancestors.

"Then it was that Gwion truly earned the title Penbard, for his voice could send a shiver down the back of the strongest soldier, and could thrill the most callous court. It was said that the Sidhe, who are often called the Fair Ones and who were no slouches at music themselves, would ride horses on the wind to hear him and would weep tears that filled rivers to overflowing when his songs were sad.

"Gwion it was who added teaching verse to the Triads - those lines that asked the questions, then answered them in threes so that all would remember.

"Not all bards were allowed to create their songs and their poems. Most words were memorized in the most scrupulous manner and passed down to each new generation. Only a great bard could create new works. Once they were polished and the creator was satisfied, the other bards learned them as part of the lessons.

"But undoubtedly Gwion's greatest contribution (aside from preserving and teaching the Druid knowledge) was his invention of several simple hand codes so that Druids could recognize each other when the Romans prevailed.

"The Ogham alphabet had been invented several hundred years before Gwion's time to leave messages and directions. They were often scratched on a tree or rock that none but a Druid would notice or understand. Gwion was adept at reading and writing it. Only the Druids used it, and then not often, since Druid rituals, doctrine and knowledge were never set down in any form of writing.

"There are twenty letters in the alphabet, each named for a tree - four grouping of five letters. If you were to write out this alphabet, you would begin each group with a horizontal line. If you marked one vertical line above this horizontal line, you would have the first letter. Two vertical lines above would give you the second letter, three the third, four the fourth and five the fifth. At that point the first grouping would be finished. You could create the second group by marking one, two, three, four and five vertical lines under the horizontal line. The third group has vertical lines that go through the horizontal and the fourth group has slanting lines through the horizontal.

"Gwion had tried several different ways for Druids to recognize each other secretly, but they had proved difficult. He stared down at his hands, thoroughly discouraged as he considered the problem.

"We don't know whether he saw the answer suddenly or worked it out slowly and painstakingly, but somehow, as he looked at the palm of his left hand, he realized that his fingers have clear dividing lines at the joints. By using these and the finger tips, each finger has four clear markings, except the thumb which has only three, making nineteen markings. Only nineteen.

"After some thought he finally realized that the fleshy part of the thumb could also be used, making twenty clear markings. Hmmm. Twenty markings. Twenty letters to the alphabet. Yes, it could be done.

"Unobtrusively, using just one finger from his right hand, words could be spelled quickly. He assigned each marking a letter, working left to right on his left hand, from thumb to little finger. It worked beautifully. All of the under-the-line letters went to the finger tips, over the line letters to the first joint, slants to the second, and through the lines, which are the five vowels, to the third. That pleased him especially, since the vowels were the most frequently used letters and would be closest to the center of the hand.

"Slowly, tentatively, he spelled 'Druid', then again faster.

"Later, others were to add to the system - whole words on the shinbone, nose and other parts of the body which had the advantage that they could be recognized from a distance and used during a performance. But it was Gwion who began the whole concept.

"When Gwion was an old man – forty years from the time when he had been the sole survivor of the Roman slaughter - he had the pleasure of ordaining his brightest and most talented pupil, and as part of the Cycle of Calling of giving him his third name. Together they had chosen the name Gwydion for him, a name close to his own as Gwydion pointed out, and that pleased him greatly.

"The original Gwydion was a great hero/god of legend, son of the goddess Don, and the father, by his sister Arianrhod, of twin sons, Lleu and Dyland who represented light and dark. To help his brother

Gilvacthwy who was sick for love of Gvewin, he disguised himself as a bard and visited King Pryderi's realm. After entertaining he asked for a herd of swine as his reward, but they were sacred gifts from the King of Annwn and Pryderi replied that he is under a pact with the people not to sell or give them until they have produced double their number. Gwydion says he will give twelve magic horses and twelve magic hounds, and they finally strike a bargain. But Gwydion has used illusion and when the horses and hounds disappear, Pryderi comes after him.

"During the fighting Gilvacthwy is able to seize Gvewin. Eventually Gwydion was caught and imprisoned and it is said that his sufferings made him a true bard. Later with his brother Amaethon and his son Lleu, he fought the Battle of Godeu against the god Bran and, using magic, called the very trees as his troops, though some taught that this was not an actual battle, but a battle of wits, for the trees – like Ogham - represented letters of the alphabet. At any rate when Bran's secret name was revealed, Gwydion won three boons for man - the dog, the roebuck and the lapwing who were also set to guard, to disguise, and to hide the alphabet secret.

"The hero Gwydion instituted a new religious system, a new calendar and tree names for the letters. Since the neophyte Gwydion had helped to develop and organize the spread of Gwion's code, and was, himself, a gifted bard, the name seemed appropriate."

Through the entire monologue a rapt Emrys sat very still. "Would you like to read the story that Gwydion wrote about rescuing the Thirteen Treasures of Britannia?"

"Oh yes. Is it one of the scrolls you mentioned having?" he asked.

I couldn't help but laugh. "Many of them," I said.

10

MERLIN

I was soon to learn why the Master had laughed, for when I left his study that night, I had almost more scrolls than I could carry. I am very excited about it. He hasn't really said, but now I'm fairly sure that he intends to let me stay.

I've been here eighteen months now and already I've learned about double what I knew when I came. Master Blaise and I hold some of our conversations in Latin. He says I understand the language very well and speak with hardly any accent. "You could easily converse with a Roman Senator," he told me. I've also learned the twenty trees which represent each letter of the ogham alphabet and how to write it and how to sign it.

I've learned about hundreds of plants that were new to me. I know what each of them can be used for, like food, medicine, and poison. Some of them are important because they feed birds and insects and animals, or because they make the soil rich so more plants will grow, or just because they are beautiful to look upon.

I know all the constellations, the five planets and when each one is visible. I know the phases of the moon and the cycle it makes through the sky. I know why it's important to perform certain rituals with those cycles.

I know the habits of all the birds and animals in these lands, and which can be hunted – when and where, and which are dangerous. And the fish? I've learned to catch one with only my bare hands!

Mathematics, memorizing ballads and triads – so many accomplishments, but so very many more to absorb.

And now all these scrolls … I can hardly wait to get started.

11

GWYDION

One day, shortly after the furtive ceremony that named Gwydion a Druid priest, Gwion summoned him to the isolated farmhouse that he was using as his headquarters, and when they were seated on wooden benches at a plank table with fresh bread and ale that wasn't too bad, Gwion made a startling announcement. "I have seen myself wandering in the castle of Arianrhod. It will be soon."

Arianrhod is one aspect of the Goddess, and it is in her castle where souls wander, waiting to be reborn. The young man's eyes filled with tears. "You've had chest pains again?"

"They knocked me to the floor. I couldn't breathe. My soul leaped out, watched my body for a time, and was called on a journey. When I awoke, I found it dark. A whole day had been lost."

"Thank the Goddess you came back."

Gwydion took a sip of ale, replacing the mug carefully so that Gwion wouldn't see his shaking hand. He wondered if he could insist that Gwion keep an assistant about at all times in case such an episode should happen again. No, it would be better to have the watching done discreetly, without Gwion's awareness that his health was being monitored.

Gwion seemed to be waiting for him to respond, so he added, "Do you remember anything of the journey?"

"After a time of searching it seemed I was called to a place of darkness. There I was shown wonders and entrusted with delivering them to a place of safekeeping."

When he did not go on, Gwydion asked, "And did you accomplish this task?"

"I don't know." The older man shook his head, thin white hair flying about his shoulders. "I saw a great light. I was close." He chose his words carefully. "I was not alone, for you were at my side, bearing the weight for me."

A gentle smile changed Gwydion's face to nearly handsome. "As I would wish to be."

"As you will be. It's a journey we must take, Gwyd, and we must go soon because the Goddess will grant me time only for this quest."

"How soon?" asked Gwydion, thinking of work not finished.

Gwion understood Gwydion's sense of obligation. "Bledsoe can teach your classes, Marddyn will go in your place as bard."

The young man rose and walked toward the door. "It's all settled then. How long do I have to pack?"

"We leave at dawn tomorrow. The mountains are cool at night, so bring warm clothes."

"The master of understatement," Gwyd laughed. "Even at noon the mountains are cool this time of year."

12

GWYDION

It was late October. The first week the weather held, but the second caught them in an early sleet that iced the steep paths and made walking treacherous. Gwydion helped his mentor to his feet after a particularly rough fall. "There's a cutoff not far from here that leads to a small village. I've been there before, and I know the folk would welcome two such gifted bards."

Breathing hard the old man answered, "Didn't I tell you? We're not bards on this trip. Check the sack you have slung over your shoulder. We're smiths." It was not a story, for all Druids received training as smiths.

Gwydion shivered as a particularly cold wind struck him. "What else haven't you told me?"

"Just that we need to cover our tracks on this one. No one, Roman or Celt, should know what we're truly up to."

"And how is this different from every other time you've sent me forth?"

The last word was nearly lost as he slid several feet. He reached back to help the old man make it across the early patch of black ice, and his fingers were clasped gratefully.

The sun was nearly down when they reached the cutoff, but Gwion was firm. "No, we aren't going that way. There's another place. Not far."

Gwydion didn't argue. He just placed one careful foot after the other and kept a watch on Gwion, hoping to catch him if he should slip again. And he trusted, for if Gwion said there was another place, it was so.

It was a shepherds' hut, nothing luxurious, but dry and warm thanks to firewood stacked neatly by the door. In the morning they would see that the view of the hilltops was stupendous, and Gwydion would replenish the firewood and bless the hearth for those to come, but now they huddled by the fire, glad that no wind touched them and that they were finally beginning to warm up.

They had stripped off wet clothes and eaten lightly from their provisions, and Gwydion had begun to think fondly of sleep when Gwion said, "Twelve days have passed since we left the settlement. You have not asked what our task will be. Have you not wondered?"

"I knew you would tell me when I needed to know, Penbard."

Gwion regarded him thoughtfully, smiling at the use of his formal title. "Do you remember from your lessons the thirteen treasures of Britannia?"

Gwydion back propped against the wall and legs outstretched, dug in his heels and sat up straighter. "Frugarch the sword that some call Caliburn, forged from metal not of this earth, Birgha the Spear of Lugh of the Long Arm, Dademi the Cauldron of the Dagda, or some say of Ceridwen, which can return life to one newly dead and where imagination was once brewed, and the Lia Fal, the Stone of Destiny whose voice cries only for the rightful ruler." He thought a moment. "Those are the four most holy - the Treasures of Tuatha, for they represent the four elements from which all is made. The stone symbolizes earth, the spear air, the sword fire and the cup water."

"It is death to touch one of them unprepared," Gwion said.

When Gwydion was sure his teacher was not about to add anything, he continued. "Of the others the drinking horn of Bran - Galed - has perhaps the greatest reputation, for it is said to heal from any affliction those who drink from it. There is also the Halter that tames any horse, the Harp of Ceraunnos which has tones that heal, and grant peace, knowledge and protection, the Ring of Gortigern that causes its wearer to speak and understand any tongue, the Mirror of Atmu that reveals the future, the Slatan Druideacht, the Staff of Seasons, which has changed summer and winter, the platter of Gwyndo Garanhir, also called the Vessel of Plenty, that can feed an army, the mantle of Tegan Eurvron, also called the Cloak of Padaen which gives its wearer invisibility, and the Gwyddbwyll Lifeboard of Gwendolau mab Ceidio, whose magic squares can control battles fought."

Gwydion had shed all signs of drowsiness. "Is this our task? Recovery of the treasures?"

"It is."

"And you know where they are?"

Gwion's eyes took on a faraway look. "I know that they were supposed to have been on Ynys Mon."

Gwydion studied his leader for signs of emotion. It would be hard on him to return to the place where his friends and teachers had been slaughtered. He saw signs of pain as thoughts, new and old, flickered through his mentor's mind.

"And if we find them? What shall we do with them?"

"Take them to a place of safe keeping. To Avalon."

Gwydion nodded. "I have heard that it's a good school the priestesses have established there, and that many who believe in the old ways have sent daughters there for training."

"It's encouraged. Even those who did not decide to stay on as servants of the Goddess will someday teach their children of Her."

"Will the treasures be safe there? What if the Romans decide to attack? I know that our women were not spared during the purges."

"For that reason the Ladies of the Isle will not yet guard the treasures." Gwion stared with unseeing eyes at the fire.

It was not long before Gwydion followed his gaze, then he too was drawn into the flames. There was brilliant light, diamond white, and a hall so vast that he couldn't see the roof. A forest of pillars twisted down to a smooth floor of glittering stones, nearly hidden by the thousands of beings who turned to stare at them. They were beautiful creatures, wearing diaphanous robes of rainbow colors, each one more graceful, more stately than any human. A path opened for them and he saw the throne and the one who sat upon it, and he gasped and shut his eyes, wondering if any mortal could bear seeing such perfection.

And when his eyes opened, he saw the fire again, and turning his head, saw Gwion. "Annwn," he said, exhaling slowly. "Annwn." The Christians would call it hell, though it was not a place of fire and brimstone. Yet it could be just as deadly, with mortal souls in dire jeopardy of never being able to escape it. Nudd on the throne. The Kingdom of Fairie.

"Who better to guard the treasures from the perfidy of man?" Gwion challenged.

"Aye," he slowly agreed. "Who better?"

13

GWYDION

The morning brought the sun and a clear blue sky. The trees were still dressed in glistening finery when they began their journey, but by noon the ice was gone. By the time the sun set they had come down the last pass and could see the sea striping the horizon.

"How do we get to the island?" Gwydion asked.

"We find a fisherman named Llewellen. There are three rocks taller than you on the beach by his house, so it shouldn't be hard to find."

"And he's to be trusted?"

"Aye." Gwion hesitated so long that Gwydion was sure his master had nothing else to tell him and had resigned himself to blind trust again, but finally Gwion spoke. "When I left the island, I was exhausted. I should have rested, eaten something, waited for morning to bring renewed strength." His smile was sheepish and soon faded with the pain of memory. "I suppose I wasn't thinking clearly."

Gwydion nodded his understanding. How could anyone think

clearly after such an ordeal? The shock at finding his friends and teachers slaughtered, the exhaustion after stamping the fires out and after singlehandedly burying those who had escaped the roundup but not the slaughter, the realization that the way of life he had trained for was finished and that from that day forth he would be an outlaw, always in hiding, and that there was no one else - no one - to go to for help and advice - all of this would be devastating.

They came to a fork in the path and it seemed that Gwion barely noticed there was a choice, taking the right-hand trail automatically. "I found a small sailboat that the soldiers had not destroyed. I was confident. I'd paddled boats across. All the novices had. We took turns getting supplies."

He stepped easily over the debris of loose rocks that looked as if they'd rolled down the mountain and landed there on the trail. He pointed so that Gwydion would see and avoid them.

"There were no oars. I'd never been in a sailboat before, but I'd watched them from the cliff tops, and it didn't look that difficult."

"And you had no other choice."

"True enough." His laugh was wry. "I got the sail up on the second try, but those who depend on fish for survival should thank the Goddess that they didn't have me sailing the boat. No amount of worthy attempts or heartfelt prayers accomplished directing the boat where I wished it would go. As the sun fell I was sailing straight out to sea. Each time I tried to turn I fought to stay upright as the sail dipped nearly to the water and the waves threatened to put an end to what the Romans had started.

Eventually I sat it out, knowing that the wind would change sometime. When it did, the moon was high in the sky - a full moon. I had fallen asleep, my arm locked about the tiller when thunder in the distance sounded.

"I came to with a start, nearly fell overboard before I realized where I was, and saw that I was now running parallel to the land. This seemed better and I was heartened until the thunder started in earnest.

The lightning was all about me, torching the sea, the distant trees and very nearly me. The rain came in torrents like the lightning. I was near drowned one moment and felt only a soft drizzle the next. Then the wind came up. The mast dropped from one side to the other, rolling the boat and throwing me about until I roped myself to the seat, praying that it wouldn't completely overturn and I would drown before I could get loose." He shook his head. "It nearly happened that way."

The path petered out. Again Gwion swung right, walking now on the grassy overhang that swept along this part of the coast. Gwydion kept one eye on the ocean, marveling at the power of the water as it beat into the black rocks below them.

"It was a huge gust of wind like a giant fist that caught the sail and spun the boat completely around. Into the air it went, then crashed down with a head-splitting jar. Up and down. Up and down. Over and over. Then the wind brought the boat down on its side. Once. Twice. Upturned it completely.

"Still roped I found myself under water. Then bobbing to the surface, but still attached. It was cold. With the last bit of strength I pushed myself up and across the bottom of the boat spread-eagled, nearly drowning from the waves and the steady pelting of rain. I couldn't think of anything at first - just tried to cling to the slippery surface of the upturned wood. But eventually I noticed that I was getting closer to the shore which gave me a little hope.

"I tried to sit up, but nearly slid off when the next wave hit. I had just recovered when the boat thudded into a mostly submerged group of rocks. Wave after wave hit, but it was wedged tight, the sunken mast acting like a giant anchor."

"That was where Llewellen spotted me the next morning, more dead than alive. He launched a small skiff, cut the rope, and hauled me back to shore. I stayed with the family for a week, recovering my strength. They were kind, completely appalled at the fate their Druids had suffered, and quick to offer any help they could give.

"Llewellen was just a young man at the time. Since then I've sent several priests who needed discretion and a place to stay. They've always helped."

That made Gwydion feel better. They weren't completely alone in this.

"Look," Gwion said softly. "The three rocks."

Gwydion could see them and the fisherman's hut too, but he could also see that Gwion was staring past them, past the white fringe that lapped the shore, past the dark blue of the sea. He was staring at the green island that rose like a giant wedge on the horizon. Gwydion didn't have to ask if that was Ynys Mon.

It was at that moment that the boy found them. He looked about eleven, but proudly told them he was fourteen. Short and wiry, and with a shock of black hair that fell into his eyes, he aimed a huge, cocky grin at them that showed perfect teeth. "I'm called Llew. I've been taught to extend a welcome hand to strangers," he announced.

14

GWYDION

It was a wonderful meal. There were two kinds of fish, freshly caught, with nicely seasoned potatoes and leeks, a dark bread still warm from the oven and ale that would hold up in the best of taverns. Though normally Druids did not partake of flesh, they ate lightly of the fish, following the policy that Druids traveling in secrecy do nothing to call attention to themselves.

Neldda, Llewellyn's still pretty wife, didn't say much, but she smiled shyly when one of them looked her way, and she kept their plates ladled full until each protested that stomachs so unused to food would surely burst if even one more bite was taken. After she'd cleared the food and dishes away and cleaned everything for the morn, she said a soft goodnight, taking the sparkling seven-year-old Brigid off to bed to hear a tale or two before settling down.

"You just have the two?" asked Gwydion, ruffling the boy's thick hair.

"I have a son grown, Colim, who has his own house down the

beach, and his own wife with one babe on her hip and another on the way," Llewellen answered proudly. "He's my right hand on the boat."

He seemed suddenly fascinated with his cup, turning it round and round. "There were two other barrens," he said finally. "A girl born dead between Colim and Llew, and a boy between Llew and Brigid who didn't reach two years. He died of fever."

Gwydion patted his arm, feeling it was a poor gesture of comfort even as he did it. "I'm sorry."

"To business." Llewellen slapped his cup down sharply, looking to Gwion in question. "Or is this just a pleasure trip? Two foot-weary travelers taking refreshment in the first house they saw?"

Gwion smiled. "Happen it's a bit more than that."

At dawn the sun tried to poke through the thick layer of dark clouds then gave up. The rain started, pelting the trees with a staccato of soft sound, and turning the ocean grey like the sky.

"And it's a grand day for fishing," Llewellen told him happily as he pointed to Colim waiting in his boat. "We're ready to go. May the Goddess bring you luck."

He clasped Gwion's hand and blinked back a tear. "Take care of the boy."

"Like my own," he promised.

Gwydion and Llew were already seated in the narrow skiff, and Llew extended a small but sure hand as Gwion stepped in and gingerly seated himself. Llewellen gave a strong push that sent the skiff into the receding waves which carried it a good way from the shore before Llew had taken even one oar stroke.

"Mama packed us food," the boy said, totally oblivious to the weather, as he broke into a fishing song, rowing in rhythm.

In the far end of the skiff, facing Gwion, Gwydion smiled and signed, 'Good voice.'

Gwion nodded his agreement, but did not smile. His eyes were on the island, and his thoughts were dark.

They were soon wet from the rain, but according to Llew the sea was calm, "and the Goddess has smiled upon us."

Gwydion, who had never been in a boat before gulped as the bow lifted several feet and fell with regularity, wondering what a heavy sea would do to them. He pulled his hooded cloak tighter and clung to the wooden seat.

"Da said in the old days there were many priests," the boy said. "They told us when the fishing was good, and when storms were coming. They blessed the harvests."

"Yes, that is true," Gwion answered absently, still staring at the island.

"They healed the sick," the boy continued. "They led the singing. They told the stories."

Now he tested, not quite sure he believed. "They went to the Otherworld to talk to the gods."

Gwydion answered this time, with a simple nod of his head.

"Then why do the Romans hate you? Those are good things."

Gwion turned his attention to the boy. He did not equivocate. "Priests have power, and the Romans fear that power. They do not want anyone to have power except themselves."

Llew shook his head like a dog and his wet hair settled, no longer in his eyes, and in his eyes was a look of challenge. "Are you afraid of the Romans?"

Gwion answered truthfully. "Yes. They killed my brother priests. I was the only one left alive."

"Yet Da says you have taught others to be Druids in secret. You must be very brave to go against those you fear."

Gwion shrugged, and there was an air of sadness about him. "Not brave so much as furtive. I cannot live my life openly like you can. That's a bad thing. I must hide my actions and my feelings and my thoughts from all but those I trust. Do you understand that?"

Llew did not rush his answer, but considered before he spoke.

"It would be hard, but I could do it. I will do it if we run into any Romans. Da made me swear to it." He glanced over his shoulder, adjusted the angle of the boat slightly. "How do you choose your students?"

"If one is touched by the Goddess, the talent will show itself and I, or one I've trained, will be there to see it."

Never breaking his steady stroke Llew nodded seriously. "One who knows. That's what Da says Druid means."

"He's right."

"But what is it that you know? Da just says everything. Do you know everything?"

"You want to know what a Druid learns?"

The unruly lock of hair had invaded his vision again, and the boy flicked his head to toss it aside. He smiled winningly. "Yes, please."

For the rest of the journey Gwion explained Druid beliefs to the boy, occasionally breaking into a dialogue with Gwydion. He said that for all that exists there is an equal of opposite power, and that Druids would not destroy something bad, but take the evil from it and restore it to the balance it had in the beginning. "We believe in the spiritual vitality of all nature."

"What about magic?" the boy wanted to know. "I've heard that Druids use magic."

"It's true," Gwion told him, "but people tend to call something magic when they don't understand it. Druids try to understand everything. We study for years and years. When we use this knowledge, many call it magic. We study the stars, the seasons and the weather so that we can know what is coming. We study the animals, the plants and the land itself. We learn healing, music, history, law and divination. We learn about man - how he thinks. We learn of the Goddess with her three faces, and of the gods of darkness and the gods of light, and we know that all gods and goddesses are but aspects of the One God."

"Do you know everything about everything?" the boy asked, awe clear on his face.

Gwion laughed. "No, truly we don't. But we try to investigate every branch of learning."

He told Llew how the Druids had been organized before the Romans came. "There were three Orders of the Wise - the judges who were also thinkers, teachers, interpreters of law, healers and Keepers of the Mysteries, the Vates who were the seers and prophets, and the bards. "Someday," he said, his eyes glowing with excitement, "these Orders will exist again, and the priests will be the leaders in every village as they were before."

"What about the kings?" the boy wanted to know, so he explained that a powerful priest/sorcerer was considered higher than a king and often was the king, sometimes even regarded as a god, for there is little differentiation among the uneducated in the one who can communicate with the gods and the gods, themselves. When the boy asked if Gwion wanted to be a king, he exchanged an amused look with Gwydion, and said, "I most emphatically do not and I would never use magic to gain a throne."

"But he wouldn't mind wearing a coat of six colors and sitting always on the left-hand side of the Heir Apparent, a favor that was once commonly granted to Master Poets in the past," Gwydion commented.

"It would be grand," Gwion admitted.

"The word 'bard' means Master Poet," Gwydion added.

"I made a poem," Llew told them excitedly. "It was for Ma when the baby died. Da said to try to make her happy. It went, 'In my boat I made a wish/ To catch a very tasty fish/ And here it is upon my dish.'"

Gwydion clapped his hands, exclaiming, "It's even a triad," and Gwion praised the lad's efforts, then told him that a bard spent years memorizing poetry so that he could tell the great tales of heroes. Llew hoped that someday he could hear the stories. Gwydion hoped that he could someday tell the stories, though he did not say so aloud. Llew asked if the stories had music, and was answered that only parts of the stories were in verse, and that the parts with great emotion were often sung with a harp or hand drum accompanying, for all bards were accomplished musicians.

"A bard is also an historian," Gwion said. "It was the custom for fighting armies to have their own bards. When the fighting started, the bards from the opposing sides would meet on a hill overlooking the battle and discuss what they were seeing. To be presented as a hero by an observing bard was many a man's goal."

The rain had finally stopped without them noticing, but when the sun broke through the clouds and glinted fiercely on the water all three felt their spirits lift. Moments later the boat glided in smoothly and stuck the sand of the shallows. The boy was quick to jump out and haul it ashore with Gwydion helping. Gwion stepped out on dry land. Directing them to pull the boat next to a large downed tree, he tossed greenery over it until he was convinced that no one would see it, and saw that it was roped to a secure tree even though Llew was sure it was above the high tide line.

"We mustn't take a chance," he said, firmly ending the debate.

Llew gave him a good-natured shrug. "Where to?"

Gwion stepped back, searching the shoreline for something familiar. "Up there," he said finally, pointing vaguely to the cliff top.

It was a short climb and the boulders held when they tested for footholds. "I can see our house," Llew said, holding his hand to shade his eyes.

Gwion gestured him back. "Yes, and if anyone is on the shore looking, they can see you silhouetted against the sky, too."

Llew accepted the reprimand cheerfully, skipping backward through tall grass.

"We'll go this way." Gwion, aided by his staff, took long strides as if by hurrying the pace he could be sure of finding the treasures.

After a time Gwydion asked, "Is this the way to the settlement?"

"No. No, we won't be anywhere near it. This is the way to the cave."

The path was tangled with bracken, but still visible even if not always passable. Several times Gwion stopped cold, motioning for silence. When he had listened and heard nothing, he seemed satisfied and started up again.

After the fifth time he had done this, Gwydion could not help but ask, "What are you listening for?",

It was the Master Gwion who turned to face him, and as teacher he asked a question in return. "Don't you feel it?"

But it was the boy who answered, whispering for fear that some presence would overhear, shivering as he glanced around with wide eyes. "It's something dark that we need be wary of."

Gwion backed him up, "Definitely malevolent," then questioned, "Are you sure the Romans don't use this island?"

"About once a year there's a patrol sent from the fort to check up like, but that's all. Da says they've never used it for anything."

Gwydion turned back to Gwion. Hopefully, "One of our own spells of protection mayhap?"

Gwion shook his head. "No. There's a feeling of magic to it as well as darkness."

The boy's eyes were pivoting back and forth, hitting every tree and bush big enough to hide anything threatening. "The Fair Ones?"

Gwion's brows creased, and he too surveyed the terrain. "Maybe. There's old magic here. Old enough to be theirs. I've dealt with them, though, and I've not felt such a touch of malevolence before."

The rest of the morning and a good part of the afternoon was spent trekking through the overgrown forest. When it became evident that they had passed a certain spot for the third time Gwion sank down on a rock, pulling his pack off. The others followed suit, wordlessly digging through their packs for water flasks, bread and cheese, and a bit of fresh fish left over from supper.

"Are we lost?" the boy asked.

"Something has confused the trail," Gwion answered. "I must find a way through it." He regarded the boy steadily. "I will find a way through it."

Llew nodded happily, not doubting for a moment that the man of power before him would do as he said. Gwydion smiled to himself at Gwion's reaction, for, personally, he too had needed this affirmation.

When they had finished eating, Gwion rose with surety. "This way," he said. They followed with confidence. It was not long before they came to a rocky place. Gwion ignored a fairly decent stream and found a bare trickle of water which he followed, climbing steadily.

It was not an easy path. More than once Gwydion slipped and skidded to a firm foothold and reached back to help the boy, but Gwion climbed steadily, his strength growing to belie any infirmities his advanced age ordinarily claimed on his body. He did not look back even once to see if they kept pace with him.

At last they caught up to him and found that they were at what looked to be a shallow pool. There was no hesitation as Gwion stepped to its center and studied the sheer cliff that backed into it. His hands were moving, the gestures sometimes broad, sometimes shallow. Llew looked at Gwydion questioningly. He formed the word 'magic' with his lips, but did not speak aloud. He and the boy settled on rocks and waited, watching as Gwion tried and discarded each spell.

They waited a long time. In the beginning Gwion had pulled his robe up through the braided cord that belted it, but it had long since sagged and the hem was heavy with water. His hands hung down at his sides now, his head bowed.

If I were to rhyme lines about defeat, that is what it would look like, Gwydion thought sadly, barely noticing as the boy slipped from his side.

It was Gwion's head snapping up that held his attention, and he saw the nod of affirmation as the now frustrated boy splashed into the water and attacked the solid cliff with his fists. Gwion was smiling, gently pulling Llew away.

"Yes. Yes, that may be it," he said, "but not that way. Like this." He placed his hands flat against the cliff at chest height, tried it again at a different place, then again. Lightly now his palms traced the rock. Settled in a place not five feet from where Llew stood watching him. "Yes. This is right. My hands fit here."

Gwydion was at his side now, close enough to hear him say, "In the name of She who wears the face of a maid at sunrise, the face of a woman at noon, and the face of a crone at sunfall, open."

Both Llew and Gwydion took an involuntary step backward as a long crack appeared, but Gwion pushed at one side of it, and slowly the rock separated.

"Quickly now," he ordered as it became wide enough to walk through. They followed him in, stepping over a rather high threshold to a dry floor.

The boy jumped through immediately, but Gwydion lagged a bit, taking the time to jam a head-sized rock into the opening. When he finally stepped in, he saw that Gwion had found a torch hanging on a wall mount. A wave of his hand, and it flamed, illuminating an awestruck expression on the boy's face.

"It's very simple. The first thing one learns in what you call magic," Gwion told him. "When we're back on the mainland I'll teach you to do it."

The incredulous look of joy on Llew's face made the journey seem entirely worthwhile, Gwydion thought, catching a second torch that Gwion tossed to him. The boy's head swiveled to see if he knew the magic too, and he couldn't help showing off. Llew grinned, thinking, no doubt, that it was a wonderful trick that all his friends would envy.

15

GWYDION

They were in a small empty cave that didn't look like much to Gwydion as he moved the torch about to see, but Gwion did not seem downcast. Confidently he walked to the far wall with Llew at his heels. Looking back to make sure that the opening was still open, Gwydion almost missed seeing them disappear behind an elongated, thick protrusion of rock from the floor of the cave. He ran to catch up.

There was a ramp, steep, invisible from the opening, and it curled down to a floor covered with water so icy that part was still solid. Gwydion gritted his teeth as the shock of it hit him and moved as quickly as he could, using one hand on the close wall of the cave to steady himself when it was slippery. Still his feet were numb before he emerged to higher ground on to a trail that climbed and dipped a dozen times before it began to spiral down again.

He stepped gingerly, afraid of meeting more water, but this time it was dry. After the first few turns they came to a long flight of stone stairs leading down, and just when he thought his leg muscles could not possibly handle another step they found themselves at the top of an open spiral of stepping stones.

No walls at the sides.

No railing.

In vain he cast the torch about, but the steps plunged so far down that he couldn't see the bottom at all. Nor could he see the top of the gigantic cavern. And just barely were the sides visible. A lair fit for a dragon, he thought.

His heart raced. A huge dragon to guard the thirteen treasures of Britain? How fitting.

No, it couldn't be. No one had seen a dragon for ages.

Of course not. There were no more dragons.

And how could there be a cavern this vast? The entire island must be hollow.

Or perhaps we're under the sea, itself? And if the rocks shift the entire ocean will pour in!

Gwion signaled a rest and sank down, so out of breath he couldn't speak.

Gwydion sat too - a little distance apart and so relieved that at first he failed to notice the ragged condition of his mentor.

A gate to the Otherworld? Of course. It had to be.

Yes, but what if all the dragons had come here? This immense cavern was certainly large enough to house a guardian dragon or two. He began listening intently for a telltale sound. Would he even know the sound a dragon makes?

Ha? But what would he do if he heard a dragon coming? They couldn't outrun it. There was no room to fight it. He had no sword. Even if he'd had a sword, none of them had any training in sword-play.

Magic. Their only hope. But he knew no magic that would slay a dragon. Did Gwion?

He looked over at Gwion and listened to his breathing. Even in the torchlight Gwydion could see that his color was bad.

70

"Are the pains back?" he asked, but it was the boy who reached into his pack and handed a water flask to the old Druid, and it was the boy who steadied his hands so that he could drink.

Gwion shook his head no, still struggling to suck air in, not wasting his breath on speech.

Gwydion wanted to ask if this was the right place. And if it was, how did Gwion know that it was? He wanted assurance that it was worth the great toll it was taking on their exhausted bodies ... and of what it would take to climb back up. Great Mother? He hadn't thought of it before. How were they ever going to get the treasures back up these horrible steps?

That was when he began to feel the dark presence of - of something. All the questions he had faded to insignificance before the new question. WHAT IS IT?

He sank back against the wall, fear overpowering him.

16

GWYDION

Gwydion cowered as he watched the old man pull himself upright.

"NO!" Gwion shouted, pushing at the vast nothingness with his torch. "NO? We will not admit Fear through the gates of our souls. OUT? I cast you away."

Behind him his shadow loomed against the wall, growing so large that soon, with only torchlight, it was visible just to the knees, and when Gwydion looked again at Gwion he seemed to have grown to match the shadow.

Slowly he rose to his feet, courage filtering back, willing to die if he must, and ready to back his leader with every resource he had to offer.

Llew rose too, his eyes huge as they darted from the magnificent Druids to the Evil form that surely lay before them. He could not see it, but he felt it and knew that it was real, not imagined.

Gwion called it fear, but fear was what they felt when they gave it credence - not the thing itself. And it WAS there. As real as the hands he felt clenched against his sides.

He swallowed. Eyes back to the Druids, and now Gwion was small again, but his face was no longer chalk-white, his legs no longer shaking.

His arm stretched out, the thin rowan staff that marked him as leader raised high. "I banish you? Draw back from the one who lays rightful claim to the Treasures of Britain."

Walking surely, saying his spells of banishment, one hand raising the torch, the other raising the rod, the old Druid started down the spiraling stones.

Stepping without looking, each step taken with certainty.

Gwydion gestured Llew to the center position again. Taking a deep breath, holding his arms out to emulate Gwion, Llew followed. Gwydion did not give himself time to think. Drawing deep regular breaths he let himself slip into the trance like state that was used for some ceremonies and kept pace.

Though untrained, Llew was also trying to control his mind. He worked very hard at imagining walls on both sides, regular steps that were even and firm, and a normal, visible floor of hard-packed dirt below. He was concentrating so hard that he failed to notice when Master Gwion stopped, and bumped into him. "Sorry."

But Gwion didn't seem to notice. "Stay here."

The steps had ended, but not the chasm. A narrow, irregular bridge of stone had thrust up from the depths below. Llew held his breath as Gwion began to cross it, brandishing his staff of rowan before him like a sword.

As if someone had opened a door, an icy wind swept toward them, and he shrank back against Gwydion as it hit, watching as the old Druid crouched and ducked his head against it.

Llew began to shake, not from the cold, but from the nameless evil ahead. He could nearly see it now. A huge black shadowy form that took its shape from nothing familiar to man, but from that dark seed of fear that each man nourished deep within. Horns it had, and fiery breath, claws and more legs than he could count.

It took a step forward onto the bridge, then another and another.

"Back," Gwion commanded, stepping forward to meet it, his chin high and firmly braced against the wind.

It did not obey. A sound like demon laughter echoed through the cave, changed to a challenging snort, then a full-throated roar as it crossed to meet the puny man-thing

Gwion braced against the wind and kept moving forward, looking tiny and vulnerable against the immense blackness of the shadow beast. Involuntarily, Llew clutched at Gwydion, burying his face in the man's chest so he wouldn't have to watch the destruction of his new friend.

"No, watch," Gwydion said, turning him gently, and what he saw were bolts of lightning leaping from the staff of Gwion, and what he heard was the beast snarling in pain.

"Be gone," shouted Gwion.

The beast had backed away some, but now it reared up on black haunches and sprang up to meet Gwion squarely in the center of the bridge. Its mouth opened.

Putrid breath could be smelled all the way to where Gwydion and Llew stood.

Fire poured out of its mouth to flame the man below.

With a nimbleness that belied his years Gwion leaped back then attacked again with a searing of white lightning that met flesh and set it aflame. "Be gone, I said."

Llew blinked in amazement. It was gone!

Gwion lowered his weapon to normal cane position. He gave a satisfied nod and stepped off confidently, calling over his shoulder, "You may follow now."

Llew and Gwydion looked at each other in amazement, trying to smother spasms of relieved shaking. When they stepped onto the stone bridge, however, fear edged in. It was a long way down, and the path was frighteningly uneven - like picking your way across a stream, but if you fell, you wouldn't get wet, you'd fall a thousand feet to death.

Gwydion was especially nonplused. Gwion had his faith and his magic and his staff, the boy had the natural agility of the young, but he had nothing - nothing but the fear of losing his balance.

Carefully Gwydion inched his way forward, studying every step before he moved. It would be easier, he thought, if his legs weren't shaking so.

Arms out. Slowly, slowly.

Another step. Whoa, not far enough. Heel off the edge. A little more.

Now change your balance. Slowly. Bring the back foot forward now.

Oh, watch what you're doing. Nearly knocked your own foot off, fool.

Slowly, now. Get it forward. Arms out, balance. Now feel the rock. Heel down. Good. Now the toe. Ease the weight forward. Careful. Straight over the foot. Good.

Now get that back foot moving. Where is it going to go? Yes, there. Nice and level. Weight forward. Oops. Slowly!

"Gwydion!"

"Shh. Don't bother me now." Can't you see what work I'm doing here? Must talk myself through it.

Next step now. Careful. Pull that foot forward.

"Gwydion, are you all right?"

He looked up. Saw the interminable bridge, his friends at the end of it, so far away they seemed hardly bigger than his hand. No. I'll never make it.

"Gwydion!"

His arms waved wildly. NO? He was falling.

17

GWYDION

Oh. Ow? Gwydion was clinging to the rock, legs and arms straddling the bridge, his cheek bloody from a bad scraping. His forehead hurt too. He wanted to touch it, but couldn't seem to move his arms. That's right, he thought. If I let go, I'll fall.

He lay there for a long time, eyes shut, utterly weary, and then he was aware that the boy was next to him, talking softly, soothingly, dabbing at his forehead and cheek with the tail of his tunic.

"Let me help. Can you sit up? Good. That's good. I'll help you. Take my hand. That's it. Can you stand up?

"Do it slowly. Yes, good. All right. Let's walk to that high step ahead. We'll do it together. That's right. We'll rest there. Keep moving. Yes, that's good."

And he was moving. Letting the boy plan each stage, his mind empty, his body obedient, his steps steady. He tuned everything out but the boy, listening to his words, responding as requested.

He did not think again until he was seated on the far side knowing the danger was behind him. Gwion was on one knee with his arms about his shoulders, assuring him that he was safe, praising Llew as his savior.

"We're almost there now," Gwion said at last, rising. "Can you go on now?"

Gwydion ducked his head in embarrassment. "Yes. Apparently, I just needed a mite of babying."

The response was, "Humph," from the elder and a barely suppressed giggle from the younger.

As if in reward for the tenacity of their ordeal the ground leveled out and the path widened. At first grateful, Gwydion's feelings changed to suspicion as the time passed. It was too easy. What were they missing? He became very alert, looking for a trap.

They rounded a bend and found that the trail forked into three trails. "Which way?" he asked.

"The center trail is the widest and easiest because it's still level," Gwion considered. "Therefore, it can't lead to the treasure." He shook his head. "At least I don't think it can. Both the others go up, but in opposite directions." He hesitated. "Right, I think."

"Let me go first," Gwydion said, taking the lead, trying to make up for the lapse on the bridge.

They had climbed for about ten minutes when the trail abruptly petered out in a small room, nondescript except for the fact that it was shaped as an equilateral pentagon. Gwion sighed and started back the way they'd come. "Wait, Penbard. This might be right after all." Carefully he began examining the walls for the fine line of a seam that would indicate a doorway.

Llew was standing in the exact center of the room. "If you stood here, you could reach out and touch all five walls."

His own examination having failed, Gwydion gave the boy a sharp look, remembered what had happened at the waterfall, and stepped to the center of the room. Taking a deep breath he began haltingly, not sure what he would say, but as the words were spoken aloud, they became strong and sure, and without thinking it through he knew that some instinct had led him to choose correctly.

Five was the sacred symbol of the Goddess, the pyramid her most ancient emblem, so it was the Goddess he addressed. He touched each of the five walls in turn, rotating slowly, reaching inside for that state of trance where the thinking mind was subordinated to the inner being that touched the god and made man one with him.

He named each of the five elements as he touched - earth, air, fire, water, soul. Turning, naming. Faster and faster, until he was spinning.

Gwydion was not conscious of what the other two were doing. Had he known, he would have been appreciative, for Gwion, seeking to increase the power of the word had crouched below his out-stretched arms, firmly grasping the boy's hands so that they formed a circle around him. They too were moving, crouching, but going in the opposite direction of his spin.

And this was fortunate, for abruptly Gwydion did become aware again, with the realization that he was dizzy, then that he was falling. The two caught him in their arms, and all three were down on the ground, but they were still falling.

The floor itself was falling!

The walls disappeared as they dropped. They clutched at one another and at the floor as they sank, for there was space all around their moving platform, and it was small enough for a single man to reach the edges, and with two grown men and a boy all occupying this small space, they were doubly fortunate that they'd fallen in a heap. Even so various appendages dangled in space and as each one realized the danger, he pulled the offending arm or leg in, sometimes unintentionally clobbering one of the others who jumped back in reflex, then clutched frantically as more body parts slipped from the edges. Long before the platform ground to a halt, they were huddled close, holding each other as much for moral support as for safety.

There was a slight thud and a minute bounce as they stopped.

Disentangling, they were quick to step off the platform, feeling grateful not to have fallen. Llew was the first to notice their surroundings. "I hear the sea." He pointed. "That way. Look, it's light too."

"We're in the mouth of another cave," Gwydion said.

Though he didn't speak aloud, he couldn't help thinking that if they'd simply walked around the island and come in this way, they'd have had an easier time of it.

He turned to face Gwion and there was an edge of bitterness in his tone. "What now?"

Llew had run to the low-hung entrance and called back to them, "We're on the far side of the island. I can see the sun setting."

As Gwion opened his mouth to speak the boy called out again. "The tide must come right inside here. It's damp everywhere and slippery."

That was startling news. Gwydion had been so relieved that he wouldn't have to repeat the bridge again to get out that he hadn't looked, but now he could see the line on the wall, clearly delineating the high-water mark. This was not good news. The line was well over his head.

"The door," Gwion was saying.

What door? Whatever did he mean?

Gwion made a sharp gesture. Llew came running, but once again they were hard-pressed to keep up with the older man as he picked his way up the back wall of the cave, using cracks and ledges and the odd handhold.

Gwion seemed to get farther and farther away, for he climbed with surety and they with hesitation. Gwydion reached back to help the boy make a particularly long step, then pushed him ahead so that he'd be able to see when Llew needed help again. They soon found themselves on a ledge that was easy to follow and led directly to the wooden door where Gwion was waiting for them.

"It's not locked," he said, "but it hasn't been opened for a very long time and it's stuck. Come help me push."

Even Llew helped, working the bottom while they worked the top. There was a hand's width of space now.

"Together now. Ready, one, two, three," Gwion urged. It gave a little more. "Again. One, two, three, push!"

All three tumbled forward as the door gave way, and before they could scramble to their feet someone said, "You're too late. You might as well leave."

The voice was so beautiful it made them think of music - more specifically, of all the lovely sad songs they'd ever heard that left one aching for more.

"I beg your pardon," Gwion said, rising to his feet. "Is someone there?"

"I said you're too late. You might as well leave."

"Excuse me. Too late for what?" Gwion asked.

Gwydion had stepped back for the torch he had left on the far side of the door. "Don't bother," the voice said to him, and suddenly it was light enough to see the room quite clearly, though the speaker's face remained hidden in shadows.

"How did you know that I wanted light?" Gwydion muttered more to himself than to the apparition. He stepped back into the room, his hand, shielded behind Gwion, drawing a sign to ward off evil.

The creature laughed. "Your puny magic won't work against my kind, Initiate."

He took a single step forward into the light and let the hood of his cloak fall back. Gwydion gasped, for the creature before him was the most singularly beautiful person he'd ever seen. He looked almost like a man, but he was taller, and each feature was more perfectly defined. The very light seemed to emanate from him, and when he moved, it was effortless, and a joy to watch.

Gwion straightened his shoulders and took a step forward to meet him, but his attention was on the boy who made a surprisingly graceful bow. "Your Eminence," he said softly.

Again there was a laugh - like bells chiming through wind.

"You needn't bow to me, Fisher Child. I have no rank worthy of a bow. In fact, if we were of the same world, we might be mates for I'm of an age near to yours."

He gave a genuine smile, and there was a radiance about him that made Gwydion feel that Llew's bow was proper even if he was young. It occurred to him that he trusted this Fair Being, and that made him emotionally back off to examine his feelings. Why should he trust him? Did not every child know stories of people entrapped in the Other World by these Faeries?

Gwion cleared his throat noisily, but the Light Bearer's attention was still on Llew. "Someday, Man Child, you will be known as Path Finder." He was looking at Gwion now, but still speaking to the boy. "Your trails will lead many to the Goddess of three faces."

Now he spoke to Gwion. "You must nurture him and see that he is taught. You have little time left before your soul is waiting to be reborn in Annwn, Penbard."

Both the advice and the fact that he knew who Gwion was startled the old Druid.

"You speak in riddles, Fair One, and your words will give us much to think on in the future, but the biggest riddle for me is who you are and why you're here."

"Ariandell," he answered. "I am here, of course, because my people would not see the Treasure of Albion fall into the wrong hands."

"Did you make the monster we met at the bridge?" asked Llew, hanging on his every word.

"Did you like that, Boy? To be sure it was a dandy." He shook his head and as the fair hair settled about his shoulders with the lightness of fine silk, he frowned. "It's never failed me before."

Gwydion decided that if the boy was bold enough to ask his question, he could certainly do the same. "Have there been many visitors here?"

"No, you're the first."

But we vanquished the beast, he thought. Who had it never failed against? What kind of a contradiction was this? He realized that Ariandell was laughing at him. He nearly slapped his forehead as he got the joke. The beast had never failed because it had never fought anyone off before.

Gwion's question was, of course, the one that got to the heart of the matter. "Where are the thirteen treasures of Albion?" He stood quietly, waiting with dignity and patience.

"I told you. You're too late. They're gone."

Gwion stared at him until both Llew and Gwydion flushed with embarrassment. "If you were truly set to guard them and they are gone, why are you still here?"

Now Ariandell's expression changed. There was cunning and furtiveness and, possibly, respect, but his sweet tones changed to thunder. "You dare to accuse me of falsehood, Old Man?"

Gwion did not back down. "I accuse you only of doing a good job of what you were charged by your king to do. You were told to guard the treasures until one came who could deliver them to their true resting place for safekeeping. I am the one."

Ariandell laughed. "You? An old man with the shadow of the Crone walking behind?"

Gwion managed to look very dignified. "The Goddess will not claim me until the treasures are safely delivered to your king. Do you think that he would be pleased at these games you play?"

"Prove it," Ariandell shot back at him. "You say you are the one. Anyone could make that claim."

"No, not anyone. I know that the treasures are here. I know that here they aren't safe from the Romans. I know what they are and what they represent to our land. I know that they belong with King Nudd in Annwyn, and I know where Annwyn is."

Ariandell made a dismissive gesture with one hand. "Deduction and gossip."

"Not gossip. I have seen Annwyn in the fire, I have seen King

Nudd in the water mirror, and I have heard him speak to me in the wakeful dream. He," Gwion paused for emphasis, "told me that I am the one."

Ariandell came so close that Gwion drew back. He towered over the old man and thrust his face down next to Gwion's, looking into his eyes. "Show me."

"Gwydion, your torch." Gwydion retrieved it and tried to hand it to him. "No, lodge it in this crevasse in the floor."

When it was done, Gwion gestured Gwydion back. As if he were lifting the flame, he cupped his hands about it, then slowly moved them up and out and the flame followed, expanding until it was the size of a huge bonfire, the flames wider than two men and so high they threatened to blacken the ceiling. "Look," he said.

18

GWYDION

All of them stared at the flames, the boy trembling a little against Gwydion. It did not take long. Almost at once the flames showed them a place fearful and beautiful - a cavern so vast that they could not see the tops of the long row of ornately carved pillars, so filled with light that they squinted against the brilliance, with gems of all colors embedded in the walls and flashing in intricate patterns.

There was a throne at one end of the cavern, carved from the rock itself and jutting out from the wall at a height slightly taller than the tallest of men, the same color as that most precious shade of blue-white diamond. Indeed, Gwydion wondered if it had been carved from one gigantic stone.

King Nudd was on his throne, his feet resting lightly on a dais of gold, his fingers pulling idly at a beard that matched the shade of gold perfectly. "Truth," he said suddenly standing, his finger pointing at Gwion. "He is the one."

Abruptly the image was gone and the flame extinguished.

Ariandell laughed and music was in his laughter. He turned his back on them. "Well, come along then."

He walked toward the back wall. There was nothing to conceal a treasure in front of it, and the wall looked solid. No one saw how he found the hidden door, but a narrow section of the wall opened and they followed him through it. They stopped in unison, staring in wonder. The room was a long one with a solid row of pillars on each side, carved to look like the trunks of oak trees, with branches extending to a ceiling of stone leaves. So skillful was the carving that it seemed they were in a real forest, walking a path between two behemoth rows of oaks. They could see no visible means of lighting, but it was light. Ariandell did not stop to admire the view, and after a moment that was too brief they scurried to catch up with him.

At the end of the room, they stepped into a great circle of carved oaks which made the two Druids feel very much at home.

"You see?" Ariandell said. "The Romans have not destroyed all the sacred circles. The heart of the island will always be here, will always be invincible."

"And will you guard this too?" Gwion asked.

"The task is for another." It was not an answer that would entirely satisfy, but it was the only one they would get.

The group stopped just short of the center of the circle. The Fair One threw his cloak back over his shoulders, lifted his chin, shut his eyes and raised his arms. In a language they didn't know he sang a haunting refrain, his voice so pure and beautiful that their hearts filled with the joy of it, and their eyes streamed with tears.

It was a moment so perfect that it seemed to them that the One God was there among them. Each of them recognized separately that this was the finest moment of his life, and was saddened, knowing that it could not last, that the bliss would fade as the god departed, and that this was why mortals were rarely allowed to glimpse such splendor. There was actual physical pain when the song ended, Gwion especially gasping at the shock of it, and it took a time to recover. When they did, there was something so brilliant between them and Ariandell that they shielded their eyes against it.

19

GWYDION

Once they grew used to the brilliance, they saw that it was a man-sized crystal egg. Ariandell gave them time to adjust, not hurrying, but when he saw that they had all recovered, he stepped forward, and waved one arm over the egg.

The crystal shell cracked horizontally, near the top, and the upper portion lifted. Inside was a plain wooden chest. Gwydion could not help but voice his disappointment. "Oh."

The one word, filled with inflection was enough to bring a reprimand from Gwion. "No, it's perfect." In spite of its size, he lifted it easily out of the egg, first gesturing to Ariandell for permission. "May I?" he asked, pointing to the lid.

"I am the guardian no longer. It is yours. Do with it as you wish."

Gwion trembled as he undid the simple clasp and lifted the lid, and the others drew near to see. "Are they all there?" Gwydion asked, reaching as if to move the top item to examine that underneath.

"No, don't touch them." Gwion looked immediately apologetic.

"They are not for us to use." He lowered the lid and redid the clasp, testing it to see if it could open accidentally, then, satisfied, he straightened up. "Yes, they are all here. I don't know how they could all possibly fit in such a small chest, and I don't know if we could get them back in again if we were to take them out, but they are all plainly here."

It was then that they realized that Ariandell was no longer standing with them. In fact, they couldn't see him anywhere. "Where did he go?" Llew asked.

"I don't know. It's as he said. He's no longer the guardian, and his task is finished."

"The crystal egg is gone too," Gwydion pointed out.

"Yes, and I have a feeling the light will soon fade now that Ariandell has disappeared, and the tide will rise to flood the cave. We should be on our way." He gestured to Gwydion who braced to lift his side of the trunk. But it came off the floor easily, and was not difficult for the two to carry.

"It should be heavier," Gwydion muttered as they made their way out of the long room and down the steep path to the floor of the cave.

"It will seem, yes, it will seem very heavy, indeed, before we're through with it," Gwion answered with surety.

"Where did this nice path come from?" Llew asked. He was right. They had struggled up the cave wall, using out-thrust rocks as footholds and handholds.

"Perhaps the path will be clear from now on," Gwion answered, a remark that Gwydion first had occasion to remember outside of the cave an hour later when they were forced on a long detour by a steep and narrow ravine that jutted from the sea to what seemed the center of the island. It was made particularly frustrating because at the coastal edge they were just three man-lengths from the opposite side, and at no point did the two sides get any closer. He grumbled so much that finally Gwion said, "Perhaps you would have been happier trying the stone bridge again? And all those steps back up?"

Gwydion was embarrassed. "No. This is infinitely better, but aren't you worried about being seen? On the way in you wouldn't let us walk openly on the shoreline where we could be spotted from shore."

Gwion grunted as he hefted the chest over a downed tree trunk. "When we reach the point where we can be seen from the mainland, we will not be silhouettes against the sky, we will be back in the trees."

"What about the fishing boats?" Llew asked, pointing.

They could see three of them. They were out of view at the moment, following the edge of the ravine, but had they been hidden before they started inland? Gwion was so upset that he put his end of the trunk down. Gwydion was quick to copy him. "Did you notice any boats when we were out on the coast, Llew?"

"Sure. One of them is my da's, and one is my uncle's."

"What about the third?"

Llew shaded his eyes and squinted. "I don't know."

"Too far away to see?"

Llew turned back to them, looking troubled. "No, I can see it, but I don't know that boat. I think it's Roman."

Gwion reached quickly for his end of the chest. "From now on we'll stay inland until we're near our own boat." Gwydion soon found that Gwion had doubled the pace, too.

20

BLAISE

The door burst open simultaneously with the knock. I looked up in surprise to see my prodigy, hair disheveled, barefoot, and in his nightshirt. "Faeries!? His voice was not quite a shout. "So this 'history' is a faerie story?"

I put the quill on its stand, put the stopper in the ink bottle and pushed away from my desk, still looking at the scroll before me, so that he would know that he had interrupted me. Then I looked up at him and stood up and spoke politely in a normal tone of voice. "Come. Sit by the fire." I handed him a fur. "And put this about you. It's a chilly night." When he had obeyed, somewhat sullenly, I added a log to the fireplace, and sat down across from him. "Aren't you supposed to be asleep now?"

"I've been reading the scrolls you gave me."

I frowned. "Keeping your dorm mates awake with your light."

"The moon is bright tonight, and my cot is next to the window." One of his legs was on a fast jiggle, up and down. "I wanted to find out what happened when they were in the cave."

I looked sternly at his leg until he stopped moving, tucking the offending limb up on the chair under his other leg. He knew that controlling his body was as important as controlling his emotions. "Faeries?" he repeated indignantly.

I saw that he was working to calm himself, in spite of his belligerent tone, so I answered him without censure. "It's not a faerie story, but the Fair Ones play a role in it."

"But there's no such thing as a faerie."

"How do you know that?"

He bit his lip, glaring at me.

"Did your grandfather tell you that?"

"No. Leave him out of it. Not one person in Dementia believes in faeries." I didn't say anything to that and after a moment he started fidgeting again. Then he became defensive. "I don't believe that anyone in all of Albion believes in them."

"That's a pretty sweeping statement," I told him. "The truth of it is that they were here before the settlers who are our ancestors came. They were called the Fair Ones because all of them were tall and well-formed. As the years passed and the settlers began to claim more and more land, they retreated to caves under the ground and eventually seemed to disappear."

"Why would they do that? It was their land to begin with. Why didn't they fight for it?"

Ah, he was settling, the emotion seeping away. "I don't know. They did not want to interact with man, and if a man stumbled upon one of their caves, he usually disappeared."

"And never came back?"

"And never came back."

He shook his head and his dark hair flew about his face. Still not convinced, he asked, "Are they still around? Have you ever seen one?

I answered his second question first. "I have not, but the Lady of the Lake has. They seem to have all gathered in one place now –

Avalon."

"But that's where she and her ladies live. Do they live there together?"

"No. If you were to visit Avalon, you would not see them. They live in a cave and unless they want you to find the entrance, you never will – no matter how long you stay."

"And they have magic?" He shook his head and revised his question, remembering that I had told him that most of what people call magic is simply observation of something that they don't understand. "Do they know more than Druids?"

"I don't know if they know everything that we know," I answered, "but there are things that they know that we don't."

"Like how to make a platform of stone drop without destroying anything?"

"Yes, and how to create an atmosphere that produces fear in those who behold it."

"So, there wasn't really a monster fighting Gwion?"

"I believe he was fighting his own fear, and the fear of Gwydion and Llew."

He stared at the fire in silence. It was late and I could not quite stifle a yawn which he saw. He seemed surprised as he stifled a yawn of his own. I stood up and damped the fire with a gesture.

He unwrapped the fur and handed it to me. "Perhaps you should keep that until morning. You'll feel the cold now," I told him.

Together we walked to the door. "Thank you," he said, turning toward his room. Before I could answer, he was back in front of me. "What's a coat of many colors?"

I smiled, laughing inwardly at his persistence. "In the olden days when a bard sang, the king rewarded him if he liked the song. He would give a piece of jewelry, meat from his own plate, a bottle of wine, or sometimes something to wear – like a coat. If the bard was a member of the king's court, he could earn a coat that might have more than one color. The more colors the coat had, the higher the honor, and once in a while, a bard became so revered that he could wear more colors than the king himself." I drew myself up and pointed down the hall. "Any other questions can wait until morning, scamp, so away with you."

21

MERLIN

I ran down the corridor as fast as I could. Master Blaise was right. It was freezing – especially my bare feet. By the time I reached my bed I could barely feel them at the end of my legs. I wrapped the fur around them several times, then pulled my blanket up and tried not to shiver.

I thought about all that he had said. Then I thought about how I had interrupted his work without apologizing, and how rude I had been, bursting in and demanding answers when he was obviously done with the school's work, and finally alone to work on his histories. And I thought how kind he had been.

He had not even reprimanded me. He should have beaten me. I deserved it. Instead, he had brought me to the fire and built it up. He had draped a fur across my lap to warm me. He should have yelled at me, and told me to return to my room at once. What was I thinking?

Will punishment come later? Suddenly my throat was so dry I couldn't swallow. What if he sends me away?

I could apologize for my outrageous behavior. Would it do any good? I suppose it couldn't do any harm. Yes, I'll do it. I'll apologize tomorrow.

Oh, I hope he'll let me stay.

22

BLAISE

Emrys was included with a group of students who were learning the words to honor our god during the various festivals, so he was at the Oak Circle and I didn't see him until after our noon repast.

He entered my office rather sheepishly and stood quietly regarding his toes until I had finished instructing a messenger about the delivery of a package. The man left, and I gestured Emrys to a chair, but instead he walked slowly toward me and stood, arms clasped behind his back as if he feared they would fly away if left on their own.

"Master Blaise," he said, finally looking up at me, "I am very sorry for interrupting your work last night, and for barging in on you demanding answers. If you want to beat me, I'm ready." He lifted his chin, and I noticed that his hair was actually combed and his tunic was brushed.

I was flabbergasted, but did not let him see it, and stood quietly, thinking, which flustered him into saying, "Should I remove my shirt,

Sir? Or my breeches?"

"Oh, please don't. Now remind me why I should beat you?"

"Because I was rude to you, Sir."

"Ah." I steepled my hands together and regarded him seriously. "Has anyone here laid a hand on you, Emrys?"

"No Sir, but then again I don't think I've done anything to deserve it before."

"No one is going to beat you here – now or ever. Come sit down. I'm weary." I led the way to the chairs.

He seemed no happier at this news, but sat as instructed. "Then what, Sir? How will you punish me?"

I saw that he truly was miserable. "I will admonish you for your rudeness, but not for your questions. You can always come to me, and you can say whatever is in your mind, whether you think I'll be pleased or not. I will never reject your questions. Do you understand?"

"Yes." He was still studying the floor.

I was close to exasperation. "What are you afraid of?" I asked, emphasizing the 'are.'

He looked up and I saw that there were tears in his eyes. "I don't want you to send me away." He couldn't look at me.

"What? Send you away? That's what has you worried?" He nodded, and I finally understood. I rose, took one of his clenched hands, pulled him to his feet, sat down in his chair, deposited him in my lap, placed both arms around him, and cuddled him close.

"I have no intention of sending you away. Not now. Or ever."

I realized that this was what he needed most – my affection. Even more than my praise and my encouragement. He was so young. And so vulnerable.

He was sobbing openly now, but he managed to say, "Really?" His eyes met mine, huge with wonder.

"Really," I told him. "You are my very special apprentice."

23

GWYDION

The sun slipped down through layer after layer of clouds, breaking through them to end the day perched on the rim of the sea and strewing the water with streaks of gold. They had sent the boy ahead, slithering on his belly to the cliff edge. He had soon returned with terrible news. "They've landed just down the beach from where we hid our skiff, and it looks like they're making camp."

"What could they be doing here?" Gwydion asked.

"I don't know. We don't often see soldiers in these parts."

"Did anyone else know we were coming here?" he asked Gwion.

"No one knew what we were going to do, and I told no one where we were going until we arrived and asked help from Llewellen."

Llew raised his chin and squared his tiny shoulders. "Da would not have told," he said defensively.

Gwion patted his shoulder. "I know he wouldn't. Come on. We'd better see if we can tell what they're up to."

A few moments later they were all lying flat on the cliff top, watching the Romans build a fire and post guards. A few of them were sent along the beach in both directions, but soon returned with firewood. No attempt was made to climb the cliff. A meal was prepared and they began eating, which reminded the trio that they had not eaten since late morning. They withdrew to a heavily treed area and pulled out the remnants of their own rations, wolfing them down with water from a nearby stream.

"Now what?" Gwydion asked.

"There's no way we can get to our boat, so I suggest we rest," Gwion answered, rolling up in his cloak. "You take the first watch, Gwyd. Wake me when the moon is high." He was asleep and snoring softly before the others had half-finished softening their own nests with pine boughs.

When it was his turn to sleep, Gwydion was not so lucky. He tossed and turned, feeling every pebble, and clenched his teeth at every night sound, holding his breath and listening hard until he had identified the animal or bird and convinced himself that it was harmless. Just before dawn he gave it up completely, nodded at Gwion on guard as he passed soundlessly, and made his way to the cliff top again.

Gwion had been half dozing as he passed, but when Gwydion disappeared down the sea side of the cliff, he jumped up, his motion waking the boy who asked sleepily, "What? What is it?"

"I don't know," he whispered. "Better wake up and be ready to run." He started to climb to the cliff top, but was back moments later. "Stay here. Don't follow me."

By the time he extracted a promise from Llew, he was well behind Gwydion, and at the viewpoint he couldn't see him. He could, however, see someone else, and it was in the worst possible place - at their boat.

It was completely uncovered, and the man - a very large man - was in the process of pushing it out to sea. Gwion didn't think the man was Roman. He was dressed in rags, his hair long, unbound and very red. Quickly Gwion checked the activity in the Roman camp which was just beginning to stir. The guard … where was the guard? Ah, there, walking toward the camp with his back to the skiff. And then Gwion saw Gwydion, moving very fast and swinging a thick piece of driftwood. He saw it connect with the back of the big man's head, saw the man fall forward into the skiff just as the tide caught it and whipped it away from the shore. Gwydion had fallen to one knee, lucky since the Roman turned back and looked, but with Gwydion down he saw nothing over the intervening bushes. "Stay down," Gwion willed.

At the same time two things happened: someone called to the Roman who turned away from the boat, and Gwion clearly heard him answer, "Don't know. Thought I heard something," and Gwydion was up and running through the water after the skiff. He made a leap just before another wave pushed the boat farther from the shore and was hanging, half in and half out when the Roman looked back one last time. But the Roman was looking at the shore, not the water, and didn't see anything.

The boy had not stayed below as he'd promised, but had crept silently to the top of the cliff, and startled Gwion as he touched his elbow. The old man fought down an oath as he struggled to still his pounding heart, and when he could concentrate again, he saw that the Romans were breaking camp, and that the boat was well out to sea. There seemed to be a struggle going on. He saw an oar raised and when it came down, the struggle stopped.

For a long time nothing changed. The boat went farther and farther out with no attempt to steer it.

Gwion realized that the sun had come up. The Romans doused their fire, packed their gear and loaded it into rolls which were strapped to their backs. Most of them were eating something as they moved out in formation along the beach, passing the spot where the skiff had been hidden without paying any particular attention to it.

"We're lucky," the boy said. "It's grass there, not sand."

Gwion failed to make the connection.

"No footprints," the boy told him.

"Of course."

"If they'd been looking, they'd see bent and broken grass."

"Or the skiff."

"No, it's too far away. We can see it because we're high, but down there they can't see it." The boy watched them carefully. "Even if they could see it, they wouldn't. They're looking at the cliffs, not at the sea. Hoping to see a path, I'll bet."

"Let's hope they're a long way from us before they find one." He watched the Romans until they disappeared around a rocky curve, lost to view.

The boy stood up, shading his eyes against the freshly risen sun. He frowned. "Gwydion wasn't very good at rowing, was he?"

Gwion got up as quickly as old bones would let him and joined the vigil. His heart pounded heavily in his chest. "I can't see the boat anymore." Urgently, "Can you?"

Llew searched the entire horizon. "No. I can't see it either."

24

GWYDION

It had taken all Gwydion's strength to shove the huge man aside so that he could free the oars. He was resting, and watching the shore to see if the Roman boat was coming after them, and watching the man which was lucky, for when the man groaned, it did not take much effort to knock him unconscious again with one oar.

He watched as the Romans moved out, felt relief when they failed to notice the skiff, and was pleased to see that they passed the cliff top where he had left his friends without attempting to climb it. When he was sure that it was safe, he slipped the oars and turned the boat. That was the easy part. What wasn't easy was rowing against the tide. He was near to exhaustion and barely making any headway and still a long, long way from shore when he heard a chuckle. "Not too experienced with an oar, are you?"

He whipped his head around, nearly losing an oar in the process, to see the unconscious man sitting comfortably in the prow, holding a blue plaid rag he had found somewhere against his forehead. The man dipped the rag in the water, wrung it out, and daubed it against the gash in his head, checking it frequently for blood.

"I mean if you're going to steal my boat," he said, "it seems to me that you ought to be able to handle it. Otherwise, why bother?"

"Your boat?" Gwydion bristled. "You're the thief, and your bold tongue won't change that."

The man laughed again. "You can't convince me you're the owner. Not the way you handle it." He shook his head, grimacing a little at the pain. "Possibly you stole it before I did, but how you ever made it to the island through that treacherous strait is the grandest of miracles, and I'd accept any wager that you won't make it back."

Inexplicably and in spite of their predicament, Gwydion found himself liking the amiable thief. "I have to make it back. You're right, I'm not the owner, but until you tried to steal the skiff I was with the owner, and I can't desert my friends."

A crafty look took over his face. "They could always arrange transportation back with the Romans, couldn't they?"

Gwydion was exhausted and doubted that he'd win a second battle with his huge passenger. Perhaps, he could win him over. "Explaining our presence to the Romans is the last thing we'd want to do. I take it from your actions that you feel likewise?"

The man stopped daubing and regarded him with good humor. "Nor do I feel it necessary to explain my presence to you. Let us just say that I have no intention of returning to the island, and the sooner you begin rowing with the tide instead of against it, the happier I'll be."

"Can't do it. Not yet at any rate. While the Romans are gone from their camp, I intend to quietly land this craft, collect my friend then head for the mainland. I could do it much faster if you'd give me some help on the oars."

"Now why would I be wanting to help you? I just told you I won't return to the island."

Gwydion looked him straight in the eye. "You're obviously a

man on the run. We have friends on the mainland - fishermen. They'll be able to outfit you for travel - food, clothes, a boat if you need one."

"I have a boat now," he answered.

"No, I have a boat now." Gwydion flipped an oar out of the holder, holding it like a club.

The large man ignored the threat and thought it over. "Friends, you said? How many?"

"Two."

"And what makes you think you could find these friends before the Romans return?"

"They're watching us now. Up on the cliff. We were up there waiting for the Romans to move out when we saw you."

"So it would be quick in and quick out?"

Gwydion nodded.

The man smoothed the hair away from his face, twisted the cloth to make a band, and tied it about his head, gentling it over the wound. "Move over, and hand me an oar." He settled himself next to Gwydion. "Now do what I tell you and we'll see if you have the makings of a seaman."

25

GWYDION

Gwion was slumped down, head on his arms, giving way to a private bout of misery. Had he brought Gwydion to a watery death? Was he to be found out by Roman soldiers? Was the treasure chest of Albion lost for all time to those who would have someday used it to restore the rightful place of their people?

"Master, look!"

It was the boy. And what fate would be this brave child's? Ariandell had called him Path Finder and charged Gwion to teach him where those trails would be. Llewellen would come looking for them. Tomorrow, probably. And what would he find? Was the boy's death on his hands? With Llewellyn and his people cursing the Druids for bringing the wrath of the Romans to them? Oh fie, what had he done?

"Master, please." The boy was shaking his shoulder gently but persistently.

"Leave me alone," he said in a terrible voice with the full-throated timbre of the bard enforcing the command.

He could see the boy back up, tentative now, confused. But resolutely he took a step forward again, his information too important to contain.

"Master, please look. The boat is coming back. We should be ready." Leaving Gwion to straighten and cast a squinting eye to the sea, he slid down the slope to their makeshift camp, and began heaving at the chest, trying to push it up the steep slope alone.

For a moment Gwion ignored his feeble efforts, straining to see if the boat was truly returning and if Gwydion really had control of it. Once he had determined the truth of the former, he didn't worry himself about the latter and made haste to help the boy. "Here now, let me get one end and you get the other. Together we'll make short work of it."

That was not particularly true. It took a great deal of effort for the two of them to work it up the steep slope, and a great deal more to ease it down the other side of the cliff to the beach. They lost their footing several times and slid, but luckily checked before plunging off the rock, and finally had it and themselves in the bushes - a scant protection against the Romans if they returned, but the best that they could do under the circumstances.

The skiff fought the tide every bit of the way, sometimes losing, sometimes gaining. When it finally bit into sand and seemed to hold, Gwydion said a short prayer of thanks to the Goddess. He was exhausted and wanted nothing more than to crawl to the nearest bush for a long rest, but instead he took a good grip on the oar and looked at his companion, fearing he would yet need a weapon.

"You needn't be wary, Landman. I'll hold the boat. You help your friends." The stranger nodded toward the shore behind them. "From the looks of the baggage they didn't pack lightly."

Gwydion cast a glance over his shoulder. Llew was making a valiant attempt, but the chest was heavy for one so small.

"Speed, Man. Or are you anxious to explain our presence to the Romans?"

Gwydion moved quickly to the front of the boat where he could turn and see his friends and the shore on either side of them, as well as keep an eye on the big red-haired man. "I'm not leaving the boat. You help them."

"No. I'm feeling a bit weak from that blow on the head you gave me." He folded his arms and crossed one leg over the other, giving every impression of a truly relaxed man.

Gwydion decided to leave matters as they were. The old man and the boy were halfway to the water. They were slow, but better to be slow than to chance losing the boat. He had a few moments of guilt as he remembered Gwion's poor health. It was surely a strain that needn't have happened, yet he couldn't leave the stranger alone.

The progress was steady until they were an arm's length from the skiff when a surge of waves hit the boy hard enough to knock him over which pulled the chest so that Gwion lost his grip and dropped it. For a heartbeat both it and the boy were swept back to shore. The chest stayed there, but Llew who was still unbalanced was pulled with the retreating water, and did not right himself until he had swept well passed the boat.

"Llew!" Gwydion cried. "Are you all right?"

There was no breath for answering, but the boy nodded and began paddling so the tide wouldn't push him farther away. "He'll ride the next wave back," the stranger said. "Try to get an oar to him and pull him in." He put one leg over the side then turned back with a look of disgust. "And don't hit him with the oar."

"I thought your head hurt too much to help," Gwydion taunted in return.

"If I don't lend a hand, the soldiers will be back for sup before your friend there gets that chest unstuck and in the boat by himself." It was true. Gwion was making no progress. In spite of their predicament Gwydion could not help a smile, but he turned to look for the boy before the stranger could see it.

26

GWYDION

This time the stranger took both oars. Working with the tide the island was soon a distant speck. The boy, stripped of his own wet clothes and wrapped in Gwydion's cloak, offered simple directions, guiding the boat away from shoals and rocks, and steadily toward the harbor.

Llewellen and Colim, still fishing in their larger boat, were not there to meet them, of course, but Brigid spotted them and called for her mother who deftly caught the line thrown by Llew and secured it neatly before she gave them a shy but hearty welcome.

"Starved, you must be," she said, hustling them toward the house. "Lucky I saved a bit of last night's stew. It will just take me a minute to heat it."

She had glanced at the stranger curiously, but it was in her nature to be gracious, and she would never have the audacity to question a Druid.

For his part he stuck with the group once he heard the word

"stew" mentioned, heaving the chest to one shoulder and bearing the burden as easily as if it were a cask of ale. At this a look with mutual lifting of eyebrows passed between Gwion and Gwydion, but as Neldda herded the group up the beach they didn't question it. If the Goddess chose such as him to serve, who were they to argue?

Neldda made good on her offer of stew, and Gwydion noticed that the stranger took three large helpings, but Neldda beamed at the unspoken praise, so Gwydion held his tongue. As the last of a fresh loaf of bread disappeared, she built the fire up and pushed them to the hearth, saying shyly that they all looked exhausted, and they were happy to let themselves be pampered, spreading the skin she handed them before the fire. They soon were all asleep. They stayed that way for several hours until Llewellen and Colim came in, laughing boisterously over "the one that got away."

Dumping wet sandals at the door Llewellen tousled his young namesake's hair, called, "Welcome, friends," then, "What have we here?" as he spotted the big redhead. Unlike his wife he had no qualms about asking. All eyes turned to the stranger, some eager, some with trepidation, wondering if the man would be honest.

"Friends call me Rob," he answered without hesitation.

"Is that short for Robin," asked Gwydion, "or a description of your profession?"

The family showed surprise at such rudeness, but not the stranger, who worked his mouth about into various expressions. Finally, though, he broke into a hearty laugh. "I guess I deserved that."

"You did." Turning to the family Gwydion explained, "Rob tried to steal our boat on the island."

There was an awkward pause while the stranger studied the floor. Llew, generous of spirit, finally added, "But then he helped us get the chest in the boat." Llewellen gave him a disapproving look, but he continued defiantly. "He rowed the boat too."

Rob flashed a smile at him. "That was partly to keep from getting whacked in the head again."

"And I'd have done it," Gwydion announced.

"I don't mind telling you, Rob, that I'm not happy to hear that you had designs on my skiff," Llewellen said, but then he spread his arms in a peace-making gesture, "however, we follow tribal laws of hospitality here, offering any traveler the comfort of roof and hearth and food from our table. Speaking of which, Woman, what are those good smells?" He looked at his wife affectionately. "Are we ready to sup?"

"As soon as Caeron and the baby arrive. I sent Brigid to fetch them when I saw you unloading the nets."

No sooner had she finished this explanation than the door opened and Colim's wife and baby daughter came in with Brigid. While Colim gave his wife an affectionate pat and bounced the child high, Neldda got the seating started, squeezing people in on the low wood benches that flanked the lengths of the table, and urging her husband to his stool at the head and Gwion to another at the foot.

Rob found himself flanked by Colim on one side and Gwydion on the other, and understood that it was deliberate. Still, Llewellen began the meal by saying, "I am Llewellen, and this is my family." He told Rob each name, going around the table and not hesitating when he reached Gwion and Gwydion which might have suggested a differentiation in family status, figuring that they would not want the stranger to know their true identities.

The chicken and mushrooms were delicious and comments were kept to praise for the cook, a brief description of the day's fishing and pleasantries about the baby who was passed from her mother to her grandmother and back several times and were happily busy stuffing tiny morsels of chicken and bread into her mouth. At the end of the meal Colim poured more ale for the men while Brigid and the two women cleared the table.

That was when Rob finally spoke. "My family is composed of fisher folk too. Well north of here. North of the Wall."

"Ah, that explains why you're at home with boats then," Llewellen said pointedly.

"And it's sorry I am that I came near to leaving you folks stranded," Rob said, stroking his red beard, nodding his head to Gwion as the elder.

Looking back to Llewellen, "Nor would I have abused your kind hospitality. My own boat was smashed on an unfriendly rock just off the shore of that island. I'm afraid I lost everything."

Llewellen leaned forward, chin on elbows and tipped toward Rob. "And what was that?"

"We have very little in our land besides rocks and fish. For certain my sisters couldn't put a meal on the table like your wife did tonight." He drained his glass and it was obvious even to Llew who quickly refilled it that he was embarrassed to admit such a thing. "At any rate several times a year we sail to Hibernia to trade. Oh, I had a fine haul - enough cloth to keep the women sewing all year and the men making new sails, also a lyre for our bard, spices that they claim came from lands far to the east of Rome and that would have livened our endless diet of fish, dried beef to do the same, hides ready to be worked into leather." He shrugged and gestured dispiritedly with his hands. "More of the like."

"What did you trade for all these things?" the boy asked.

"The only thing we have a true abundance of, lad. Fish!"

This time they all laughed with him. When it had died down, he continued. "On the way home a squall caught me. I lost the mast as well as the sail, and nearly lost my life. There was no way to control the boat, of course, and for days I drifted as the current took me. I'd never seen a sight so grand as your island and was thanking the Goddess for her benevolent guidance when I hit the rocks. The only thing I could save was my own skin and lucky I was to do that."

"That you were," Colim said, and all around the table there were nods of agreement.

Except from Gwydion who leaned forward, tapping his glass on the table for emphasis. "You managed to leave out one small detail,

Rob. Seems you've neglected to tell us why the Romans were hunting you," his voice raised enough to bring the women back, "and why you didn't want them to see you."

27

GWYDION

Rob tossed his head back and took a long drought of the tasty ale that Llewellyn had brought out to compliment his wife's fine cooking.

"Ah, but can I trust you, or will your tongues wag tales when I've gone?"

His free hand shot out to grasp the shoulder of the rising Colim and forced him back to his seat in an almost companionable manner. "It's NOT you fine fisher folk I'm concerned about, you see."

He smiled, his face nearly touching Colim's, then he released his hold and twisted, rising to face the younger Druid who had also risen at the insult. He spread his arms wide and shrugged an apology. "From the People of the Sea you're not. Nor you," he nodded at Gwion, still smiling affably. "Trust must be earned. It canna be plucked from a stranger's orchard, nor sown in a stranger's field."

Gwydion poked a wagging fist at the big man's chin. "This is all the trust you'll get!"

Rob did not pull back from the fist, but leaned closer. "Do you think, you puny whelp, that you truly could threaten me?"

They were all on their feet now, except Gwion, but it was his voice that commanded, "Sit down. All of you. Sit."

Slowly they obeyed him - all but Rob who faced him proudly, chin high, shoulders squared.

Gwion let him wait, eyes locked onto him, never wavering. "Rob," he said at last. "Rob mac Tave."

The big man sat down very slowly. He tipped his cup. Found it empty. Licked at thick, dry lips. "Where have you heard that name?"

"That bard you mentioned - the one you were bringing a lyre to - is his name Padua? Did he lose an eye at age eight to a Roman rapist while trying to defend his mother?"

"Aye, it is the same man."

Gwion did not hesitate, though Gwydion flinched at his revelation. "He is one of my priests."

A look of incredulity crept over Rob's face. With a hushed tone of the utmost respect he said, "Penbard."

"Be careful," Gwydion warned. "We are not using our own names on this journey, nor such a title."

"Nor am I," Rob shot back. "Discretion suits for both of us. Can you say the same?"

"Now that I have a reason for it."

Though Gwydion seemed satisfied, Colim was still rankled. "Yet before we swear to such discretion, I would have the story of Rob mac Tave."

It was Gwion who answered. "Do you know of the Fianna? The Fianna Eirinn - warriors of Hibernia," he said for the benefit of Llew. Gwion raised a hand to forestall any protest from Rob. "Not just warriors - the greatest warriors, Llew. They were first organized four hundred years ago by a king named Fiachadh, and in King Cormac's time led by the mighty Finn mac Coul the most famous of all Fenians."

"I have heard of him. He was a great warrior."

"More than that. To be a Fenian one must also be learned in many arts, including poetry, and must renounce all loyalties to family and tribe. Ah, and the tests one must pass.

"It is said that a man must stand in a knee-high pit with only a staff of hazel to defend himself as nine warriors hurl their weapons toward him at the same time.

"If he survives that, he is chased through a forest by armed men with not more than the length of a tree to separate them at the start.

"If he is unwounded and if he has not damaged one single branch of the forest nor loosened a single lock from his braided hair, he may go on to the next ordeal which is to run at full speed, jumping over a branch that's as high as his forehead, stooping under another that's as low as his knee, and pulling a thorn out of his foot without breaking stride."

This had all been addressed to Llew, but now Gwion's eyes found those of the stranger. "It is said that Rob mac Tave is the greatest of all Fenians now living."

Llew was regarding Rob with something between enthusiasm and hero worship, but his older brother was still probing. "If you are the Fenian Rob mac Tave, you were not telling the truth about your people."

"I told you only part of the truth, Colim. My mother is from Hibernia, the sister of four Fenians, the daughter of a Fenian. I grew up in the village I described - my father's, but visited with her people every summer and joined the Fenians when I was not much older than Llew here. Every year I go to my birth village, taking supplies to them, bringing back fish."

"So let's hear why the Romans were after you."

"They spotted my mast-less boat, saw my trouble, and took the time to rescue me and my gear. They believed my trading story - the same one I told you. But one officer had been asleep, curled up behind something and out of sight. When he woke, he unfortunately recognized me from a skirmish we'd fought up north somewhere. Then and there he wanted to hang me for piracy. I suppose we'd raided for cattle. The Romans seem to take that personally. That might not have warranted instant death, but apparently I'd killed someone who meant a great deal to him too."

Llewellen had filled his cup. He nodded gratefully and drank. "So while they were debating whether to try to rig up a noose on the mast or to simply throw me overboard, I made the decision for them. I spotted the island we were passing and jumped. I can hold my breath longer than most and I did that, staying under as long as I could, surfacing only to look for the island, but they must have been watching the shoreline, for as soon as I caught my breath on shore, I saw them turn the boat.

I ran to the rocks, hoping to find a way up the cliffs, making my way around a curve that would hide me from view. I found your skiff by ramming a knee into it, decided it was well hidden, and found a good spot behind a couple of large boulders part way up the cliff and not far from it. Then I fell asleep - exhausted from battling the ocean for days and from the swim. Woke up early the next morning and you know the rest."

"I thought Luguvallium had been deserted by the Romans," Gwydion said to Gwion.

Llewellen answered. "Sometimes they send a garrison there from the Wall. They don't usually stay long." To Rob, "Did you hear anything? Do you know what they were doing or why?"

"Happen I was lucky to get away with my skin intact. We had little time for pleasantries."

Gwion stood. "We'd best get some sleep. We'll leave well before the sun rises."

"Won't you stay and rest a day or two?" Llewellen asked. "You look like you could use it if you don't mind me being blunt about it."

"With Romans close about I don't want any suspicion cast on you

116

or your family, Friend. Rob, you must go too, for the same reason."

"You're right about that. I wouldna want harm coming to your fine family because of me." He tugged on a leather string that hung about his neck, soon producing a pouch that had been hidden in his shirt, and spilled the contents - a man's ring set with a large stone of amber, four gold arm bands, and two women's hair clips, one in silver with a large ruby and four small emeralds, the other gold with tracings of Celtic knots. "You wouldn't know of a boat for sale, would you, Llewellen?"

28

GWYDION

The moon had come, ridden high then sunk out of sight before any of them got to sleep that night. The only boat that might be for sale was owned by an elderly neighbor who threatened yearly to go live with his daughter in Deva, "where I'll sit by the fire. When it rains, I'll laugh at the rest of you, knowing how wet and miserable you are."

"You can't handle his boat by yourself," Colim said.

"Let me be the judge of that," Rob countered, so Colim and Llewellen took him to meet Wayllan, a large jovial man who limped badly from an old injury and was nearly blind. "It would be doing me a favor to take it off my hands," Wayllan admitted. "Seems every time I put out I must scout the nearest three taverns to find a crew, and most of them aren't happy working for a cut of the fish we haul in. That's what they get - I've no gold to be handing out - but they grumble about it and slack off when I'm not paying attention."

"She's a beauty," Rob confided to Llewellen when he finished his inspection, and they sat down to an hour of bargaining. Each point had to be emphasized with a swallow of ale and by the time the two had finished an enormous quantity had been consumed.

"Still don't know how you're going to handle her by yourself," Llewellen said as they neared the house. He was holding on to Colim who was holding on to him, each with the pretense of helping the other walk steadily.

From the doorway Gwion spoke. "Perhaps we can help. Gwydion and I have come up with an idea."

Gwydion, standing behind him, did not look pleased, but then he'd lost the argument the two had been having ever since the others had left. He saw no reason why Rob mac Tave should be involved in their future. Reluctantly he moved aside so the others could pass, but he did not sit down at the table with them, but remained standing at the door.

Colim stifled a yawn and Llewellen returned it openly as Rob gave the Penbard his full attention. "Have you a firm destination?" the old man asked without preamble.

"I thought to go west across the sea, then north, hugging Hibernia's shore and seeing what goods I can gather for a day's labor here and there."

"Then east to Caledonia?"

Rob nodded.

"The day's labor here and there … it could take weeks. Am I right?"

Again Rob nodded.

Gwion stroked the thin hairs of his beard thoughtfully. "What if you were to earn enough gold so that you could hire help to man your boat and replace the goods lost? And shave off a week or so?"

Rob leaned back. "I'm interested."

Of course you are, Gwydion thought, folding his arms and leaning against the wall. But he stayed silent out of regard for the Penbard.

"Take us south around Gwynedd and Dementia to the Severn Sea, and east to the mouth of the Severn River. We will be your crew and before we depart, we will help you find sailors to accompany you north again."

"Tis a fair plan, Penbard, with the one wee imperfection."

Gwydion found himself scowling at the implied criticism, then fully angry when Rob went on to explain that the imperfection was the two of them as crew. He controlled his emotions, however, at a sign from Gwion. "We will be happy to learn the way of boats. It's useful knowledge - something that all Druids should learn, perhaps. What do you think Gwyd?"

He stifled the reply he wanted to make. "Yes, it could be useful."

Rob diplomatically ignored the fact that Gwion was of such an advanced state of age and deterioration that he could do little of the practical work and concentrated his criticism on Gwydion. "I've seen you row. Hopeless." He shook his head. "It would take months to train you."

Gwydion had to bite his tongue to keep an angry oath down, but Gwion ignored the tension. "You were prepared to sail by yourself. Isn't some help better than none?"

The silence was too long to be comfortable.

"He doesn't want our help," Gwydion snapped.

"For sure I didn't say that."

A very high-pitched voice asked, "What if I went with them? There isn't anything I don't know about boats."

"You?" Llewellen said to his youngest son. "Why would you be wanting to go?"

This was the question that Llew had been asking himself ever since they had gone to see about the boat. He couldn't tell his da about Ariandell and the words he'd spoken. "The Path Finder," he'd said, and with those words Llew had felt like he'd been hit over the head with his destiny. It felt so right.

He wanted it so much. How could he explain it to a man who

thought the world revolved around catching fish? He certainly couldn't tell him about the magic and how he wanted to learn it, for he must prove to the Penbard that he could hold his tongue.

Could he tell about the singing, and how he knew there were songs inside him wanting to come out?

Could he tell of the fierce wanting to learn the ways of the outside world that the two Druids had whetted?

He could not say it was a thing of importance to know of the Treasures of Britain, for he was not supposed to know of them, but could he make his da see the necessity he felt for the task of transporting them to their proper resting place? He'd be good at it. He hadn't choked when the monster appeared on the bridge, nor when the Faerie had appeared, nor when they were only a cliff away from being discovered by the Romans.

Could he say how alive it made him feel? That fear of discovery created an excitement all its own that he wasn't sure he could live without now that he'd felt it?

That it was a task he'd started, and would like to see through to the end? Yes, maybe that was the way to approach it. He had to say something. They were all staring at him - all ready to dismiss the whims of a child. "I - I would like to see the job we started finished, Da, but even more I would like to be a Druid," he finally blurted out.

Both Colim and his da uttered oaths, and across their faces flickered emotions of surprise, of fear, and of dismay. Yet neither of them wanted to criticize his wanting - especially not with two Druids listening and Llewellen settled at last on, "You're young for such a decision, Boy."

"No, I'm not young," he corrected. "I'm just small for my age." He took a chance and made a lucky guess. "The Penbard was about my age when he began the studies."

They all looked to Gwion to say something, and he did not disappoint. "I was even younger."

"Don't you have to have some calling for such a thing?" Colim asked. "You can't just decide you want to be a Druid with no talent for it."

Again they looked to Gwion, the boy anxiously holding his breath, but it was from another quarter that he received unexpected support.

"I think there is talent," Gwydion said. "He has a passable voice. You might make a bard of him. And he comported himself well. There were moments …" He'd been about to say, "of danger," but thought better of it "… when even a man grown might have turned and run the other way, but young Llew proved brave and steadfast. And once when it seemed we were doomed to fail, it was Llew who became the Path Finder."

Gwion smiled, nodding to show Gwydion that he understood the reference. "I would be happy to train Llew if it is acceptable to you, Llewellen."

"And I would be happy to accept Llew in my crew," Rob added, remembering the boy's skill at steering them through the rocks.

Llewellen had completely sobered. He stood, then stepped away from the table. "We'd best all try to get a little sleep. You, especially, Llew, for if it's leaving you are in the morn, you'd better be first up. Have the firewood neatly chopped and stacked, a bucket of fresh water drawn from the well, and it wouldn't hurt to gather some of those late wild flowers on the upper hillside for your ma. She's the one who'll be missing you most."

29

MERLIN

I've just learned about the enormous sea that Gwion and his friends are about to face. Before this I've seen only the Severn Sea which separates Cambria from the Summer Country and Cornwall. My grandfather's castle was in the town of Maridinum, not far from the shore of the Severn. Sometimes, when it was storming and the wind was whipped up, the waves came in high, but it never seemed threatening.

The sea I've just seen hits the cliffs with such force that it tears rocks from it. The waves can be twice as tall as a man and I've learned that if one is out in a boat the waves can be as high as an oak tree. The sound it makes striking the land is like the booming of the deepest drum or thunder marching across the sky. And supposedly the weather and the sea were mild while we were there? Oh, and no matter how long you stand on the shore, or how much you squint, you cannot see anything but water. I asked if there was land across from us, but none of our elders would venture a guess, for no one had sailed west far enough to see.

Three of the older students took eight of us (all under nine years) on a walking trip. Well, to be honest, the first day we were in a boat, rowed by a few of the small folk who live in the swamps around us. Mother and I had come in a larger boat, so we were higher and farther away from the fish and animals that make this water home. But the boys and I saw many of them, oh, and birds, and felt that we were part of the water too.

When we left the boats, we headed southwest for several days until we were on top of the cliffs, looking at water as far as we could see. We spent a week there climbing up and down, searching the beaches for shells and small shellfish and strange little beasts that lived in tidal pools. We lived off the land on the entire trip, learning to make snares to catch rabbits, to find bushes that held succulent berries, to discover which greens were edible, to find fresh water that trickled down the cliffs in many places, and to catch fish. An old man from one of the first villages we passed showed us how to make a net and how to cast it and drag it back, hopefully full of fish.

We slept out under the stars in bedrolls, which were basically just a blanket we rolled to carry an extra set of clothes and any food we found, and before we went to sleep we searched for planets and constellations, pointing them out in voices that got quieter as the minutes passed because one-by-one we dropped off to sleep.

It was exciting to sleep outside at night. I'd never done that before. It was also exciting to see a new kind of land and to learn that we could live off it.

We came back just in time for supper, then I met with Master Blaise to discuss the trip, and now it's off to bed where I will learn what's happening in Gwydion's story.

30

GWYDION

A morning that started dark and cold, and above all too early, soon turned into a glorious day. The sky was that dark blue that only comes in autumn and offers perfect contrast to the reds and golds the trees are wearing. On the coast the temperature was milder than in the mountains and fall was later in coming. No hint of snow here - even a promise of lingering summer.

Neldda had been up long before the others. She had prepared a solid breakfast and packed as much food as the family could spare for the seafarers, and she had done it all blinking back her tears. Gwydion wondered if she had tried to sleep at all after Llewellen had gone to bed and broken the news that their youngest son would be departing on the morrow. She was wordless through the meal and wordless when they were loading the boat. It had appeared on their mooring just after a faint dawn had given color to the sky, and Wayllan and the friends who had sailed it there helped Rob and Llew check it out, then waved a cheerful farewell and good luck, and headed back to their homes.

Just as they were saying their farewells to Colim and Caeron who had come to see them off and had gifted Llew with a good knife, Neldda broke through the group and pressed a soft new cloak of blue wool into Llew's hands. "You've a need of it," she told him, "for you've outgrown your old wrap. It was going to be for your birthday with a design embroidered down the edges, but you'll have to do without the fancy trimming."

"It's beautiful," Llew told her. "Thank you."

"I wasn't up working by firelight like your ma," Llewellen said, "but I've a bit of something for you too." From his own neck he slid a long, thin strip of leather threaded with three small, but lovely fish worked in silver.

"I shall wear it with pride and think of you every day when I polish it," Llew said. His voice was steady, belying the tears that threatened to spill from his eyes.

Gwydion was looking at him proudly, pleased that he had spoken for the boy, and surer than ever that they would make a good Druid of him. And that, for hours, was the last moment that he had the leisure for a thought of any kind, for orders were soon given, with more and more following, and he tried very hard to obey them. He had determined that if he had to suffer Rob mac Tave's presence on this part of his journey, he would give the man as little to complain about as possible. He had also talked himself into being enthusiastic about learning to sail.

Learn he did. By the time the boat had rounded Dementia he could raise and lower the sail, keep it from being shredded by the wind and pretty generally at the correct angles to get where they were trying to go, and Rob had pronounced him "passable" with oars. It was a learning experience for all of them. Gwion was becoming quite the fisherman, trolling lines from the stern that he checked frequently, baiting the lines himself, and proud of each day's catch that often fed them adequately. Llew had formal lessons each night, memorizing and repeating back the lesson of the day before, and sometimes they worked on simpler ballads, though without a harp the music itself could not be taught. They all enjoyed the songs and sometimes all sang along with Gwion. Rob turned out to have a surprisingly good baritone and seemed as anxious to learn as Llew. In turn he taught them ballads of Hibernia and a few battle songs of the Fianna.

The weather held for them. The skies were stacked with clouds that swelled and billowed like the sail of their boat, and none faded to grey, nor gathered enough moisture to dump it back to earth. Yet as the days passed crisp became cool and cool became cold, and more and more of the trees were bare. They shivered out in the boat, wearing all the clothes they owned, and sometimes wrapping the spare sail around Gwion. The old man said nothing in complaint, but his teeth chattered and his skin looked blue, and sometimes they felt the need to stop on shore to build a small fire, to walk the numbness out of their feet, and to drink heated wine.

They were near Maridinum when the weather changed. Everywhere they looked it was grey - the sky, the sea, the shoreline. The wind picked up. Rob and Llew fought to keep the sail in line as they rode newly churned waves. Sleet fell, icing the lines and their fingers impartially, and visibility dropped to nothing.

"Can't we make the shore?" Gwydion shouted over the wind.

Rob's answer was lost when a huge wave broke over the bow, flooding the boat with icy water. He grabbed a bucket, as did Gwion, and both bailed furiously as he repeated the question.

"We couldn't see the rocks," Llew said when it was obvious they still couldn't hear the answer. "We're better off heading for open water."

Another huge wave hit, this time spinning the boat and tipping it so that the sail touched the water before righting.

"Lucky we have the chest tied down," Gwion said to Gwydion as they clutched at the railing, clinging with all their strength, but

127

Gwydion wasn't listening, he was sliding away and reaching to help Llew who also clung to the rail, but happened to be hanging on the outside of the boat.

He reached for the boy's belt and gave a massive heave, jerking him up and over, but there wasn't time to check his condition.

"Sail coming!" Rob shouted, and he lunged to catch it, struggling with all his might to secure the lowered cloth against the wind that was trying to jerk it away and shred it. Gwion added his weight and they soon had it down and tied, but now the boat was completely at the mercy of the waves, for Rob's attempts to steer seemed in vain.

The boat was tossed into the air like a child's toy, landed on the crest of the next wave, rode it down into the trough, and got flooded by the next.

The other three couldn't do anything to help Rob. They were too busy clinging to the rails.

"Rope yourselves down and bail," he roared. This time they heard him.

Unsteadily, riding the sea like a bucking beast, they tried.

Gwydion had to help Llew who was so light that the wind threatened to pluck him off and sacrifice him to the sea.

"Are you all right?" he finally managed to ask.

"Just wet and cold, but not much more than you," the boy said bravely, then tried to lift Gwydion's spirits. "It won't last long, Gwyd. We'll be all right. Tend to your own ropes."

Gwydion did, but first he checked Gwion, tugging on the ropes to make sure they were secure. "Need help, Master?"

"Trying … he muttered, his teeth drumming a staccato rhythm, "… trying to remember the words to harness the wind."

Gwydion tied himself loosely enough to sit close to the old bard and began to bail. Softly he began to sing.

Gwion's head snapped up. "That's it. Yes, that's it."

He threw a bucket of water back to the sea and spread his arms wide, his strong voice joining in.

Crouched over the rudder, Rob shouted, "Singing won't help. Bail!" but they ignored him.

Llew worked with a cooking pot, his motions steady as he dipped it down, scooped, and threw water over the side, but he listened carefully, and finally shouted, "You've done it? The waves are calming."

Rob gave the two a doubtful look, but called, "Raise the sail, Llew. We're on our way to a warm fire."

Rob had made a confident prediction, but a wrong one, for when they finally reached shore some two hours later, it was not a warm fire that awaited them, but a cold reception.

They had secured the boat, had helped Gwion to his feet and out of the boat, then walked him until the stiffness was gone. Meanwhile Llew had rounded up a pile of damp wood, hoping to start a fire when a blood-curdling shriek pierced the silence.

The sleet had turned to a steady snow, but without the wind to whip it about, it was gentle enough to see the nine bodies hurling toward them, swords drawn.

All nine were shouting now, using the sound to stir themselves into a battle frenzy.

Three of the four about to light the fire froze, but the fourth - Rob - sprang into a crouch between the two groups and pulled his sword.

"Get to the boat and cast off," he cried, meeting the first attacker with a lunge that spitted him.

Rob pulled the sword free and side-swiped the blade across the chest of the man next to him.

Before the blood began spurting and the man falling, he had back-handed his blade through the neck of the man following and the freed head flew off, rolling to a stop in front of another who jumped it.

Off balance that attacker landed on his knees to meet a thick tree branch swung at his head by Gwydion who had not obeyed Rob's command. It stunned him enough so that a second and third blow were meted out. The fourth was interrupted when a sword sliced his weapon in two.

Gwydion was left with a useless stump. Useless, unless you shoved it into the man's eyes - which Gwydion did.

Unfortunately, the sword hand was poised to cleave Gwyd's skull in two.

"I said get to the boat," Rob thundered, hacking the arm of Gwydion's attacker off at the elbow.

Gwydion, watching the pulsing blood spurt, felt sick to his stomach and fell to his knees, retching.

It was a good position to observe that the man he'd downed with a stick of firewood was also on his knees. In fact, the man had reached one arm back and looked about to throw something.

Gwydion grabbed the arm and twisted hard.

Not hard enough. Instead of struggling, the man turned into him, the knife blade now inches from Gwydion's face. But Gwydion still held the knife arm and he was straddling the man, smelling his foul breath.

Gwydion was not a trained warrior with the reflexes of an athlete.

The man startled him when he spit in his face and Gwyd relaxed the hold enough so that he ended on the bottom as the man's strength rolled them.

Worse, the knife blade was close enough to draw blood at his throat.

Aid came unexpectedly from his half-sized companion who ripped two handfuls of the attacker's long hair straight back, yanking as hard as he could.

This gave Gwyd the release he needed to push the knife away, and Llew mashed down hard on the man's arm with his foot and kept it there, still pulling the hair, until Gwydion could extract the knife from his fingers.

With a massive shove the warrior thrust to his feet and out of the grasp of both of them.

He turned, searching for his sword, only to run straight into the blade which Gwion was holding stiffly with both hands.

When the man fell to his knees Gwion didn't budge and the sword ripped through bones and flesh as his own weight dragged him down, shearing a path from his abdomen to his chest. Only then did Gwion let the sword angle drop.

It took all three of them to pull it out.

Wearily they looked around. There were now eight bodies on the ground in various stages of dismemberment. The ninth man was running away and was nearly out of sight.

Rob was going from one body to the next methodically checking to make sure they were dead. When he had finished, he wiped his blade clean on the grass, shoved it back in his scabbard then turned on the others, his anger so palpable that they each took a step backward. "When I give an order," he said, "I want it obeyed. Instantly. NONE OF YOU," he thundered, "are capable of giving me any aid in battle. Therefore, none of you are capable of making a decision about it. DO YOU UNDERSTAND?"

Llew swallowed hard and ventured, "We killed one of them."

"YOU WERE IN MY WAY? If I hadn't had to watch out for you, the one you got would not have almost caused the death of Gwydion. And the one who got away would be lying here with the others." He seemed eight feet tall, and he bore down on them and they cowered, unconsciously drawing together.

"You may be in command of our spiritual journey, but on the boat and anywhere that danger threatens, I am your commander, and if you don't all agree right now, on the spot, I'll put your precious chest ashore and sail away."

Both Llew and Gwydion looked at Gwion to see if he would agree, but he was so exhausted from the storm and the battle and the emotional devastation of eight bodies, one of them slain by himself that he hesitated and did not answer straight away.

In a quieter voice Rob added, "The runner will be back, you

know. And this time he'll bring enough men to kill us all."

Gwydion matched his tone. "Why? Why did they attack us, and why will they come back, and who are they?"

Rob spat. "I don't know, but we got attacked because we're not of their people. And why they'll return is easy to answer. One word - revenge."

He turned and walked away from them, back toward the water where the boat waited. "Are you coming?"

"Yes," Gwion answered for all of them.

Rob did not turn back, nor did he stop walking.

"And we agree to your terms. We will obey you, and we will let you determine when a situation is dangerous."

Rob faced them, hands planted firmly on hips, his eyes narrowed. He did not seem pleased to have tamed them so. "Yes, you will."

31

GWYDION

They were still wet and now more miserable than ever with the cold wind blurring the shore with swirls of snow. Llew sneezed.

"Are we going to stop soon?" Gwydion asked Rob. "We've got to get warm."

"If we can ever get a decent wind that will get us well away from them." Rob's head nodded toward the shore.

"Them?" Gwydion asked dully.

"You don't see them?"

Gwydion stared at the shore, carefully now. The beach was empty, but back by the tree line he finally spotted movement, and gave a sharp cry as he counted them. "There must be over a hundred of them."

"I'd say closer to two hundred."

"Who are they? I didn't recognize their colors."

"Nor did I," Rob responded. "They aren't Dumnonii."

The cold, the wet, and the futile battle had lowered his spirits, but now true despair as dark as the slate-grey sky seeped into Gwydion. "What can we do? We'll freeze before the wind turns. Look at Gwion."

The old man was crouched down, his back to the wind, but even from the other end of the boat, they could see him shivering violently."

"The boy too," Rob said, whispering. "He didn't get a chance to get warm after his dunking."

They watched as the boy blew on his hands, wrapping one with the other, balling the fingers of the inside hand to a fist, then switching hands, the fingers coming out of their coil slowly.

Rob looked back to the shore, to the boy and the old bard, then out to the open water.

In a low voice, so that the others couldn't hear, he confided, "I've been trying to figure out where we are. It's still too cloudy to get a direction from the sun. I didn't think we'd been blown out of the Severn Sea. I thought we were on the south coast of Dementia. But if that's right, what are they," he indicated the warriors, "doing there? Do you see the problem?"

Gwydion shook his head. "No."

Rob was surprisingly patient. "If that's Dementia, we're going east toward the marshes of the Summer Country like we should be."

He waited for Gwydion's nod of understanding.

"But what warrior tribe exists in that settled and populated area? Where did they come from? Have they killed all the people in their path?"

Gwydion shrugged, as confused as Rob. "It doesn't make sense."

"It does make sense if we landed on the north coast of Dumnonia," Rob continued. "It isn't heavily populated and a new tribe could have avoided the Dumnonii."

"So that's where you think we are."

"I do now." He stared at the shore. "So if that is Dumnonia, we're going west. We could end up west in the endless ocean."

Gwydion shuddered, wondering why he'd ever thought learning to operate a boat might be pleasurable. "So until we're sure where we are, we have to keep the shore in sight which means we'll freeze to death."

Llew stood up and came to them, and they were surprised when he spoke, because they hadn't thought he could hear the discussion. "What if we turned away from the shore just long enough to become invisible to the warriors?"

"If we can see them, can't they still see us?" Gwydion asked.

"No, Llew's right." Rob was already turning the boat away from the land. "We'll sail until we can't see the warriors. You see, the land is high - we'll have no trouble seeing it. Then we'll turn again and run parallel to the shore. They'll lose sight of us, and they'll wait - probably all night, thinking we might be trying to trick them into leaving. They'll never see a tiny boat like ours."

"I hope you're right," Gwyd muttered, sitting down next to Gwion.

"Llew's right. Trust the Goddess, Gwydion. Do you remember what Ariandell called him?"

"I know. The Path Finder. A much more important question is one for you. Can you hold out that long?"

Gwion smiled a sad little smile. "I suppose I'll have to."

32

GWYDION

They spent the whole night out on the water, sailing under a full moon that periodically fought through the clouds for a few minutes, but never could they catch a glimpse of the stars that might have oriented their direction. Finally they slept with the sail dropped, the anchor out, and the boat rocking them like babes in a crib.

The snow had stopped falling just after Rob turned the boat, and as the sky darkened it actually got warmer instead of colder. At first this worried Gwydion, for he remembered hearing that when one froze to death, he didn't actually feel cold, and he thought this might be happening to them, but eventually exhaustion wore fear down, then fought it out with the discomfort produced by sleeping on unpadded wood, and finally claimed the round.

In the morning Rob confirmed that they were now going north. "How do you know?" Gwydion asked.

"Druids study the stars, don't they?"

"Yes."

"So do men of the sea. The pole star directs us."

They kept going until late afternoon. "Look!" Llew shouted, pointing at the barely visible land. The others looked and saw that it seemed to end. "We're back at the Severn Sea."

They followed the curve of the land, battling the sail as they changed direction, and when Llew and Gwydion had finally followed all Rob's directions with the sail and found that they had time to look around, they were coming in to a sheltered cove. That night they ate hot food, dried their clothes, and got warm.

The next morning they found themselves nursing a fevered Llew. The wind was fierce and cold, so Rob and Gwydion gathered wood and lashed it together for a quick lean-to while Gwion doused Llew with medicine from his pack.

Inside the shelter he held Llew's head in his lap, alternately pressing a cold cloth to the boy's forehead and pouring melted snow water down his throat.

For hours the tiny body shivered in spite of the fire and the extra cloaks that covered him, and sometimes he raved deliriously, his words making no sense.

Rob and Gwydion slept a little that night, but Gwion watched the boy all night in spite of offers from the others to relieve him.

In the morning, when his fever still raged, they agreed that they couldn't travel. Gwydion tramped through the trees gathering firewood, and worried about barbarian attacks.

Rob proved his skill at knife throwing by downing two rabbits. He skinned them and began a stew. Gwydion added the last of their onions and a twist of salt to it. It began to smell so good that Gwion left the boy for a few minutes to walk over, sniff at it and fish a chunk of meat out with a stick to see if it was done.

When he had gone back to the boy, Rob whispered, "Gwion still looks weak, but under the old layer of skin he's strong as a bull."

Gwydion nodded his agreement. "I was very worried about him after the storm, but with each adversity he seems to have gotten stronger. Still ..."

"Still what?"

Gwydion swallowed, looked away finally looked back. "Still, his spirit will soon leave his body. I think ... shortly after we reach ... our destination."

"You're saying he's dying? That getting to wherever you're going is what's giving him strength to go on?"

Gwydion couldn't answer. His throat was so tight it hurt. He nodded again.

Rob didn't say anything, but there was an aura of anger about him. He stalked off toward the boat, climbed in, sat down, and stared out to the frothing sea.

It wasn't until the next morning, while Gwydion was heating leftover stew that the fever broke. Llew sat up normally - no thrashing, no spasms of shivering - and said, "Something smells really good."

Gwion stood for the first time in hours, yawned, stretched. "It certainly does." He took several stiff, uncertain steps toward the fire before returning for the staff that sometimes served as his cane. By the time he reached Gwydion two large helpings had been dished up.

"Hope that's not for the boy and I. He should just have the broth and I could only eat half of that."

Gwydion put half of one portion back into the pot and handed it to Gwion, then dumped the other back and carefully scooped so that there was only broth. "You sit and eat. I'll help the boy."

"Where's Rob?" Llew asked, and, "Where did we find this shelter?"

"Rob's hunting for supper. Are you strong enough to hold the bowl? Here, I'll help you drink from it."

Gwydion saw how surprised Llew was by his own weakness, but didn't comment on it. "Rob and I built the shelter ourselves." He laughed at the ramshackle structure. "Think we ought to set up shop?"

Llew laughed too. "You'd shame the profession of carpenter."

Head-to-head they looked into each other's eyes with affection. "You frightened us, Llew. You were very sick."

He glanced at Gwion. Saw that he was sleeping where he sat, his unfinished bowl of stew balanced precariously on his lap. "Good. This is the first sleep Gwion's had since you came down with the fever. He's been at your side constantly. Wouldn't let either of us take a turn." He reached over and deftly removed the bowl.

Llew fingered a leather bag, hanging from his neck. "Did he gather the herbs for this bag? I can smell how strong they are."

"No. Well, maybe, long ago. He put the charm together from things in his pack." He smiled as he remembered Gwion, searching through the pack, finally dumping its contents in the snow, picking packets out making different piles with packets to be returned to the bag, packets to use immediately as medicine, packets to use as charms. "You'll find other charms tied to your ankles and arms."

"I can feel them. Will you help me? I need to find a bush."

Gwydion pulled him to his feet and supported him as Llew faltered at his first steps. He was visibly shaking. Before Gwydion let him take another step, he tucked his own cloak about the boy. "Lean on me. It's all right."

It was as they made their way slowly back that they heard Gwion's shout of alarm. Then came silence which alarmed Gwydion so much that he lifted the boy and ran the last few steps. The lean-to came into view, and also the warriors, dozens of them, one of them holding Gwion firmly with a long knife blade at his throat.

33

GWYDION

Gwydion ducked back into the trees, pulling the boy with him, and crouched behind a bush while he considered what they should do. He had no weapons, and even if he had one, he was vastly outnumbered. The old master's throat would be cut before he took two steps into the open.

Perhaps … he risked a peek over the bush. No, the knife was sheathed and someone was in the process of tying ropes about his master's hands.

Llew was too weak to be of any help in a rescue attempt, too weak to make a run for it. Perhaps they could make their way around to the boat. He could put Llew in it, cut the rope, and give it a good push toward open sea. Llew could sail it by himself.

He looked at the boy to see if he was well enough. Saw a drawn white face and large dark eyes wide with fear. Awkwardly he patted the boy's shoulder in an attempt at comforting.

Once more he risked a look into the clearing. He stood on his toes. The boat? Where was the boat? He stepped to the side, head still craning to the empty sea, still seeing nothing. Then a weathered hand clamped over his mouth, and jerked him down.

He fought, chest hammering, but he lacked the strength and slowly, silently he was turned to face … Rob!

For a moment they glared at each other, blood pulsing rapidly, still clutching at each other. Then Rob signaled for silence, picked the boy up, and gestured for Gwydion to follow.

The forest was dense, providing a natural cover. Gwydion thought surely they would stop to plan some course of action, but Rob kept moving, breaking into a run as they got further away. After several futile attempts he got close enough to pluck Rob's sleeve. "Where are we going?" he panted.

Rob pointed ahead. "The stream. Hurry, some of them are following us."

Gwydion needed no further prodding and plunged in after Rob, ignoring the pain of icy water.

Harder to ignore the gouges to his ankles, toes, and shins as he slid on the rocks of the streambed. Twice he went down, bruising his hands and soaking his robes, but still Rob stayed in the water. "How much longer?" he asked, dismayed to find his voice as shaky as his body. The wet and cold were causing spasms of shivers.

"There's a hill. You can see it ahead."

It was not much of a relief. It was rocky and steep, and by the time they reached the top, Gwydion was gasping for breath.

"We'll rest here," Rob said.

"Thank the Gods." Gwydion collapsed on the ground next to the boy. Rob had put him there gently, and covered him with his own cloak. Gwyd hoped he was truly sleeping, but after that bone rattling run considered it more likely that he had passed out.

Rob was standing at the edge of the plateau, staring west. "They've made no move to leave. Probably hoping we'll double back and attempt a rescue."

Wearily, Gwydion pushed himself upright. "You can see our camp?"

"That's why we're on this hill."

"Gwion can't be comfortable tied up like that, but he's all right. They're talking to him."

Rob didn't look at him. "They may be after information."

He said it like it was an important statement, but Gwydion couldn't grasp his meaning. "So what?"

Rob finally turned to him. "If they think he knows where we've gone, and he doesn't tell them, he may be tortured."

Gwydion sank to the ground again, hammered down by the thought. He didn't say anything for a long time, then, finally, "Even if we could rescue him, the mission is lost. They've evidently taken the boat somewhere … and the chest."

"No. I scuttled it."

"What?"

"I killed a deer this morning. I thought we'd be leaving, so I was in the boat, stowing the meat when they came. They didn't see me. I didn't let them see me," he corrected. "There were too many of them to take on, so I stayed hidden until it occurred to me that, at the very least, they would search the boat for valuables, so I scuttled it and swam to a point near you. Yes, I'd seen you pull Llew to a hiding spot."

Gwydion was still trying to comprehend. "You sank the boat?"

"Just a few small holes. Well placed. Easy to pull the boat up and repair it when they've gone."

Gwydion gave him a pleased smile. "That was well done."

Rob gripped his shoulder with one hand, motioned for silence with the other, and pointed until Gwydion saw what he was looking at.

There were six of them, walking slowly, three on each side of the stream, their eyes searching the brush for signs of passage. They had bows and arrows slung across their shoulders and swords hanging from their belts, and two of them had knives in their hands. In spite of the cold their chests were naked except for a crisscross of leather that probably held the knives. The two men above were on their stomachs now, peering cautiously over the edge of the hilltop through a screening of leaves. A groan came from behind them.

Instantly Gwydion scuttled back to Llew, whispered for silence, helped the boy to a sitting position.

Rob finally joined them. "They've gone. Still it's best to speak softly."

Llew nodded. Gwydion asked, "What now?"

"One of us should keep watching. I'll do it. Why don't you see if you can round up something to eat that doesn't need a fire?"

"All right, but what about Gwion?"

"We'll wait until they're sleeping. They'll have guards posted, but maybe we can disable them."

Gwydion understood that Rob would disable them straight to Annwn, but he didn't argue. "I can help."

Rob started back to his lookout. "And?"

"And what?"

"And when do we get supper?"

Gwydion smiled, and shoved his exhaustion aside. "I'm on my way."

34

BLAISE

Sometimes Emrys wants to skip over the steps that lead one to a conclusion. I often need to evaluate in the middle of a lesson whether his quick mind has leaped to the correct answer because he has already done the evaluation in his head, without my careful plan to lead him there, or whether he's bored with the subject and wants to move on. Perhaps it's a combination of both. At any rate he keeps my mind nimble by trying to constantly challenge him.

He thinks that I spend all my spare time writing the history of Albion, but I spend a lot of it thinking about how to teach him. There are fundamentals he has to understand, or if he already knows them, to look at them in a new way - from the Druid viewpoint. I believe that some of his previous teachers failed to teach him to think about what he was learning. It was enough that he could memorize and repeat it back.

There's a lot of memorizations for us, but behind each triad and each song is an explanation of the world about us, and these must all be understood or the memorizing does no good.

Yesterday we got into an argument about the Treasures of Tuatha which represent earth, air, fire, and water – the four principles of our faith – our pledge to the gods to care for and understand the importance and the purity of these elements.

"If these four treasures are so important to the Druids, we should have them, shouldn't we? He gave me a piercing look. "Do you have the Treasures?" he asked.

I shook my head, no.

"Does the Merlin?"

"No, they're not in Gaul with him."

"In Avalon? With the Lady of the Lake?"

"Yes, they're in Avalon, but not with the Lady."

"The Faeries have them? Do you mean that the entire journey of Gwion and Gwydion that I've been reading is for naught? That the Treasures were just moved for the Faeries? Why couldn't they do it themselves? What was the point of it all?"

"I'm not sure why the Faeries couldn't move it themselves," I told him. "The point, however, is that they were moved from a place where the Romans or others of ill intent could reach them to a place of absolute safety."

"It sounded to me like the cavern on Ynys Mon was safe enough. Finding it seemed nearly impossible, and the narrow bridge they crossed, the fear monster they fought, the door to the hidden room – all that they went through they did because they knew it was there, but some stray fisherman or Roman soldier might have somehow found the cave and sheltered there for a day or two, but they would not have found the inner realms."

"You could be right – or completely wrong."

He made a pouting face.

"Consider this, Emrys. At that point in time Gwion was the only man who knew where the Treasure was. Now, because of him, we know."

"What good does that do us?" he exploded. "What good are the Treasures if no one can use them?"

"There has been no need for the Treasures, but it is said that some of them will be used someday to save Albion."

His eyes were round and very blue, but he stopped arguing, so I continued. "It is not said that Faeries will save Albion, it is said that a great king will – a man."

He started to shake and began to speak in a voice that sounded far away. I grabbed for a scrap of parchment and a quill, wanting to take his words down exactly, but they stopped after one brief sentence that chilled me. "I will find them for him," he said.

35

GWYDION

They feasted on cranberries that day, and nuts. Gwydion knew all the places to look, for it was not the first time that he had depended on foraging to assuage hunger. He had learned from the best - Gwion, himself, who had taken him along on many furtive missions to recruit and to meet with those who taught the Druid way in distant locations. As the Penbard had come to trust him he had been sent alone as the Penbard's representative, so he had learned to read the land for its bounties and had come to understand what their teachings meant about respecting the land and working to nurture it.

"You'll have just one task tonight," Rob told him as the sun dropped.

"You mean other than staying out of your way."

Rob grinned. "Ah, you remember now, but the test will come when you see that I'm badly outnumbered, and it looks like I'm near to losing the battle."

Gwydion swallowed the retort he wanted to make and spoke

through clenched teeth. "And my task is?"

"Getting Gwion out. You stay with him at all times - no matter what happens to me. And memorize the way back to this spot. You may have to bring him by yourself. I'll join you later." He did not add, if I can. He didn't have to.

"And what can I do?" Llew asked, his voice muffled under a warming cover of pine boughs.

"Stay here," they both answered. "You have to be strong enough to move quickly in the morning. If we're successful, we'll be moving out."

36

GWYDION

It was still dark when Rob awakened him. It was still dark when Rob and Gwydion silently surveyed the enemy encampment. And it was still dark as Gwyd crept close to the sleeping Gwion. His knees were shaking, and he was sure that the thunder of his heartbeat would wake the warriors he passed.

A burly man next to him rolled over, and he dropped to the ground, holding his breath, waiting for the cry of discovery.

When nothing happened, he began to breathe again, shallowly, though he wanted to gasp for air.

He counted to ten slowly.

Still nothing.

He got to his feet carefully, wishing the campfire wasn't so bright, and made his way passed the man. Passed two more.

And there was Gwion.

On his knees he shook the old man gently, making sure his own face was clearly visible as he pressed a hand over the sleeper's mouth to signal silence. That hadn't really been necessary he realized, as he felt the gag that bound Gwion's mouth at the same time that his eyes popped open.

He looked alarmed, then reassured as he saw his friend and nodded. Gwydion slashed the ropes that bound his wrists and his ankles, but pressed him to the ground as he looked about to make sure that all were still sleeping.

There had been two guards on watch. Before he had started toward Gwion he had seen Rob cut the throat of the near one, soundlessly lowering the body to the ground. The other would prove harder to take, for he had been walking back and forth along the beach.

He stared hard at the beach now looking for movement, and seeing none, hoped that meant that Rob had been successful.

His eyes swept the camp, saw and heard only the signs of sleep.

Cautiously he got to his feet and helped Gwion up. The old man swayed and he caught him. Aye, the ropes had been tight. His feet were probably numb.

Half lifting him, he chose the clearest path through the sleepers though it took them away from where he wanted to head. The cover of the trees got closer.

They were going to make it.

And then his heart thudded as a tall man next to them lurched to his feet, shouting something that he couldn't understand.

Now the camp was alive and moving, each man with a weapon, and he swung his knife with his free arm and felt it connect in the soft tissue of the tall man's stomach. He pulled it straight up to free the blade.

The man groaned, and fell, his fingers cradling the bloody hole.

Dragging Gwion toward the trees he noticed that the space that had seemed filled with angry, sleepy warriors was now relatively clear.

See what fear can do to the imagination, he chided himself, then noticed that he was lifting Gwion over a dead man. There was an arrow protruding from his chest, and now that he was looking down, he saw a veritable path of such arrows, each pinning an enemy to the ground.

Rob must have a bow with arrows, he thought, though he hadn't seen any in the boat.

Another thought. Startling! Maybe it was the enemy shooting at him and missing, striking their own men.

Much heartened he moved faster, then stopped so suddenly that Gwion lurched and fell. Heart thudding, he moved only his hands, extending them helplessly over his head as a strange bowman stepped out of the darkness, directly into his path.

Gwydion wondered what it would feel like to be shot and hoped the shot was clean and killed him at once so he wouldn't be left dying from a slow, excruciatingly painful wound. They might torture him if he lived, and, worse, torture Gwion.

These were the thoughts that ran through his mind in the brief second before the archer said, "Get down, Cymbrogi. I can't get a clear shot with you waving your arms in front of my face."

He obliged, shaking with relief.

The archers - for there were more than the one - made quick work of the warriors, using the bright light of the fire to find their targets. There was nowhere for the warriors to run. Gwydion saw that only the sea kept them from being surrounded, and those few who reached the sea died before their knees were wet.

37

GWYDION

Just after Rob had killed the second guard and slipped back into the trees, he had found himself surrounded by strangers. He would have fought them, but there was an aimed arrow ready to loose not three feet from his heart. Slowly he lifted his hands to show surrender, wondering where these warriors had come from. No, he corrected himself. They are not the enemy warriors. By their dress they are Celts.

The leader spoke softly, confirming by his tongue the truth of it. "Who are you? You that the Trinovantes have chased near to the Quantock Hills?"

"Traders," Rob answered just as softly, mentally cataloging their location and pleased in spite of his predicament, for they were close to where they wanted to be. "A storm blew us out of the Severn and back again. When we put in, a small party of warriors attacked us. We killed all but one, but he brought the warriors you see before you, and they've been following us along the coast ever since. Yesterday they captured our friend."

"It's revenge they want then?"

"That's why they didn't kill the old man. They hoped to lure the rest of us back."

The leader was watching the camp as Rob spoke. "Your comrade is cutting the bindings of the old one now. The Trinovantes have no good reason to be on our shores. We'll help." Quickly and quietly he deployed his men, so that when the Trinovantes alarm went out, they were ready, and their arrows flew.

Later, when the sun had brought a warmth to the morning, they helped carry the boy back and made a funeral pyre for the dead. "You called them Trinovantes," Gwydion said. "Why are they here and not in the East where their tribe belongs, and why do they not wear Trinovantes colors?"

The leader answered after throwing his torch into the flames. "Trinovantes scum. We've heard rumors that this group broke from the tribe when it cowed to the Roman brutes. They've cut a path through the heart of Albion, leaving widows all the way."

"But to what purpose?" asked Gwion. "Were they trying to raise an army?"

The leader spat. "It's certain they didn't stop to ask for recruits. We feared they were after our boats. We've been waiting for them."

By afternoon the boat was raised. By evening there was deer meat, rabbit, and partridge cooking on spits, and when bellies were full and spirits high and a vast quantity of mead had been drunk, there was singing. Rob joined in happily, his pleasant voice leading one melody after another. A solo was requested and he answered with a rousing drinking song that demanded a chorus and was given one. When a second was requested, he remembered that Gwydion had not participated, and said, "It's my friend you should be asking, for his voice is as fine as a bard's."

Everyone turned expectantly to Gwyd who shot a look of annoyance at Rob, for he had purposely avoided the singing, trying to look busy as he catered to the needs of the boy and of his master. "Na," he said. "The heart must be light to sing, and tonight mine is heavy with worry for my son."

Llew was still lightheaded, but caught on instantly to the need for caution and played his role. "I'll be fine, Da. Just let me lay my head in your lap as I did when I was small."

Gwydion smiled at him, and helped move him to the new position, thinking he had gotten out of that neatly when Gwion surprised him. "Sing one for the Gran Da, Gwyd. I've a mind to hear the song Morgwnny taught you."

Gwydion did not understand it. The last thing they wanted was to be identified as Druids, and this was a complicated ballad about the winds that really demanded a harp to do it justice, yet Gwion urged him on. "Sing, Son. Sing."

Gwydion drew breath and began the haunting melody, noticing that the man who had been tapping on a small hand drum got up and disappeared into the darkness. No matter that. His drum wasn't needed. By the time he finished the first verse there was total silence, a respectful silence, made sweeter by the upturned faces in the firelight, each turned on him with rapt attention.

In the middle of the second verse a harp joined in, chording in all the correct places, and finding the lovely counter-melody that made a strange and beautiful harmony. This was a man who had played this piece before and knew the ins and outs of it. He was scarcely aware that his own fingers were sending a message quite different from the vocal one, using the secret coding of the Ogham alphabet.

A hush of respect followed on the heels of the last note, then a rousing cheer, finally interrupted by the harper in a voice that carried over the others, "And are you knowing this one, then?" He chorded a quick introduction for a question/answer ballad designed as a duet then began the tenor part. On cue Gwydion's baritone answered, and the two wove the story back and forth much to the enjoyment of the others.

There were two more songs from them, and in between, while bantering with the group, the harper replied to Gwydion in the finger alphabet, so now they had the knowledge that he, too, was a Druid. Gwydion had prompted the group to join in the last song - a fitting way to end. Now he yawned openly. "We've all had a long day. If we're to be on our way when the sun rises, we'd best sleep now."

"True enough," answered Ider, the leader of the group, who had identified himself during the second round of mead. "Let's finish the cups, Cymbrogi, with a toast of friendship."

"And of thanks," added Gwion, "for you've done naught but aid us since we met."

"Fine hosts we'd be had we done else." He polished off the last of his cup and tucked it in his belt. "We'll be seeing you on your way in the morning then and see you aimed the proper way if you'll be telling us where you're headed to do your trading."

Gwion caught the undertone that implied disbelief. If they were really traders, they should have had some goods to offer in a situation like this and he took the opportunity to rectify the error. "We've goods for the brothers at Ynys Witrin, and would be pleased if you'd point the way." He saw that Rob was going to say something, and gave a slight shake of the head to keep him quiet. He had also noticed that some of Ider's men wore the cross of the Christian church so he purposely used the term, "brothers," which was ambiguous enough to suggest either the Monks or those who studied the Way.

He was not surprised to hear the harpist speak up. "The tides are tricky there with low ground that floods and disappears into the water only to sink boats in its shallows, and marshes that look solid but are passable, and mists that make the island disappear. I know it well, and if it's all right with you, Ider, I'd be happy to guide our new friends there."

Gwion was quick to say, "And happy we'd be to have you as guide."

Ider did not seem the least bit suspicious now. "So be it," he said, and after a night that seemed too short to the party of 'traders,' they were seated around the fire again, breaking their fast with cold leftovers from the night before.

After another round of thanks Ider walked them to the boat while his men broke camp. "You're lightly packed for traders."

Rob jumped in before anyone else could answer. "We lost everything but the trunk that was tied down when the storm hit."

"That would explain it," Ider said carefully. Casually he draped an arm about the shoulders of his bard. "Dinacat, tell the Lady of the Lake that Ider of the Dumnovii sends his greetings and will always light the fires for the old gods. Ask of her if his daughter fares well, and if she's still serious about her lessons."

They were at the boat now. Rob jumped in, reaching a hand to Llew who was well enough to walk on his own now, but still weak enough to need the assistance. On the other end Gwydion had just finished lifting him up and had reached back to help Gwion when Ider shocked him. Still speaking to Dinacat he said softly, "Tell Her that Ider has helped the priests of the Goddess and sends them to Her with your own guiding hand."

Gwydion hoped that their identities were not as transparent to all the men, and looked to see how Gwion would handle it.

The old man smiled and raised his hand. "The blessing of The Goddess upon the House of Ider. Be proud that you have helped Gwion the Survivor and Gwydion, his successor."

Ider smiled, obviously pleased to have gained their confidence. "With my people you will always have a place of refuge and welcome."

38

GWYDION

Gwydion's head was reeling. He had never heard Gwion name himself to a stranger before. Ider was probably a safe enough confidante, but would he tell his warriors? Or his Council? Or his wife? All of his men knew their destination. If just one person with a Roman connection - a sister who had married a Roman soldier, a brother who had served the Legion - if just one, told whom they had rescued, they would be pursued. Why, they could bring devastation to Ynys Witrin - a slaughter like Ynys Mon. Whatever was the Penbard thinking? Even though Rob had now saved their lives several times, they had not divulged their secret. Until now.

While he worked the sail, he studied Rob to see if Gwion's name had meant anything to him. Maybe he hadn't heard. Or maybe "Gwion the Survivor" was a name he didn't know. He'd lived most of his life out at sea. He might not understand the significance - might not know that Gwion the Survivor was a man openly hunted by the Romans. Maybe he thought "the survivor" was something Gwion had tacked on out of pride as a man would say, "I'm Eric the Red," if his hair was red, or "I'm Perdd the Strong," if he had a reputation as a mighty warrior. "Survivor" could mean, "I've survived many years - I'm an old man."

Rob was giving him some kind of look now. What could it mean?

He had his answer a second later when Rob shouted, "Watch the sail, Gwydion. You're daydreaming again."

He trimmed it carefully, knowing he had to pay attention. Their very lives could depend on it.

Can we depend on Ider? And what of Dinacat? Can we depend on him?

He was still staring absently at Rob who answered the stare with a loud, "And I'm thinking it's a grand day to be alive? Not cold like it has been."

"Aye," he shouted back, only vaguely aware that it was a day warm enough to lay his cloak aside if he'd not been riding the wind on the water.

For a moment practicality intruded on his thoughts as he automatically checked on the boy. Llew was sitting on the roped chest not far from him, his face turned into the wind, his black hair blowing behind him, long and unkempt, but his cheeks had color again, and his dark eyes danced with the pleasure of feeling well enough to journey and enjoy it. His face turned as he felt Gwydion's gaze and he smiled broadly. "Gwion named you successor, Gwyd. Did you know?"

He shook his head, leaving the boy to wonder whether it was in answer to his question or just to indicate that he didn't want to talk. No question that the boy had understood. Gwion the Survivor must have been talked about in his household!

How many households knew that name, he wondered? Gwion was a legend in Powys where he had grown up, and in the adjacent Dyfed where much of his learning had taken place. In fact, all of Cambria knew the name and much of Logres. Why, it was highly likely that Ider would consider it the best of material for bragging the first time he had a drop too much of ale. Gwydion pictured a crowded tavern, someone calling Ider a liar, and Ider backing the truth of his statement with fists. Soon everyone in the tavern was involved, with cups and brew flying, benches overturned, and bodies piling up. When it was over, all would agree that a grand time had been had, and the cause of it would spread through Dumnonia, bringing the name of Gwion the Survivor to every tongue.

Gwydion shuddered.

The old one was in the bow, talking earnestly with Dinacat, and he listened intently, trying to catch what they were saying, but they were speaking quietly, and the wind carried the sounds away. The boy leaned closer. "They're speaking of Dinacat's training," he told Gwion.

"Aye? And what makes you think I care?"

His words were harsh enough that Llew drew back again, and didn't answer except to shrug his thin shoulders.

That made him sorry that he'd been so sharp, and now he tried to make up for it. "We have some time now. Are you strong enough to continue your lessons, Llew?"

The boy's eyes danced. "Oh, yes."

Gwydion began the lessons as near as he could remember to where they'd left off, and soon Dinacat and Gwion joined in, then Rob from behind him, but all the time he was asking questions and prompting the boy to think his answers through, he was wondering that he, who had barely finished his own training, was to be named successor, and he was anxious to find time alone with Gwion to question him.

The sun had become a red ball floating just above the horizon when Dinacat stood and pointed. "Look - the Quantock Hills. Our journey's near end, but we should put in and camp on this side of them, Rob, for I'll need the sun to find my way round them and through the marshes to the island."

"It's fine by me," Rob answered, swinging the tiller around, but looking at Gwion for confirmation. Gwion must have given it, but Gwyd was too busy with the sail to notice.

A little later he was busy gathering wood for a fire, then helping Dinacat cook a meal that by their standards was hearty. Ider had seen that they were well supplied. Not entirely trusting that they were in safe country, Rob had spent most of the evening on guard duty. Gwydion relieved him while he ate and slept. It wasn't a long time - the moon had just hit its high point when Rob woke and took over, but the others had long been asleep, so he never did get a chance to question Master Gwion.

39

GWYDION

With the dawn came a waist-high mist that was so thick, Gwydion couldn't see his feet. He thought they'd probably wait until the winter sun burned it off, but Dinacat surprised him by directing them all to the boat. "We won't be able to see where we're going," he griped. "I thought it was treacherous here."

"Oh, it is," Dinacat agreed cheerfully, "but I know the paths where it's shallow, and we'll stay well away from them."

He couldn't argue with that, so after boosting the boy up he took his place at the sail, and when Rob cast off, he was ready to do his job.

It was eerie. They sailed through fog so thick that they couldn't see ahead at all. Dinacat stood in the prow of the boat, calm and silent, but Gwydion noticed him staring up and to his right, and when he looked, he could sometimes catch a brief glimpse of the Quantock Hills running parallel to their course before the mist blotted their outlines away.

Uneasy, Gwydion began to invent vicious scenarios. One ended in ambush as Dinacat led them into a Roman trap, but the others involved natural disasters - grounded in an endless mist, crashing into jagged rocks that speared then sank the boat, thumping into some unidentified object just hard enough to toss him into the water and watching the boat sail away because no one heard his cries.

Indeed, the silence was unnerving - possibly the worst part of this ordeal.

Where were the dark birds that braved the winter?

Maybe they had twisted about and were sailing out to sea. He turned to look at the reassuring hills, but they were gone. How long since he had last seen them?

Where were they headed?

How would he know if they were being led into a trap?

Why didn't the mists burn off as the sun rose ever higher?

Though it was difficult to tell without being able to see the sun Gwydion thought it was about noon when the old leader came over and sat down facing him. "You have questions for me."

Gwydion hardly knew where to start and fumbled his flask to his lips for a long drink of water to hide his confusion.

Gwion didn't wait for a question. He smiled gently. "You're worried about trusting Ider. So worried that you forgot to look into his heart, but I looked, and I found the soul of a man who has come to life many times, a man who has lived as a priest in more than one of these lives, a man who believes in the old ways. He has told his children stories of Gwion the Survivor and made a hero of me, though the praise is undeserved. True, some of his followers are Christian, but they are not fanatical - more Cymbrogi than Roman."

Gwydion nodded. If Gwion felt the man worthy of trust, he must respect the decision. He glanced at Dinacat standing tall in the prow, leaning forward out over the water as if he were actually able to see the depth.

"He took his training at Avalon," Gwion said, following the

direction of his gaze. "I'm satisfied that what he says is true. I asked questions that only a trained bard and someone familiar with the island could answer."

"And Rob? What do you see in his heart?"

Gwion smiled fondly. "He's a true rogue, but once committed to something, he'll see it through."

"His tongue will wag at the first ale house."

"Perhaps, but by the time he reaches an ale house, the treasure will be safe, and we will be long distant."

"But he'll know where it is."

"He won't be able to find Avalon a second time."

Gwydion would not give up his perverseness. "He's a good sailor. I'll wager he knows exactly where he is and how to return."

Gwion shook his head firmly. "No, Gwyd. He would find Ynys Witrin and one of the oldest abbeys of the Christians, but the veil of Avalon would open for him no more than the veil of the Otherworld of Faerie would open to Dinacat."

"And the boy?" Might as well hear what Gwion had to say about every member of their party.

Gwion's eyes twinkled. "Ah, for our little Path Finder, I shouldn't be surprised to see King Nudd, himself, giving welcome!"

40

GWYDION

It was not the King of Faerie who greeted them as they stepped ashore, but it was the earthly representation of the Goddess, Herself - the Lady of the Lake. "Dierdra? You honor us," Gwion told her, clasping her hands affectionately.

Gwydion was still shaking his head as he was introduced. From the moment that Dinacat had raised his arms to part the mists it was as if a gifted bard had embellished the scene. The fog vanished with not even a wisp of remnants. The sun striped the water with bands of silver and shone in a sky of pure, cloudless blue. Cornflower blue, he had thought. That's what his sister had called the color, oh, years ago. He smiled, remembering his sister with fondness, so wrapped up in a pleasant memory of childhood that Llew had to nudge him twice to get him to pay attention to what was happening.

"Look, Gwydion. Spring has come early to the island."

Dinacat had overheard the boy. "Ah, but it's always spring here, lad."

"Now don't be filling his head with your bard tales," Gwion corrected. "But the island is famous for its apple trees, and they do bloom unseasonably long."

You could smell the blossoms even before you were close enough to see that the trees were not laden with snow, but with flowers. The trees rimmed the shoreline, obscuring the dwellings, and behind them rose a tall, flat topped mountain of green that dominated the entire island - the Tor. He caught his breath. The Tor of legend where all ceremonies of importance were conducted, the Tor that housed the realm of Faerie, that opened its secret crevices for Gwyn and his hounds to ride forth seeking souls.

That was all he had time to reflect, for Rob was shouting to help with the sail and lowering it, and he had to catch the boom and secure it. Rob had been clever. They coasted in to shore without having to use an oar, and as they breeched the land, Rob hopped out and roped one of the posts, then lifted the large boat as if it were weightless, and dragged until they could step out on dry land.

There wasn't an age line to mar the Lady's face, nor was she stooped, nor did she show any other sign of being old, yet there was something about her that made her seem ancient, like a towering oak that spreads vast branches over a village and has heard the secrets of its people for many generations back.

She was beautiful. Her hair was the color of honey, not bound, not curled, flowing straight down to her waist. She was probably too thin, but the long blue robe draped her gracefully and seemed to flow like water as she moved. She was of average height, but small boned, so she seemed delicate next to the Druids, and diminutive next to Rob. Her eyes, under thin arched brows, were grey, a dark grey that matched the winter sea, and seemed just as fathomless.

Surprisingly it was Rob who bowed to her first. "Lady," he murmured, dazzled by her presence. The others were quick to follow suit as Gwion introduced them. "I'm glad to meet you," she said to Gwydion. "Your work has been praised by many." He was too surprised and tongue-tied to answer. She clasped Dinacat's hand as she welcomed him home, and she turned a radiant smile on the boy. "Llew. You are young, but you've done a man's work on this trip. You are thrice welcome here."

"How did she know about us?" Llew whispered to Gwydion as she hugged Gwion. She took his arm affectionately and the group moved off.

"They say she looks into a mirrored pool and sees everything she wants to," he whispered back.

They passed three large buildings. "The school," she said of the first. "Sleeping quarters," she said of the others. There was nothing to make you look twice at the school, but Gwydion stopped and let the others pass him while he looked it over. Many kings and queens, as well as Druids and Priestesses, had studied in that building as young men and women, though it was a secret place now. He wondered if mists had hidden the island before the bad times, or if they had been called by the Lady.

He caught up in time to hear Gwion tell her cheerfully, "It's good to be here again." It must have been good for him. He was walking with the stride of a man half his age, his back straight, his shoulders back. His voice had power again. Too long we've been in disguise, Gwyd thought.

Rob sidled up to him. "So what kind of a place is this?"

"It's a place of power. Can't you feel it?"

"What I feel is a rumbling in my belly. It's been a long age since breakfast."

As if she had heard him, the Lady turned and announced, "We've a simple meal prepared. I hope you'll join me."

They entered a small, two-roomed house, its back nestled right into the foot of the Tor, its portico overlooking an endless orchard and the beach far below. The blossoming trees seemed an expansion of the white capped waves. There was a table just large enough for the six of them, set with fruit, a soft white cheese, and thin crusted bread just out of the oven. There was both apple juice and wine, but Gwydion noticed that the Lady drank only water. "Won't you join us in a glass of wine, Lady?" he asked, after working up his courage.

"No thank you, Gwydion. My ladies and I drink only of the water from the Holy Well."

Llew managed to swallow the enormous chunk of bread he had in his mouth. "What makes it holy?" Gwydion kicked him under the table. "Lady," he offered belatedly.

She took no offense from his informality. "It's holy because it's a gift of the Goddess, Llew."

The boy remembered his lessons from the boat. "But isn't all water a gift of the Goddess?"

She smiled. "Yes, but some is sacred, springing from land sacred to Her. The River Hafren, which runs close to your home, is one of Her sacred rivers."

There was no more talk of rivers. Gwion began to question the Lady about her students, and the meal was finished while she told him of the work being done, the results in nearby communities, and of various promising individuals. She spent the rest of the afternoon introducing him to new students and saying the things she could tell only him and Gwydion.

Dinacat took charge of Rob and Llew. They climbed to the top of the Tor and walked in the circle of the standing stones, not easily for Llew because the wind blew so hard that it threatened to snatch and hurl him down the mountain. He was glad to feel Rob's firm grip on his shoulder. Even Rob felt the power of the place, becoming strangely silent as they walked the circle and reached tentatively to touch each stone as they passed.

That night a dinner was given in their honor and everyone on the island attended. Gwion was asked to sing, and the Lady's bard passed his own harp to the Penbard, an honor that was lost on none.

Gwion plucked a few chords, checking the feel of the instrument and smiled in satisfaction at the pure quality of the sound. Then he strummed a harsh chord of discord and those who were murmuring in anticipation at hearing the Master fell silent. The chord turned into an eerie wail, and his voice entered as a cry of mourning for the death of the Iceni King Prasutagus.

Those who knew the story leaned forward in anticipation, and those who didn't soon joined them as the sad story came of the Iceni alliance with the Romans. There was a moment of hope as the will was sung out, leaving the kingdom jointly to the king's two daughters and to the Emperor Nero, so that the Iceni would continue to peacefully coexist with the Conquerors.

Llew, enthralled, later swore that he could hear Roman soldiers marching, as the Penbard told of the startling Roman reaction to this news. Led by Catus Decianus, he whose name became synonymous with evil, the Romans plundered the royal household.

Gwion's fingers struck the notes and drew pain from the harp as the king's widow, Boudicca, bore the strokes of the whip. She did not cry out at this injustice, but as her daughters were raped, her screams of agony filled the room, and when the Romans left, her screams gathered the Iceni, then united tribe after tribe, until a vast army stood behind her. And the screams of the harp sounded human.

The music changed to the strident sounds of battle. Donning helm and sword, she led the charge, her long hair streaming unbound in the wind as her horse thundered toward Camulodunum. Her sword plunged again and again, dripping blood, until the city was razed and all the infantry massacred. Yet this triumph was not enough, and the battle fury carried her to Londinium with her army screaming to drive every Roman from Albion.

Again the sword struck. The harp crackled as the city flamed and burned, and finally she stood on the ashes, her soldiers cheering, yet her heart flamed brighter than the fires had. She turned her horse toward Verulanium and a third city was destroyed.

Vowing vengeance on Nero, himself, she led her triumphant

forces to Wroxeter and the Morgian flew over her forces, filling her warriors with battle lust. The clash of swords rang out on the harp. The horses shrilled and the ravens flew overhead then settled on the piles of dead. But, alas, the dead were not Roman this time, and in one cold afternoon there were thousands of widows keening in the Tribes.

Boudicca took one last look, and her tears fell at last. Her daughters put aside their swords, gathering their mother for a last embrace, then crying, "Albion, oh lost Albion," the three dived on their own swords and died. The last sad notes stopped suddenly, and there were no dry eyes on the faces of those who listened.

"The Iceni retreated to Ynys Mon," Gwion said softly. "A year later the Romans slaughtered them in retribution, and among those killed were those being trained as Knowing Ones, along with all their teachers. Not only was the knowledge of Albion being erased, but that of Druids everywhere, for Ynys Mon was the school of schools for those from Gaul and Iberia and everywhere there were Druids. The Romans had decided that there should be no Wise Ones left in their World." His voice faltered as he fought to control his emotions. "They nearly succeeded."

"But thanks to one man - you, Penbard, Gwion ap Gwynedd, the knowledge did not die and new Druids have been trained to replace the old," said the Lady of the Lake, rising solemnly and holding her arms high.

Everyone in the room rose in salute, their hands beating together, their voices lifted in praise. Gwion shook his head, but the cheering drowned out his protests, and he was very obviously moved by the tribute. Still, he was uncomfortable with the accolade, for he had spent thirty years in hiding, teaching secretly, assuming other identities. "Enough," he said, signaling for quiet. "Thank you, but that rousing cheer far accedes anything I deserve. Now I would like to hear some of the rest of you, especially our new students."

The Hall Harper took over, much to Gwion's relief, starting a song that had a lovely chorus and many verses which were performed solo by eight of the newer students. The rest of the evening was lively, and nearly everyone took a turn performing - even Rob. Though tired from their long journey, it was such a relaxed evening that they all enjoyed it and were surprised to see how late it was when the Lady thanked everyone and sent them off to their beds.

41

GWYDION

A day of good food, warmth, and festivity had done wonders for Llew. He woke early, before the stars had left the sky, the good, sweet fragrance of apple blossoms drifting in through the open window. He had been given a room alone in the men's dormitory and he took a moment to look around appreciatively. He'd never slept in a room by himself before, and though in truth it was small and furnished sparsely, to him it was as grand as a castle. Lying there he could see the morning star crowning a sliver of moon. It was as if the Goddess, Herself, was guarding her champions, and he smiled and stretched and sat up so that he could watch her disappear into the lightening sky.

He wondered what it would be like to watch the sun rise from the top of the Tor. At first it was just a vague thought in the back of his mind, then it grew to overwhelm the other random thoughts, and before he had considered the consequences, he was pulling his trousers and boots on.

He opened the door and peered left and right down the hallway, but saw no one. Walking as silently as he could, he headed for the stairs, then through the main hall and out the door. It wasn't barred, he noticed - probably because everyone here was trustworthy.

He found the trail he'd followed the day before, but looking at the sky, he thought he'd better hurry, so he ignored the switchbacks and climbed straight up. By the time he reached the top it was very steep. Remembering the violence of the wind, he crawled across the top until he could reach the circle of stones where he could hold on. Only then did he look up at the sky and see that he was just in time. The stars had entirely disappeared in a wash of light and the sky was streaked with shades of pink.

He sat quietly enjoying the show that seemed staged for him, alone, and moved only occasionally to brush aside the hair that was blowing in his eyes. And that was what he was doing when a particularly strong gust of wind struck him. Twisting to maintain his firm grip on the stone, he suddenly realized that it was moving, and he was falling down through the hole that opened in the dirt below him, and he was screaming.

Rob was sharing a room with Dinacat. Toward dawn he awoke. Instantly alert, he sat up, knife in hand, then smiled and lay back again. Even in his sleep their guide projected like a bard, but this time it wasn't the pleasant tones of song, it was the thunder of snoring. He shut his eyes. Tried to think of something else. Slow prolonged snort. Three short snorts. His eyes flew open. He concentrated on finding a pattern in the sounds. Just as he thought he had it, the rhythm changed completely. He sat up again, stood up, leaned both elbows on the window sill and stared out. A man could find peace here, he thought, with no need to have your guard up all the time.

He watched the stars fade until he wasn't sure they were there anymore then caught a movement in the courtyard below.

He watched absently, then with every fiber of alertness. Why would two men be carrying something so obviously heavy when no one else was up and about? Then he realized that the two were Gwion and Gwydion, and that the object in question was their precious chest. He looked back at the reverberating bard, and shook his head at his own foolishness. Might as well go down and help them. He wasn't going to get anymore sleep this night.

Gwydion had had no trouble sleeping soundly, and was indignant when someone shook him awake. "What? WHAT?" He pushed the hand aside, saw only darkness and turned over, trying to snuggle back to his dreams.

"Gwyd, wake up. It's time. And be quiet about it."

He was alert now, but not cooperative. "Gwion? What is it?"

"Our quest is near over." Gwion smiled. "Or would be if I could get your attention."

He sat up slowly, rubbing the last remnants of sleep from his eyes. "You have it."

"Come then. 'Tis time we rid ourselves of the treasures."

Gwydion pulled his tunic down over his head and, a moment later, stuffed it into the trousers he had pulled on. "Do you know where to go?" he asked as he pulled his boots on.

The answer he got wasn't the one he wanted to hear. "The Goddess will guide us."

As they crossed the courtyard furtively, not wanting to explain their mission to anyone, Gwydion began to hope that Gwion knew what he was doing. The chest had never seemed this heavy.

As they started up the serpentine trail that led to the Tor, it seemed even heavier, so that when Rob stepped in next to him and said, "I'll take the back end. You go up front and relieve Gwion," he found himself grateful and not even startled.

42

GWYDION

Before they reached the summit, at the place where the wind began its wild attack, Gwion stopped them and indicated that they should sit. He, himself, remained standing, staring long at the pink tinged sky, then equally long out over the valley which was just becoming clearly visible. There were sheep grazing near the path, balanced on the steep slopes like tiny white clouds and Rob smiled to see them. "I could fancy myself staying here to care for them. I tended sheep for my grandda one fine summer."

Gwion squatted before Rob, staring so intently into his eyes that he found himself extremely uncomfortable. He actually had to concentrate to keep from squirming. "Aye, there's a purpose for you being here," he said at last, "but it's not as a shepherd that you'll find the peace you search for."

Gwydion lifted his hand as if to warn his mentor, then dropped it, swallowing objections to what he sensed was coming.

"It's now you must choose, Rob mac Tave, and I'll not try to influence you. A boat, gold, and our thanks go with you if you walk back down the path. We will trust you to remain silent about who we are and where we've been, for you're a good man, and you've earned our trust. If that is your choice, you will have our blessings."

The only reaction was a stubborn lift of the chin.

"You cannot walk away, then change your mind and turn back. Not ever," he added.

Rob might feel uncomfortable, but he was not intimidated. He understood he was about to be challenged, and a Finian never walked away from a challenge. "And if I choose to take my end of the chest and walk up the path?"

"You would be choosing to be one of us. Years of schooling would lie ahead, then, when you truly understood the power of the Goddess, years of dealing with others secretly. Your reward would be the gold of truth not of coin, your home would be wherever you were needed." His stern face spread into a smile. "And I must admit that you have skills we could put to use."

Rob stood up and folded his arms, one foot resting on a boulder as he leaned out over the mountainside and stared down at the beached boat. After what seemed a long time, he turned and shrugged his massive shoulders. "There are many who'd tell me it's a poor choice I'm making, but I've never yet walked out in the middle of an adventure, and now's not the time to be starting." He stationed himself at the back of the chest, looking expectantly at the others who were quick to join him.

They fought steadily through the wind, and the climb was rough enough that Gwydion was thankful at Rob's choice, for he doubted that he and his frail mentor would have been able to handle the weight of the chest while trying to keep their footing. As it was, he kept a careful eye on Gwion and stayed close behind him, ready to drop his end and catch if a misstep sent the old bard tumbling.

They had just cleared the last height and stepped out onto the flat top of the Tor when they heard the boy's scream. All three of them knew instinctively that it was Llew, and all three of them ran toward the standing stones where the scream had come from.

What they saw was one stone twisted askew and a deeply plunging hole where it had stood.

43

GWYDION

Gwion and Gwydion were quick to reach the edge of the hole, but Rob was even quicker, dropping his end of the chest and sprinting passed the others. He was sitting, legs dangling in space, mentally calculating the width of the hole against the width of his shoulders.

"Wait," Gwydion said. "We need a rope to tie around you."

"You can throw a rope down after you run back down the mountain to get one," Rob answered. "I'll not be letting Llew stay down there alone in the dark." His arm muscles tensed to push himself off.

"WAIT!? This time it was Gwion, using the bard's voice, and Rob froze. "Listen," he said in more normal tones.

What Gwydion and Rob hoped to hear - screams from below - was not forthcoming. What they did hear was the thunder of hoofs, and before they could react, they saw the horses coming across the flat of the mountain top, nearly upon them.

There were a dozen, black as night, each matched to the next, and all three of them remembered stories of the Otherworld where dark riders snatched the souls of men. This memory came in a flash as the horses skidded to a stop, surrounding them. "I'd be listening to the Penbard if I were you, Rob mac Tave," their leader said. "That path spirals down, getting narrower as it reaches the bottom. You'd be stuck firm before you were half way down."

Rob was on his feet in an instance. "Who are you? How do you know my name?"

As if rehearsed the dozen threw off their hoods in unison and now Rob was even more amazed. These were not men. The perfection of their features, the grace of their movements, the light that seemed to come from within made each shine with beauty. He felt fear creep in to dwell deep in his belly. It was such an unfamiliar sensation that he felt ill and turned his head, swallowing the bile that rose. No, he would not be sick in front of them.

"Rest easy," the leader said. "There's a wider gate." He swooped down and pulled the Penbard up in front of him and started off. Immediately two others pulled Gwydion and Rob to their horses' backs and followed, and when Rob saw that neither of the others was struggling, he stopped trying to push the rider off, thinking that was probably best anyway since there was no saddle and no bridle, thus, no easy way to control the horse which, in the way of horses, would be wanting to follow the others.

There was one more command before the speed had him grasping desperately at his companion to keep from falling off, and that was to bring the chest. He assumed it was carried out. He didn't dare look back, for what was just ahead - the edge of the Tor - was upon him, and now the horses ahead were soaring into space and disappearing over the rim.

And now he was falling. No, he was flying. Feeling light and strangely elated. So that he was sad when the hoofs lightly picked up the hillside below.

They were on a path now, steep, headed straight down. No, a

road, wide enough so that all twelve were abreast, but where was this road when they were all spiraling up the mountain? They should have crossed it a dozen times.

He couldn't help but think the horses were magnificent. He had been on horses before, but none that moved like lightning, none that had a gait so smooth. He was actually enjoying himself now, so exhilarated at the sheer rush of speed that it was a shock when the road made a sudden turn and he found himself hurtling at the side of a cliff only ten paces away.

There was no time to stop the horses, regardless of the remarkable skill of the riders.

There was no time and no room for his remarkable reflexes to kick in and roll off the horse.

There was time only to stiffen, to grip his companion in a grasp that must surely have produced pain, and to shout. And a dim perception that Gwydion to the right of him was also crying out in fear.

They hit the cliff broadside, all together.

44

GWYDION

Gwydion's scream died when they slipped through the solid rock as if it had been gossamer. He was shaking, gripping the horse's mane hard, and had shut his eyes, but when there was no collision, they popped open and he saw that they were in a wide arched tunnel that sloped gently downward.

He had been holding his breath too. By the time he had filled his lungs twice the smoothness of the tunnel had changed. There were carvings of tree trunks edging the sides and overhead there were branches meeting and twining together so that no one tree was clearly visible. He noticed that through the carved leaves he could see light.

There was no change of pace and the horses were still abreast, but the trees changed, stepping off the walls to become three dimensional and on either side was a veritable forest of stone trees. He thought they were going deep into the heart of the mountain, yet it was daylight.

They went a score of paces. The trees were no longer stone, but real oaks, and Gwydion was wondering if they were back outside. Then he remembered the cave on Ynys Mon and how Ariandell had made it seem brighter than sunlight, and decided that this was faerie light and these were faerie trees.

He thought how pleasant it would be to jump off the horse and wander through this wonderful forest. He would touch each tree he passed, feeling the life force from oaks that had seen several hundred years or more. Oaks that towered hundreds of feet high. Trunks so wide that a man could not put his arms round about and touch his fingertips.

Oh, the Romans had been brutal to the oak groves, chopping and burning, and where once there had been thousands upon thousands of glorious oaks reaching to the stars, there were only isolated trees, giants hidden amongst other trees dwarfed by their youth.

He made a silent pledge to the Goddess to begin carrying acorns with him as he traveled, planting them frequently in every likely place. He could envision Logres a hundred years from now with oaks nearly as tall as these.

They stopped abruptly and his reverie ended. Though he saw nothing but trees for miles in all directions everyone climbed down from the horses, acting as though they had arrived somewhere. From behind one of the trees a youth appeared and took the leader's horse. The others followed as if they'd been roped together. Gwion indicated the chest on the ground. "Gwydion, Rob, would you ...?"

You bet we'll carry it, Gwydion thought to himself. Until Gwion has placed it in Nudd's hands. He didn't trust any of the rest of them.

At first he was so concerned with the chest that he barely noticed his surroundings, but gradually he realized that the trees were no longer real, that their tops were so high that they were no longer visible, and that the floor he walked on was no longer dirt, but a mosaic of gems, dazzling an array of brilliant colors. He and Rob were somewhere in the middle of their small group, with Gwion near the front, and he saw finally that they were in a huge crowd of Sidhe, wearing beautiful diaphanous robes.

As they walked the crowd parted before them, and now he realized that they were in an immense room with jeweled walls. He could see the throne, and it was just as it had been in the visions - sparkling, a diamond jutting out from the diamond wall behind. On the throne, without question, was King Nudd. Only King Nudd could have such beauty and radiance that the beauty of all the other Fair Ones seemed suddenly dim.

Gwion was executing a graceful bow. Gwydion was determined not to let go of the chest, but he did the best he could to imitate his leader, and behind him he felt the chest drop a foot as Rob followed suit.

Now that his eyes were cast down from the glorious creature above, he saw a saucy figure sitting on each side of the golden dais where Nudd rested his feet, and his heart leaped in gladness. Llew? Llew, alive and safe? And smiling as was Ariandell on the opposite side.

Nudd leaned forward, gesturing them to rise. "You have come at last, Penbard."

Gwion straightened slowly, but as he stood he took on the mantle of power, and stood so tall and straight that he could look Nudd on his raised throne in the eye. "Aye, I have come at last."

Nudd laughed. "An age could have passed and I would still be here, but I wasn't sure you'd live long enough to make it."

"Man has a tendency to endure if it's important - even when the odds are against him," Gwion countered. "I am pleased to see that our young companion was not hurt when he fell into your strange doorway."

The king smiled down at the boy who returned his smile without any of the trepidation that saturated Gwydion. "Not the first time the lad has been the Path Finder, nor will it be the last." His gaze went passed Gwion and settled on Gwydion, then Rob. "The Sidhe have never mistreated guests. Indeed, the Celts learned the arts of hospitality from us."

"'Tis the stories of those who could not escape your hospitality that worries us," Rob shot back at him, and Gwydion could not help but admire his courage, foolish though it seemed.

For a moment the light about Nudd grew so brilliant that they were forced to look away again, but the king spoke in a gentle manner. "You need not worry, Rob mac Tave. Both of you will be on your way to Avalon soon enough, and the boy with you."

Now his gaze turned to Gwydion, and the scrutiny was near unbearable. He held himself very still, standing tall, and keeping his gaze level. He had noticed that Gwion had not been included in the assurance. "It's a worrier, you are, Gwydion," the king said at last, "but sometimes you have to trust - to put your faith in others, and this is a lesson you should take to heart, for only when you learn to truly give, will you truly reap the rewards of receiving."

It seemed he should say something, but he wasn't sure what would be appropriate. "I - I will remember what you've said, High One. I will think on it carefully."

"You will need to learn that lesson before you can be a great leader, and you best think on it quickly, for leadership will be upon you sooner than you know." He gave Gwydion no more attention, his head turning to Gwion. "You may ask."

Ask what, Gwydion wondered. Ask where they were? Ask how the boy came to be here? Ask why Ariandell had a place of importance? Ask how he knew them all by name?

But Gwion understood. "We have come to ask a favor of you, High One, a favor that should benefit man, but would also benefit the Fair Ones." He paused, and Nudd nodded his head, indicating that he should go on. "Inside the chest is what man calls the thirteen treasures of Albion. With the coming of the Romans they are in grave danger of being destroyed, and I seek a place of sanctity where they will be safe through the coming centuries. Thus, I ask you to guard these treasures until such time that man can safely reclaim them."

"Why would I have any interest in what will be called the dowry of Olwen, and why would I bother to guard them for you?"

Gwion stared at him with such intensity and with so many changes of expression that it seemed there was a silent communication. At last he said, "Already the Sidhe have retreated far into the mists. If you do not wish to disappear completely, it is to your advantage to help the Cymry."

This time it was Nudd who was silent and thoughtful. Gwion waited him out, resisting the temptation to add to his words. Finally he said, "You give these wee treasures to us willingly, but what makes you think we'd be giving them back?"

"There will come to pass a time when a Merlin is so mighty in powers and so in need of the treasures that some of them will be claimed. I have seen this. In water and in fire I have seen this."

Gwydion noticed that Gwion didn't say anything about trust.

Nudd laughed. "What you say is true, but have you also seen the price you'll pay."

It seemed impossible, but Gwion seemed to glow with power as Nudd did. "I am ready."

"Then open the chest. We will see the treasures. Gwydion, step forward. You will witness for mankind. Ariandell, you will witness for the Sidhe, so that both givers and guardians know exactly what the chest contains."

Slowly, with utmost care not to damage the elaborate fastenings, Gwion slid them loose and opened the lid while Gwydion and Ariandell moved to a position behind the chest. With shaking hands the Penbard reached for the first object. Gwydion almost shouted, no - don't touch them. It was death to touch them unprepared. Had Gwion thought of this?

What was prepared?

What exactly did prepared mean?

Meeting his eyes Gwion spoke softly, just to him. "I'm ready, Gwydion." He pulled out the first object, holding it high, using his bard's voice to reach all of the vast audience. "The Mantle of Tegan Eurvron to make the wearer invisible." Ignoring appreciative murmurs from the crowd and folding it carefully, he laid it aside and reached for the next object. "The Stone of Lia Fal which proclaims the rightful king."

Gwydion was watching Gwion closely, looking for signs of weakness and saw none. His hands were no longer shaking. He stood tall, his voice strong. Carefully he put the large stone next to the mantle and drew the next item. "The Mirror that reveals the future." This one brought a gasp from the Sidhe as it caught the light and flashed a thousand images, clear and brilliant. Gwion gently placed it face down. The light settled and there came a soft sound of breath released.

Gwion was holding a rather nondescript ring high. "The man who wears this ring will understand and speak the language of all men on earth." He put it next to the other treasures and reached into the chest again. "The Harp of Teirtu which plays wonderful music by itself."

The harp was beautifully carved, but it was silent until Gwion placed it on the floor and there came a resonant chiming of chords that made him catch his breath at such a lovely sound. Then it was gone, and a collective sigh from the musically gifted audience took its place.

"The Halter of Clydno Eidyn which can make any horse run like lightning," Gwion said, holding up the next item. There was nothing that looked magical about it. It was a halter like any other.

"The Gwyddbwyll Board of Gwendolau," he continued, "said to make the game pieces come alive." Gwydion watched as he set it beside the halter, and remembered the stories that tied men's fate to the board. He stared at the beautifully carved pieces with such awe that he nearly missed seeing the thin staff that Gwion was showing.

"The Staff of Seasons which will change the bleakest winter to a green season of plenty."

Almost to make up for his lack of attention Gwydion stared

intently at the next object. "The Horn of Bran Galed - the Horn of Immortality." This was a drinking horn, made from the tusk of some fabled creature, and its carvings were very ornate and very beautiful. Gwydion wanted to look at it closely, but of course he couldn't.

"Ah, the Chalice of Plenty." Gwion shook his head in admiration, and held the next item high. "The Hamper of Gwyndo Garanh which can feed all the men in the world thrice times nine."

How ordinary it seemed, thought Gwydion. Not beautifully decorated like the horn, but so simple that it would be at home in any farmhouse.

Gwion laid it down carefully and reached for the next object. "The Cauldron of Dyrnach Gawr, or of Dagda, or of Ceridwen, often called the Cauldron of Rebirth or the Cauldron of Knowledge," Gwion said reverently. "This will return life to the newly dead."

The Sidhe seemed to lean forward as one body, straining to see the vessel clearly. It was a very large, bronzed cauldron - so large that Gwydion wondered how it had ever fit in the small chest. But how had the Lia Fal or the spear that Gwion pulled out next?

"The Spear Birgha of Rygenid which never misses, nor fails to slay," he told them.

Still holding the spear in one hand, Gwion pulled the last item from the chest with the other and held it before them. "The Sword of Ryderch Hael, or the Sword of Gwrnach the Giant as some say, but as all say The Sword of Light which can kill flesh or spirit. To draw it with no need means death for all."

Gwydion swallowed and hoped that this was an occasion where it needed to be drawn. Evidently it must be, for no one dropped. All had understood the necessity to verify the contents of the chest before it changed hands.

At a nod from Nudd Gwion began putting the objects back in the chest. Both Gwydion and Ariandell stepped forward to help, but he waved them back. "Thank you, but it is a job for me alone." Gwyd didn't know how Ariandell felt, but he was perfectly happy to comply. In spite of the difficulty that the size of some of the objects presented, Gwion had them all back in and closed the lid in a time shorter than Gwydion could have imagined possible.

Ariandell made a gesture with his fingers and two of the Sidhe stepped forward and lifted the chest. He made a formal bow to his king. "Witnessed, Sire." Hastily, Gwydion copied the bow and added an echoing affirmation of his own, then stepped back to Rob's side as the chest was carried away.

"It will be safely held for the one who comes to claim it," Nudd told them. "Ariandell, please see that our guests are delivered safely to the path." He stood in dismissal, ruffling Llew's hair as he passed. "You too, Scamp. Off with you."

Though they were being urged to leave, Gwydion hung back for Nudd had stopped to say a few private words to Gwion. When he saw the old bard sink heavily to the steps, he stepped around his escort and rushed to his side. "Can't - can't get my breath, Gwyd," he apologized.

Gwydion unclipped the pin holding the Penbard's cape, hoping the loosening of it would help him breathe, and propped him to a straighter position, holding him in place with one arm about his shoulders.

The other hand was fishing in his belt for a small vial of a pungent and sharp herb. He broke it open and held it under the Penbard's nose, and for a moment it seemed to help. "Your time has come, Gwyd," he said in a stronger voice. "It will all be up to you now."

His entire body jerked hard once, as if he were a puppet and someone had pulled a string, and sharp irregular breaths were punctuated by air sucking gasps.

"Move back," Gwydion said, aware that his friends and the Sidhe escort were crowding around. "Give him air."

All but one, King Nudd, obeyed. He leaned closer and stretched his hand down toward Gwion. "It's a choice I'll offer but once,

187

Penbard. Take my hand and you'll sing with us forever, but no man will hear your voice again."

Gwion smiled, the ragged breathing shallow, and his eyes opened wide. "Tis a kind offer and a generous one and I appreciate the honor, but I'll not be taking you up on it, Sire. Already I've lived longer than most, and it's a yearning for rest and a bit of peace that I want, before it's time to step on to the Wheel of Life again." Once more he gasped and a weak hand found one of Gwydion's and barely was able to grasp it. His eyes found Gwydion's. "Take care of them."

King Nudd had stepped back and waited. When Gwydion's face was streaked with tears and Gwion had long ceased to breathe, the king repeated Gwion's last words, looking fiercely at Gwydion as he spoke. "Take care of them, Gwydion. The souls of men are in your hands now." He turned and strode away, and when several of the Sidhe would have taken Gwion's body up, it was Rob who shouldered them gently aside and gathered Gwion's body up into his arms, his tears matching Gwydion's.

As soon as Gwydion was on his feet the boy flung himself into his arms, his small body shaking from sobs, but seeing Ariandell and the waiting Sidhe, Gwydion soon realized that they were uncomfortable with death and the sorrow of men and had no sympathy for it. "Llew," he said shaking him gently, "time enough later for tears, but now it's time to go." He fell into line behind Ariandell, his arms about the boy's shoulders, propelling him forward, and just behind him came Rob with his sad burden.

None of them remembered exactly how they reached the foot of the path that wound up the Tor. It didn't concern them at the time, and later it seemed a blur of trees and walking and paths. The only thing they knew for certain was that there had been no horses involved, but whether they had climbed up to the entrance they had used before, then back down the winding path, or whether they had come out close to the bottom, they could not remember.

They were met at the foot of the Tor by the Lady of the Lake and all of her women. There were no questions asked, and it was obvious that the women expected what they saw and were prepared. The Lady gestured for them to follow, and the entire procession made its way to the same room she had received them in the day before. Rob laid Gwion on her own bed in a smaller room just off the main chamber, and the women went to work, preparing the body.

Later that day Gwion, now on a stretcher of yew, was carried by Druids as all in the community snaked up the winding path of the Tor. On the top, in the very center of the standing stones, the stretcher was laid on a tall wooden platform and Gwydion, robed for the first time as the Archdruid, commemorated Gwion's soul to the care of Arianrhod until it was reborn, and the Lady added her own words. "The rhythms of life are complete, and it is as the Death Crone that I bid you tend this soul."

Each of the women tore the skirt of her gown, and a haunting thrum came from their throats to be echoed a moment later by the harps and flat hand drums of the bards. Gwydion took a torch from one of the other Druids and thrust it into the pyre. The flame spread quickly, for the wind never died on top of the Tor, and the music and the mourning sounds continued until there was nothing left but ashes. Slowly they formed into a long, single-file line and made a procession down the Tor, and all that time the music never stopped.

45

BLAISE

"Later it was said that even the Sidhe mourned the passing of the Gwion the Penbard, Emrys, and that in his memory their song followed the procession down the Tor and continued so that all could hear their magical music for the entire night."

"What happened to the others, Master Blaise?" asked my young apprentice.

"Gwydion proved an able successor to Gwion, continuing the secret recruitment and training of Druids. He lived to see a time where Druids were accepted openly again in the north.

"Rob mac Tave stayed in Avalon for many years, learning Druidic lore then traveled the north as a bard. It was said that before he left Avalon, he had trained the younger bards in certain Fenian techniques of self-defense and assault that occasionally proved useful to a secret order, and that Gwydion called upon this group when such was needed.

"Llew, called Path Finder, was also trained as a Druid. He was one of those rare ones who could see what was to come, and spent many years at Gwydion's side as an advisor. It was said that he often returned to Avalon, and on each visit he disappeared for a time and no one knew where he had gone except the Lady. On her deathbed she shared Llew's secret with her successor. 'Llew visits his friend, Ariandell,' she said.

"Thus ends the story of Gwion and his successor Gwydion. Many able men followed, secretly teaching Druid lore and guiding tribal leaders." His face was shining, framing the smile that lit even his eyes. "Do you have more questions for me?"

"Yes. Gwion was called Penbard and that title is given to the Master of Music, but Gwydion is called Archdruid. Was that title born by Gwion too?"

"Yes."

"Was either of them called the Merlin?"

"No. Eventually the Druid High Priest came to be called the Merlin, but not that far back in time."

"I see," he said. The dinner bell rang, and he dutifully rose to his feet, and put the last scrolls away. He looked toward me for permission to leave, and I waved him away.

46

BLAISE

Emrys was nine when he had his first long vision. We were sharing a fire in my study at the end of a winter day. I'd shown him a map - a concept he'd grasped easily, and been excited by. "It puts it all in perspective - easy to see how the Roman Empire spread, and how it shrinks with Barbarians at the very gates of Rome. I'd had no idea that it was so large and our island so small. I understand now why troops were pulled from Britannia to defend their city. Why, we're at the very edge of their world, and I had thought we were larger and more important."

"Yes, man tends to think that events center around him."

Carefully, he placed another log on the fire. "I think a man has to start somewhere. A piece of land grounds him and gives him defini-tion. If he can grow the size of that land, it increases his importance to those around him. If he gains enough to have a kingdom, he can be a king. That's why the Saxons ..."

He stopped talking. His eyes went blank and rolled up, and his body stiffened. I was at his side, kneeling when he started shaking, and I eased him against the chair back, and ran for wine across the room. I added herbs that would help and sat across from him again, waiting for him to wake.

It wasn't long - less than an hour. He groaned, flailed, sat straight then buried his face in his hands, rubbing his eyes. "Here drink this. It will help."

"Master, I saw ..."

"No. Don't talk until you feel better. You had a vision. Don't worry, you'll remember." I had the cup to his lips. "Drink now. All of it."

Another ten minutes and he was himself again. "Master, I have to tell you. I have to tell you now," he said urgently.

"Yes, but slowly. What was the first thing you saw?"

"A large hall full of men. There were long tables with benches where the men were sitting." His eyes narrowed and he gripped the arms of the chair. "They had finished eating, I think, but there were drinking horns. Half of the men were dressed strangely. Tunics, long leggings with thongs wrapping about them, bare arms in spite of the cold, with gold armbands - a lot of gold, horns on their helmets."

His story was coming faster and faster. "Slow down, Emrys. Give me all the details you remember."

They were interspersed with our Celtish men, all dressed in fine clothes with many jewels flashing in the torchlight. One of them, a Celt, wore the twisted metal choker that showed tribal leadership - a thick gold torque. He was in the center of the head table, with two large men - men of the strangers - on either side. The one at his right hand stood up and raised his cup as if to drink a toast. I don't know what he said, but at that ... that signal ... each of the strange men stood. The man with the torque tried to rise, but the man on his left pressed him back to his chair and pinned his arms."

His eyes swam with unshed tears. "Then each of the strangers pulled a knife from his leg wrappings and cut the throat of the man next to him. A few tried to fight, but they had no weapons. The man with the torque was screaming, and now they pulled him to his feet and shoved him to the door. I watched him mount and ride away. No one followed. There were tears running down his cheeks."

The tears spilled and ran down Emrys' cheeks too. "One of the men slain was one of my uncles - my grandfather's named heir."

Our bards were to call it "The Night of the Long Knives," and no night had ever held such treachery. Vortigern, who called himself the High King, was the man wearing the torque. The Picts from the North had joined forces with the Irish across the sea causing such devastation that Vortigern was hard-pressed on all sides and finally sent for aid from the Saxon, Hengist. Hengist and his brother Horsa brought boatloads of men to help, and with their aid the Irish and the Picts were driven back. Vortigern had promised them land on the southeast coast where they could build a home and the gathering was at Caer Caradduc to celebrate the victories and to plan for the future defense of the realm. All of Vortigern's supporting kings were invited, and all came or sent noble representatives who could speak for them. The Saxons were invited too, with offerings of friendship for their loyalty.

But Hengist felt the small strip of land granted him was niggardly and vowed to take all the land they wanted and punish Vortigern for the poor gift he had made, so when the group assembled, the Saxons laid down their swords and axes at the door next to the shed weapons of the Celts, but kept long knives hidden in their clothing, and at Hengist's signal they took their vengeance, leaving Vortigern alive to tell the tale and to know that he had met his conqueror.

It took two weeks before we who lived on the Isle of Glass heard the story confirmed - a short time in those days before king's messengers rode the highways, but this was devastating news and all of Britannia mourned the deaths and cursed the Saxons. Hengist had made his move boldly, thinking it would destroy Vortigern and lay Britannia open to his conquest, but it did quite the opposite, drawing the normally independent and quarrelsome Celts together in their grief and hatred.

And of all of us, many trained in the art of prophecy, only Emrys had seen it happen.

47

BLAISE

I had Emrys train with our best seers for the next few years, so that he could control the aftereffects. No one, could entirely control when a vision came, although there were exercises and herbs to bring them on. Still, it was no sure thing, and one might be trying to see one thing and get quite another in its stead.

By the time Emrys was twelve his Druid training was half done, having progressed through ten years of work in only five.

He had memorized nearly all the triads that taught our history, knew most plants and herbs, knew how to prepare potions and how to heal the sick, lacking only the practical experience of working with patients. He had learned about the celestial bodies that moved through the night sky. He had learned the Ogham alphabet and could finger spell a message with great speed. He had the rudiments of our ceremonies, though he had not conducted any. He understood the importance of music and how we used it to soothe, inspire, instruct, or inflame the listener. He had made his own drums and played all the rhythms well. From reeds he could make a decent flute and play, and he had just made a beautifully finished harp with a true tone. His playing was improving daily.

For the most important instrument - the human voice, I had sent him to our best bard at the court of King Gorlois of the Dumnonii where he spent six months studying nothing but singing. I was pleased to find upon his return that his voice was true, and he that had learned a great number of ballads.

Describing the court of Gorlois and his wife Anna to me, he mentioned their young son, Cador. "He will be a strong supporter of the king who is coming," he said, and immediately went on to a new topic.

I stopped him. "Emrys, what you said of Cador - how do you know that?"

A surprised expression played on his face for a moment, and he smiled sheepishly. "I - I just know. It's not a vision, exactly. It's just something I see, like when you look at a tree and see that it is an oak, or when you look at a star and know it's part of Pisces."

"But those are things you learned and memorized."

"Yes, I see the difference, yet I know this as surely as I know the oak."

I studied him. Still young, a boy unfinished, long limbs he hadn't grown into yet making him clumsy, hair so dark it was nearly black - and shaggy, needing a good trim, but the eyes unmistakable - sometimes blue, sometimes grey, always knowing. They were eyes that gave him a surety well beyond his years, timeless eyes that looked both back and forward with ease. Eyes so old they could have seen the beginning of the world, and so far-seeing that they might see the end. Finally I said, "You must learn to keep these insights to yourself when you are in the world of men."

"Here, too?" he asked.

"No. I will always be grateful for such foreknowledge."

He laughed. "When I am away, I always guard my tongue. Men

probably think me slow witted, because I think so much before I speak."

I ruffled the unruly hair. "I'm very glad to hear that."

It wasn't long after that conversation that we had another of interest. He came in quietly, waiting until I had finished talking with a group of older students, not saying a word himself. I could tell, though, that he was disturbed and dismissed the others as quickly as I could. "What is it, Emrys?"

"I dreamed of the king you call Vortigern again."

I braced for bad news, but there was only silence. "And?"

"I don't know. I just keep seeing his face, then things that don't make sense."

"Tell me. Maybe I can make sense of them."

"There's a white dragon, and a red dragon, and a bear. Oh, it's just all mixed up. A flash of the king's face, then the others, then I wake up." He shrugged apologetically. "I go back to sleep, and get the same thing again … and again … and again."

"Dreams don't always mean something," I said carefully, not wanting to sound condescending, for he knew that. "Sometimes it's just indigestion."

"I know, but it's disturbing because it comes over and over which suggests that it's something important, but I can't understand it."

"You may find it repeating until you do understand it." I thought about the images he'd described. "I've heard that the Saxons sometimes fight under a banner with a white dragon." He looked up hopefully. "And it is said that Ambrosius Aurelianus and his younger brother will come back to fight under the red dragon."

"Yes, yes," he said, his eyes vacant. "King Uther Pendragon. He is …" he faltered uncertainly.

"Important?"

"Yes, he will be." He shook his head. "Tell me who they are. Now I have the names, but I don't know anything about them."

I told him the story as I'd learned it. How Vortigern had killed the king they called "The Last Roman" to claim his throne, and killed his oldest sons, and how the younger had been spirited away to Brittany for safe keeping, and how some pinned their hopes on these two boys as well as their support and waited for the day they'd come back to save Britannia.

He nodded. "And that's where I will have a role to play."

I looked at him in surprise.

"That I know now. As soon as you told the story, I knew."

"Like a tree that you know as an oak?"

"Yes, like that."

I told him about the letter I'd had from his mother then. "It's time, she says. She will be taking her vows soon, but first she wants to see you again, so I'm sending you home to Maridunum for a visit."

"Yes, it's time," he answered.

"Time for her to take her vows?"

"Time for my story to begin," he said.

What was I to say in the face of such surety? "You will be careful?"

"I promise I will return to you."

That seemed enough at the time, but within a week, I wondered if I should have forbidden the journey.

48

BLAISE

I sent Jostyn with Emrys. He was near to being finished with his training, so near that I was already contemplating his placement, trying to match his talents, the needs of various communities, and my needs for information. He rode well, he had the ability to think quickly on his feet, and perhaps, most important, he was a large man, large enough to discourage a possible challenger and trained to fight if need be. It turned out to be a wise decision.

There was no problem until they had reached Maridunum. The weather had cooperated with an early burst of spring temperatures without the usual accompanying rain. The horses were swift. They met no challengers on the road. The inns were welcoming, generous with rooms and food once the travelers had proved their worth as bards.

King Maelgwyn of Dementia greeted them - if not warmly, at least with a chill courtesy, inviting Jostyn to favor the court with song at the evening meal. It apparently didn't occur to him that his grandson would also be capable of entertaining. He curtly informed Emrys that his mother had already taken her vows, but had arranged with the Abbess to receive her son when he arrived. "Go to the convent early tomorrow and ask for her."

"I will, Sir. Thank you," Emrys replied, wondering if he would be welcome a second or third night if necessary.

They were dismissed immediately, with no questions to Emrys about his schooling or his progress. At least a steward was summoned to show them to a modest castle room. Not what Jostyn expected for the grandson of the king, but Emrys shrugged it off and seemed pleased that facing the king had not been an ordeal.

Jostyn fully intended to give Emrys the featured role while entertaining that evening, but Emrys refused. "I'll accompany you on a hand drum, but that's all I'll do. I won't sing for him." Jostyn might have argued, but for the firm look on Emrys' face.

The entertainment that evening went flawlessly, but was cut short when a contingent of soldiers from the usurper, King Vortigern, arrived. They were welcomed with courtesy and a hint of unease, but all seemed to go well. Jostyn kept his ears open and learned that they were unexpected.

There was much speculation as to the purpose of their visit. Most seemed to think that it had something to do with the rumors that Ambrosius was raising an army in Brittany, and that they were there to gain pledges of support. All the whisperers were certain that Ambrosius would come in force to win back the kingdom that had been stolen from his father. Jostyn heard one exchange that disturbed him. "Your bards are young," the commander commented. "Not my bards," King Maelgwyn replied. "They're just traveling through."

His son, also named Maelgwyn was less circumspect, however, and had drunk far too much wine. He added spitefully, "Let's hope the young bastard keeps right on traveling. He has no place in this court."

The commander seemed much too interested. "A bastard, is he?

Who's bastard?"

The answer was spoken with contempt, the words slightly slurred. "My sister's," and at that point the two moved off, too far away for Jostyn to hear more.

The next morning they walked through the town to the convent. Emrys rang the bell and asked for the Lady Ninianne. "Here she is simply the Novitiate Anna, not a princess," the cowled woman announced in an unfriendly tone of voice. Emrys told her he'd been sent for and smiled sweetly. "Come back at noon. I'll have an answer for you then," she said, shutting the door firmly.

Promptly at noon they returned only to hear disturbing news. "Soldiers came." This time the sister was too upset to be less than forthcoming. "They took Sister Anna, though the Prioress protested most firmly."

"Where, Sister? Where did they take her?" Emrys asked.

"To the king, they said." She went on distractedly, "What is the world coming to when soldiers can come here with no respect to steal our sisters away?"

Emrys was as upset as she, and it was Jostyn who spoke words of comfort. "It's probably fine, Sister. We'll go to the king, and don't worry, he'll see us. We're guests at the castle." He might have added more, but Emrys had already darted away, and he needed to run to catch up.

He tried to speak to Emrys, but Emrys was in a dark mood and in too much of a hurry to waste time on words.

When they reached the castle, Emrys told Jostyn to return to their quarters. "Wait for me there. He'll see me."

"Perhaps the king wanted to be present during your interview with your mother. She may be with him."

"No," he said curtly, already walking away. "She's not with him."

"How do you know that?" Jostyn asked, but Emrys kept on

walking and didn't answer.

49

BLAISE

Jostyn waited impatiently for hours, but Emrys did not return. Perhaps, they'll all show up together for dinner, he thought, but a quick glance around the dining hall showed King Maelgwyn alone. Now he was alarmed. He slipped away from the table and ran back to their room to see if Emrys was waiting for him there. The room was empty.

On the way back to the dining hall, he was fortunate enough to run into Prince Maelgwyn, returning from the privy. Worry made him bold enough to speak. "Did you enjoy the music last night, Sire?"

"The music? Oh, it was fine enough."

"Thank you, Sire. Have you, perchance, seen young Emrys, my companion, about?"

"The bastard?" He laughed heartily. "I saw him. Hauled off by the soldiers, he was."

"What? His grandfather has imprisoned him?"

"No, that's not the way of it." He laughed again. "It was King

Vortigern's soldiers that took him. They rode off hours ago." He walked away, still chuckling.

Jostyn wasted no time. He went back to their room, packed, and made his way to the stables where he had the horses saddled.

He was lucky enough to find a talkative guard at the gate. "The High King's soldiers? Left at sunset, they did, and if you asked me, I'd say they were riding fast. They finally found what they'd come for."

"And what was that, do you think?"

"Oh they've been looking for a bastard with no earthly father." He nodded knowingly. "The walls keep falling on the castle Vortigern is trying to raise, and it seems they need a bastard. So they'll stand up, you see?"

"Sorry, no. I don't see. What would a bastard have to do with raising the walls?"

"Why, as a sacrifice … an old custom, they say."

Jostyn gulped. "A sorry custom if it's true. Which way did they go?"

"If I was you," the guard answered, "I wouldn't be riding after them."

"Of course not," he snapped. "I was looking to avoid them."

"In that case take the road east, then south. They're going north."

"My thanks," he offered. "May the gods protect you."

He rode off quickly, and when he was out of sight, circled the city and rode through the hills until he found the road that went north.

50

BLAISE

Emrys had been waiting for admittance outside King Maelgwyn's private chambers when he saw Vortigern's guards approaching. He felt no warning, just annoyance, for if they wanted audience with the king his wait would be even longer and it had already stretched into hours. He settled on the bench, his back against the wall, worried about his mother. When a rough hand clamped on his shoulder, he still had no other concern, and looked up in annoyance.

"It's him," the soldier said. "The bastard."

He couldn't imagine how that fact could possibly interest the guard and he thought of several immediate retorts, but knew enough about soldiers to keep quiet.

"Is it true?" the soldier pressed.

"Sir? That I'm a bastard? Yes, it's true."

"Who is your mother?" the soldier asked, not releasing his grip. "Come, the truth."

Emrys lifted his chin, refusing to be cowed by the question. "My mother is Ninianne, daughter of King Maelgwyn, now known as Sister Anne, for she's taken Holy vows."

"And your father?"

"I don't know, Sir. That is the truth."

"She never told you?"

"No, Sir."

The man hauled him to his feet roughly. "You're to come with us."

Emrys planted his feet wide apart and stood tall. "Not until I've spoken with my mother, Sir. Then I will gladly do as you ask."

"You won't find her here," the soldier answered. "We'll take you to her. I know where she is."

It was clear to Emrys that the soldier was not fabricating. He instantly realized that these were the soldiers who had taken her, not his grandfather's men. "All right," he answered with dignity. "Lead the way, Sir." He fell in behind the Leader and did not find it strange that the rest of the escort followed closely on their heels. If anything, he was relieved that he didn't have to face his grandfather.

At first he thought they were going to the chamber that had been hers when he was a boy and lived there, but they passed it by. In the courtyard they headed for the stables and he was given a fine horse which pleased him. Perhaps they were going back to the convent. But they passed that, too, and headed off on the northern road. They were riding at a fast pace which suited him, but he spurred the horse forward until he was next to the leader to ask where they were going.

"It's a place where we camped two nights ago. She's waiting for you there," he was told. That seemed strange to him, but still he had no feelings of foreboding, and he was sure that if there was danger, he'd have known it.

Two hours more they rode. Darkness was beginning to drench the sky, but ahead he saw fires, and then tents, and he was satisfied.

The horses were handed off and he was marched to a tent - quite a grand tent it turned out, with warm furs on the cot and more on the floor, and a lantern that cast a soft light. She was sitting on the cot, still in a traveling cape, with an empty plate in her hand, but rose when they entered and set the plate aside. "Emrys!"

He fell to a knee before her and reached for her hand, but she pulled him up into her arms, embracing him firmly before pulling him back to look up into his face. "You've grown so." It was true. On the last visit he had faced her eye to eye, but now he could have rested his chin on her head.

"Are you all right?" he asked. "Have they mistreated you in any way?"

"No, Emrys. I'm fine," she shot a fierce look at the soldiers, "except that I am forced to go with them. To see the High King, they say."

Emrys turned to the men. "Is this necessary? You have me as hostage, you don't need my mother."

"No," she said quickly. "Take me, but release my son. He has done you no harm."

"Nor have you, Madam," the Leader answered. "Yet it is best to take you both. I assure you that you will be treated well on the journey. Now it is time for you to sleep, Madam, for we will have an early start tomorrow, and it is time to feed your son and find accommodations for him."

"Can't we stay together?" she begged. "It's been such a long time since I've seen him."

"No. That would be impossible. It's best to keep you separate."

And that was the way it was for the rest of the trip. They were not allowed to converse from then on.

Still they were not mistreated, and Emrys had no feelings of foreboding which he was sure he would have felt if they were truly in danger. The opposite, if anything, for there was a clear feeling of destiny, or, to be more precise, he felt that this was the beginning of the role he was meant to play out in the future.

They did not move swiftly, but at a pace set for his mother's litter. He was sorry to see that she was curtained off, unable to enjoy the countryside, for the weather still held, and every shade of green wove through the forests and hillsides and fields, and there were the first flowers of spring all about them - tiny bursts of white and yellow and lavender, and streams swollen with winter melting, racing toward rivers that rose high against the banks. He took advantage of his captivity, quite enjoying the chance to learn the land that he had studied on maps, noting each village and each crossing, imagining the report that he would give me at the end of his adventure.

51

BLAISE

Jostyn rode his horses to exhaustion the first evening, finally camping at the side of the road when it was obvious that his horses could go no farther without rest. It was midmorning on the next day when he heard the sounds of horses ahead. He reigned in, looking about, then followed at a slower pace, keeping the sounds constant in front of him until he saw a hill ahead. Leaving the road, he spurred the horses straight up, stopping just short of the crest. Quickly he looped the reigns through the limb of a tree, and took the summit on foot, taking care to crawl over the utmost rocks until he had a clear view of the road ahead.

He spotted Emrys immediately, mounted and surrounded by soldiers. Farther back he saw the litter, also surrounded. A litter? That would slow them. And it might be the Lady Ninianne. These must have been the soldiers that took her from the convent, not King Maelgwyns' men, as they had assumed.

Not much chance of rescue with so many soldiers maintaining

vigilance. He would have to stay back, being careful not to be seen, and hope that the night would bring an opportunity. He'd have to try something. This couldn't be left to fate with Emrys' life hanging in the balance. He wondered if Emrys knew.

52

BLAISE

The journey took six days. Here there were no Roman roads, for the Romans had never conquered Cambria. The road they followed narrowed to a trail that snaked up through mountain passes and down into valleys, with treacherous switchbacks that slowed their progress as they continued winding north. Towns became villages then thinned to small scattered settlements with just a few buildings.

In the lower regions they ran into fog, coming off the Irish Sea that Emrys knew lay west of them, but the heights gave them sight of magnificent mountain chains as far as they could see. It was colder, but the gods were kind and there was no wind. Emrys was glad of the warm cape that wrapped him and the furs that covered his mother. With these aids it was tolerable.

The night skies were magnificent with a fiery sun dropping like a red ball behind the mountain peaks, bringing in its wake a sky black and crisp with stars.

Their destination, Dinas Bran, meaning the king's fortress, was a tall, flat-topped mountain with a commanding view of the land all around and the sea to the north and west where there was a good-sized town.

There was a road that came in from the east, Emrys saw, where men were hauling loads of cut stones in heavy wagons, urging the small mountain horses on and up.

He saw, too, as they began the steep zigzagged path to the crest, that there were many places where water trickled from the stones - too many places, and with a perfect clarity he suddenly understood why the foundations of the fortress were falling.

At the top the tents were pitched a final time, and a meal was prepared. There was no dining hall, no building at all yet - just groupings of tents, and walls about the rim that were in various stages of completion, some sections as tall as eight feet, some just two feet high, and some that had once been tall, but had fallen. Emrys saw men working by torchlight, driven by overseers who shouted directions at each team, and he saw too the frustrated looks on the faces of the workers.

He'd been kept separate from his mother, with no chance of conversation since the initial exchange of the first night, so when the soldiers came to get him, with her in tow, he was pleased and smiled.

She had no answering smile for him. He understood that there was fear buried deep beneath the seeming calm.

She was a tiny woman, thinner as she aged, but she walked with her shoulders back and her chin up and a royal dignity that gave her height and power. She needed no crown, no torque, to look a queen. With pride in her, Emrys copied what he saw, his stride measured to hers, his back straight his head looking neither left nor right, but ahead with confidence.

His mother glanced at him sideways, thinking she understood his bravado, but it wasn't that on his part. He was preparing to meet his destiny.

They were taken to a large tent of yellow silk - the largest that

Emrys had yet seen. The High King's standard flew before it, the wind lifting and fluttering it, and he saw his mother hesitate, staring at this brazen display of the red dragon banner that had never been Vortigern's to display. He felt her anger and knew it was shared by all the nobles and most of the people. They approached two guards who held spears crossed and stood like Roman columns before the entrance. Words were exchanged with their guards and the spears lifted. Their escort stopped them just inside and waited to be summoned.

The tent was well lighted with torches on each pole, and hung with thick tapestries to keep out the chill. A brazier burned brightly in the center of the room. The floor was thick with furs. There were three men seated behind a long table and behind them in long dark cloaks stood the priests. Emrys considered making the hand signals that would identify him as one of them, but held back, with the feeling that this was wrong. He was not one of 'them.'

From his vision he recognized Vortigern in the center - would have known him even if he had not worn the thick gold torque. He had the thought that the actual Vortigern had greatly aged from the one in his vision and looked haggard from worrying. Sitting on one side of him was a young man, surely one of his sons from the look of him. On the other side was a greybeard, a man made hard from many battles, with scars on his forehead and one cheek to prove it.

They were gestured forward. His mother sank into a graceful curtsy. He followed her example. "Rise," Vortigern said curtly, then, "Boy, who are you?"

There was no hesitation in his answer. "I am Emrys of Maridunum, grandson of King Maelgwyn." He gestured toward his mother. "Son of Sister Anna who was formerly the Lady Ninianne, daughter of King Maelgwyn." Quickly he added, "Sir."

"I understand that you no longer live in Maridunum?" asked the King's son.

Emrys thought it best not to mention his school. "Lately I have been at the court of King Gorlois," he answered, hoping that the point would not be pressed, and that they would assume he was being fostered there.

Vortigern was giving his son a look that said plainly, 'Let me handle this.' He turned his attention back to Emrys. "Your father? Who was he?"

"I don't know."

"How can this be?" the King demanded. "Did you never ask?"

His eyes did not wander, but met the King's evenly. "I did ask. I did not receive an answer, Sir."

Now the King turned his attention on the Lady Ninianne. He spoke curtly. "And now I ask the same question of you, Madam. Who is the boy's father?"

Like her son, she met his gaze levelly. "I am a good woman, Your Highness. I have been a devout Christian for many years, and I've taken vows. I've not told this story before, but I will now, and I swear on all I believe, that it is the truth."

She did not falter in her delivery, and her gaze did not drop. "One day I was in the garden below my rooms. My ladies were in sight, as always, but not at my side. A young man came and sat down beside me without asking my leave. I turned to admonish him, but all about him was a golden light, and I was filled with wonder. We spoke of the flowers and the fountain, and he made me laugh at the antics of my kitten.

"Later, I asked my ladies who he was, but they looked at me strangely and said they'd seen no one." The torchlight lit her dark hair with tones of red. As if conscious of it, she pulled at her cowl and tucked the hair back into place. "He came many times after that, always when he could speak to me alone, but always when my ladies were present."

For the first time she looked down. "He came to me at night too, holding and touching me gently, never waking my lady companions." She looked up, her eyes filled with tears. "I think he was an angel."

There was a stirring among the priests. One of them proclaimed, "The boy has no earthly father."

"That's right," she answered. Emrys reached for her hand, and she gave it gladly. There was turmoil inside him at her story, but he had learned the Druid way well, and no emotion showed on his face.

The King stood. "Thank you for your honesty, Lady Ninianne. You will be escorted back to your convent at first light."

"And my son with me?"

"No. I have use for your boy."

"He's a good boy," she protested. "His interest is in books and study. In time we hope to see him join a monastery. He'll do you no harm, Sir. I swear it."

"We're done here," he said to the soldiers, ignoring her plea. "Prepare an escort for the lady, and have the boy brought to me at high sun. I'll be at the wall with the workmen."

They were taken back to their tents, separated as before. Emrys was thankful that his mother was to be sent home, more thankful the next morning when the party left. This time it did not look so much like she was a captive. It seemed a guard of honor, and he knew that she would come to no harm.

53

BLAISE

Jostyn had followed Emrys, but had seen no chance for a rescue during the long journey. When they arrived at Dinas Bran, he knew he had to make a move and soon.

For a while he watched the busy scene from a neighboring hilltop, observing the fortifications, the many soldiers, and the equally numerous laborers. Gradually he formed a plan and began immediately to implement it.

The east side of Vortigern's hill was heavily forested and that was where he headed. He camped, fireless, that night in a thick grove of trees, and in the morning he changed, layering his clothes to keep off the chill, with his oldest on top, then smoothed a warm hat over his light brown hair, and tucked a knife into his boot. He left his good cloak behind along with their instruments, hidden under a bush, but took the scant remainder of his food, which had been reinforced several times as he passed through the mountain villages. He left the horses tethered, with feed bags for nourishment and with long blankets for warmth, held on firmly by their saddles.

As he moved toward the trail that led up the mountain, he used his knife to mark trees so that he would have no trouble finding the horses. His final mark went on a tree that came to the very edge of the trail. He would be able to see it easily, even in the dark. He hoped that no one else would notice it, but if someone did, it was a single slash that would signify nothing to the observer.

He found a thick coppice of shrubbery and hid there, watching those who passed until he spotted the opportunity he was looking for. It came within the hour. Two men were struggling, straining to haul a heavy load of rocks up the steep trail, no soldiers in sight. He waited until they had passed and were a little way farther up, slid out of the bushes, and ran noisily to catch up with them, panting as if he had run a long distance. When he reached them, he slid in to the rear of the wagon and added his bulk to push from behind. "Ho? Where'd you come from?" asked one of them as they both felt the load lighten and turned.

"Sent me from below," he panted. "They thought you could use the help and I was unlucky enough to have no load of my own." He grinned. "Threatened to skin me alive if their horses passed me, and I hadn't caught you."

"And they'll skin all of us if we don't get a move on," one of them answered picking up the pace.

As they went round the next bend, they heard horses coming from above and moved to the side of the path, pulling off it entirely a moment later when they came to a place wide enough to hold the cart. There were twenty mounted soldiers, ten in front of a closed litter, ten behind. The driver of the horses pulling the litter slowed as they passed, and a curtain was pulled aside as the occupant stared out at them. Jostyn gave no sign of it, but he recognized the litter as the same one that had held the Lady Ninianne, and now he saw that it was, indeed, she. Alone. Emrys was not in the litter with her, and scrutinizing the soldiers as they went by, he saw that Emrys was not with them either. So she doesn't know, he thought. She has been sent back so there will be no outcry from a mother watching her son on the sacrificial stone.

54

BLAISE

It seemed that everyone was busy this morning. Everyone but him. The workmen were at the walls, unloading and stacking stones, mixing mortar and spreading it, while the soldiers and overseers directed. The priests were huddled near Vortigern's yellow tent, their dark robes flapping in the wind like ravens diving in to feed on carrion, their eyes glittering, darting frequent glances at Emrys who was huddled over the remains of a night fire, keeping as warm as he could while he ate the bread and cheese the soldiers had provided.

There were two soldiers guarding him, but not watching closely. They were talking in voices kept low so he wouldn't overhear. Even so, he knew what they were saying. The moment that the High King heard the priest pronounce him a child with no earthly father, Emrys had understood what they intended to do with him.

The shedding of bastard blood was an old superstition. He'd read about it, and he knew that there was no magic in the deed. It would prove a failure if it was allowed to happen. He also understood that the priests were afraid. They had no power here. Their spells had not worked, and if something didn't change soon, they were doomed.

One of them had suggested finding a bastard with no earthly father, not dreaming that they'd actually find one. It had been suggested to buy time, to keep them safe from the High King's anger at their failure.

Emrys hoped that he could save them as well as himself.

He also wondered what the truth was. Who was his father? Not for an instant had he believed the story his mother told, but he was glad that she'd been able to convince Vortigern. Even though it made his own situation more difficult it lent his mother a virtuousness that many had denied her, and he had no doubt that the soldiers would be repeating the story until the whole country knew it as truth.

At the same time that he felt pride in her performance, he also felt disappointment. All the doubts that had tormented him since he'd been old enough to understand leaped to the surface.

Who was his father? Someone so shameful that she would not tell his name? A slave or a servant? Definitely someone who wouldn't or couldn't marry her? Why not? Because he wouldn't be accepted. Because it was someone who would shame the royal household?

Someone who did not deserve a king's daughter. Who was it? Maybe someone who already had a wife and another family. He could have half-brothers and half-sisters, and perhaps that was why his mother had always wanted him to take vows - so that he would not be able to marry someone who was his own sister. Could that be it?

Or had some ruffian raped her? Someone who cared nothing for her, who didn't even know that a son had come of the union? Someone who had come through the town one day and left the next, then laughed about his conquest? No surely, not that, for she would have told her father, and he would have sent soldiers and brought the man to justice. No, surely not rape by a stranger. Rape by someone else? Someone close to her father whom she dared not name? No. That didn't feel right to him. She had never seemed ashamed and that would probably bring shame. Who was it?

He shook his head and turned away from the fire, trying to distract himself. He found a perfect distraction. A laborer was handing rocks to another man. His back was to Emrys but Emrys knew that back very well. He should. He'd followed it all the way to Maridunum!

He did not betray Jostyn with an outward show of interest, but watched that group of workers idly. Jostyn saw him looking and took a moment to pause and drink from a flask he retrieved from his belt. Before he had the flask in hand his nimble fingers had formed letters in the secret ogham alphabet. "Are you all right?"

Emrys signaled back just as quickly. "Yes. Do nothing. Wait."

A few moments later the soldiers were telling him to rise. It was time. Yes, time to meet my destiny, he thought, and was so sure of it that as soon as he spotted Vortigern he quickened his pace, knelt in front of him, and announced himself. "My Lord, it's high sun and time you learn how to keep your walls from falling."

Vortigern signaled him to rise and looked at the child with amusement. "You're an eager one, Emrys. I've seen grown men in your situation beg for their lives."

"Spilling my blood will not make your walls stand, Sir. You've heard what my father was ... angel or demon." He let the words hang until he saw that they had been absorbed. "It is as his son, with his power, that I tell you that beneath these rocks there is a pool of water that must be drained, for in that pool there are two dragons - one red, one white - who battle each night, shaking the foundations that your masons have tried to build." The next thing he remembered was a blinding pain.

55

BLAISE

When the word spread that the High King had sent for the bastard, the soldiers left their posts to watch, and the laborers took advantage of the excitement and followed along. Jostyn pushed his way to the forefront, determined to make a grab for Emrys even if it meant his own death.

He heard Emrys tell the king to drain the water from a lake beneath the surface of the mountain, then watched as Emrys shook and his body stiffened. He saw the whites of his friend's eyes as they rolled up into his head and listened as the voice of power touched him.

Emrys spoke for a long time, and not much of it made sense to him. Spoke of dragons – red and white, he did, representing Britannia and the Saxons, and foretold that in the end the Saxons would triumph.

But before that would come the Boar of Cornwall, or perhaps it was the Bear of Cornwall, for he used the Latin 'Artos,' and this being would trample these Saxons underfoot.

He spoke of eagles and lions, comets and constellations, king-doms rising and kingdoms falling. Then came a long description of what was to befall the Britons until the very end of time. The heavens would quake, the stars battling as the seas rose up, and the winds would deliver arrows of fire to the stars.

It seemed he would never stop, but finally the voice of power gave way and the body weakened, and Emrys fell to the ground in a faint. Vortigern said, "The boy might prove useful," which was a relief to Jostyn. Then he had the soldiers carry Emrys back to his tent, and sent one of his priests along to tend him, and ordered his engi-neers to drill for water and rig pumps.

In the general confusion that resulted Jostyn followed those carrying Emrys, and took a sheltered position between two tents where he could safely watch those who came and left.

A second priest entered carrying supplies and Jostyn stealthily took a circuitous route to the back of the boy's tent and listened as one of the priests listed the herbs he had brought. The other shortly had it brewed into a steaming drink. Jostyn had not specialized in herb lore as Emrys had, but he knew enough to be sure that none of the ingredients were harmful.

He heard one priest say, "Help me by propping him up while I try to get him to drink this." Apparently Emrys was still unresponsive. "The same voice said, "Keep holding him. I'll spoon some into his mouth. Hopefully he'll swallow it. That will help keep the headache at bay." They must have been successful, for the same voice said, "That's all we can do for now. He needs to sleep it out."

Jostyn saw them leave a few minutes later and heard them instruct the guards to leave the boy alone and let him sleep. Quickly he slipped away, going to the work area that held supplies.

It didn't take him long to find the sacks of flour that he'd ob-served earlier piled by a makeshift kitchen. No one was watching as he used his knife to slit and empty one of them, and no one questioned him when he took the long sack and walked away.

He made his way to the back of Emrys' tent again and slipped several fastenings loose, crawling in under the flaps. There was torchlight, so he made his way directly to the cot where Emrys slept the sleep of little death, as they called it at the school. Emrys was tall for his age, but the weight of a man had not kept pace with his height, so it was easy to wrap him inside the sack, lift him to the back flap of the tent and, after peering out to make sure no one was about, roll him under.

He followed and re-staked the fastenings, smiling as he thought of the rumors that would fly about the devil making his son disappear. Then casually he hefted the sack over his shoulder and made his way to the path.

56

BLAISE

Emrys first became aware of the fire. He was cold and tried to scrunch himself closer. That was when he realized that he was so tightly wrapped that nothing happened when he tried to move. At first he thought he was tied up, then realized he could move his hands inside - inside the blankets. Yes, they were blankets wrapped about him tightly. Blankets. So who was keeping him warm?

Slowly he moved his head from side to side. He saw no one. He was apparently alone. Not in a tent. Outside, in a forest, with a campfire. He managed to free his hands. Pushed himself to a sitting position. And lost consciousness as the pain filled his head.

Someone caught him as he fell. Hands lowered him to the ground again, and patted the blankets back around him.

The next time he woke he could see sunlight dappling through the trees. The fire was still burning brightly and someone pressed a flask of water to his lips. He drank thirstily, slurping, and felt embarrassed as water slopped over and ran down his chin. A cloth, not too clean, mopped up the overflow, and a face came into view. "Jostyn," he whispered, not intending to whisper, but it was the loudest sound he could produce.

"Shhh. Just rest," Jostyn told him. "You're safe."

He woke again when the sun was higher. It was still blotted by the trees, but he was sure it was the same day, and he felt stronger. As long as he stayed flat, the headache was tempered, but when he tried to raise himself, it struck again.

"I have hot broth," his friend told him. "Can you drink some if I help?"

He mumbled, "Yes," carefully, trying not to move his head, and a cup appeared. He felt stronger when the long process of drinking with the support of Jostyn ended. "What happened?" he asked.

"You were brought before Vortigern. Before he could kill you, you told him there was water below and that he should drain the pool."

"I - I remember that."

"Then you went into a trance and talked for a long time, making one prophecy after another."

"What did I say?"

"Do you remember any of it?"

"No."

"Well, you pretty much gave the entire future history of Britannia, ending with the destruction of the world."

Emrys smiled weakly. "Is that all?"

"You said that the Boar – or Bear of Cornwall would crush the Saxon's white dragon, but in the end the white dragon would triumph over the red dragon."

"And Vortigern was unhappy at that outcome, I'll wager."

"Well, the immediate result after you collapsed was that he called for pumps to be set up, so he believed what you said about the water. He also decided to keep you alive and had you carted away." Jostyn's eyes twinkled. "I stole you out from under them though. Didn't really think you wanted to become Vortigern's pet prophet."

"You were right."

"We're not away yet." He looked Emrys over carefully. "If you think you're strong enough we'll put some distance behind us in the morning."

Emrys was nearly asleep again, but he managed to be encouraging. "I will be." He also managed to say, "Thank you," and he hoped he had said it aloud.

57

BLAISE

A full month later I was pacing my study - something I did often of late - when word finally came that Emrys and Jostyn were riding in. They hadn't come to our island by boat, but had taken the long way, using the hidden trails, some of which were causeways always under water and dangerous to those who didn't know the way. I took the stairs at a breakneck speed and was in the courtyard to meet the horses. "Thank the one great God!" I greeted them. "We've been very worried about you."

They looked tired, bedraggled and dirty, but I was too eager to hear their story to allow them rest yet, and escorted them straight up to the study, and sent for food. It arrived minutes later, and I set them about eating, and said I wouldn't listen to anything until they had nearly finished it. There was no argument.

I noticed how relieved they were to be home. Their journey must have been harrowing.

"We heard about the boy who prophesied on the coming of kings and the end of the stars," I told them, "and we knew his name was Emrys. A boy with no earthly father, the story was - a boy who would be sacrificed so Vortigern's walls would stand. I was afraid it was you."

With his mouth full, Emrys nodded, and Jostyn said, "It was. I thought it would be the end of him."

"Eat, eat," I told them. "We also heard about dragons fighting - red with white - and how that represented the Saxons and the Celts, and that Vortigern called all the lesser kings in with their armies. There was a great battle in the north, but because of the boy prophet, the High King was ready and defeated the Saxons who broke the treaty. No one knew where the boy was, though there have been stories and the High King has soldiers searching for him."

Jostyn had cleaned his plate with the last bit of bread. He swallowed a mouthful of wine and asked, "Would the stories be that the boy's unearthly father had rescued him?"

"Why, yes. Now why don't you tell me about that."

Jostyn did, describing how he had boldly carried Emrys off in a flour sack over his shoulder, and how he had followed his trail back to the horses and put all the supplies and instruments on one of them, with himself propping the boy in front of him on the second until they had gone a safe distance, and how Emrys had taken two full days to regain consciousness, and how they had seen soldiers on all the roads, so had made their way slowly through the forests and hills, avoiding trails and roads through the entire journey until they were safe in the Summer Country. "Came as fast as we could," he finished, "but thought it was better to stay hidden than to risk capture."

"You did very well, Jostyn. I thank you, as does everyone at the school. You proved brave, steadfast, cunning, innovative, and took the initiative at every opportunity. I wish we had dozens with just half your abilities."

For once Jostyn had no words. His mouth hung open for just a moment. Pleasure lit his eyes, but before it could spread to the rest of his face, he bowed his head. "Fate," he mumbled, then a stronger voice as his head came up. "I figure that God has a plan for young Emrys, Master. It was fate that took him to the High King and fate that brought him home."

I nodded. "I'm sure you're right, Jostyn. And it was you that God used to administer the bringing home part." Now it was time to get to business and to send Jostyn away so I could have a private interview with my star pupil. "I suggest that you get as much rest as possible during the next week, beginning right now. Come to me in two days and I'll give you your new assignment." I walked Jostyn to the door, and gently squeezed his shoulder in a gesture of final thanks as I ushered him out.

I turned to Emrys. "What do you have to add to this report?"

"Not much, Sir. I don't remember anything that I said when the spell came upon me." An expression of serenity took over his face - not a common expression for him. "I was never afraid, though Jostyn feared for me," he said. "Somehow I knew that going to Vortigern was my destiny, and that I would come out of it intact."

"You said as much before you left. Do you recall? You told me you were going to begin your destiny." He smiled at that, but I couldn't help but think that it was the one straw I could grasp when I was so worried about them. "What about your mother? Did you get a chance to talk to her?"

"No, not really. Once in the presence of soldiers, and a second time with the whole court listening. Vortigern sent her home before I was supposed to be sacrificed. I was glad of that and watched to make sure that she was, indeed, taken away. That time it seemed she was escorted with honors and not a captive, just as Vortigern had promised."

"I will see that she has word of your safety."

"Thank you."

I studied him for a moment. "I notice that you don't honor King Vortigern with his title."

"I did in front of him, Master, but I was raised to doubt that he had any right to the title of High King except as a murderer."

"What do you know of that, Emrys?"

"Only what you told me. That he murdered two of Emperor Constantine's sons - Moyne and Constans, and that the younger boys, Ambrosius and Uther, were spirited away to Brittany before he could murder them too. Then he claimed the throne and invited the brothers Hengist and Horsa of the Saxons here to fight the Picts and Irish, and, of course, anyone who might claim that he had no right to the leadership.

"He learned that was a mistake during the Night of Long Knives - the night I saw in my first vision, and now, because he lost the trust of the tribes, he's scrambling to gather all who will heed the danger to fight the Saxons. It is also said, by the people, not by any at either court I've observed, but by the common people, that Ambrosius is now a man ready to claim his rightful place in Britannia - that he's been raising an army and building a fleet."

"So your grandfather follows Vortigern reluctantly?"

"As do all the southern kings who visited his court. Or Gorlois' court, for that matter."

I poked at the fire until a log caught and began to flame brightly. "It's all true, Emrys. And you - you will have a role to play when Ambrosius comes to power, but that's still several years away. Meanwhile you must finish your training so that you'll be ready, and, for your own safety, I'm sending you away.

Vortigern's busy battling Saxons right now, but it won't be long before he has even more soldiers out looking for you. I think three days will see you rested and ready to leave, and if you are not well enough to go at that time, you are to tell me."

"I'll be ready, but Master, where am I to go?"

"To a group of Druids who rule the continent. They're in hiding because of the fighting going on, but organized as we are, and knowledgeable about what is happening all over the Empire. You will find them in Brittany."

58

BLAISE

It was seven years before I saw Emrys again. He wrote to me with a regularity that surprised me, entrusting the sealed scrolls only to Druid bards and priests who were coming to Ynys Witrin. He wrote of the voyage across the narrow sea where he was so seasick that he remembered only the initial casting off. The rest of the journey he was in a cot below decks, either heaving into a bucket or about to heave into a bucket. I wasn't surprised by this report. It's a common problem for our seers.

Once he was on land the sickness abated, but not for several days. The second part of his journey - on horseback - was easier, but he was not in any shape to remember many of the sights he passed. He apologized for this. "I should like to have described the land itself and its people, but I'm afraid I was riding in a fog, though the sun shone brightly."

He did describe his new community. "It's on a river, but so hidden in the forest that one cannot see it from the water which is good because, since so many soldiers have left to fight the Barbarians, there are frequent uprisings against the Romans in all areas of Gaul, and we have no desire to be caught up in local disputes. The buildings are not of stone like the ones on our island, but of timber, so that they blend into the surrounding forest. The paths that lead to Carnates are not roads but trails."

He had a small hut to himself which suited him though it had "not one luxury." He was in classes, but felt rather alone, since there was no one there who was as young. It took him a year before friendships developed, but it seemed that the older men began to value his insight and eventually sought him out for discussion on the many diverse subjects that a Druid must learn. Before long they began treating him as an equal.

It was about that time that the Merlin, himself, took an interest in him. Merlin is the title of our High Priest. Most of them had lived in Britannia - traditionally on the Isle of Mons, until the Romans purged the Druids from its shores. Later they hid in various places as the need arose, including our Glass Isle, but the last two Merlins had followed the Romans to the continent and lived in Lesser Britain which they felt was closer to the center of the political problems that concerned them.

"Merlin is very old," he wrote. "I think he must know everything there is to know, for there is not a question that I put to him that does not have a ready answer. Then I smile at my own naivety, for I honestly do know that he can't know everything, for no one can. Answers to one question bring up new questions. What a dull world, if one could really know it all? Where would be the joy in discovery of something new?"

Emrys was confirmed as a full Druid priest after just three years in Brittany. He wrote about the initiation - not, of course, about the ceremony which was one of our secrets, but about his feelings. "I was afraid that they'd misjudged me, and that I wasn't truly ready for the tests, but I found that I answered the questions easily, as if I had always known the answers, and the dreaded ordeal soon turned joyful.

The others who went through the ceremony with me have all been sent away to new postings, and at first, I was disturbed to find that I was the only one not fit to be given this honor, for Merlin explained that I was still young and needed seasoning. Naturally I interpreted this as meaning I was too immature to be taken seriously by others, and I was devastated. I spent a week in self chosen seclusion, too ashamed to present myself to the others, but at length Merlin, himself, sent for me and, Master Blaise, you will not believe this, but he has chosen me to be his special assistant."

Of course I believed it. I had done the same with Emrys.

"Though travel is difficult for the Merlin - he must go slowly in a litter - he has taken me to the courts of the brothers, King Ban of Benoic, King Hoel of Amorica, and King Bors of Brittany, and he told each of them that from now on when they have need of him, I will be his voice."

For nine months now he has let me receive couriers, make assignments, write to those who have asked for help, deciding myself what should be done in each case - even when it was a king asking, and I have served in his place as judge. Truly, he listens as I tell him my decisions, but he has questioned none of them for a full seven months now.

"That is the exciting news. The sad news is that every day Merlin's condition deteriorates. I am considered one of our most skilled healers now, and truly I can do nothing but alleviate his pain, nor can the other healers.

"He wants me to go to the secret camp of Ambrosius Aurelianus, in whom he places much hope and confidence, but I have managed to postpone it. I don't want to leave him when his health is so poor."

I read this last dispatch with sorrow for Merlin, but pride - oh, such pride - in Emrys. I understood, knowing that he had no suspicion whatsoever, exactly what Merlin was grooming him for.

59

BLAISE

The next letter came on the heels of the last, in the same packet that contained the official announcement that went to all Master Druids and to the kings who still followed the old ways.

"For one who is supposed to be a seer, I've been completely blind," he wrote. "Oh I knew that it would come someday, but to happen so soon!? I smiled as I read those words, rather amused that for once our lesser seers in the school had seen the truth that Emrys - my brightest and strongest seer - had missed.

"I knew that Merlin was dying," he continued. "That grand old man, with his wispy white hair, and his bushy black eyebrows that were always so startling in the frail face, died quietly, with all the elders gathered around him. I was there too, of course, sitting at his side, holding one thin hand, while Bertrano, whom I was sure would be his successor, held the other.

"The conclave met in the great circle of oaks while the pyre embers were still smoldering. Bertrano, tears running down the deep grooves in his face, held the document that Merlin had signed confirming the appointment of the new Merlin and, Master, the Merlin chose me.

Me, as his successor. Me?

They circled around me, each one naming me Merlin as he passed, and then they burned the document so there would be no written evidence.

I hardly believed it and was in such a state of wonderment that I barely remember what happened from then on, yet at the same time, Master, I felt strangely comfortable, as if I had known all along that this was to be. After the ceremony I questioned Bertrano, wondering if some would object to my appointment, but he told me firmly that it simply wasn't done. When the Merlin spoke, everyone obeyed - such is the respect for the holder of the title.

"But I have only nineteen years," I told him, still perplexed that I wasn't made to argue for the honor.

"You have the wisdom of the Merlin," he answered firmly, and then he pledged his personal loyalty, vowing to help me in any way I could use him. How grateful I am that he should stand by me so firmly. I have made him my assistant, and will leave him, and all the affairs of the Merlin, in his able hands when it is time to leave. That will be soon. I must go to Ambrosius within the week, and though I haven't told the others, I have seen that it will be many years before I return. The Merlin is returning to Britannia, Master Blaise, and the banner of the red dragon will be with me."

60

BLAISE

Merlin was led to the secret compound of Ambrosius by the master bard appointed to the camp. His name was Alyfin and he had attended the conclave that made Emrys the Merlin. He had brought a scroll from Ambrosius requesting the new Merlin's presence as soon as it was convenient. He presented it shortly after the ceremony, and then congratulated Merlin with a huge smile and a hug. "I knew it would be you."

"It's just the pride you feel for an old student talking, Master." Merlin looked him over from head to foot. "It seems that camp life agrees with you. You've gained twenty pounds of muscle since I've seen you, and it looks good. I'll bet you could wrestle a bear and win now."

Alyfin laughed heartily. "When you live with an army, it keeps them respectful if you train with them."

"Just remember the twenty-odd years it took you to become a master and try to avoid getting into a real battle. I'd hate to lose you before all your songs were sung."

"You've naught to worry about, Merlin. The very second a battle begins, I'll be way above it - up a hill where I can see it all." He laughed. "Someone needs to be able to describe it later."

The two rode with a small party of six Druids, all carrying instruments and dressed as traveling bards. King Bors' oldest daughter was marrying soon. If any asked, they were entertainers on their way to the wedding. They spent most of the day on forest paths roughly paralleling the river.

At dusk they came to an inn at a ferry crossing and spent the night singing for their supper. Merlin was the youngest, but held his own with harp and drum and song, then retired with the others to the small room tucked under the rafters. There were two beds and they slept soundly, three to a bed, on mattresses stuffed with new straw which were thankfully free of lice.

In the morning they hurried their horses onto the large raft and were poled to the far side of the river where they found an old Roman road that led straight through rich farmland for miles and miles. In the late afternoon they headed into the hills, making their own trail to the west, and passing only one solitary shepherd with his flock. As the sun began to set they came to a trail and followed it west, then north as it cut through a shallow valley of farms. "They grow food for the camp," Alyfin told him.

Not long after that they topped a final hill, and found a long wooden wall that stretched as far as they could see in both directions. Following its edge to the west, they soon came to a gate where they were challenged by soldiers. Alyfin let his hood fall back and was immediately recognized. "Ah, we've been looking for you, Bard, and it seems you've brought your friends. We'll sup with music tonight, eh?"

"You'll not be able to escape it," Alyfin called back cheerfully, "but we'll hope for a wash and short rest first."

"You know the way," he was told. "And he'll see you as soon as you're sufficiently clean and polished."

As they passed through the gate Merlin saw a well-organized camp, fortified with manned guard towers all along the wall which circled the compound. There was a large communal building for meals, smaller buildings to house the men, a stable and pasture for the horses - and Merlin had never seen so many horses in one place before, an armory with the noise of smith's hammering, an exercise yard where many men were drilling with swords, and a long field where a cavalry unit was practicing pacing and turns. He saw in an instant that the entire valley was filled with men gearing for war.

Alyfin led them to a barracks building where he was met by a soldier named Garad who assigned them rooms, brought them fresh water for washing, wine for their thirst, and bid them welcome. Merlin washed and changed out of his dusty clothes into fresh linens. He wasn't surprised when Alyfin appeared clean and re-garbed and told him, "It's time to meet Ambrosius, Master. If you're ready?"

"It seems I've been waiting for this moment my whole life," Merlin answered him, and the two strode off quickly.

Headquarters were in a small rectangular building of two stories. He saw that the Banner of the Red Dragon hung on a tall pole above it, and he smiled. This is where it should be, he thought. There were no guards at the entry and they went in to a central chamber with a large stone fireplace, chairs about it. There were also several tables with benches, one strewn with maps, and another that Merlin wanted to get a better look at. It, too, seemed to be a map, but was built to be three dimensional, the mountains and lakes, rivers and towns minia-tures of the real thing. He knew by the shape that it represented Britannia, and it seemed a vast improvement over parchment.

A tall man came out of a room on the right side of the building, a sword sheathed at his hip. His hair was a pale yellow and hung loose to his massive shoulders. His smile was wide, showing perfect teeth, and his blue eyes lit with pleasure as he spotted Alyfin. "Welcome back, my friend," he said, moving with a soldier's quick grace to embrace Alyfin. The eyes narrowed suddenly as he looked at Merlin over his friend's shoulder, and he stepped back sharply.

Alyfin missed the change in him, returning his greeting, then introducing Merlin, quite oblivious to the intensity in the man's gaze. "Merlin, this is Prince Uther," he finished. Merlin muttered a pleasantry, but it was lost as Uther strode across the room to the chamber on the other side. "Ambrosius!" he all but shouted, pushing open the door.

His brother had barely risen from his desk when all four of them were in his room. "This," Uther said, hissing the word as he pointed to Merlin, "is the new Merlin."

He stared at his brother so intently that his glare forced Ambrosius to stare back. Then Ambrosius blinked, as if remembering his manners, and turned his look to Merlin and Alyfin. "Welcome back, Alyfin, and welcome to our camp, Merlin. We have need of your wisdom."

"Where are you from, Merlin?" It was Uther asking, and he pronounced the name as if it tasted bitter to his tongue.

Merlin answered him first. "Originally Maridunum, Sire. On the border of Dyfed and Powys." He did not miss the look that passed between the two brothers, but he ignored it. He assumed that Uther's ill manners were due to his youth. He turned to Ambrosius, but as he said, "Thank you for your kind welcome, Sire. I have long wanted to meet you."

Strange visions began flickering before his eyes, coming faster and faster, like horses galloping by, and the room whirled.

When Merlin awoke, he discovered that he was lying on a cushioned bench, and as he tried to sit up, he saw that only Ambrosius was still in the room with him. There was no mistaking that he was the brother of Uther, though his hair was dark and his build a bit slimmer. "Sire?" Merlin said, trying to sit up, but succeeding only in getting his elbows under him. The prince was quick to lend a hand, helping him lift his shoulders, but insisting that he stayed seated when he tried to rise.

"Here. Drink this," Ambrosius said as he offered a cup of wine. "I can see why you were named Merlin."

"Did - did I say something, Sire?"

An easy smile lit his face. "Quite a lot actually. You said the Pendragon would fill the land just as a blazing comet fills the sky, and that the son of my brother would be the king all others were measured against until the end of time." He gave Merlin a sharp look. "I suppose that means that I will have no son of my own."

A flash - of something - came back to him. Without thinking, he said, "Your son will have no throne, but will be remembered as - as the king maker - and his name will become legend," and as he said it, he knew it as a prophecy that would be true.

Ambrosius looked away for a moment, then back. "I have trained the finest troop of fighting men since the Romans. I've also negotiated agreements with many of Britannia's kings who will support my troops with additions of their own. I have a fleet of ships being loaded with supplies as we speak, and my men will board these ships in three days. In my mind all is ready to take my kingdom back from the usurper, but I do have one question, and it is for you, Merlin."

"I will gladly answer it if I can, Sire." Merlin's head felt clearer than before, and his heart soared with the news he had just been given.

"Will you come with me? I would like to have you at my side."

Merlin had known before coming to the camp that he would go, but he was very pleased to be invited. "Of course. I would not want to be anywhere else."

"But your new responsibilities?"

"Will be ably handled by those left behind."

"That pleases me."

Emboldened by the implied praise, Merlin did not hesitate. "May

I ask you a question, Sire? Actually, more than one."

Ambrosius smiled and deliberately used Merlin's own words. "I will gladly answer it if I can."

"Have you been back to Britannia since you were a child?"

"Yes. Once. When I was about your age, maybe a year or two younger."

Merlin was remembering the series of images he had seen as the vision was coming to him. "Did you go to Maridunum?"

"Yes. Not as myself, of course. I went with King Gorlois of Dumnoni and a small party of his men. I was disguised as his squire."

"Did you happen to meet my mother, the Lady Ninianne, daughter of King Maelgwyn of Dementia?"

There was a long pause while Ambrosius studied the floor. "Did she tell you about me?" he asked in turn.

"No, she never mentioned you. It was when I first saw you - there were visions, like quick pictures flashing across my mind, of you with her in the cave."

He didn't ask what cave. He nodded. "Those would be true visions. I loved her, but I could not ask for her hand, nor take her away with me. Her father was loyal to Vortigern at that time, and I dared not reveal who I was." A sadness spread across his face. "I did not know about you, Merlin. If I had known, nothing would have stopped me from stealing her away, even if it had started a war that was twenty years premature."

He knew the answer. It was one of those feelings that he was so sure about. Still he had to ask the question. "Are you saying that you're my father?" He felt struck by wonder, and hope that was so strong that he could scarcely breathe.

"How old are you?"

"Nineteen, Sire."

"That would be about right, I imagine. Yes. Yes, that would make you my son."

Merlin's smile was broad. "I've imagined many men as my

father, hoping with some, appalled by others, but never have I ever imagined anyone as perfect as you, Sire." This was not idle flattery. Already he had seen that Ambrosius had a commanding presence and an ability to analyze a situation and act swiftly. He was a man whom men would follow. He was also kind, and this was, perhaps, even more important, for this would cause men to work for his approval and to return his good intentions with pride, admiration, and love. The smile faded and his chin lifted. "But I will keep your secret. It would do neither of us any good to announce it."

Ambrosius shook his head. "Uther knew immediately. He was quite jealous at first, assuming that you had come to stake a claim on the throne, but I assured him that I would never formally recognize you. He seemed appeased by that ... and by the fact that you named him king in your prophecy, but I would not trust his good will for you, Merlin. You should be careful around him."

Merlin nodded in agreement. "How did he know? Is he, too, a seer?"

Ambrosius laughed aloud. "Hardly." He looked Merlin up and down. "You don't know, do you?"

"Know what, Sire?" Merlin was worried that his sight had failed him and that Ambrosius knew it.

"I won't say anything, and you won't, and Uther most certainly won't, but others will see and wonder, and when they see that I honor you with a place at my side, they will speculate, and the rumors will begin."

"Sire? What is it that they will see?"

"Why, that you look just like me, Merlin."

61

BLAISE

It took four days of preparation, not three, and a day of hard riding before they met the ships at the port. There was another full day of loading weapons, horses and men, but they sailed that evening with the tide.

They were not on the water for a full hour before Merlin, as on his first voyage, was deathly ill and gripping a bucket. To him the journey was interminable - he could not judge how long it took - it seemed weeks, not days. He heard that the winds were favorable and that they were making good time, but he could not have verified it.

The ships rounded Cornwall and made their way through the Severn Sea, landing close to the old deserted Roman Fort at Caerleon. This was the rendezvous point for the southern kings, led by the brothers' most loyal supporter, King Gorlois. He had lookouts watching for them, and as word spread thousands of soldiers, and all the villagers who lived in the area, flocked out, lining the road, and the walls of the fort to catch a glimpse of the man they were about to fight for.

Merlin had cleaned himself up as best he could before he left the ship and donned his robes as High Priest. He was pleased to be asked to ride at the side of his father, though Uther, who rode at the other side, frowned and ignored him. "I'm sorry you were so ill," Ambrosius told him.

"Apparently crossing the sea isn't easy for any seer," he answered.

"Do you feel better now?"

Merlin was sure he was still green and surer still that no food would stay down for several more days, but he answered bravely. "Almost back to normal, Sire. Thank you for asking."

Uther rolled his eyes.

"I've wanted to ask you about your mother," Ambrosius continued. "Is she well?"

"Her letters say she is, Sire. She joined the Christian Holy Sisters just before I left for Lesser Britain."

"Ah." The sound was drawn out, long and sad.

"A Christian?" Uther snorted. "Yet she allowed you to be trained in the old religion!"

"If she'd had her way, I'd be in a monastery now," he answered.

"Then how did this happen?" Ambrosius asked, indicating my blue robe.

"I had many Christian tutors, but none of them proved satisfactory. I believe she was at wit's end when Master Blaise said he'd take me on as a student."

"A good man," Ambrosius said.

"A very good man," Merlin agreed.

Then came a sound of cheering that filled the air as fully as if clouds of sound had dropped to the ground, and they slowed to a pace that would allow the spectators to get a good look at them. Uther gave a running count of the number of fighting men he saw, and Ambrosius smiled, waving. The cheering became even louder.

The pendragon banner flew before them - a long stream of white, with the red dragon. Merlin thought about the last time he had seen this banner. It had been at Vortigern's camp - before his tent, and how it had seemed small and insignificant compared to the one they followed.

They had gone less than a mile when King Gorlois, riding out from Caerleon with a group of seven southern kings, met them. "Ambrosius? Uther!" he hailed them. He indicated the crowd of cheering people. "As you can see, all of Britannia bids you welcome."

Ambrosius smiled. "You have done well, old friend."

"How many soldiers?" Uther, ever the practical one, asked.

"Thirty thousand with more on their way. Two days more, and another five thousand should arrive, but I should warn you that three legions of peasants have come to fight too, though they are untrained and armed only with staves and pitchforks."

Quickly he introduced the other kings, all of whom were excited to finally meet Ambrosius, and all of whom looked impressed as they surveyed the soldiers from Lesser Britain who were holding their lines in orderly files. Indeed, Merlin thought, they were as impressive as the Roman Legions had been, for they had been trained in the Roman way.

Ambrosius greeted each king with courtesy and thanks for his loyalty, and praised them all for coming to his aid.

Merlin had not expected to be included in the formal greetings and had dropped back to give the kings room on the road which was made narrow by the crowds who strained to hear the kings, but King Gorlois spotted him. "Emrys, it's good to see you again. And in such exalted company? We'd like to have a song or two, though I don't know that we'll have the time for it."

Ambrosius heard him, and said, "You haven't had the news yet? Emrys is now Merlin. He will sit in council as advisor."

Gorlois lifted an eyebrow in surprise and saluted his former bard. "Well done, Em … Merlin. I knew you had amazing potential, but this? At such a young age. Congratulations."

Merlin felt lucky to be on horseback. He knew that if they'd been on the ground, he'd have been the victim of one of Gorlois' bear hugs, and the man was so massive that there was nothing gentle about him.

When they rode into the fort Merlin saw that it was a ruin, unused since the Romans who had built it had left. Stones had been scavenged and the walls were down in many places, but Gorlois had seen that the rubble was removed, and the camp was orderly. Tents spilled out, surrounding the fort and all along the curls of the river, but he had saved room inside for Prince Ambrosius and his men to set up camp. This they did quickly, and a council was held as soon as they had refreshed themselves.

Everyone agreed on three things - that Vortigern would hear that Ambrosius was coming, that he would be riding south with his army to meet them, and that speed was of the essence. Their attack would not be a surprise, but if they could fight before Vortigern had time to gather support from the Saxons on the southern shore, they would have the advantage.

Uther wanted to march the next morning, but Ambrosius declared that he would take one more day to make sure that food and medical supplies were organized to travel as fast as the army, so it was the second morning before they marched north.

The road was in good condition and they made excellent time, their numbers swelling as they were met by those coming in from Dyfed and Powys in the west, and from the mid-section of Britannia in the east. Just as Gorlois had told them, they were joined by thousands of peasants from the towns and farmlands. Ambrosius had his soldiers assigning weapons to the stronger men, giving the weaker responsibilities on the supply train.

Merlin's job was to organize wagons of medical supplies, and to scout for those with any training in healing. There were a half dozen healers from Lesser Britain who had training for injuries, along with ten Druid healers who had volunteered to help, and he assigned his new recruits equally among them so that each had several assistants.

He also chose one hundred strong peasants to act as carriers, and had them practice working in twos. They would search out the injured on the battlefield and bring them to the healers.

Merlin was happy to have something to do that would help Ambrosius, and pleased to be included as advisor and friend, for the prince kept him at his side as often as possible. Yet there was something disconcerting - a rumor he had heard, more and more often it seemed as recruits swept in who had once allied with Vortigern. They were saying, "The magician is here. Vortigern's magician." He had always hoped that no one would recognize him now that he was grown to manhood.

He especially didn't want to be identified with Vortigern, and he wished that he had made his prophecy publicly for Ambrosius, so he would be identified with him instead. He could only hope that some opportunity for pronouncement would come soon.

They were camped for the night near Viroconium when more troops rode in from Rheged and Northumbria to join them. With them were a dozen men who had defected from Vortigern at Dinas Bran. Their spokesman, a man named Canus, told the council that Vortigern had, indeed, heard that they were on their way. He had ordered his troops south from Mount Snowden and was hoping to lay a trap for them in a narrow gorge near Doward.

"Let's be sure to get there first," Ambrosius said, and the rest of the council nodded agreement.

His message delivered, Canus was looking about at those assembled when he spotted Merlin, and walked a few paces toward him. "It's you, isn't it? All grown up, but I'd recognize you anywhere. You're the one they call Vortigern's Magician."

Uther jumped to his feet. His dagger was out and a second later one arm was holding Canus firmly while the other held the dagger across his throat. "What are you saying, Canus?"

The man gulped but held to his convictions without struggle. "King Vortigern had us searching for the boy - for young Emrys - for more than a year after he disappeared. He wanted to keep him at court because he could make prophecies."

Behind Canus, Uther's eyes narrowed and he stared at Merlin. Abruptly his arms dropped away from Canus and he advanced on Merlin, every inch of his body threatening, the knife still poised, but this time at Merlin's heart. "I told you we couldn't trust him," he said with a glance of triumph at his brother.

Ambrosius made no move to help either his brother or his son. "Merlin?" he asked with deceptive calmness.

"Yes, Sire?"

"Perhaps you would explain what our new friend, Canus, is talking about."

Merlin walked a few steps toward the prince, glad that he could move to the side and didn't have to go through Uther. It didn't occur to him to tell anything but the truth. He looked around at all the assembled kings - there were thirteen now, and saw that the majority were in agreement with Prince Uther, ready to call him traitor.

He spoke slowly and carefully, knowing that he could be imprisoned and exiled from his father if he said the wrong thing. He took a deep breath, and in the powerful voice of bard began. "When I was twelve, my school received word from my mother that she was about to join the Holy Sisters. She requested that I visit for a last time before she took her vows, so I was sent with a bard named Jostyn to Maridunum.

"We arrived safely, but before I could see my mother, both she and I were taken captive by Vortigern's soldiers. We were brought to the fortress he was trying to build in northern Gwynedd, kept separate from each other, but not mistreated.

"When we were taken before Vortigern, he asked my mother who my father was, and she told him that I had no earthly father. A man

had come to her, she said, a man who no one else could see - an angel
…" he looked closely at Ambrosius, "… or a demon, she did not
know - only that she had lain with no earthly man, but found herself
with child."

At this the kings stirred, glancing anxiously at each other, and
then at Ambrosius to see how he took this news, but he was perfectly
still, not looking away from Merlin, not even a glance for his brother
who still had the knife poised to strike.

"Vortigern sent her away, instructing his soldiers to see that she
was escorted back to Maridunum. He did keep his word, Sire. She
reached her home with no mishap.

"Then he asked me if I knew who my father was. I answered that
my mother had never told me before, which was true, and that I
believed her, for she had never lied to me."

Merlin watched as the prince settled back, his posture less rigid,
but his eyes never left Merlin's face.

"I soon learned," he continued, "that what was well for her was
not so well for me. Vortigern's priests were at a loss to explain why
his walls kept falling down. After many weeks they had concluded
that he must go back to the old ways, sacrificing a boy with no earthly
father and burying him under a cornerstone. Soldiers had been sent
throughout the kingdom to find such a boy." He smiled wryly. "It
seems that my mother had obliged him. I was scheduled for death the
next noon."

"And how did you weasel out of that to become Vortigern's pet?"
Uther prodded, waving the knife in Merlin's face.

Ambrosius made a sign and he backed away a little.

"I had seen water seeping from the mountain as we climbed to the
building site. I told him that he must pump the water out.

"Then, truthfully, I don't remember what I said, but the sight
came and spoke through me. According to Jostyn who had followed
and disguised himself as a worker, I went on at length about dragons -
red and white, battles, triumphs, and great kingdoms coming in the

future.

"I collapsed and Vortigern had me carried to a tent for healing. Again, I remember none of this.

"Jostyn saw his chance a little later and carried me away, hidden in a sack slung over his shoulder. When I awoke two days later, we were at a campsite well away from any habitation. Very slowly and carefully, staying away from all trails and villages, we made our way back to the school in the Summer Country.

"Master Blaise had heard that Vortigern's soldiers were out searching for me and were determined to take me back to him. That was when I was sent to the old Merlin in Lesser Britain - for my own safety."

"I see," Ambrosius said.

"Who can vouch for the truth of this story?" Uther asked at almost the same time.

It was Canus who answered first. "I was there. Some of the men with me were there too, and it's as he said. He was brought to King Vortigern to be sacrificed. He was a known bastard with no father … or so they said - those guards who heard the story from his mother, I mean.

"I, myself, heard his prophecies, and that was a wondrous thing. This small slip of a boy … he spoke like nothing I've heard before or since. Couldn't make sense of most of it. All about dragons and bears and kings who would come and do great deeds … but the king, he seemed to understand. Heard him say it meant the Saxons would be beat, and he - the red dragon - would be the one to do it.

"He wanted the boy saved and at his side from then on, but when the High King went to the tent where they'd put him for healing, it was empty, and was he mad! Had the whole camp searched, hung the guards, sent soldiers out in all directions with orders to find the boy and return him unharmed. I, myself, was sent west to check the coast. Like I said before, King Vortigern searched for him for more than a year."

"Thank you, Canus. You should make sure your men are fed and ready to march at first light." He watched as Canus, escorted by soldiers from Lesser Britain, left. Then he turned to his Council. "We should all be ready to move at first light. I'd like to beat Vortigern's soldiers to the ambush site. Uther, send scouts out now."

As the kings moved to join their men, Merlin heard Uther ask, "And Merlin? Do you want him watched?"

"You may do as you want, Uther, but I am assured of his loyalty."

Uther stalked off to follow orders. Merlin figured Uther would be too busy with the coming battle to do much harm, but he would do as Ambrosius had long ago advised him. He would watch his back.

62

BLAISE

The River Wye ran in a deep gorge through the Wye Valley and they followed its course with utmost speed. At times the valley widened to meadows bursting with spring flowers, but generally the slopes were steep and heavily forested.

Ambrosius picked the place where valley had narrowed to gorge and waited, hiding the Cambrians on their surefooted ponies in the forested heights along with the foot soldiers and the armed peasants, and keeping the cavalry back in the wider valley until the trap was sprung.

He sent Merlin with Alyfin to watch in safety from a high outcropping of rock, and sent Uther ahead with a small troop hand-picked from the fastest of the cavalry. It was their job to engage the enemy in a skirmish that would end as they quickly turned to flee, luring Vortigern's army to chase them into the gorge where the rest of the troops were ready to spring the ambush.

It worked exactly as Ambrosius had hoped. By high sun Uther's men were galloping back through the gorge with Vortigern's men on their heels. His soldiers were confused when Uther's men reversed, then shocked as they smashed into the rest of the cavalry. As the High King's soldiers looked to the hills for refuge, they saw the foot soldiers and the Cymri riders swooping down on them from both sides.

Some tried to turn and run, but stumbled into their own men. Most were well trained and ferocious though, and put up a real fight. From his height Merlin could see that there were hordes of Saxons coming to reinforce them, swinging their huge axes as they joined the melee. And he could not help but notice the crows. The sky was black with these harbingers of the goddess as death crone, though the battle had just begun. They know, he thought, and they are ready to feast.

Merlin lost sight of Ambrosius and his banner. All he could see was the Saxon tribes who had joined Vortigern.

Ferocious with horned helmets.

Swinging huge axes.

Pushing the Britons back.

He looked at Alyfin in alarm, then remembered his history lessons. In the olden days the Druids from one tribe of Celts met the Druids from another, shouting insults back and forth if they could not solve the conflict among themselves, and finally stirring the armies behind them into heroic action.

Merlin moved closer to the ledge. Without thinking he raised both arms high and shouted - an undulating, high pitched sound that rose over the noise of the battle, so startling the fighters that they stopped fighting for a moment and raised their eyes.

For just a flicker of time there was no sound, then someone shouted and pointed, "It's the Merlin? The Merlin is with us!" and he saw Ambrosius pushing forward, his banner carrier right behind, his sword flashing and men falling and pulling back before him. And there was Uther, sword slashing death, bearing down on Vortigern's forces, and some of them were running, with the horses pounding after them. Then more were running, until all of Vortigern's armies were in full rout.

Alyfin grabbed his arm and the two ran along the cliff top, trying to keep pace with the fighting men below.

They lost sight as the armies rounded a curve, then caught up to the rearguard and saw ahead the old Doward fort. It was not occupied, nor well cared for. Merlin could see several places where the walls had crumbled, but it would suffice for Vortigern's purpose. He watched as the last of the Usurper's men scrambled in and saw the great gates closed and barred.

He noticed that the sun was low in the sky now and was surprised, not having realized that so many hours had passed.

Doward was a wooden citadel halfway up the rock of a craggy mountain, the natural terrain lending to its invulnerability. The mountain was flat topped and steep with sides that looked unclimbable. In front of the walls there was a double rampart and a ditch. There was only one way in, he saw. Or out.

Though he and Alyfin were scrambling down the mountain he was still high enough to see that not all of the Saxons had headed for the fort.

A group had passed it by and was heading up the valley, and he saw that Uther had the cavalry in pursuit.

Ambrosius was grouping his forces to surround the citadel, and already setting up a campsite. The massive catapults dragged from Brittany were set into place and began lobbing stones into the walls at the points where they had crumbled and were weakest. They succeeded in breaching the wall in two places.

By the time he reached the valley floor, Merlin saw the crows settling into the gorge behind them, and saw, too, the burial parties as they marched by. His crew was bringing in the wounded, and he and Alyfin hastened toward the tents where his healers were already at work.

For the rest of the night, they tended injuries without stopping.

Around midnight Prince Ambrosius came by with words of praise for the healers, who had not stopped to rest, and for the injured. Each man received his full attention. If he didn't know them personally, he asked their names and where they were from, and which king claimed their allegiance. It took several hours for him to get through the tents, and Merlin finally drew him aside. "You should rest, Sire. It's not over yet."

"You're right, Merlin." He dragged a tired hand through his hair. "We held a Council. Sorry not to call you, but I thought you'd be of more use here."

"I wouldn't have come."

"I can't afford a long siege. We were all agreed on that."

"Would it come to that, Sire?"

"There's no way in. The Citadel's position is much too strong, with the cliffs and the walls and the height in Vortigern's favor. I don't want to see my men killed trying uselessly to storm the ramparts." He looked so exhausted that Merlin feared he would not make it back to his own tent. "And I hear from prisoners that there are several wells inside and that the fort is stocked with enough food for six months."

"What will you do then?"

Ambrosius patted his arm. "What I have to," he said. "Good night, Merlin. Try to get some rest yourself."

63

BLAISE

The next morning Ambrosius had all the dead searched for weapons which he distributed to those men who had come with axes and pitchforks. He saw that our men were buried, but he had all of Vortigern's dead brought before the gate and burned, giving the men behind the walls a show of what he would bring to them.

On the second morning Ambrosius sent a messenger under a flag of truce, giving the High King a chance to surrender. All who swore allegiance to Ambrosius would be allowed to leave peacefully.

On the third morning Vortigern had the dead messenger's body flung over the wall, throwing the head separately. Ambrosius watched the broken body roll down the steep cliff and heard the obscene splat as it landed in the ditch.

He had spent years learning and practicing battle skills, but this was his first actual battle. Somehow his teachers had missed the detail that men would die. Glory, they had stressed, not the sick feeling that had filled him as they identified each dead body and placed them in long rows of newly dug graves in a hillside field of wild flowers. Nor had they mentioned the horrifying cries of the wounded that had gone on for days now. Sadness - soul sickening sadness was what he had felt.

He saw the look of dread on the faces of his men at the sight of the bloodied head of his emissary which had bounced high out of the ditch and landed on the battlefield.

This - this deliberate calculated butchery - this was enough. No more. Not one more man in my army will die today, he vowed to himself.

He turned away, his face hardened with resolve, and called for his archers.

The first round of flaming arrows was aimed at the two breaches in the wall, which had been hastily piled high with what looked like firewood. That made sense. Doward was a quickly prepared refuge, a former Roman outlook, not a place where anyone actually lived.

The second barrage of flaming arrows went directly into the fort.

From then on the arrows went as fast as the archers could reload and release. Each had an assistant to hand him the flaming arrows.

Before long the smoke was thick and the flames were high behind the walls. Still it was an hour before the gate opened and men began pouring out, some with their clothes in flames.

Ambrosius did not let them go. They were shot as they came, this time with regular arrows. Then no more came. The fire burned itself out behind the stone walls of the cliff and the fortification, but the sky was dark with smoke long after the flames were gone. Our soldiers were sent in to check if any were left alive. They searched for a long time. They found no one.

64

BLAISE

On the fourth morning Ambrosius started east, but before that he had Merlin brought to his tent. "Did you hear that Uther was back?"

"I didn't know. Did he catch up to the Saxons?"

"Some of them. Hengist is dead. He was captured, then beheaded, but his men were allowed to go with the understanding that they stay north of Hadrian's Wall."

"What is the likelihood of that, Sire?"

"I don't trust them. Octa and Eosa are still alive, and they're fierce leaders. We will ride east, fortifying and leaving soldiers in the outposts against any threats from the Saxons or the Picts."

"Why east?"

"I want to meet with the northern kings and have them swear oaths of fealty. There were more than a few who didn't come in support. I'm hoping that they just waited to join the victor, and that they're not in open rebellion. We'll march with Roman speed," he said, "but take the time to honor the gods with thanks and feasts. If all goes well, I'll be in Londinium in three or four months."

"Where you'll be crowned High King," Merlin told him, smiling.

"Is it the 'Prophet of Ambrosius' speaking?"

"Yes, but it doesn't take a prophet to know that you are the savior of the Celts. The soldiers - the people - they all love and support you. We'll have a triumphant procession into the city."

Ambrosius gave him a wan smile, then fell silent.

"Sire? Many of the wounded are ready to return to duty. Those who aren't will be cared for in Deva. One of my healers will stay with them, and be given enough carriers to see that they arrive safely."

"Good, good." Ambrosius was studying the dirt floor as if it were very important. Finally, when Merlin seemed resigned to silence, he looked up. "You're not going with me. I have another job for you, with two dozen men as escort."

Merlin had hoped to study the refortifications that Ambrosius planned. He was interested in the building process, but he answered, "I will be pleased to do what is needed, Sire." He waited.

Ambrosius studied the floor again. At length his eyes met those of his son. "I think it's time that you visited your mother, Merlin, and I want you to deliver a message for me."

Merlin did not let Ambrosius see how startled he was. "I'll - I'll be happy to see her again." When there was no response, he asked if the prince had a letter to deliver.

"No, no letter," he answered. "It is better not to have anything in writing." His chin lifted, not without effort, and his eyes lost their blue and seemed dark in the flickering light of the torches. "Tell her … tell her that there has never been another woman. Tell her that I would have her come to Londinium with you … that I would make her my wife and my queen."

Merlin regarded him with sadness. "I will tell her, Sire, but I fear it's too late."

"Because she's taken vows?"

"Because she's very ill."

"How … how do you know this, Merlin?"

"It's a feeling I've had for a week or so. I didn't want to burden you."

"Go to Maridunum. Go and make sure," he said. "And Merlin …"

"Yes, Sire?"

"Make haste."

65

BLAISE

Merlin was in Maridunum for just over a week. It was as he feared. His mother was very ill. Seemingly she had waited just to see him. "I prayed," she told him. "I prayed that you would come before I died."

He would not lie to her with false hope. "It seems that your god listened to your prayers," he answered, sitting on the stool next to her bed and clasping a damp and clammy hand.

"He's your god too. I know you believe that, Emrys."

"God is in all the gods," he told her, "and all the gods are God."

She gave a weak laugh, but it set her to coughing, and the cloth she pressed to her mouth was covered in blood when she pulled it away.

"Mother? Have they brought a doctor to you?" He soaked a clean cloth in her wash basin and bathed her face gently, then pressed the cool cloth to her forehead. She seemed so delicate - so small. Had she always been that small, or was it just because he was a man now grown?

"You are trained as a healer," she said. "Surely you can see that there's nothing to be done for me."

He knew she was right. "Are you in much pain?"

"Some," she admitted.

"I can do something about that." He opened the bag that hung from his belt, extracting herbs from packets of cloth and poured fresh water into a pot that he set to boiling over a brazier. Then he crushed the herbs and stirred them into the water, sniffing and tasting until he had the mixture he wanted. With one arm he supported her to an upright position, and with the other he brought the liquid to her mouth and helped her to drink.

"Thank you," she said when the liquid was gone. "I will rest now."

He stayed at her side for the seven days she lived. Her cell was austere with no comforts, but there was a window which looked out over the hills of Maridinum and they were lush with the greens of spring and visible from the bed.

Someone brought him a chair, and he rested when she did, which was not often. He told her about the old Merlin and some of the things he had learned. He sang songs to her - long ballads telling the old stories, ballads of love and hope and bravery.

He told her how he had come to be the new Merlin and how alone he had felt when he realized the weight of the responsibility put upon him.

And finally, he told her what was happening in the north, how he had come to know Ambrosius and had come to serve him. "So the tyrant Vortigern is dead, along with his Saxon queen," he finished.

He didn't expect the questions she asked. "Was it hard for him? Lighting the fire?"

He didn't have to ask who she meant. "It was hard, but it had to be done. A long siege would have killed many more men."

She was silent at that, and when he looked for a response, he saw that she had fallen asleep again. He let her sleep.

On the fourth day he had lowered the curtain to keep the rain from coming in, but they could hear it drumming on the roof. Her eyes still burned with fever so he kept a cool compress on her brow. He had just changed it when she said, "Tell me about him."

"My father?" he asked a bit absently, since he was checking her pulse.

She gasped, staring at him intently.

"I know all about it," he told her. "He told me himself."

"You can't know about it. Your father doesn't know of your existence."

He settled on the stool as she watched him warily. "He knows and I understand the circumstances. He had to leave you, though he told me if he'd known of my impending birth, he'd have started a war to claim you if necessary. He loved you. He still loves you."

She was more concerned with the effect on him. "How did he find out? Why did he tell you?" She coughed twice, but waved his cloth away. "What did he tell you?"

"Look at me. Picture him. Now look at both of us with the eyes of a stranger and tell me what you see?"

She shook her head stubbornly. "I don't know."

"Uther saw the resemblance immediately. He knows, but no one else is sure. Oh, there are rumors. We discussed it. I am not to be recognized as his son, for I am Merlin, and my role is as advisor, not as prince and certainly not as king. Uther will remain his heir."

It was later that same day. She came suddenly awake, the groan escaping her lips before she could stop it.

Merlin was ready and came to her side immediately with the brew that would ease her pain. "No," she told him. "Not yet. I want to talk to you and I can't think when you've dosed me." Before he could ask what she wanted to talk about she said, "Tell me about him."

"He's a good man. A very good man. He's thoughtful. Concerned about the hardships of his people. Well educated and able to discuss weighty subjects with a scholar, but he keeps the common man in his sight too, discussing how the land might yield more potatoes with the man farming it, how different grains flavor the bread with a baker, or how to make a taller wall secure with a mason.

He was raised in the Roman way and trained his army like a Roman Centurion. His soldiers would do anything he asked of them and the kings of Britannia who joined us had no hesitation in supporting him either.

Though he let them think they were contributing to his plans for battle, they would have done whatever he suggested." She gave him a wan smile, so he continued, hoping not to tax what strength remained to her. "His plans to secure the country will work. He will be crowned soon. In Londinium."

Her eyes shone. With imagining it, he wondered, or because of the fever? He moved the chair closer, his hand going to her brow. "I'm fine," she said. "Tell me more. Will it be a grand ceremony with all the kings of Britannia there to swear allegiance?"

"Definitely. He's securing the borders along the wall and bringing the northern kings to heel … as we speak. They'll all come for the ceremony. The Archbishop Dubricius, himself, wearing his finest robes will place the crown on his head, and I will be there wearing a new robe to place the torque around his neck. In fact, everyone will dress in their newest and best, the colors like a rainbow, the jewels flashing like the lightning outside. Who would miss it?"

He saw the look of pain cross her face, and it was not physical. Now was the time. "Mother, he asked me to bring you there. To Londinium. To see him crowned." He paused, then pronounced each word slowly, "To be crowned with him. As his queen." She drew in a sharp breath. "He has never stopped loving you. He wants to marry you."

"Ahhhh." Her head fell back, sinking deeply into her pillow. "I - I'm ready for your medicine, Emrys."

It had brewed and steeped. He pulled it off the brazier and poured it into a cup, studying her face as he came back. She had her eyes tightly shut as if she would keep him out of her thoughts, and when he lifted her to drink and she opened them, he saw that they were filled with tears. "Mother?" he asked anxiously.

Slowly she drank the brew. "Let me sleep now," she answered.

Fervently he hoped that the proposal from Ambrosius would do for her what his medicines had not.

66

BLAISE

Indeed, the next day she seemed stronger, though she avoided the discussion he hoped for. At noon she sent him away, asking for time alone to think, and when he returned at sunset, she was humming a tune that brought back childhood memories of her arms about him as she rocked him in a chair by the hearth. She asked for his medicine as soon as he entered. When the cup was empty she went right to sleep, and her sleep was peaceful and lasted the entire night.

The morning brought wracking coughs - the worst yet. When the bout was finished and she lay weak and helpless, her skin as white as the sheet she lay on, he tried to give her medicine, but she refused. "It will ease the coughing," he told her.

"The coughing will be over very soon," she answered. He saw that her pupils were enormous, making her eyes look black, not their usual blue. She reached for his hand with both of hers and held it to her chest. "Emrys, are you sure you don't want to be a prince?" Her voice was a whisper.

"That is not to be my role," he answered.

"That's not what I asked, Emrys. I asked if you wanted to be a prince. Or a king. Would that please you to rule the kingdom?"

"When I was a boy, I wanted to be more than a bastard. I wanted to be recognized as a prince like my cousins, though I never thought to be a king. But now? No, definitely not. It's not power or glory that I shy away from, for I will have both. My name will be remembered for centuries to come. When men forget the name Ambrosius, they will still remember the name of Merlin."

She drew in a sharp breath and he realized that the voice he had spoken with had come from the sight. "You know that? You're certain?"

He nodded. Slowly. "I will help make three men king - Ambrosius, Uther, and the greatest of all kings - Arthur."

"Arthur?" There were shadows under her eyes, he saw. Shadows that deepened as he stared. "Who is Arthur?"

"Uther's son, Arthur, hasn't been born yet, but it is he who will unite the kingdom and drive out the Saxons."

For a long time she said nothing, then in a stronger tone she finally spoke. "I can't accept his offer."

"You will get stronger," he answered, though he didn't believe it.

"Even if that were true, my answer would be no. It would surely make problems for all of us and for Britannia if I were to become his queen."

"How could that be, Mother?"

"Already, you've told me, men whisper of the resemblance between you. If your mother suddenly became his wife, there are those who would campaign against him, some maybe for you."

"Men would not willingly call a bastard king."

"Men would make trouble over it, nevertheless."

He knew she was right, but he said. "Surely you deserve some happiness in your life. And Ambrosius too. He loves you so."

The coughing started again. The sheet was red with blood. "Mother, please drink this."

She drank, and slept. Merlin took a clean blanket, wrapped her up, and carried her to his chair. He held her in his arms, rocking her gently, thinking how she had once held and rocked him, and once more he sang to her.

She woke just as the sun cracked the horizon. Her face was beautiful in the new blush of day. Her voice was so weak that he dropped his ear to her mouth. "Thank you for being with me. I love you." He thought she was finished, but she had one more thing to say before she slept her final sleep. "Tell him I never stopped loving him."

67

BLAISE

Merlin had her buried two days later in the churchyard, next to his grandfather who had died three years before. His cousin - the King of Maridunum, and his brothers were marching with Prince Ambrosius, but their wives and children were all present. Everyone from the convent was there for the service, of course, as well as the two dozen men Ambrosius had sent with him. He had expected that, but he was surprised to see that the whole town came to honor her. He had not realized that she was so loved and wondered if it had happened because she was loved as the Princess Ninianne or as Sister Anna.

It certainly did not occur to him that most of the townspeople had turned out to see him, for he did not realize that the soldiers he had left on their own were proud to accompany the Merlin, and had spent the week bragging that he had prophesied a great future for Britannia under Ambrosius, and that he had helped the Prince to win the battle against Vortigern by standing on a cliff and exhorting the soldiers on to heroic efforts just when things had looked bleak for them, and that the Prince who would soon be crowned High King had made the Merlin his chief advisor. Merlin was never one to consider his own fame.

He did not think it strange that the mother of one high in the old faith was given a Christian burial. She had chosen that path and he honored it. Privately, he had also spoken the Druid blessings over her and rejoiced that her soul would come back for the next life she chose to live.

He spoke kindly to each of his aunts and his cousins, not disremembering, but choosing to deliberately ignore any slights they had given him as a child, and told all who asked about the greatness of Prince Ambrosius.

Nor did he in any way short the celebration of her life, held after the service at the castle. He stayed for the entire feast, sang several of her favorite songs to honor her, and toasted her memory with both ale and wine, though he drank very little of either.

He was there until the last straggler had either left the castle yard or fallen asleep at the table. Then, when he was sure that everyone was done with honoring her, he made his way to his old bedroom and slept soundly.

The next morning he told his soldiers that he needed one more day in Maridunum, but dismissed them to arms practice in the castle yard.

Taking bread and cheese from the kitchen, he wrapped them and placed them in his pack, then made his way to the stables where he saddled his own horse and rode out of the gate, speaking only to the guard whom he informed about his whereabouts in case someone should worry.

He took the road alongside the river for a way, approached the mill, and spurred his horse up the steep trail to the cave, stopping only to pour libations for the old god of the spring.

The cave was just as he remembered. Everything he had stored there was still in its place, and it was swept clean. Someone must be caring for it.

There was wood laid out for a fire. He lit it with a motion and sat looking at the flames as he ate the food he had brought. Along one of the walls stored in a chest were the books of his childhood. He opened the chest and spent the afternoon remembering and reading. When the sun was low he rode back down the mountain.

He heard someone coming and reigned his horse in, waiting quietly. Whoever it was certainly wasn't worried about being quiet, walking noisily and whistling to himself. He waited. As the figure approached, he saw that it was a boy, maybe eleven or twelve years old, and when he saw Merlin, he waved and called out. "Good afternoon to you, Master."

He smiled. "Good afternoon to you too."

"Well met," said the boy. "I've been sent to see if you needed anything."

"No. Thank you." He decided he liked the look of the boy who was all knobby knees and elbows, but had a thick head of blonde hair that made him quite handsome. "You are?" he asked.

"William. I'm one of the miller's sons."

"Ah, Walter is still turning out sons?"

"Yes, Sir."

"Perhaps there is something you could do for me."

The boy looked quite eager at that. "Glad I'd be to give service, Master."

"Could you watch the cave for me, keeping it clean and ready for me if I should want to come back to stay for a time? There would be monthly coins in it for you."

"I already do that, Master," he answered proudly, then added a cheeky, "but I wouldn't argue being paid for it."

"Then it's you I should thank. You've been doing a grand job of it. I'll leave two years pay with your father and let him dole it out."

He beamed a shy smile. "Thank you. And Ma says I'm to bring

you back for supper if you'll come."

"I'd be honored," Merlin told him. "You set the pace."

The boy turned and started off at a walk he thought suitable. The pace suited Merlin, for with the darkening sky he moved the horse at a slow walk that seemed safe on the steep slope. The Miller and his wife and large brood greeted him effusively when they arrived, pleased to see the quiet boy grown up to hold such a resplendent position, and pleased that he remembered them fondly. Supper was a merry affair with stories told on both sides, and singing, and ale served cold and crisp.

68

BLAISE

I was very pleased when Merlin and his escort arrived at the school a few days later. He was still thin, but now taller than I, and the young features had sharpened. I was surprised to see that his nose was of the shape they called Roman, but his hair was still straight and black and his eyes still changed from blue to grey.

After catching me up in all the news, he promised to keep the letters coming so that I could continue writing my history.

I had dispatches for him from Lesser Britain, and set him up with a desk and supplies in the building that had always been kept ready for the Merlin's use whether or not he had chosen to live there.

He stayed for nearly three months. Each evening we met at my fire, sitting in comfortable chairs and sipping wine as we talked, and our discussions were filled with the exploration of ideas and just as challenging and comfortable and exciting to me as they had always been.

Twice Merlin officiated at important ceremonies. The first was on our island in the great oak circle where those initiates who were to take their vows as Druid priests were honored and accepted into our ranks. There were six of them.

The second ceremony took place on the larger neighboring island of Avalon where our priestesses lived and were taught to honor the Goddess - she who wore three faces representing the phases of life: the maiden, the mother, and the death crone. Merlin had been there several times before for ceremonies, but as a young boy, and he had been an observer, not a participant. This Beltane he and the Lady of the Lake, who was the High Priestess, conducted the ceremony.

He told me how mysterious it seemed, knowing that Avalon was so close, but not being able to see it because of the surrounding mists. These mists were always present, and though the island was the largest in the area, it was always hidden in the mists, with only the towering Tor visible from a distance.

All the lights had been extinguished so that when the boats pulled into shore the only sensory perception was that of smell. Before they saw the shadow of the land, they could smell the fragrance of the apple blossoms that Merlin remembered so well.

As they stepped ashore the clouds parted, giving them the sole light of the moon. It was full and bright that night so the procession that wound up the Tor above the mists to the standing stones did not stumble in the darkness.

The Tor was the tallest mountain in the south of Britannia, a beacon of rock that was visible even from the waters of the Severn Sea, and sailors used it as a locator. The Christians had a story that the Tor was the landmark that had guided Joseph of Arimathea, he who had walked with the Christ, to the shores of Ynys Witrin where the first daub and wattle church was built.

They were welcomed by the Druids and given land by King Aviragus, and at least in this place the Druids and the Christians were still friends, for the Druids had agreed that there was one God and that the Christ was an honored teacher of truth.

There was still a church on this land, though it was much grander and larger than the original, and they too had a school - two schools, one for boys who were taught by the monks and one for girls who were taught by the nuns. We, who led these places, met occasionally, though the students and their teachers were confined by both groups and never mingled, each staying to our own lands.

Merlin told me that from the height of the Tor where the ritual Beltane fire was lit to signify the returning of the light, he could see answering fires springing to life throughout the countryside for miles and miles, and the sight was thrilling.

The words were spoken, asking for the blessing on land and animals, so that both would be fruitful. A few minutes later they could hear the music from Dragon Island and they knew that the dancing had started.

In the cities the Christians who had outlawed the Beltane rituals had succeeded in stifling the ceremonies, but out in the countryside the old ways persisted, and as the fires roared couples crept away from the music and the dancing and into the shadows - to celebrate the oldest of rites between man and woman with no shame for the results, for any man and any woman could come together for this celebration with no repercussions, and a child born of the Beltane celebrations was honored as blessed by the gods.

Indeed, Merlin talked much of Beltane thereafter, and I noticed that the discussions seemed to center around the Lady of the Lake, she who was the physical representation of the Goddess. The Merlin was not her counterpart in this aspect, for the Druids did not take on the form of the God, but the Lady had the trick of being the Goddess when she desired.

This was not the same Lady who had been High Priestess when Merlin had gone to the isle as a young boy. She had been a lady of great age who had worn the title for many years until her death just three years ago. This was her successor - the Lady Vivianne, only five or six years older than Merlin.

"During the ceremony she was tall and powerful," Merlin told me, "though that was surely a glamour, for later I was surprised to see that she was a tiny, delicate creature, only as high as my shoulder."

"The former Lady was like that too," I answered. Studying his face I saw a hundred emotions flicker as he considered her. "And is she beautiful?"

"The most beautiful woman I've ever seen. Her eyes are huge and dark, like a fawn's. When she looks at you, it's as if she could see your soul. Surely she reads your thoughts as clearly as a scholar reads a book."

"Some say the Merlin can do that too. How did you feel about that?"

"I have to admit it's disconcerting. It would be devastating if you had something you wanted to keep hidden from her."

"Merlin? Are you blushing?"

He skirted the question. "I'm not sure that the dignified Merlin should have been gaping at her beauty like an awkward schoolboy. Worse, when she knows it, but I'm sure she's used to that reaction. Her hair is a wave of black curls that fall to a waist thin enough to put my hands around."

"And did you do that?"

He looked startled, even guilty.

I realized that before me was a man, that he had grown physically just as he had grown in knowledge. "Well, after all, it was Beltane. You're a young and comely lad in spite of the dignity of your high priesthood, and she's a young and beautiful girl."

"Not a girl," he argued. "A woman, in every way."

I let the pause hang in the air until he finally answered. "Yes, she guided me in the art of becoming a man." He blushed again.

"This was your first?"

I was not surprised when he nodded. I don't believe that Merlin had ever before thought about the pleasure a woman can give a man.

"My first was at Beltane too," I told him. "Though I wasn't

fortunate enough to gain the attention of the Lady of the Lake."

"We talked all night … after. I did not realize how pleasant it is to talk to an educated woman, Master Blaise. She is so … so wise."

I noticed that during the next week Merlin sought her wisdom three more times.

Merlin shared the Lady's thoughts with me. "Vivianne is very concerned about the Christians." I did not fail to notice that he now spoke of her as 'Vivianne,' not using her title, but I let it go without teasing. "Ever since the Emperor Constantine adopted Christianity as the religion of the Empire, Christianity has spread with the conquest of the Romans."

"Britannia has long had Christians," I reminded him. "Since shortly after the Christ, when Joseph of Arimathea arrived with his missionaries to spread the word to our land."

"Yes, but Constantine also insisted that a unified form of Christianity was to exist, and enforced it with the Council of Nicaea in 373. Since then the Pope has become more powerful and has enforced their edicts with the threat of excommunication."

"As happened with Pelagius," I said, nodding in understanding.

"Germanicus and his council saw that Pelagius, with his gentle teachings of the love of Christ, was punished and brought into line with the Pope's desires."

"Yet much of Britannia still believes in the Pelagian form where man can actually choose his own behavior without having every little thing punished as sinful by a priest."

"Vivianne fears that more and more of the Christians here follow the Pope now."

"What they follow and what they believe are two different things," I told him. "We haven't been much bothered by the Pope since the Romans left."

"But now Ambrosius has brought an army from Brittany."

"Don't many of the soldiers follow Mithra, Merlin? He is the god of the Roman soldiers of old."

"Those who follow Mithra no longer do so openly. I observed that even while we were still in Ambrosius' camp in Lesser Britain. There was a ceremony before we left to bless the soldiers, but it was a hidden affair with only the known believers present." He smiled. "Except for me. Ambrosius and Uther both attended, and I was taken to observe at my own request. Everyone there was hooded, so that none could recognize their brothers. The Christians don't approve of Mithra. They consider it a pagan religion."

"They consider us pagans too, and accuse us of human sacrifice." Both of us shook our heads wearily at this old story, then we smiled at each other for having the same reaction. "I thought Ambrosius followed the Druid way," I continued. "If he doesn't, this may be cause for alarm, and the Lady is right to worry."

"Ambrosius is not an overly religious man. He believes that the people of Britannia should be able to worship the god they choose without fear of reprisal. He had me conduct a ceremony for the safety of our army in the circle of oaks which he maintained inside the camp wall, and he had me stand where the armies could see and hear me during the battle with Vortigern. But," he paused emphasizing the word, "he went to mass that same morning that I blessed his troops."

"Hmn. Not taking any chances, was he? Got blessings from everyone."

"Yes, and Vivianne's not worried about that. I assured her that he will allow all religions but will support us. She's more concerned with the new breed of priests Rome is sending. The talk of sin is a constant reprisal with them. If the crops don't come up at the right time, it's because the farmer has sinned, not because he planted late, or because it was a cold spring. If a woman fails to produce a son for her husband, it's because she's sinned. If a child is sick with fever, it's because either he or the parents sinned. If ... well, you understand what I'm saying."

"The new priests cast an anchor about each man's foot, and force him to drag it around. Yes, I've heard such preaching upon occasion, but the priests on this island still seem Pelagians at heart. I didn't realize the sin casters were becoming common."

"Nor did I, but Vivianne has heard many stories of their repressions - from sources throughout Britannia. She has seen things with the holy eyes of the sight too." He reached to flame the dying fire, then looked at me, his eyes suddenly blazing in anger. "Hibernia will be the first to suffer from the Christians. She has seen a man who will cast out the Druids." He paused and his eyes narrowed. "And then he will come here."

69

BLAISE

A few days after that conversation Merlin's guard arrived. He had summoned them from Caerleon where he had sent them to help with the refortifying, but now, he told me, it was time he was on his way to Londinium. "Was there a messenger?" I inquired.

"No, but Ambrosius will be there in a few days for the coronation, and he requested that I come." Apparently he just knew, without a message. I wasn't surprised.

"I'd like to see The Giant's Dance on the way, so we'll leave in the morning."

He was referring to the ruins of a large stone circle on the Salisbury Plain, which was built hundreds of years before the Druids began passing down legends. No one knew who built it, though some said Bran, himself, had raised it. "It's impressive," I told him.

"I've heard that," he agreed. "I will need to understand how the stones were raised."

"You will? Why is that?"

"I want a monument of importance for Ambrosius."

"From what I hear all of Britannia has welcomed him gladly and will feel joy at seeing him crowned. Do you really think he needs a monument to his victories? Wouldn't that remind people of his Roman heritage at a time when no one thanks the Romans for deserting us? Don't we want to emphasize his Celtic mother and her truer claim to rule our tribes?"

Merlin answered, "Both heritages are important, I think."

"The Dance marks the movement of the stars," I continued. "Did you know?"

His brow creased and his hand rose to it as if in pain. "It will not mark the triumphs of Ambrosius," he answered. "It will mark his grave."

70

BLAISE

Merlin reached Londinium the day after Ambrosius had arrived and found the city busy with preparations for the crowning on the morrow.

Everywhere he looked things were being swept, washed, or polished. Thousands of red dragon banners had appeared, hanging from windows, walls and roofs, so that it seemed the whole town was fluttering.

Bakers were turning out loaves of bread and sweets to make the mouth water. Chickens, ducks and geese were being plucked. Cows, oxen, sheep, and pigs were turning on spits, wafting delicious scents that brought every dog and cat to watch the turning, darting in when it was safe to catch a dripping.

As soon as the farmers unloaded their vegetables and fruits at the marketplace, they were bought and carried off to the kitchens where maids scrubbed and chopped.

Garments were washed and brushed and hung to air. Fine ladies kept their maids busy bringing dress after dress to be tried on, and when one was decided upon, out came the chests of jewels. Those who had daughters dressed them in their most flattering colors, hoping they would catch the eye of the king. He was said to be handsome and charming, so the daughters cooperated fully, knowing that the High King's Counselors would be urging him to marry and produce an heir as soon as possible.

It was Uther who answered the knock on the king's door. He was in a high state of excitement. Instead of the usual scowl he greeted Merlin with a friendly slap on the shoulder that nearly knocked him over. "He'll be glad you're here. He tried to talk us into waiting for you, but we made him see sense. Won't do to wait any longer than necessary for the crowning."

He had been ushering Merlin toward a closed door which he banged on loudly with the handle of his dagger, before pushing it open and calling, "He's here. Now there's no reason to postpone." This time he pushed Merlin who found himself in the bath chamber where Ambrosius was soaking in a large metal tub.

"Your Highness," Merlin said, bowing.

"Oh, stop. You don't ever need to stand on ceremony when we're alone. You know that."

Merlin peered at him through the steam, exaggerating his movements as he looked about. "I wasn't sure if we were actually alone, Sire."

Ambrosius laughed at this - a wonderful laugh that would have made any listener want to join in. "Ah, Emrys, Emrys? I'm very happy to see you. If I weren't wet, I'd hug you."

"And I you, Sire. I trust that all went well in the North?"

"Every king swore allegiance, and every king is here to swear before all at the ceremony tomorrow."

"No wonder Uther was so effusive. That's wonderful news. And the wall? The fortifications?"

"I left teams of soldiers in each place, each working under a

Master Mason, and each with instructions that when finished, the team should move on to help at the next location. When all four teams arrived at the fifth designated spot, half of them went on to help at the sixth, and so on. By the time I left the last place they were only one spot behind me. And, of course, each place was garrisoned and provisioned before I left."

"And the Saxons?"

"Only one minor skirmish with an advance party under Uther. He had it settled before the army arrived. At least for now, it seems they'll follow my orders and stay north of the wall."

"So you are triumphant. Are you happy? Pleased? Satisfied?" When Ambrosius did not immediately answer, he continued, "Worried? Frightened?"

"All those things," he said. "Happy to be rid of Vortigern and his Saxons. Pleased that the country will accept me gladly as High King. Satisfied to be taking the place that was rightfully my father's. Worried that it will be difficult to keep all the factions content. And frightened - yes, frightened, that I may not be worthy of the responsibility."

Merlin dismissed these concerns with a wave of the hand. "I'd say you've done all right so far. You've been here less than six months and you've already defeated the king slayer Vortigern, driven the Saxons behind the wall, refortified Caerleon and the north, united a few dozen factious kings as your supporters, and tomorrow all the people of Britannia will have you crowned High King. I fully expect that at the end of a year the Picts, Scots, and Irish will be gratefully subdued, all the Saxons will have either sworn allegiance or gone home, and that Gwynn ap Nudd, Himself, will be offering you the Thirteen Treasures of Britannia, and possibly a herd of his fleet, red-eyed horses."

Ambrosius laughed until tears ran down his face. "Ah, Merlin, it's good to have you back."

He called for his manservant who brought towels and fresh

clothes, and as he dressed he gave Merlin some of the details of his travels through the north. Then he dismissed the servant and gestured toward a bowl of fruit on a table in the bedroom. "You must be famished. You had a long journey. Come, sit." He sat across from Merlin and poured two glasses of wine while Merlin helped himself to a ripe apricot.

"Now tell me about Ninianne. Did she come with you?" Though he sat comfortably, there was a tension in his posture that betrayed the importance of this topic.

Merlin didn't know how to tell him, and started gently. "You know I told you she was very ill."

"Yes, yes."

Merlin saw that it was all the king could do to keep from shaking the answer out of him. Better to get it said. "She died in my arms."

The king leaned forward heavily, elbows on the table, hands supporting his bowed head. His shoulders heaved, but for a long time there was no other motion, not even when he said, "Tell me," in a voice filled with anguish.

"Her last words were, 'Tell him I never stopped loving him.'"

Again, his answer was silence, and Merlin understood that he was too emotional to speak, so he described her last days and her funeral, emphasizing how the people had loved her and turned out in mass to honor her.

"But even had she been well and strong, she would not have come, Sire, and that was for your sake as High King." He heard the king's sharp intake of breath and continued quickly before he could be interrupted. "She was a princess, after all, and she understood the fragility of any kingship in our land, with its long tradition of individual tribes and tribal warfare. Vortigern called himself High King, but ruled by force, not by allegiance.

"The very idea of one king over all is a new one to us and completely foreign to a people who have avoided cooperation with each other for centuries. She knew that if she were to become your queen, it would add to the dissension - possibly even rupturing your newly established court."

Ambrosius could hold his tongue no longer. "What nonsense? How could this be?"

"Because it would be known that she was my mother, and since you and I apparently resemble each other enough to have already had tongues wagging for months, she did not want to be responsible for rendering the relationship you have with your brother." The king's brow was furled, his lips pursed. "Nor did she want me in the middle of such a fiasco."

Many emotions played out over the king's face, though he was silent, and stared away from Merlin into the fire. When he finally looked back, it was to study Merlin intently, and then, finally, to ask, "And what of that? Are you anxious to claim your heritage? Would you be king after me?"

Merlin went to his knees before the king, his hands lifted and imploring. "No, Sire. Truly, no. I haven't changed my mind since we last talked of it. Uther will be king after you, and his son after him, and I will serve all three of you in any capacity you need me, and none will hear me admit who my father is."

Ambrosius captured Merlin's hands and held them in his own. Leaning forward he kissed Merlin lightly on each cheek. "My son," he said. "I am proud that you are my son. For both our sakes I wish I could recognize you formally. But for Uther, I'd do it, I swear."

For the first and only time Merlin said the word, "Father," then he rose and pulled away. "I will never call you that again. It will be our secret until it can do neither of us harm, nor cause trouble for Uther."

Using the power of the Merlin, he drew himself up, taller and more imposing and his voice strengthened. "I will never be king, but I will make a king of Uther's son who will be remembered through all of time - a king whose every action will cause the birth of a new legend, a king who will prove a model to all kings who follow, a king who will inspire men in all the known worlds to come and serve him as knights of his realm, a king who will make a kingdom that will never be forgotten."

71

BLAISE

Early the next morning the noblemen of the realm and their families squeezed into St. Paul's modest church in the center of Londinium. The army and the people of the city lined the streets, and those in the square before the church strained to hear through the open doors what was said.

The churchyard had been reserved for the original supporters who had trained with Ambrosius in Brittany, and most of them could actually catch glimpses of the happenings through the numerous narrow windows that graced the long sides of the building every few feet.

As the king and an Honor Guard, chosen from his generals and those who had particularly distinguished themselves in battle, made their way slowly from the Tower to the church, Dubricious, the newly chosen Archbishop, and Merlin came to the altar through a side door.

Merlin had just met him, but immediately liked the man and knew that they would work well together out of mutual respect. He was pleased that Dubricious was not of the new school of Christians that so worried Vivianne. They could easily judge when the procession got closer by the cheering of the crowd as the king passed, and they smiled at each other as the king drew near.

The Archbishop was dressed richly in robes of gold and pearled white. Merlin was dressed simply in the long blue robes of a Druid, and deliberately moved behind Dubricious, letting him draw the eyes of the nobles and their ladies whose brilliantly colored robes and flashing jewels gave the plain church a festive air.

As the honor guard entered the church Merlin saw that Uther led the procession. He was every inch a soldier, in bearing and in dress, though his golden armor was dress armor, lightweight and not meant for battle, and his green tunic was floor length and not designed for fighting. His countenance was somber, yet he could not hide the smile that constantly crept from his eyes to his lips. Entering after him were some twenty soldiers, Ambrosius, then twenty more.

Uther climbed the steps to the altar and took a place beside Merlin. The soldiers came to stand behind them, facing the congregation, then Ambrosius came slowly up the steps, his golden tunic studded with a smattering of gleaming gems, his long cloak of purple velvet trailing behind. Kneeling before the Archbishop with a quiet dignity, he bowed his head, his dark hair hiding his face.

Archbishop Dubricious was not a man to take advantage of those before him with a lengthy sermon, and mass for all who wished had happened several hours earlier. He spoke, in a voice that easily projected to those in the courtyard beyond, of the grave responsibilities of a king to protect his people, and called for his god to bless Ambrosius and his newly forged union of tribes.

Merlin stepped forward, holding a silk cushion with a simple crown of gold resting on top, and he too blessed the High King and the people of Britannia, and his voice was the equal of the archbishop's. Then Dubricious took the crown and placed it on the head of the king, and from an identical silk cushion now held by Uther, Merlin took a carved torque of gold and fastened it about his neck, then bade him rise.

Ambrosius turned to face those in the crowded church, and the people erupted in cheering so loud that every bird in the city took flight. It went on for a long time, long enough for the newly crowned king to draw his brother forward, his arm draped about Uther's shoulders, then to thank Dubricious and Merlin, and then to go to the soldiers and have a quiet word with each.

When, finally, he came to the front of the altar once more, he signaled for quiet. The word passed through the crowd outside until all was still enough for the High King to be heard. "People of Britannia," he said, "you are one now - of many tribes, but united against a common enemy, sworn to honor a High King, desiring, most of all, peace. A time will soon come when our roads will be safe to travel, our shores will be safe from raids, and our lands will be safe to plant and harvest.

"This will come because we are - at last - one people." His arms lifted as if he too was blessing those before him, and once again the people cheered.

Uther stepped forward and shouted, "Long live Ambrosius, High King of Britannia," and the people responded, "Long live the King! Long live the King!" The chant was soon taken up and repeated through the churchyard, and the square, and through all the streets of Londinium.

Then Uther shouted, "Oaths of fealty will be given. I call before the High King, King Gorlois of Dumnonia." Gorlois came forward with his family, the first to swear fealty, and then came every king, called one by one to bow before Ambrosius and swear the oath.

At the end of this royal procession came the South Saxon king, Octa, with his sons, and his oath was sworn as well. Merlin could not help but wonder if he would be the first to break the oath. He knew that Uther trusted him not, but Octa had convinced the High King that all the South Saxons desired was to farm their lands peacefully and had volunteered to give his support against any invasion. Ambrosius had warned his nobles and his soldiers that Octa was to be treated with courtesy.

Throughout this procession of kings, which had taken nearly two hours to complete, those who were outside waited patiently, then cheered as the ceremony ended with the Honor Guard, the High King, the nobles, and finally the soldiers parading before them once more.

Those soldiers who had kept the crowds back along the street, fell in behind, letting the crowd loose to follow, and they all proceeded toward the Tower Castle where musicians were already playing, and platters of food were being set at long tables overlooking the river.

Later there was dancing, and jugglers, and acrobats, and bards who sang new songs about the mighty feats of Ambrosius. Merlin too had a new song of a long-awaited king who came in triumphs from across the sea, and when his harp struck the last jubilant note, the people rose to their feet and shouted their approval.

Ambrosius seemed greatly moved by this tribute from the son he could not openly claim and immediately presented him with a ruby studded gold dragon ring from his own finger as a reward. It was common for a king to reward a bard who did well – often with jewelry – but Merlin in turn was moved when he realized that the pendragon ring, rather than a lesser trinket, came partly as a private acknowledgement of their true relationship.

There was wine at the high tables and ale for the rest, and at no time did servers stop offering it. The celebration lasted all afternoon and evening, long into the night, and no fights broke out, and no arguments or disruptions in spite of the many who were in their cups. For once it seemed that all of Britannia had found a joyous cause for celebration.

72

BLAISE

Merlin stayed in Londinium for nearly five months, indulging an interest he had long hoped to master. Working alongside Timoreus, the Master Builder who had supervised the training site in Brittany and the refortifications along the wall and in the northern kingdoms, he learned the fundamentals of construction. They enlarged the Tower, making it into a castle fit for a king as well as a fort large enough to house and train soldiers and strong enough to discourage enemies, and they built a wall around the entire city, with walkways for patrolling lookouts, and armories every few hundred feet to house men and weapons and to provide sheltered stairways to the walkways.

Merlin learned how to cut and join wood, and how to make mortar and how to apply it so that walls were solid, and how to cut stone and lift it into place. He learned about stress and pillars that would allow a large span of roof to flow overhead with little support. He learned to see what pleased the eye in a building and how to enhance the beauty with decorative touches.

Once he had the fundamentals, he was also allowed to design and supervise the building of several projects - the stables, a bridge over the Thames, a long section of the wall with protected slits for archers along the walkway, and the huge kitchen for the castle.

He spent hours drawing designs for what he hoped might be future projects - castles, hill forts, and whole cities, then spent even more hours going over the plans with Timoreus who encouraged his imagination and rewarded his innovations with enthusiasm.

Timoreus could build anything, but always copied what had been done before, not being adept at new design, himself. He did not begrudge Merlin's talent at all, but made Merlin carefully examine the structure, sometimes even building miniature models so the two could test whether the building would stand or fall.

As a very young man Timoreus, who was well into his fifties at present and considered old and venerable, had made a pilgrimage to Rome at the suggestion of his grandfather, a master mason. His father, who was also a master mason, had argued that he needed the son to help in the building of a church, but the grandfather was insistent, saying that Timoreus would learn skills that would someday be helpful to his trade.

It was he who had secured a place on a trading vessel for his grandson, and the boy proved his usefulness, employing his skills as a carpenter to anything on board that needed repairing throughout the journey. When a storm caught them off the coast of Iberia, breaking the mast and splintering the bow as it tossed the uncontrollable vessel into a large jagged rock while they were frantically rowing toward land, it was Timoreus who supervised repairs and had them underway again in only a few days.

The captain was so grateful for his expertise that he cheerfully arranged a date to pick him up in Ostia for the journey home.

"Ah, Merlin, you've heard your whole life of the glories of Rome, and it's true - all true." Quickly he sketched an aqueduct and explained the principle of transporting water from mountain streams.

While Merlin was studying that and remembering that he had seen a Roman one in southern Cambria, Timoreus sketched a pillared temple, then a Roman arch, then a bath house. "Have you been to Aquae Sulis? It's well worth a trip to see the baths there."

"I've seen the baths at Caerleon," Merlin answered. "Indeed, a wondrous sight even though part is in ruins."

"As is Rome, itself, but still you should go there."

"Worthwhile, I'm sure," came a new voice, and Ambrosius entered Merlin's chamber, "but I'm afraid there are other places I need to send Merlin before we have the leisure to add a trip to Rome." He studied the drawings, and asked many questions which Timoreus was delighted to answer. When Timoreus left, a half hour later, he studied his son for a moment before asking, "You've enjoyed working with Timoreus, haven't you?"

"Very much. Construction is not something taught at the Druid Schools - perhaps it should be," he mused.

"When we truly have peace, I think I'll let you build a city for me. Possibly near Salisbury. That was where I was born, you know, and where I lived until we were whisked off to Brittany."

"You decide where you want it, and I'll build it happily."

"Possibly farther south. It would be good to have a center that looks out to the sea. I fear the Saxons will outgrow their border and push west, so a stronghold there would be advantageous."

"When I travel that way again, I'll look for a good hilltop."

Ambrosius was silent for a while, studying Merlin's model of his dream city, then he picked up the drawing of the Roman arch and asked if Merlin could make an arch of stones. "It reminds me of the Giant's Dance, near Salisbury."

"I took the time to study the Dance on my way to Londinium," Merlin told him.

"Did you? And what did you think?"

"It's magnificent. Much more primitive, of course, than what we've been building, but the size of the stones ... well, it's phenomenal, especially when you think how long ago it was built. I'd like a chance to repair it - to lift the fallen stones. I've also thought of a few improvements." Quickly he sketched his idea.

"All right," Ambrosius said. "You may do it."

Merlin had been standing as he sketched, leaning over the table, but at those words a shadow passed over him and he sank to a chair, remembering that he had told Blaise it would be his father's grave, and realizing the death would not be long into the future.

"Merlin? Are you all right? You've turned a fair shade of white, and your hands are shaking."

He looked up slowly, and it seemed to him that the High King was fading away as he looked. He shook his head, willing the vision away, meeting his father's eyes steadily. "Sorry. I think we forgot to eat tonight. I didn't realize I was weak from hunger."

Ambrosius went to the door and summoned a servant, sending him for food, "And be quick about it," he said. "No stopping to flirt with the cooks."

Looking once more at Merlin's drawing, the High King commented, "You know, I've heard that in Hibernia there is a stone circle worth seeing at Killare. It's said to be the heart of the land, and it's holy to the kings."

"I've heard of it - the Dance of Killare."

Ambrosius was perfectly serious when he said, "I'd like you to tear it down. You'll go with Uther when he sails to attack the fortress. Killare is a stronghold built on a mountain top and said to be impregnable, but I have complete confidence in my brother's ability to take it. It's time the Irish were taught that their piracy is unacceptable. And destroying the Stone Dance," he added, "will demoralize them more than conquering the impregnable."

"I will do as you ask, Sire," Merlin told him.

73

BLAISE

A week later Merlin left Londinium for Caerleon where a fleet of ships awaited Uther and his soldiers. Earlier he shared a quick breakfast with Ambrosius and Uther, where the king instructed Uther to make this conquest rapidly. "We can't afford the time for a siege, so do what you have to do to avoid that at all costs. I don't trust the Picts in the north or the Saxons in the south, though both have sworn loyalty."

Uther made a disparaging sound. "That for the word of either. I trust them less than you do, so I'll plan on meeting you at Caerleon in a month's time."

"I'll be there," Ambrosius told him. "I think that at least for the first year of my reign I must show a strong army presence around all of our borders, so I need you and your men back as soon as possible." He regarded his brother with a twinkle in his eye. "I'm only giving you a month so you can't sew your seed all over Ireland. It wouldn't do for you to be challenged for the throne by a bastard son in the far future."

Uther flicked a bold look at Merlin. "I've always tried to be cautious about leaving bastard sons at large. Unlike some."

There was a rare flash of anger from the king. "We've discussed this. There is no threat to you from this quarter. See that your tongue does not provide one."

Uther's face flamed in embarrassment for being reprimanded in front of Merlin, but he apologized and Ambrosius accepted it, not noticing the look of hatred he flashed toward Merlin. To further rub the wound, the king instructed, "After securing Killare Merlin will tear down the Dance of Stone. You and your men are to provide help and follow any instructions that he gives in this mission."

"It will be as you command," Uther said, giving a formal salute. "May I have your permission to leave, Sire? I want to make sure the war machines are packed securely."

"Of course." Ambrosius broke off the formality, stood up, and stepped forward to hug his brother. "May the gods be with you. Come home safely, Uther."

"You can be sure of it," he said with the cockiness that Merlin usually associated with him. He also took advantage of the king's hug to send another warning look at Merlin, and Merlin realized that he would soon have trouble with his uncle.

In silence he watched Uther leave. "I should probably check my pack again, and find my horse." Still, Merlin lingered, his finger tracing the rim of his cup, and he remained seated.

"Don't let his bluster upset you," the king told him, sitting again at the table. "He's rash, but his heart belongs to Britannia, and in the end he will always do the right thing."

"I know. He will listen to the words I say, but not take my advice, and he will never trust me."

"Not as I do, perhaps, but he will find that unlike Lesser Britain, Britannia revers the word of the High Priest of the Druids. I am confident that he'll come to respect you." When Merlin didn't say anything, he continued. "When the battle is done, you must insist that he send his soldiers to tear down the Dance."

"I will."

"I don't care if you choose to pack up every stone and bring them back with you. Make him help."

"I will."

Merlin was looking at his father with an expression that he couldn't understand. "What is it?" he asked at last. "What is bothering you?"

Merlin couldn't tell him that it was the last time he'd ever see him. What he said instead was, "Thank you for welcoming a bastard son to the high table, Sire. It has been a privilege to serve you and to know you."

Ambrosius laughed. "That's awfully formal."

"Sorry. I guess Uther got me thinking how I might have been treated if you hadn't accepted me open heartedly."

"Merlin, I'm proud that you are my son. I've told you before that I wished I could honor you as such."

"Sire, truly, I have all I want as the Merlin, but I can't help but feel glad that it turned out that you are my father."

It might have been that the High King was overwhelmed with emotion, and there might have been a tear or two blinked back. "I'm as glad as you are," he said, standing and pulling Merlin to his feet. His hug was just longer than courtesy called for. "Now, away with you. We both have things to accomplish today, and we'd best get started."

"Be careful, Sire."

"And you."

Merlin left, but when he reached the doorway, he could not help looking back once more.

74

BLAISE

The ride to Caerleon seemed brutally fast to Merlin who was not used to long hours in the saddle. In all the time he had spent riding with Ambrosius to battle, or to Londinium, to Caerleon, or to Ynys Witrin, the pace had been reasonable and the rests frequent.

He had barely slid off his horse, clinging to the animal to still his shaking legs, when Uther ordered them back in the saddle and on to the harbor. When that ride was finally over, he wasn't sure he could even get down off the horse. It seemed an impossible task to ask a leg that was so sore to swing up, over the saddle, and down as far as the ground.

Luckily his high position as King's Counselor came with a squire, and Ralf was not an unthinking young lad, but a man mature enough to understand that Merlin was no cavalryman. "How bad is it?" he asked, surveying his master without the slightest hint of the humor he probably felt.

"If you were Irish, I'd to beg you to put me out of my misery."

Ralf did laugh this time. "It's a good thing I'm not Irish then." Straight to business, he commanded, "Put your arm around my shoulder and I'll pull you off."

Merlin obliged, but still cried out in pain and didn't care who heard him. He was sure there was no skin left on the inside and back of his thighs. Then he noticed that Ralf had him in a semi-standing position and was asking him to walk toward the tent that he had already pitched.

He tried to walk but ended up being dragged five feet for every one step he took. At the entrance he bent, meaning to just duck his head, but lost his balance and fell to his hands and knees. He crawled forward, collapsing face down on his bedroll, but was still coherent and asked Ralf to bring his pack.

A moment later he heard, "Here it is, Sire."

Without moving he described what he wanted and Ralf soon had the correct jar of ointment out of the pack and close to his face. "Yes, thank you. That's it."

Ralf surveyed him for a moment with a wry expression. "Now I suppose you'll be wanting help to apply it."

"If you would be so kind."

As soon as the ointment was spread over the painful areas, he felt the relief of numbness. Ralf told him he'd be back with food as soon as he rubbed the horses down, but Merlin said, "No. Just let me sleep."

It seemed that he and Ralf had just exchanged those words, when Ralf was shaking him awake. "Sorry, Sire, but the ships are loaded with weapons and horses, and the men are starting to board." Again he offered food, and again Merlin refused. He knew that nothing he ate would stay down once he was on the sea.

Others said they were lucky. The Irish Sea was known for its wild waves, but for Uther it was relatively calm. Merlin thought they were being facetious, since he'd spent the entire journey hunched over a bucket, but when Uther told him the same thing, he realized they were serious. As far as he could tell, Uther did not have a sense of humor.

The sea had been so rough for him that once they were on land he was glad to see his horse - until he weakly lifted himself into the saddle and his former injuries painfully blotted out the memory of his cramping stomach. He was about to climb back down, but at that moment Uther rode by, giving him a disdainful look for his weaknesses, so he gritted his teeth and held his seat.

An hour later he considered asking Uther for permission to stay where he was, or at least to walk slowly along the trail they were forging, but he knew that Uther would have to leave men with him - men he could ill afford to lose.

It was also at that point when he heard someone say, "Of course, we'll win. The Merlin, himself, is here to cheer us on." He sighed, realizing that though he could leave his uncle quite cheerfully, he could not desert the men.

Killare was said to be impregnable, and, indeed, it might have been, but the young Irish king, Gilloman, for some ill-advised reason decided to ride forth and attack on a wide plain with a river at his back.

It did not take Uther, with his experienced troops, long to drive the Irish into the river where they either surrendered or were slaughtered. Merlin was riding at the rear and stayed back with the other healers when the battle began. There was no standing on a hilltop to inspire the soldiers, though he did trill the ancient Celtic ululations, the high-pitched cry to battle, that was meant to strike terror into the heart of the enemy.

The fighting was over almost before it had begun, the casualties few, and the injuries light. It's true that Merlin actually forgot his own pain while supervising the treatment of the injured, but it's also true that when Uther ordered his men to mount up and continue on to occupy Killare, he considered asking if he could borrow Ralf's sword for the sole purpose of sinking it into Uther, who by then he considered his own, personal tormentor.

He spent another night lying on his stomach, but this time he was in a bed, and said stomach was full, for he had eaten a light meal (standing up), and Ralf had once again administered the numbing cream to his nether regions. He slept long and deeply, having ordered Ralf to wake him only if they were under attack again.

It was the evening of the next day when he shakily made his way down a flight of stairs, allowing his nose to lead him to the hall where the soldiers were filling their bellies with fresh pork and bragging of their personal exploits in the battle. Merlin heard Uther complain to someone that they had dragged their new siege engines all the way from Londinium without the opportunity to try them out.

He spotted one of the healers and gingerly sat on the bench next to him. He soon learned that the pork was delicious, that all the injured were doing well and that with only minor adjustments he was not too uncomfortable to sit. "What of Gilloman?" he asked. "Was he killed?"

"No, he actually escaped. Uther sent a troop after him and there was a second battle near the gates, even shorter than the first, but he managed to escape again, and no one saw where," the healer answered.

Merlin reached for bread and found it still warm from the oven, and every bit as delicious as the pork. "Have you seen the Dance of Stones?" Merlin had been in no condition to look for it when he had finally reached Killare.

"Oh, aye. It's at the top of the hill we're on, not far at all. Looks like a crown on a giant's head."

When Merlin had finished his meal, he stepped outside and found the moon bright and the evening mild. Walking seemed a pleasant change from riding on a horse or a ship. In fact, it felt good to stretch his long legs. To one side of the fortress he found a path that wound up the mountain. He followed it, relieved to be away from the noise of men. It was not that Merlin didn't like people, it was that he'd been extremely solitary as a child, only some of the time self-imposed, and he had learned to enjoy the peace of being alone with his thoughts.

The healer had been right. The circle of rocks on the crest of the hill did look like a crown. It was not as large or as imposing as the Giant's Dance on Salisbury Plain, but he could feel the power of the place. He would see that the capped stones were torn down as Ambrosius had requested, but even if they were all hauled away, there would still be a feeling of holiness here.

Slowly he walked into the circle, then around it three times clockwise before moving to the center. It was a ritual of power, the circle, whether oak or stone, the symbol of the universe - the wheel of life cycles, and the words he spoke were to draw from the force of the macrocosm down to the microcosm that was the self at the center, the words from the prayer of Talhaiarn. "God, thy protection, and in protection strength, and in strength, reason, and in reason, knowledge, and in knowledge truth, and in truth, justice, and in justice, love, and in love, the love of God, and in the love of God, the love of every living thing."

There was an altar in the circle and a navel stone, but he was drawn to neither, yet as he knelt in the grass the moonlight seemed to brighten and he noticed the outlines of a large, flat rectangular stone, nearly buried in the grass. He began pulling the grass away, and as it came loose he felt a pulsing, as if the stone was alive. It seemed to shimmer with rainbow colors in the moonlight. The very air wavered like it does on a very hot day under a burning sun, but it was moon-light, and it was cool.

He laid both hands on the stone when he had cleared it. A thrumming sound came and he looked about, then realized that the sounds came from the stone. He knew of stones like this from his homeland, and wondered if this stone had been brought from there. More, he knew that this stone was the heart of the Dance.

Something seemed to draw his eyes to the star-filled sky. As his gaze fell on the heavens he saw it - a falling star that trailed a tail of fire across the star basin, and coiled like a striking dragon. He knew then that it heralded the death of the Pendragon.

He rose stiffly, hands pressing hard against his face as if he could push the grief out through the pores of his skin, but once on his feet, he mastered his emotion and made his way down the trail quickly. The courtyard was full of soldiers, including Uther, and all were staring at the fiery spectacle in the sky. "Merlin," Uther called when he saw him, "what does it mean?"

Merlin went to one knee, bowing before Uther. "It means that your brother has died and that you are the new Pendragon and High King, Sire."

As the word spread every soldier knelt to his startled uncle. "Hail, King Uther," Merlin said, using the Druid priest's voice that all could hear, and they shouted back, "Hail, King Uther."

Uther stood with his chin up, still gazing at the sky, without seeming to hear the homage and showing no outward emotion, but as Merlin looked, he saw one tear, sliding down the king's chiseled face. He had just lost his brother.

75

BLAISE

Very early the next morning horns blew to muster the men, and Merlin staggered out of his warm bed to see what was happening.

Uther stood before the assembled soldiers. "We will leave for Britannia early tomorrow morning," he said. "That gives us one day to tear down this fortress so that it is never occupied against us again." He spotted Merlin. "How many men do you need to tear down the Dance, Merlin?"

"Fifty," he answered after a moment's thought. "We should replace them with another fifty at high sun and another fifty, four hours later."

"That many?"

"We're taking one of the stones with us - the heart of the Dance." He added, "The heart of the Irish." He saw the exasperated expression on King Uther's face, then saw the flicker of understanding.

"And where are we taking it?"

"To the Giant's Dance," he answered without hesitation. I will rebuild it as King Ambrosius requested, and it will stand as his memorial when we have buried him there."

Uther gave him a look he couldn't read. "It will be done as you say." With barely a pause, he signaled. "Commanders, to me," and they came to receive specific assignments for their men.

Merlin took his soldiers up the mountain quickly, then set the first forty to pushing the stones over, which was not an easy task. Most of the stones were half buried so deep trenches had to be dug around part of the bases before they would budge, and sometimes it was necessary to rope the tops and pull them over.

The other ten men he used to cut timber and make a sturdy sled, while he, himself, wove a strong harness of ropes, and as men finished their assigned tasks, he set some of them to digging around the giant heart stone to loosen and free it, and sent others for a team of horses. Then, when all was ready, he put the men about the sled to hold it securely, wrapped the stone with his harness, and tied the loose ends to the horses' saddles.

Working the horses and their riders in rhythm, he had the stone on the sled much sooner than he expected. He roped the stone securely to the sled, then put half the horses in the rear and started down the mountain path. The difficult part here was to keep the stone from overrunning the front horses, and in the beginning - on the steepest section - they looked to lose it, and only the skill of the riders, answering Merlin's shouted instructions, kept it secure.

In this way, slowly and carefully, they slid the stone down to the level ground below, then bedded down for the night. In the morning they found that it was harder to pull the stone on level ground, but easier to control it. Merlin added horses and riders as needed through-out the day, depending on the terrain, but most of the way was level or downhill, and by the evening they had reached the sea and dragged the sled onto the deck of a ship with the aid of a wide and long, gently inclined ramp, built just for the occasion.

Uther was impatient, of course, but kept his word to his brother, and supplied fresh men and horses whenever Merlin requested them.

Merlin spent the night securing the stone and raft to the ship, knowing that the decks would roll even in a gentle sea. When they sailed the next morning, he asked one of Uther's commanders to keep a constant check on it, knowing that he would soon be in no condition to do it himself. That turned out to be a wise decision, for once again Merlin befriended a bucket, neglecting all other duties.

76

BLAISE

When they landed at Caerleon they learned that Ambrosius had been poisoned by drinking from a well while visiting his holding in Winchester. Nor was he alone. Everyone who drank from that well died – nineteen in all. The poisoner, a Saxon posing as a servant, had been captured. He confessed proudly, and Gorlois, who had taken command until Uther returned, had executed him. Gorlois had then returned to Londinium with Ambrosius' retinue to await Uther's arrival.

Uther, wanting to be crowned as soon as possible, took his troop and immediately rode for Londinium, but before he left, he ordered the commander at Caerleon to aid Merlin with whatever he needed to haul the giant heart stone to the Giant's Dance.

Merlin took advantage, knowing that most of the reconstruction of the fortress was finished. He ordered the Masons and their laborers to join him, as well as pressing an escort of soldiers to accompany them. Most fortunate was the fact that some weeks before Timoreus had been sent to speed the rebuilding of Caerleon, so he was there to greet his friend and agreed immediately to come along.

It took three weeks to haul the massive stone from Caerleon to the Dance on the plains of Salisbury. Whenever possible they used rivers to float it, but still it had to be dragged over much of the terrain, and Merlin was thankful for the aid of Timoreus and his laborers who had an expertise at this from experience, unlike the soldiers of his crew in Hibernia.

When they finally arrived at the site, they found a rider with a dispatch from Uther, asking Merlin to come to Londinium for the crowning. He spent the next day making sketches for Timoreus, revising occasionally at his suggestion, and by evening the Master Builder had his completed plans, and was ready to begin the work of lifting and securing the fallen stones. Merlin left the day after that, not wanting to tempt the ire of the new king.

He arrived in Londinium a day later where he learned that his timing was impeccable. There was one day where he was drawn into the final plans for the coronation. Uther was crowned the day after that with most of the same noble families present who had all too recently attended the crowning of his brother.

Once again Merlin was paired with the Archbishop Dubricious. He enjoyed a long talk with him before the ceremony, and Merlin was pleased to find him, not just tolerant to the Druids, but someone who would be an active friend.

Noticeably absent was Octa and his Southern Saxons, along with several of the northern kings who guarded the border against the Picts, which worried Uther enough so that he planned immediate excursions to visit those absent, taking, of course, a large army, so that they might be persuaded to acknowledge his authority over them.

The new king was not greeted by the people as enthusiastically as Ambrosius had been. Still the cheers were loud enough to be pleasing, and the celebration was just as grand. The only shadow that fell upon the occasion was a private one felt only by Merlin. It came twice that day.

The first time was during the ceremony of homage. Gorlois, always first to support the king, was first in line and presented his wife, Ygerna. This was the first time that either Merlin or Uther had met her.

Merlin found her striking. Tall, with a straight back and a head held high, dignified, graceful of movement, her bearing that of the queen she was. She was the much younger sister of Gorlois' first wife, Anna, mother of his grown son, Cador. Anna had the ancient Celtic female blood that made her queen of the land and her husband the consort. Her Romanized husband had no illusions about how he held the land in spite of his Christianity and his masculine oriented upbringing, so one year after Anna's death, Gorlois married her sister who had inherited her title. In spite of the practical circumstances, he was delighted with her.

Indeed, what man would not be, for she was a good twenty years younger than he and very beautiful as well. Her hair was the lightest shade of red, a few curls peeking from under her headdress. Her eyes were probably grey, but looked lavender in the muted light of the church. She had high cheekbones and unblemished skin where one might have expected freckles. Merlin was quite taken with her combination of power and modesty.

Then he saw that Uther was looking at her as if stricken by a bolt of lightning. A shadow blotted Gorlois to nonexistence just as the sun passed from behind a cloud and streamed a blast of light through the window to focus on the Queen of Dumnonia and the King of all Britannia.

Merlin felt that shadow as heavily as if an angel of stone had fallen from the carved pillars of the church to pin him to the ground. He swayed, and might have fallen if Dubricious had not reached to steady him. The shadow passed as the King and Queen of Dumnonia sank to their knees and swore their homage.

The second time that Merlin felt the wings of darkness came

during the feast. He had been seated next to Ygerna - a delight to him, for he knew with the surety of sight that it was important to him to know her, and with conversation came the knowledge that a keen intelligence lay behind the sparkling eyes and the luminous complexion.

She spoke to him, not as a queen, but as a priestess, for she was also that as the lady of her land, and she seemed as eager to know her High Priest as he was to know her.

In some senses - her place in the king's court, for instance - she seemed very young and inexperienced, eager to learn what was expected of her and apparently not getting much help from her husband, but in other senses she had a wisdom far beyond her years, a true sense of the bond between king and land, and how that created a bond between the folk and their rulers when both the land and the folk were nurtured and cared for.

One of the bards was singing a song of yearning for love lost. His voice was true and the story he wove was one that brought tears to the eyes of many, including Ygerna. Merlin felt the dark sadness, then realized he was feeling more than the music, and when his eyes rose, they met those of Uther who signaled for him to come near. Excusing himself to Ygerna who paid him no mind, so absorbed in the song was she, he did as commanded.

Uther requested that he sing next, so when the applause had ended, he had picked up his harp and was ready to replace the bard. He chose a song well known to all that celebrated the exploits of a long dead king and was greeted with cheers as he struck the first few notes.

He was halfway through the first chorus when he saw that Uther had moved to his seat and was engaged in earnest conversation. He saw Ygerna laugh, and Uther smile, and Gorlois frown.

By the second chorus when Ygerna laughed again, Gorlois leaned across her, trying to engage the High King in a private conversation, but Uther included Ygerna by explaining something to her and she looked, not to her husband, but to the High King, and as the explanation went on and on, Gorlois sat back again, arms folded in fury.

Merlin rushed the tempo of the song, finishing with a flourish, and gave up the podium to another harper. He could not very well take the king's chair, so he returned to his own, standing behind Uther, and deftly inserting a comment as soon as it seemed appropriate, speaking and gesturing to include Gorlois as well.

Ygerna, as eager as Merlin to end the impasse, complimented him on his song and looked to her husband, saying, "Though you told me many things about the Merlin, you neglected to tell me how accomplished his voice and harp are, My Lord."

Gorlois answered with a compliment to Merlin. Gesturing to Merlin's wine glass in front of the king, he added, rather pointedly, "You must be thirsty after that performance."

Uther could have handed Merlin's wine to him, but took the hint and excused himself, vacating Merlin's chair with a bow of his head to Lady Ygerna.

77

BLAISE

The kings met in council the next day, and Merlin listened as each reported progress in fortification. He said nothing unless asked. Uther had made it clear to him immediately before the meeting that he was not to volunteer advice. He found this amusing since he was supposed to be the king's advisor. Truly, though, Ambrosius had organized his kingdom well before his death, and the kings had few difficulties to report. This pleased Uther well and all were invited to bring their wives and dine with him in the newly built dining hall of the Tower Castle that evening.

Merlin was playing his harp as the kings and their ladies arrived, and saw that they were dressed as elaborately as for the crowning, the colors of their gowns and cloaks rich, their jewels gleaming in the torchlight. A cheer came up when the newly crowned High King arrived – not a prolonged and hearty cheer, but a polite recognition that seemed to please him. If it had been a gathering of soldiers, his applause would have been deafening of course.

He passed through the crowd, speaking a word to those selected to join him at the high table. Once he had seated himself on the dais everyone else quickly found places for themselves, and the servants entered with the first course.

Merlin noticed that King Gorlois was seated on Uther's right and the Lady Ygerna on his left, with her stepson Cador on her other side. She was dressed modestly all in white with small pearls tucked in the piles of her hair, and one large single pearl at her throat. Though others had colorful gowns and elaborate jewels, trying to capture the attention of their new monarch, it was Ygerna who drew his eye and deservedly so, for her beauty shown like the single pearl she wore.

Although she maintained her regal posture, he saw that her eyes were downcast. Her movements were graceful, but never overt, doing nothing to cause undue attention. Her demeanor was demure and so proper that no one could criticize. Gorlois tried valiantly to engage his king in conversation, but Uther could not take his eyes off Ygerna, never turning toward her husband for more than a few seconds.

As the evening progressed Gorlois signaled for wine more and more often. He stopped trying to speak to his king and stared around him at his wife, his expression by turns angry and sullen.

When her husband failed to rescue her from the king's undivided attention, she tried to include Cador in the conversation, but his new wife, Mariana, was too young to understand what was happening and responded by jealously reclaiming him.

Cador did understand, but he loved his wife very much and wisely chose to support her rather than his stepmother. He did flash a look of apology to his father, along with a 'what-could-I-do, she's-the-one-I-need-to-keep-happy' shrug, but as far as Merlin could tell, Gorlois was so intent on his cup that he didn't notice.

Merlin tried to help keep peace too. He sent one of the servants for Alyfin and had him take the harp for a rousing song that commanded attention. Merlin sang next, moving along the tables until he stood immediately in front of the king, who due to the force of his singing was now looking at him.

He finished in the same spot, then began a ballad that contained a hero story – a long hero story with many hardships to overcome, many battles to fight, and love to nearly lose, then find at the last moment.

Merlin stretched every part of the story, even when he saw the king's fingers tapping in annoyance. Ygerna flashed him a grateful smile when he was finished, and the applause was so prolonged that Uther was obliged to award him with a golden bracelet from his own arm.

He went back to his harp, fully expecting the king to rise and retire, signaling an end to festivities since the serving of food had ended long before and the wine was coming only sparsely, but it was not to be. Instead, he engaged Ygerna in a conversation that evidently required frequent responses, and at each of these her downcast eyes looked up to meet his and finally locked on them.

At this response his hand touched and then rested upon her arm and his gaze grew even more intense. She did not seem able to look away.

The guests stared in fascination. All other conversation stopped as they absorbed the tableau. Gorlois' face took on a red glow, whether from the wine or embarrassment it was impossible to say. He rose unsteadily from his chair, and at that moment Cador acted, saving the day as he deliberately reached for his wine glass, and clumsily knocked it over into Ygerna's lap.

She jumped up, dabbing ineffectually at the red stains streaking the pure white of her gown like blood on snow. Cador was on his feet too, apologizing, and now Ygerna was gesturing toward the stains and moving toward her husband, and taking his arm. Uther rose and gestured them away, his eyes never leaving her as Gorlois escorted her out, then he looked at Cador, said a few quick words to him, turned on his heel, and left. The evening was over.

78

BLAISE

There was another council the next day, this time including the garrison commanders. Uther did not trust the Picts north of the wall or the Saxons in the southeast. With a new king in command, it seemed a good time for either or both of them to stage an uprising – a testing of his power, and he wanted to take no chances on having a border overrun.

Merlin was listening as Uther was promising reinforcements to young King Lot of Lothian in the Northeast when the squire, Ralf, entered and handed him a note. He was surprised to find that it was from the Lady Ygerna, requesting his presence at her tent. Both Gorlois and Uther were fully engaged with the topic at hand, and Merlin, knowing he was there simply as a formality to honor the memory of Ambrosius and was not really needed, left the chamber quietly.

Ralf was waiting for him at the door. "I know where King Gorlois' campsite is, Sire. I'll take you there."

Merlin stood still, staring at him until the young man was quite uncomfortable. "Sire?"

"Did you then read my message?"

"No – no, Sire. I would not presume." He did not seem all that flustered. "It was the Lady's maid, you see. She asked me to deliver the message. The Lady is apparently not feeling well and has request-ed that you come. I took the liberty of getting your bag with your healing supplies." He held up Merlin's bag. It held packets of herbs and ground powders, all clearly labeled, and a few surgical instru-ments, as well as bandages. Merlin did not usually carry it unless he was traveling or accompanying the army. He nodded his approval.

Gorlois' camp was set up a half mile from the Tower, his stand-ard flying from about two hundred tents. Ralf took him straight to the largest – a blue silk, striped with white, where two guards were posted. One of them pulled the flap aside and held it while he entered. Ralf was left on the outside with the guards.

Ygerna was seated on the bed, fully dressed, and she rose to greet him. In the next breath she asked her maid to leave them alone, and when the woman looked hesitant, she gave her a stern look and commanded, "Now," and the woman scuttled away.

"You're not feeling well, My Lady?" Merlin asked when they were alone.

She backed away and sank to a chair, indicating that he should sit too, but as soon as he was seated she jumped up and began pacing a small circle before him. "My husband said I should pretend to be ill. So I won't be able to attend another dinner with the king, you see."

"Ah, and you want me to pretend to be healing you."

She sank down on her knees before him, taking his hands in hers. "I wouldn't presume to ask."

"I don't mind the pretending. It would be better for all con-cerned."

Her grey eyes filled with tears. "You saw how it was then?"

"The whole court saw how it was," he answered honestly.

Her hands fluttered to her face, hiding the tears that began falling in earnest. When she had gained some semblance of control, her eyes met his and he saw that she was angry. "I didn't ask for this!"

"I know," he said softly, working comfort into his tone.

"Oh, Merlin, what can I do? I realize I don't know you well, but you hold the title of Merlin which makes you my spiritual advisor, so I feel I can ask you. What can I do?"

"It seems that your husband has advised you well. The High King can hardly make you uncomfortable if he can't see you."

She drew in a sharp breath and sank to her knees again. Looking down at her hands clasped in her lap, she said very softly, "But that means I can't see him either."

Merlin leaned back, studying her. Gone was the perfectly controlled young queen. Before him was a very young woman, distraught with unforeseen emotions. "I see that there is a bigger problem than I had thought." After a moment he rose and pulled her from her knees to her feet, then seated her carefully in a chair and poured a glass of wine, which had been set conveniently on the table by the chairs. He handed it to her. "Drink it." He poured himself a glass and sat across from her. "Tell me how you came to marry Gorlois and what you think of him."

Obediently she took a sip. "He's a good king. Always loyal to Ambrosius, and he worked hard to gain the allegiance of other kings for Ambrosius. He's not as certain of Uther. Thinks him a bit hot-headed."

"True enough," Merlin said encouragingly.

"He was married to my oldest sister, Anna, who chose him as her consort to rule Dumnonia. I was much younger than Anna – and Gorlois – so I didn't really know either of them well. When she died, I inherited her title as Lady of the Land, and Gorlois arranged to marry me. He's – he's been kind." Merlin noticed her emphasis on the 'been'. "But sometimes he seems more like a father than a husband."

"You feel what for him?"

"Usually, affection. I would not act in a way that harms him or his pride." She took another sip of wine. "We have two daughters – pretty little girls, but he pays little attention to them." Her eyes found her lap again. "He's truly Roman that way, thinking only boys are important."

"And yet, he chose the Lady of the Land," Merlin pointed out.

"Oh, he's astute. He knows he must have the loyalty of the tribe."

After a moment of silence, Merlin asked, "And how do you feel about Uther?"

She didn't answer directly. "I went to the marketplace yesterday. I was allowed to go out of the tent then, you see. I was not a prisoner, as I am today. Oh, Gorlois saw that I had a guard to keep me safe from harm, but they didn't interfere with my shopping, and later when I wanted to climb the wall so that I could see the whole town before me and the countryside beyond, they let me go, staying a distance back so that I'd have privacy.

"I was amazed at the vastness of the city that went on and on with hustle and bustle everywhere. Then, as I gazed out at the great forests and all the shades of green in the pastures and farmlands, a voice came from right next to me, quite startling me. 'Which view do you like best?' he asked. I turned to face him, and saw that it was Uther. Without thinking my heart set my voice to answer, 'The one before me.'"

The wine was near to spilling as she twisted and twisted the goblet. "Oh, Merlin. What can I do? He is the man I was meant to be with in this life as I was in all past lives, and as I will be in all lives to come. I know this, and he knows this. We clasped hands and we saw what has been and what was meant to be." She set the goblet down on the table and reached for my hands. "It's not just my body that aches for the love of this good, strong man, but my very soul."

Merlin knew, without doubt, that her sight of things that had been came from the Goddess. It was not the wild, imaginings of a woman infatuated with a king.

A queen sat before him, the equal of the High King, and in some ways the stronger of the two.

He also knew that she was right. She belonged with Uther, ruling at his side, and flashes from past visions of his own were remembered, and he realized that before him stood the mother of the greatest king of all.

Still holding her hands, he stood, his visions flooding his mind and growing him until he towered above her. "It shall be," he said. "You will be his queen, you will rule at his side, and you will be the mother of a king destined to be remembered for all time."

Yet he was the king's advisor, a man of wisdom who should not act in rashness. He leaned down close to her, his face just inches away. "It's not yet time for you to take your place at his side. You must wait, Ygerna. You must wait. All that your husband asks, you must do. In fact, you must anticipate what he desires, and meet those desires, being the best wife and queen that he can imagine. Already the gods of jealousy and suspicion have taken hold of him.

"You must not give him reason to let these gods drive him to an act that will damage his allegiance to the kingdom. You must be strong and bide your time. Can you do that, Ygerna?"

She stood to face him, her back straight, her chin high. "Yes. If you have spoken truly?"

"I have seen you at Uther's side."

"It is a sure prophecy?"

"It will be as I have said."

"Then, yes. Thank you, Merlin." The image of the queen-to-be dissolved and she hugged him. "Thank you, thank you."

79

BLAISE

But the Wheel of Fortune turned, and it was too late for Ygerna to work her magic on Gorlois, and too late for Merlin to advise the king to be wise and wait. That evening, when Ygerna did not attend the supper Uther had arranged for the commanders and their wives, he was visibly impatient and dismissed them all after an extremely abbreviated evening.

Just as Gorlois arrived at his tent, the king's token arrived – a large square amethyst, set with diamonds, along with a note expressing his hope that she would be well soon.

This set off a dark storm in Gorlois, and with it came the order to his troops to strike down their tents. Within the hour he and Ygerna and all of his men had left the city and were riding fast and furiously for his lands in the west.

It was done quietly, and so quickly that, until morning, no one realized that they had left. When Merlin heard, he sought out Uther, and the king was furious. "How dare they leave without permission?"

he shouted. "Gorlois has turned traitor and he will pay for the insult."

Nothing Merlin said could persuade him to desist from such a course. He became so angry with his advisor that he ordered him away. "Go to the Giant's Dance and finish the work you started," he commanded. "I have a battle to prepare for." By noon the city was nearly emptied of soldiers.

Merlin did as ordered, and in the days that followed tried to forget Uther's rashness as he threw himself into the task of lifting giant stones.

Uther laid siege to Gorlois' castle at Dimilioc, and there were skirmishes fought when Gorlois sought to break out. Meanwhile, Ygerna had been secreted a few miles away at Gorlois' castle at Tintagel, an impregnable stone fortress on an island with only a narrow causeway to the mainland.

Two months passed with no advantage to either side. Then one day Uther, himself, rode into the Giant's Dance with a small escort.

Merlin kept him waiting while he finished the ticklish job he was supervising, which happened to be the placing of the last top stone. An hour passed as the stone was eased into position and the supports removed.

He was aware that Uther was impatient, but saw, too, that he was impressed. "It's magnificent," he said when Merlin finally approached.

"Yes. It should be ready for commemoration on the Summer Solstice. Will you be able to attend?"

"I'll be here. With the soldiers," he added.

"The battle goes well then?" Merlin asked.

"No."

"You'll give it up?"

He gave a tight-lipped grimace. "Never." He swung down off his horse. "I thought Celts were known for their hospitality. Have you no wine to offer me?"

Merlin bent his head, but did not bend the knee. "Please follow me."

Not until the king had been refreshed with drink and food and a bowl to wash the dust off did he speak to Merlin again, but finally he walked back to the Giant's Dance with him and the two watched the sun set and the first stars appear. Merlin pointed out several of the astral phenomena marked by the stones, but saw that Uther was not much interested. "What is it, Sire? What brings you here?"

"Why you, of course," Uther responded. "I've been told that you are the only one who can make me well."

Merlin studied him. Indeed, he did not look well. He had lost weight. There were deep circles of darkness under his eyes. Earlier Merlin had noticed that his hands shook. "You apparently don't sleep well."

Uther's eyes widened. "How – how did you know that?"

Merlin ignored the question. "There's nothing physically wrong with you. I can't make you well when you're not sick."

He was angry. "Ambrosius said you'd always be there to help me, but I can see that he was wrong. Just as I expected."

"Exactly what did you expect, Sire?"

He was thoroughly agitated. "That I could never trust you. At the worst that you would gather supporters and make a claim to the throne."

"Don't you know that I have no interest in being a king? I am the Merlin, and that is all that I shall ever want to be."

"We'll see," he said smugly.

Merlin let his cape loose to flap in the wind and the sound it made would have ended most conversations, but Uther didn't budge. "Is there more?"

"Yes. That I could never count on your help or your support."

"A good advisor does not tell the king what he wants to hear, but what he needs to hear," Merlin retorted. "Your brother understood that. How is it that you ignored that lesson of statesmanship and must be constantly reigned in?"

"How dare you?" he shouted.

"How?" Merlin thundered back. "Because, now that your brother has died, I'm the only one who will dare. You should stop acting like a stallion in heat and make amends to Gorlois, who was the most valiant and loyal friend your brother had."

"I? I should make amends to him?" Uther sputtered. "It was his insult – his sneaking away like a thief in the night – that led to this war."

"Be honest, Uther. It was your injury to his pride – to his dignity – that led to this. You cannot court a man's wife and not expect a falling out." He looked ready to shout again, but Merlin continued quickly, "And already I've heard that the soldiers grumble at attacking those who fought at their side such a short time ago."

"You're mad, Merlin. I will listen to your lunatic ravings no longer." He stomped off angrily, and Merlin, no less aggravated, let him go.

80

BLAISE

When Merlin stepped outside his tent the next morning, he was not surprised to see that the king's tent had been struck, as well as those of his guard. All that was left of them was a cloud of dust to the north. That surprised him. North? Gorlois' castles were to the west by the sea.

He was working on the altar stone when he noticed a horse riding toward them, and saw that the rider was Ulfin, Uther's squire. "Hail, friend," he called out when Ulfin was close enough to hear him. He stepped out of the stone circle to meet him, and Ulfin slipped down off the horse.

"Don't know what you said to him, Merlin, but he's in a rare fit this morn."

"I can well imagine. It was not the friendliest of interviews."

"No? Well, it seems His Highness wants another chance at persuading you."

"Persuading me to what?" Merlin asked.

"To help him out of his sorrowful temper."

"Ha? I'm the last to do that."

"No, you must listen to me, Merlin. It was I who convinced the king to come to you. He can't go on like he has been. As his squire I've seen the tole it's taken on him. He's up pacing his tent night after night, not sleeping two winks. He won't eat. I can barely get him to take a little wine or water. This has gone on for weeks, mind you. He can't keep it up. I'm surprised he hasn't collapsed on us yet."

"Why did you ride north?"

"North?" Ulfin seemed confused. "Ah, we just went to the king's barrow. He's there now – maybe paying respects to his brother, maybe praying to his ghost for advice. Can't say. But I can say that I convinced him to talk to you again."

"You think you're doing me a favor?"

The sun was in his eyes, and Ulfin squinted as he looked up at Merlin. "Nay, I think I'll be doing him one."

"Well, I'm glad somebody's confident," Merlin grumbled, but he signaled to Ralf and soon their horses were saddled and the three were riding toward the barrow.

Uther was alone and pacing when they reached the burial mound – his guards giving him a wide berth as they sat around a campfire. All three dismounted, but when Ralf and Ulfin led the horses toward the fire, Merlin found himself approaching the king alone.

"Have you come to apologize?" the king asked, arms folded stubbornly, eyes narrowed.

"No. Are you going to fight me?" Merlin took a wrestler's stance and held it until Uther laughed.

Still laughing he shook his head at the futility of the situation, then put his arm about Merlin's shoulders to lead him inside the barrow. "You are quite mad, you know."

"It's been mentioned before." A smile came to Merlin's lips. "And I must be near to barking at the moon to offer my help to you."

A look of genuine gratitude was offered to him. "What can we do?"

"Above all, what is it that you want, Sire?"

"I want to see Ygerna. To touch her. To love her openly. To make her my queen."

"Is it enough if I tell you that the sight has been given to me, and it will be so."

"I don't want to wait until Gorlois is dead from old age." After a moment's thought he added, "Nor do I want him killed. But I must hold her in my arms soon, Merlin. I must!"

Merlin looked at him steadily, a plan already formulating. "Go back to your camp. Give me ten days, then I will send Ralf to Ulfin with instructions. You must give me your word, Sire, that you will do exactly as I tell you when the time comes."

"Yes. Yes, I will," he said eagerly.

"One thing more, King Uther."

"Anything, Merlin."

"When it is over, I will ask you to do something, and you will do it with no argument." Merlin waited patiently through the long pause that followed.

"Aren't you going to tell me what it is?" he finally asked.

"No. I will tell you that it will not harm anyone, nor harm the kingdom."

There was no careful consideration from Uther. He had what he wanted, did not care about the cost, and answered immediately. "You have my word."

81

BLAISE

Dimilioc had been a pleasant place when Merlin had last seen it as an apprentice to its Master Singer, Gerd. Set on a high plateau, its pastures were lush with tall grasses of softest green that seemed constantly moving to a perpetual breeze that blew in from the ocean. Large rocks so dark they seemed black, formed a thousand islands in the grass – bothering the sheep not at all, but continually irritating those who tried to farm.

The castle had seemed a place of welcoming comfort to all those coming down the old Roman road, its gates always open like a wide smile. Now it loomed high over the surrounding pastures and farms, the walls a good ten feet higher than when Merlin had lived there, and the gates were slammed shut. Men were stationed at even paces around those walls, and even though Merlin was looking from the top of a distant hill, he could see that they were armed and alert.

The castle was ringed on three sides by Uther's camp, with a high cliff at its back. By the look of it Gorlois still controlled the top of the cliff, for it was his standard flying there. Merlin's hilltop was to the south. He had no intention of riding into camp and had Ralf set up a small tent for him before he sent him off to find Ulfin. He decided he had enough time for a nap and took advantage of it, so a few hours later, when he heard horses outside, he was startled awake and a bit disoriented until Ralf poked his head into the tent and jabbered, "Sire. Sire? 'Tis the king, himself, who awaits you, Sire."

Merlin grumbled, but tossed his blanket aside, rose to his feet, splashed water onto his face from a bowl Ralf had set out, dried his face on his sleeve without looking for a towel, and stepped outside to a bright afternoon sun. He squinted, nodded his head vaguely toward the king, and asked Ralf to fetch a skin of wine and four cups. Then he gestured toward several of the rocks. "We might as well sit while I tell you what we're going to do."

As soon as Ralf had delivered the wine, he sent him scurrying for his saddlebag, and watched Uther as he lifted the cup to his lips. The king looked better, he decided. His faith in Merlin's words seemed to have affected his regimen, for now there was a healthy glow to his cheeks, his eyes were eager, and he no longer looked weak.

The saddlebag was soon before him. Merlin reached in, pulled out a roll of parchment, and undid the binding. There were three sections, each about a foot square. He passed the first to Uther. "I'm not much of an artist, but the sketch you see will at least give you an idea. This is Tintagel where Gorlois has sent Ygerna. It's a very unusual and beautiful place in the spring and summer, but in the late fall the wind takes over, blowing cold into every crevice and no matter how much wood is burned in the fireplaces and braziers, one never truly gets warm.

Generally, Gorlois moves his court to Dimilioc in the fall, leaving only a few guards and servants to tend the castle. Since it's now close to Midsummer you might think the weather will be good there, but the wind never stops and seems designed just to pluck you off a cliffside. The wind," Merlin said, "will be our first enemy.

"As you can see, Tintagel is basically an island with just a thin bridge of land to the mainland. One man set right here," he pointed at the intersection of causeway and mainland, "can beat off an entire army unless an arrow gets him, but it would have to be a pretty lucky arrow since the causeway is so narrow that only one horse at a time can ride onto it, and the height of the walls is over the guard's head.

What makes the whole thing even more formidable is the height of the land. It's a cliff that overlooks the sea on the mainland, with no real beach below. The whole island is also mostly the same height as the cliff, though on parts of it there are trails leading down to the sea. The widest trail leads to the docks. Gorlois does a fair share of trading when he's not off fighting battles."

"Is that how we get in?" Uther asked. "By boat?"

"I considered that," Merlin told them, "but there is always someone keeping a sharp lookout for boats and for sure we'd be spotted. Also, we're going in at night. No one would attempt a landing at night. There are rocks that have made a regular graveyard of boats. It takes a sharp hand and an even sharper eye to make a landing there."

Merlin passed a second parchment around. This one showed a close view of the causeway. He pointed to the bottom of it. "There's a trail that leads here, below the houses on the cliff top. No one should be on it at night, but if we do meet someone, don't stop. Keep riding as if we have a mission ahead. We'll leave the horses on this side of the causeway and go in by foot. Here. When the tide is low, there's a narrow path along the footings. It leads to a trail on the island that most the soldiers don't know about, though the servants do. There's a wine cellar and several caves used for storage down low, and it's just possible that we may run into someone." He held up two fingers. "That's the second danger - the possibility that someone from the castle will be using the trail tonight."

Uther's eyes got brighter. "Tonight then? We'll go tonight?"

"The moon's nearly full. It should give us some visibility. We can't use torches. The path is steep and narrow. We won't be able to see it well. That's the third danger, and also the fourth. Waves hit the island all the way around, including the causeway walls. If the wind's bad and the sea's rough, the waves will wash over us again and again along the base of the causeway. If we survive that, the bottom third of the trail will be wet and slick."

Ulfin groaned. "I hate getting wet."

Uther ignored him, sounding positively enthusiastic. "Are there more obstacles?"

"The trail leads to the postern gate. I imagine a servant will open the door to us if it's locked." Ulfin groaned again. "If it's a guard," Merlin continued," you may have to kill him, though I'd prefer it if you just rendered him unconscious."

"Once in the castle what happens?" Uther prompted.

Merlin passed the third and last sheet of parchment to them. "This shows a layout of the castle. Just inside the postern gate is a stairway. Half way up is the Steward's room and above that is the main floor lookout, with windows facing the sea to the north and west and south. Hopefully there will be only one guard on duty there at night and his attention will be engaged keeping an eye out for ships.

The rest of the guards should be stationed where they can see outside threats and won't be looking for an inside threat. The guard-room and guards' sleeping quarters are by the main entrance at the causeway. At the top of the stairs next to the main lookout the castle proper begins. I'm fairly sure that I've remembered the main rooms correctly, but I'm not sure about the number of rooms on the third level. I had quarters in the fourth and top level with the servants.

I do know that the room on the third level that is farthest west – you see, I've marked it with an 'X' – was the room that Gorlois and Anna, his first wife, slept in. If nothing's changed, that's where Ygerna will be."

Ulfin was frowning. "Assuming we make it all the way up the cliff, the minute that we knock on the postern gate and someone sees us, he'll alert the guards and we'll have a full-scale battle. I'm also assuming that since Gorlois has seen fit to guard his wifely treasure, he'll have a good number of well-trained guards near her at all times. What about that, Merlin?"

"Oh, that's the fun part," Merlin answered him. "We're going in disguise."

82

BLAISE

Merlin had known immediately how to get Uther inside the castle. But after sending Ralf to Londinium, he spent five of the ten days agonizing about whether he should do it. Later, when everyone in the kingdom knew his name and reputation, he felt no qualms about his decisions. He was so sure he was right in all his actions, so sure of his visions, that there was no doubt. But Merlin was at that time a very young man without much experience who had the responsibilities of heading all the Druids, not only of Britannia, but of the settled world, and now he had taken on the added responsibility of king making.

Oh, he knew that Uther and Ygerna were destined to be together, and that they would make the babe who would become the greatest king of all, but was he really supposed to make that happen now? He could wait for the wheel of fate to decide the outcome, but what then? Would the outcome really be the same? What if a different child was born? What if there was no child at all? Ah, but was it vanity that made him want to forge ahead? Was he so sure that now was the time?

Merlin used all the strength of Druid training during those five days - secluded, fasting, purifying himself, casting visions and searching them for truth, then analyzing his very soul for the answer. At the end of those five days the doubt was cast away.

Three more days passed until Ralf returned, having followed Merlin's specific instructions to gather what was needed. He let the man rest a day, then the two set off to meet Uther.

The four men ate a light supper, and then dressed as Merlin instructed them. It had been easy for Ralf to find cloaks and saddle cloths with Gorlois' Cornish symbols, for he had left Londinium in such a hurry that some of his baggage had been left behind.

Nor were the horses a problem. A large grey, resembling Gorlois' horse was in the king's stable, ready for borrowing, and the others, of nondescript color, were already at the Giant's Dance for the taking.

The only problem for Ralf was finding a ring that looked like the one that Gorlois always wore. He finally bought a large rectangular ruby and had a goldsmith set it, paying well for quick service.

Merlin combed and cut Ulfin's hair to look like that of Sir Brastius, whom he resembled, and was satisfied that he could pass for the man at a distance.

With dye made from berries he darkened Uther's fair hair and curled it, padded his shoulders, and instructed him to keep gauntlets on so that the fine hair on his arms wouldn't show.

Working with a mirror of polished bronze, he drew lines from the edge of his nostrils down to his chin to age his face and glued on a stubby beard like Sir Jordan wore. Other than a cloak, Ralf wore no disguise. He would stay with the horses. As a final instruction he told them all to put on the hoods of their cloaks and to keep their faces in shadow as much as possible. He added, "Let me do the talking. I am good at imitating the Cornish accent, and can do the bass of Sir

Jordan as well."

It was only a few miles to the gully that led down to the base of the cliff opposite Tintagel. The path was steeper than Merlin remembered. At first his horse balked, refusing to go down, but Ralf came close and slapped its rear as he passed and whether that did the trick or its instinct as a herd animal took over Merlin never knew, but at last it followed the others.

At the bottom of the trail, alongside the creek which was swollen enough to flood the path in several places, Merlin took the lead. The moon had not cooperated for the night was dark, cloudy with the hint of a storm coming. This did not concern him. It actually might aid to keep them hidden. Merlin moved slowly, letting the horse feel the way when he couldn't see the path, and the others stayed close behind.

Before they reached the foot of the causeway the rain started and the wind picked up. They were about thirty feet from the causeway when Merlin drew up and dismounted. The others followed his lead, each handing the reins to Ralf. Merlin backed him into the overhanging cliff which curved slightly inland at that point. "It won't be completely dry here with the wind whipping the rain in, but at least the waves won't reach you and they won't be able to see you from above," he said in a low voice.

Ralf settled a feed bag over the head of each horse. "This should keep them quiet," he whispered. "Good luck."

"And to you," Merlin replied.

"No talking," he said to the others. "Stay close and remember it will be slippery." He peered around the cliff, looking up to see if he could spot any activity. There were lights in the castle and at each end of the causeway – one at the castle entrance, and one at the guardhouse on the mainland, but as far as he could tell no one was looking down at them and the lights weren't moving.

Keeping close to the shadowed cliff, he moved quickly and was pleased to see that Uther was right next to him. Ulfin was only slightly farther back, but caught up when a massive wave pounded the rocks just below and broke in a high splatter that soaked all of them.

Merlin shook the water out of his eyes, clung to the cliffside with both hands, and continued going, his steps slow and tentative until he felt a punch in his arm and turned to see Uther gesturing for him to go faster.

The king was right. This was the spot where they were most vulnerable, because from both the causeway and the castle they were visible if anyone happened to be looking. Merlin took a deep breath for courage, and increased his speed, stepping from one slippery rock to the next, sliding his feet and clinging to the wall, silently telling himself over and over that they would succeed. His visions had shown that. He was sure of it, so there was no reason to fear.

Unless, of course, he'd misinterpreted the visions. Enough, he silently told himself, and pocketed his misgivings. He needed every bit of concentration to simply move forward.

He learned quickly to brace himself every fourth step, for at that point the waves pounded into him, covering him completely to the waist. The third time that happened they nearly lost Ulfin, but Uther grabbed his arm, slamming him back to the wall, and Ulfin managed to get a grip and hold until the waves pulled back.

As they inched closer to the center the wind picked up. The waves came as high as their shoulders now and the sound of the water was deafening. He looked back at the other two to see how they were faring. In the rain and the darkness he couldn't see more than a dark outline of Ulfin. Uther had his teeth clenched, but plodded forward relentlessly and that pushed Merlin to keep moving. He was grateful to all aspects of his god when they finally succeeded in reaching the island.

This time Merlin wasted no time, starting quickly up the trail that snaked north and west to the open sea. Not that all sides of Tintagel weren't surrounded by sea, Merlin thought as he struggled to find secure footing up the slippery slope.

As they climbed higher the waves could no longer reach them and he was grateful, but the sound they made crashing below was loud and constant. It must be the storm, he thought. He remembered that the sea sang a constant song here, drumming against the rocky shore, but he had forgotten how dramatic it could be.

They were moving slowly, buffeted by the wind so that care had to be taken at each step, even though it was less slippery as they climbed higher. He realized that they were fortunate, indeed, to have been so drenched by the rain and the waves, for if the wind had been able to lift a cloak, they'd have flown off the wall like seabirds.

By the time they reached the postern gate the storm seemed worse than ever, the wind shrieking a startling treble to the pounding base of the waves. He wasn't sure as he rapped on the locked gate whether anyone inside could hear him.

He pulled his hood tight around his face and checked to see that the other two had done the same. He was pointing to his ring finger to remind Uther to flash it if anyone questioned their identity when he heard someone lifting the bar on the far side of the door. A moment later it opened a crack and a face peered out at them. It was the Steward, himself – a face that Merlin knew well from his apprentice-ship.

In a deep accented voice Merlin commanded, "For pity's sake, let us in, Hanno. We're about to drown out here."

"Sir Jordan, what?" At that point he made an obsequious bow, backing up as he did so. Merlin took advantage, pushing in with his back to the steward. Holding the door open, he let Uther and Ulfin pass him.

They both started up the stairs and Merlin followed with the steward trotting noisily behind. Uther continued past the observation room without being noticed and quickly crossed the grand hall to the staircase that led toward the bedrooms.

Merlin pulled Ulfin toward the receiving room. "We'll be in here, drying our cloaks at the fire. Something to warm our bellies might be nice. Is there still soup on the fire?" He heard Ulfin grunt in affirmation.

"Right away, Sir," Hanno said, moving toward the kitchen.

"Take some up to King Gorlois before you go serving us."

"Yes, Sir." He was at the door, but turned back, "Will you be staying the night, Sir? Should I get a fire going at your hearths?"

"Nothing would please us more, but our king and master has it in mind to be back with the troops by cock crow."

He started off toward the kitchen. Merlin heard footsteps coming toward them from the corridor that led to the lookout post. This was what he had feared.

He threw his cloak off and pulled his sword, standing to the left of the doorway. Ulfin, to his credit, followed suit, taking a post to the right, but the steward intercepted the guard.

"Back to your post, Man. It's just the king coming for a conjugal visit, and Sir Jordan and Sir Brastius warming up by the fire." He didn't hear the reply, but the footsteps sounded again, going back toward the lookout.

Now he wondered how Uther was faring and peered out of the room and up the steps. He was in time to see that Uther had reached the third floor and knew that under the cloak Uther had his sword ready. His other hand – the one with the ring – held his cloak tightly about his neck as if he was cold. A guard was stepping toward him, sword in hand.

But at that moment Merlin saw Ygerna coming along the hallway toward them, a red robe thrown over her nightclothes, her walk urgent and purposeful.

The guard was looking at her now, which was fortunate because the top of the stairway was brightly lit with a wall-sconced torch, and Uther was under the light, a smile on his face. To her credit she didn't stop, but Merlin saw the look of startlement on her face as she recognized the High King.

Stepping quickly between Uther and the guard, she threw herself into Uther's arms. "Welcome home, Sire," she said softly, and Uther, with his head down near her shoulder hugged her and turned her down the hallway, keeping his face averted.

She looked back at the guard as she led him away, "You may stand down, Marcus. Go get some sleep. We will be safe from harm with our Lord home and ready to protect us."

There was another woman, her maid, Merlin assumed. Ygerna laughed a joyous laugh. "Merrila, you may sleep in your own room tonight." The maid slipped into another room and had disappeared before the two passed it.

If she had whispered, "Yes, my Lady," it was so soft that Merlin couldn't hear the words.

The great relief that Merlin felt was something he'd never share with anyone, because he had never shared the worry.

What if Ygerna had changed the way she felt about Uther and had cried out to the guard?

What if she hadn't changed her mind, but was so startled by his unexpected presence that she'd cried out?

Or, even though she had feelings of love for Uther, she had decided that she could never betray her husband?

Oh, in his mind he had played out every possible scenario and had worried about each of them, so the relief he felt was so physical that it made him weak in the knees. What an amazing, self-assured, wonderful, quick-thinking woman she was. What an incredible High Queen she would make!

Merlin and Ulfin slipped away from the door as the guard came down the stairs, passed their room, and went off down the corridor that led to his sleeping quarters. A few moments later the Steward passed them, carrying food and wine up the stairs.

Merlin crept to the doorway again and listened intently. Apparently Ygerna answered the Steward's knock, thanking him for his thoughtful service. Moments later he came back down the stairs and headed back to the kitchen.

When he arrived with wine and soup for them, both Merlin and Ulfin were standing before the fire with their backs to the door and hands outstretched to the flames. Their long cloaks had been spread out to dry. Using a deep voice, without turning, Merlin said, "Just set the tray on the table, Hanno." When he heard the soft clunk of the tray, he added, "You may retire now. We'll be fine, and there's no telling what time we'll be leaving, so we'll show ourselves out."

The footsteps faded away down the stairs. Simultaneously Merlin and Ulfin sighed in relief and seated themselves at the table. Hot soup and mulled wine had never tasted so good. Still, they knew better than to completely relax.

After a few moments quiet reflection, Merlin was up on his feet and pacing, understanding that he'd never be able to rest until they were safely out and far away from Tintagel, and Ulfin nervously checked the doorway every few moments, listening for any signs of activity.

They passed nearly two hours this way. At midnight the guard changed at the observation post. Both of them had their swords out and ready, but neither the new guard nor the old came near their room, content to exchange a few words about the violent weather before the one took up the post and the other shuffled off to sleep.

Merlin was relieved that they had seemingly been forgotten, but the relief was short-lived, for there was a sudden commotion at the main gate. He could not hear what it was about and worried that Ralf had been discovered with the horses.

Now there were many voices and the sound of many footsteps coming along the corridor toward them. He and Ulfin jumped to the doorway, swords drawn. "We'll lay him out here on one of the tables," a voice Merlin recognized as Cador's said as they entered the main reception room.

"What happened?" asked a guard.

"He led a raid into the King's camp," the first voice answered. "There was a burst of fighting and he caught a sword in the chest.

Then it was all over as quick as it started."

Another voice added, "They let us take his body."

From above came a cry of dismay – a female cry, and Ygerna was running down the steps, her hair unbound, her red robe flying. Other doors opened and soon her female attendants were beside her as she flung herself on the body of her husband.

83

BLAISE

Hanno was chugging up the stairs, barefoot, slinging a robe over his shoulders as he came. "What has happened? Sir Jordan?" Nervously, he glanced back at the small room where Merlin and Ulfin were hiding.

The real Sir Jordan answered in a gruff voice. "What has happened is that your master was killed in a skirmish and we have surrendered to the king's men."

"But – but how can that be, Sir? The Master was here, sleeping with his wife. With my own eyes I saw him and unlocked the postern gate – to him, to Sir Brastius, and to you, Sir Jordan. The Master went right up these stairs and Lady Ygerna welcomed him."

All eyes turned to Ygerna who, at those words, looked up at the assembly with tear-streaked face, her eyes and mouth round with horror, her hands flown to her cheeks. Then her eyes went to the top of the stairs, and we all saw Uther standing there.

"What treachery is this?" cried Sir Jordan, drawing his sword.

But Merlin was faster. His sword went back to his belt and with one hand he mussed Ulfin's styled hair and with the other, he pulled off his beard and pocketed it. Ulfin sheathed his sword too, and the two of them slipped to the back of the crowd as Uther made his way slowly down the stairs.

"Do none of you churls bow to your king?" Merlin shouted and sank to a knee, his head bowed. Those around him slowly followed suit until only Sir Jordan was left standing.

His eyes had settled on Merlin. "Merlin? Merlin, you are here in Tintagel? It was your doing, wasn't it? Your evil sorcery? I understand it now. You cast a glamour and made yourselves look like us." He had momentarily forgotten the king and was so angry that he advanced on Merlin."

Merlin rose to his feet with dignity and used the voice that would cast fear into the hearts of all but the strongest of men. Indeed, Sir Jordan stopped moving toward him. He didn't retreat, however, so he wasn't entirely cowed. "There was no sorcery, Sir Jordan. Men see what they expect to see."

Hanno was not to be stopped. "But I saw the ring. He had the Master's ring."

Uther held his hand up so that everyone saw the flash of the ruby. "This ring? Is it like one of Gorlois'?"

Sir Jordan spun about to face him. "I repeat," he said, "what treachery is this that brings the wrong king to the bedroom of the queen?"

Uther had his sword in hand and had nearly reached the bottom step when Merlin strode to his side. "Treachery?" he said in a voice that carried to every corner of the castle. "The treachery is not on the part of the High King, but on the rebel, Gorlois, who had the audacity to forsake the king he had sworn to protect and defend. It was his disloyalty that was traitorous."

There were murmurs as the servants and soldiers turned nervously to one another.

Uther rose magnificently to the occasion. "The war is over. Those who supported Gorlois in his malfeasance are to swear oaths to me and will be forgiven." He stared at Sir Jordan until the man wisely decided that it was more prudent to change his allegiance from his dead friend to his powerful king. He bent his knee and swore the oath.

The other soldiers came quickly, relieved to join the High King again. Most of them had fought with Ambrosius and some had fought under Uther. One by one, they swore to protect and defend as well, nudging each other to get to the front of the line.

When it was done, Uther gave orders to the Steward to see that the body was prepared for burial, to the Captain of the Guard to dig a grave, and then called for Ulfin to ride back to his campsite to bring back his personal guards.

"And make sure that everyone – on both sides – understands that the fighting is over. The army is to wait at the camp until we can join them. Tell them no longer than three days."

Everyone melted away to their separate tasks until only Uther, Ygerna, and Merlin were left. Carefully Uther placed an arm around the queen's shoulders. "We will bury him tomorrow. On the day after that we will wed. Merlin, you will perform both ceremonies before all, and then we will ride for Londinium where a second ceremony will be performed by the archbishop. Ygerna, you should think of all you need to pack. We won't be coming here again." He held her gently and slowly led her back up the stairway.

That left Merlin alone in the huge reception room with the body of Gorlois. For a long moment he looked at his old friend, the bear-like frame shrunken now in death. He knew that he would honor the man who had readied Logres for its true king with kind words at the burial ceremony. Let his jealousy and rebellion be forgotten.

Oh, and thinking of things forgotten, Merlin clapped his hands to his brow. Not even the king had remembered that Ralf was hiding below with the horses. He'd have to ride out through the storm and bring him back to the castle himself.

Grumbling quietly, he retrieved his cloak and headed for the guard station. He'd ask for a horse on the other side of the causeway and ride along the cliff until he came to the first path down, then double back for Ralf. At least this time, he wouldn't be lashed by waves and clinging to walls the whole way.

With Ralf in tow Merlin was back at Tintagel in time to take a seat right next to the roaring fireplace as breakfast was served.

Ralf had spent a night where cold and fear alternated making him irritable. He had heard the noise of men riding in and the commotion in the guardhouse and had feared the worst when they clattered over the causeway. He was sure we were discovered and spent hours debating whether he should take the horses and run or wait for us on the chance that we had slipped away safely.

Merlin tried to set him at ease by telling him he had done well to wait, and assuring him that the king would not forget his service on this night, but Uther, coming to the table with Ygerna, ignored Ralf and spoke no words of kindness or thanks. As soon as they had thawed out properly, he and Merlin found the steward and followed him to a warm guest room where they collapsed and slept until the sun was near to setting.

Ralf helped Merlin to brush his clothes and wash, then the two made their way to the burial site where the mourners and the curious villagers from the mainland had taken posts. The rain had finally stopped, and the sun had broken through the clouds and was settling slowly toward the ocean in a sky streaked with pink.

Solemnly Merlin watched as soldiers brought the body of Gorlois to the grave. Ygerna came next, walking just behind, dressed in a gown of deep blue, holding the hands of her two young daughters. As she took her place at the grave, her proud head high, her dark head scarf blowing in the wind, and her cloak blue like the ladies of the Holy Isle, Merlin could see her as priestess trained and Lady of the Land she held.

Uther and his guard, who had arrived while Merlin slept, came and took a place at the opposite side of the grave, and his eyes never left her.

Merlin began his song, beating a rhythm on a small hand drum, and the story of Gorlois and his place in the history of Logres held all in wonder. All the women were in tears by the end of it, Ygerna included, and the oldest girl, Morgausa. Merlin saw from her face that she had loved her father, and saw too that she glanced speculatively at Uther every so often.

The younger child, Morgana, did not cry - possibly too young to understand that her father was gone from her world. She had no glance for the king, but stared at Merlin during the entire ceremony, her dark eyes drinking in his every word and gesture.

It was all finished just as the sun dropped into the sea and Merlin made the final gestures that would send Gorlois' soul to Annwn and the peaceful finding of a new life.

The soldiers lowered his body into the ground and began to fill the grave from the mound of dirt. There was a startled noise of discordance from Morgausa, and she broke away from her mother and ran to the edge of the grave, pulling at the shovel of one of the soldiers.

Four of Ygerna's ladies reached her at the same time, struggled with her briefly, then pulled her away, back toward the castle. At Ygerna's urging a fifth lady took Morgana's hand and followed.

The little one looked back over her shoulder, her eyes not on the grave, but still on Merlin, and he felt … something – some power that struck him to startlement with the unexpectedness of it. As she moved farther and farther into the distance he realized it was the touch of her soul.

84

BLAISE

The wedding ceremony was to be at noon in the main assembly room. Merlin had grabbed a bun directly from the kitchen to break his fast and had taken it outside where he had found a convenient rock to sit on. His rock was close to the edge of the cliff – well away from the commotion of setting up for a wedding and cooking for a feast.

He sat for a time looking down at the massive waves that crashed on the rocks below and erupted with a constant spray of white foam that leaped back up toward the sky. They were pounding an irregular beat that had him totally absorbed, thinking of music which would suggest the power of the sea. Before he had half finished his bun, he was interrupted. "They tell me you're the Merlin."

"That's correct." He turned to the voice and saw Morgausa, a miniature of her mother, with the same straight posture and regal bearing. Her hair, though, was a brighter red, and he wondered if Ygerna's had been that color when she was that age. She must be about nine or ten years old.

"Do you really know the art of magic?" She was demanding an answer with not a bit of shyness or politeness.

Her boldness amused him and he smiled. "What is magic, but knowing things that most men don't know?" he asked.

There was no answering smile. "I want to learn magic. Will you teach me?"

"No."

Her eyes narrowed. "What if the king demands it?"

Merlin was still smiling. "The king will not demand it. If he did, I would refuse him."

She became so angry at his refusal, at his smile, at his power, perhaps, that she stamped her foot. "My mother could make him ask, and you WOULD do it."

Merlin stood up, making himself very tall, and she took a backward step. The voice he used had the power of sight in it, though it came so suddenly upon him that he hardly realized it himself. "You will learn no magic from me to make you Queen of the Dark Arts. I will never help you. Go away and bother me not again."

She looked suddenly frightened and he saw that her eyes were not grey like her mother's, but very green like a cat's. She turned and ran back to the castle where she stopped and stared at him. Very deliberately, still using power, he made a pushing gesture with his hand. She gasped and stumbled backward, then disappeared through a doorway.

He turned to look back at the water again, wondering at the feelings that made him harsh with a child. He put the bun to his mouth again, but couldn't taste it, so he wrapped a napkin around it and put it in the pocket of his robe. He'd lost his hunger. Queen of the Dark Arts?

He'd used those words. He knew in his heart that he was right, but he had no specific vision of her. It was more of a feeling that came so strongly that he knew he had the truth of it.

The child, Morgausa, was one he'd need to deal with in the future, a truly unfortunate situation, but for whom he didn't know.

For himself? For the girl? For her mother? Worse – for the king and the kingdom? No, the warning feeling gave no hint of answer. He knew only that there was an evil feeling about her.

85

BLAISE

Merlin kept the wedding ceremony simple and short on Uther's request. All of the guests were seated at the banquet tables. They rose when the king entered and stayed standing as Ygerna came to his side. She had chosen an untrimmed gown of rust velvet, her only jewelry understated diamond earbobs. Her expression was one of sadness and her gestures hesitant which managed to suggest she was mourning for Gorlois while going through with a wedding that was a duty not a choice. Her bearing was always so queenly that at the same time she conveyed the impression of being an extremely suitable bride for the High King.

Uther seemed to pluck from her this trick of sadness, looking to his guests as if he had been forced to this war and this marriage against his will, and was merely doing the honorable thing.

Merlin knew that hidden from the observers their hearts were singing, but as he spoke the words that would twine their lives together for all time, he too acted the part of the reluctant priest, his expression as sad as theirs. Only when he sang the final song did he allow his voice to travel to the flight of joy, marking their lives with the song of Logres that would triumph during their reign.

Indeed, it was the right note to strike, for when they all sat down to feast, the first toast offered was from Sir Jordan and it was a toast for happiness. Merlin had found the hall's harp so there was music as well as food and drink. He finished a ballad of love to enthusiastic applause and returning to his seat at the table reached for his goblet.

Cador came and sat down so heavily that the bench they shared tipped. When he had recovered his nearly spilled drink, Merlin faced him, wondering where his loyalties would fall. He started to express his sympathy, but Cador interrupted.

"I think this wedding is as difficult for you as it is for me. At first I saw only the red of treachery, but after hearing you speak at the funeral, Merlin, I felt healed. I'm grateful for your words. You both honored my father and tried to heal the breach of those who had fought each other."

Merlin was surprised to be so praised. He studied Cador's face, looking for truth. "I wonder," he said, "if the soldiers and their families will truly forgive King Uther."

"If I can do it, they can do it. I swear to you, Merlin, that I will cause the king no trouble. I will prove my loyalty to him as my father proved it to his brother."

"So it will be, my friend. I have seen you at his side."

Cador rose. "I will honor my father's memory. All of my life he told me that our hope lay in uniting our tribal lands under one king – that it was our job to bring the people together to make our land strong. I want him to be remembered, not as a man disloyal and squabbling, but as the man who paved the way for the Pendragons."

"He will be," Merlin answered, not quite believing it.

Cador turned and walked away, shoulders squared. Then for the first time Merlin felt the joy that Cador had loosed. He had worried that there would be hatred and recriminations. He was feeling proud, recalling his prediction about Cador, and a little smug until he realized that someone was watching him. He looked around and caught the eye of Morgana.

Since it was still afternoon both of Ygerna's daughters were present. Merlin had found himself watching them frequently. The elder he dismissed. He was just keeping an eye on her in case she tried some sort of mischief, but she seemed the model of decorum and grace, smiling and talking when directly addressed, but hands in her lap, alert, and looking about her pleasantly when not.

The younger daughter was more interesting to him. She had the dark coloring of her father, but was tiny and delicate looking, her frame not as big as either of her parents. She was probably about five years old, maybe six, but definitely no more than that. Merlin tried to think who she reminded him of, but couldn't grasp an image.

It was several weeks before he did realize who it was, and then it was a total surprise to him. He had traveled to Avalon, and the moment he saw Vivianne he realized that Morgana looked like her. When he remarked upon the resemblance, the Lady laughed. "I'm not surprised," she told him. "My mother and Ygerna's mother were sisters, one ruling the land and one ruling here."

But at the wedding feast Merlin was still trying to puzzle it out and failing. There was beauty in her young face, yet she was not perfectly formed like her sister, and not yet as poised. It was obvious that she was uncomfortable at her mother's side, and when Ygerna did try to engage her in conversation, she shrugged her tiny shoulders and didn't say much in reply. Her nurse was on the other side of her, but more interested in flirting with the soldier next to her than in entertaining the child.

Morgana seemed glad to be left alone with her thoughts, and her dark eyes locked onto Merlin's often. He wondered if it was because of the music. She listened to that attentively, obviously enthralled whenever he sang.

He would have to send a good harper to the king's hall. Perhaps the child had some talent.

He would definitely have a word with Ygerna and suggest some training for her if she hadn't already begun an instrument.

When the nurse finally did gather her up, she nodded to Merlin as he stood strumming the chords for a new song – nodded as if they were old friends and she was bidding him a silent farewell.

Silently he nodded back to her and smiled, but she had no answering smile. Her eyes, in fact, were harsh as they appraised him. He found this extremely disconcerting. It seemed that Ygerna had given the world two daughters worth watching, and since Merlin knew that already she carried the seed within her of a worthy king, he suddenly realized that all of Ygerna's children would be important to Britannia.

86

BLAISE

Before they set out to join the army the next morning, Uther summoned Merlin to the room he had shared with Ygerna. Merlin had, of course, been in the room before, and everything about it reminded him of Gorlois. It was no wonder that Uther was anxious to be away from Tintagel.

The two were alone, Ygerna off somewhere supervising the last-minute packing. "Sire?" Uther was staring out the window at some distant point on the sea and Merlin wondered if he had spotted a ship. "You wanted to see me?" Merlin persisted.

Finally Uther turned. The look he gave Merlin was not at all friendly which made Merlin wonder if he had done something to offend, and that made him angry, for he had done everything that Uther had asked and more. Everything! "Sire?" he asked again when no response seemed to be forthcoming.

Still Uther stared at him. Almost insolently Merlin folded his arms and leaned back against the wall. "Are we then at leisure to stare at each other all morning? I thought we were trying to make an early start."

Uther took two steps forward, picked a bronze goblet off the table, drained its contents, and then threw it violently against the wall right next to Merlin – who did not do him the courtesy of flinching. "Strange mood for a joyous bridegroom," Merlin said.

"Why didn't you know?" Uther finally said – though a hiss might describe better his tone.

"Know what? That people would gossip. Of course, they will. That's the nature of people, and it will get worse. When they learn that Ygerna's with child, some will whisper that Gorlois was his father so he can't be your heir, and others will whisper that he can't be your heir because he's a bastard. It's only to be expected."

Uther took a moment to digest this. Apparently it hadn't occurred to him. His next words stunned Merlin, for this was the man who had so longed to hold Ygerna in his arms that he had made himself sick with desire. "Why couldn't we have waited one more day?" he asked, emphasizing 'one more day' with lengthy pauses between each word. "Then Gorlois would have been dead, and there would have been no risk and nothing to gossip about."

Merlin straightened up and left the wall. "One more day?" Then, incredulously, "One more day, Uther? If we had waited one … more … day, the son Ygerna bears would not be the king who will unite and bring such glory to Britannia that all other kings will be measured against him. If we had waited one … more … day, it would have been a different babe."

Uther shook his head in denial. "Merlin, I want you to go far out of my sight. I will not have you near to offer your confused visions as advice. I will come to the Giant's Dance on Midsummer's Eve, and you and I will honor my brother. Then … then I don't want to see you again. Ever."

"I will gladly go, Uther. But you will see me once more at least – when I collect that which you promised me. When the child is born, I will come to take him away, and you will do nothing to hinder me." Merlin waited for the curt nod of acknowledgement that came before he turned on his heel and left the room – without permission.

87

BLAISE

Merlin was still furious when he arrived at the school. "What a wretched, ungrateful dolt. How can he possibly be related to Ambrosius? How can he possibly be the High King?"

I was sitting before the fire in my study. Merlin was pacing the room, making its rather generous proportion seem small.

When he finally appeared to be done fuming, I said, "Does it really matter? So what if he's too foolish to listen to you. You've accomplished what you set out to do, haven't you?"

I set my wine carefully on the small table next to my chair, leaned back, and crossed one leg over the other. "Your visions have shown that Uther is important only because he sires our future king of kings, so be done with him. Go be the Merlin for a while and let him run the kingdom without you."

"What if he ruins the kingdom as he runs it?"

"Again, what do your visions show you? The babe will most certainly still have a kingdom to run." I gave him a small smile.

"There have been many kings who've run a country without a Merlin at their sides."

Merlin paused, stared, flopped down in the chair across from me. He started to chuckle and it turned into a full-throated laugh. "I've turned into quite a peacock, haven't I?"

"It's not the first time I've had to reprimand you for strutting."

"I suppose that's why I burden you with all my concerns. You're the one person whom I trust to keep me on the path when I threaten to cut through the forest."

"I'm honored," I said dryly.

"I did have word from Timoreus that he has put the finishing touches on the Giant's Dance which leaves me free to catch up on Druid affairs."

"Did I mention that I have many scrolls addressed to you from all over Britannia and Gaul? So many that I'm running out of room to store them?"

He laughed again, this time at the pathetic face I was making. "All right, Master, but do you think I have time for a cup of wine before I tackle them?"

Merlin stayed with us for several weeks, sorting his many messages and sending instructions industriously. We heard that Uther and Ygerna had reached Londinium with their entourage and taken up residence. True to his word, a second wedding ceremony was performed by Dubricious to please the Christian contingent. Merlin managed to not only stay put and finish those tasks which were necessary, but to "consult" frequently with our Lady of the Lake, Vivianne. I must confess, I teased him about that and managed to draw a blush every time.

Midsummer's Eve found Merlin at the Giant's Dance, and I was fortunate enough to be with him. I had very much wanted to see this huge circle of stones, and I found it very impressive. To this day I can't imagine how Merlin was able to raise the giant slabs, let alone top them with massive lintels, even though he explained the process to me. "I used music, chanting in rhythm, with the men pulling on ropes to the beat." I just shook my head in wonder.

I do know how he was able to use the position of the sun and the moon and the stars, so that at regular times they would appear framed by the stones, for their timing was something that all Druids study, but this pleased Uther and struck wonder and whispers about Merlin's magic in the many soldiers who had accompanied the king.

Indeed, I thought the whole army must be there, though Merlin assured me that posts throughout Britannia were still manned at full strength. It was an amazing tribute to Ambrosius to see so many men there to honor him, for each man there had truly chosen to come.

Even Merlin commented on Uther's wisdom in that. The army had not been ordered to come, they had been invited, and that so many accepted the invitation was an honor to Ambrosius that none could have foreseen. Well, perhaps Merlin could have, but this time he hadn't.

I had hoped to meet Queen Ygerna, but because Merlin insisted on staying well away from them and their tent, and since they stayed only the one night and started off for Londinium soon after sunup the next morning, I missed my chance. I made my own observations about the royal family during the ceremony, however, trying not to let Merlin's stories color them.

Morgausa was, indeed, a beautiful young girl, physically very like Ygerna, though she showed every indication that she would grow into a woman even more beautiful than her mother. Her features were slightly less pronounced, meaning the cheekbones were not as prominent, the mouth was a little smaller, the eyebrows had less point. The flaming red hair was brighter than her mother's and would have attracted attention even if she was not the queen's daughter, and her young body had already taken on some of the curves of woman-hood.

She had the same proud carriage as her mother, but there was not a bit of humbleness to soften it. She was already turning heads and she knew it and used it, eyeing the younger, better-looking soldiers with teasing looks and amusement at their reactions. She was only nine years old, but looked thirteen, and acted like an eighteen-year-old barmaid. They would have to keep a close watch on that one, I decided.

Morgana, as Merlin had said, was tiny for a six-year-old. There was no plumpness left from babyhood. She was fragile looking, and seemed glad to hold the hand of her nurse, as if she were drawing strength from her to meet the looks of the curious.

Her complexion was darker than that of her mother and sister – as Merlin had said, she was more like Gorlois in that aspect, but her hair was not dark brown as I had thought it would be from his description, but a combination of her parents – the black and the light red making a rich auburn. The hair was definitely her best feature, already hanging in thick curls to her waist.

I imagined her running with that magnificent hair streaming like a banner behind her, and quite enjoyed the image. Her eyes were a dark chocolate brown and they took in everything that was happening with solemn regard. When Merlin was around, her eyes, unwaveringly, found him and devoured him almost – what? Hungrily. That's the word. It was as if she had a hunger for his words, his songs, his very gestures, and tried to draw it into herself and keep it for a memory.

Merlin's description of Ygerna seemed accurate to me, but I must add to it the happiness that shone in her face. At the moment her life must have seemed perfect to her. She was the queen of all Britannia's queens with all the wealth and honors that come with the title. She truly loved her new husband, and it was clear that he likewise adored her. She had two lovely daughters, and a son was on the way. I wondered if she realized that, and decided that she must know, for she had that glow that the joy of fecundity often causes in women. Yes, she truly was a lovely woman and complimented Uther in all ways.

I hadn't seen Uther since he was a young boy. He had blonde hair and a rugged face that would probably seem attractive to a woman. Indeed, I had heard rumors of the many women who had tried to entice him to marriage before he met Ygerna, and the many, many women who had been content to bed him, though, strangely, I had not heard of any illegitimate children.

His carriage was definitely that of a soldier. I saw enough of him on horseback to realize that his special expertise was cavalry. He sat a horse like a centaur, his control over the beast perfect, but so softly done that it was invisible.

His soldiers seemed well trained too, and obeyed him instantly and without question. Merlin had said that many of them disagreed with his recent civil war, yet I could see that they respected his ability as a warrior and would let him lead them. When they rode or marched in formation as they did both coming and leaving, the Roman background in training was obvious to me, for I had observed Romans for myself as a young man when training as a Druid in Gaul.

In all I was rather pleased with the royal family, though when I said so to Merlin, I had to endure a lecture about the king's pitfalls, and when that was done, I had to hear again about the dangers he felt about Morgausa.

The day was splendid and the ride home was very pleasant, so I quite enjoyed myself, feeling lucky that his tirade didn't last long.

Altogether Merlin stayed in Ynys Witrin for three months. Just after the summer solstice he began for the first time to grow a beard, and six weeks later it was quite respectable. He had let his hair grow to shoulder-length too, and I had to agree that he looked like a different man – a much older man, which, of course, was his intention.

He asked if he could borrow an apprentice and together, we decided upon a sturdy boy of thirteen years named Lleon who came from the old Roman town of Viroconium in Powys. The boy had dark hair like Merlin, and his same stringy build. We were sure he could pass as this elder Merlin's son.

Merlin chose two of the sturdy mountain ponies favored by Cambrians for their skill on slippery mountain trails, and loaded their packs with medicinal herbs and powders. He would go as Calisca, a healer, on this journey. If anyone asked at the school, we did not know where the Merlin had gone. He had wanted time alone to study and meditate.

Even I didn't know where he was really going, but I knew that it had to do with the coming of the prince who would someday be the High King of Britannia, and of course I did hear the whole tale later.

88

BLAISE

Calisca rode slowly north with his son, Lleon, traveling occasionally on the Roman roads which were still the main thoroughfares, but more often on the trails that led from village to village. They never went hungry. There were always illnesses to treat and injuries to tend with consequent invitations to a meal or sleeping quarters.

Lleon proved a cheerful and uncomplaining companion, eager to learn medicine which he picked up quickly, soon helping to gather and prepare herbs in the small leather pouches Merlin preferred.

He was also keen on traveling, commenting happily on each new sight and keeping eyes and ears open to absorb information gleaned from each new acquaintance. Merlin encouraged this, knowing that people talk in front of a youngster when they would be reticent with an adult.

Lleon did not know the true purpose of the journey. He did know that he was very fortunate to have been chosen to accompany the Merlin. So, he determined that he would do everything asked of him to the best of his ability.

Lleon was supposed to learn not only on this journey, but on any journey he took in the future. He should learn not only healing, but about the countryside they were passing through, looking for landmarks that he could recognize should he be sent there again.

He should learn about the people he met. What were their occupations? What crops were raised? What goods created? What sold? How did they feel about their fellow villagers? The chieftains and kings of their territories? The High King Uther and his new wife?

What about religion? Did they follow the old ways or listen to those preaching about the Christ? Did they welcome and honor bards in their villages?

How safe did they feel? What was the main threat if they didn't? Was it the Saxons or the Irish coming from the sea? Or bands of pirates? What about the Picts to the north? Was there trouble there?

And this information should be shared with Merlin or with his other superiors so that action could be taken if necessary. Merlin was very pleased to find that the boy was a natural gatherer of gossip and easily got people to tell him their opinions.

Also, Lleon should try to make friends, so that if there was need, he would have a place of refuge.

Merlin was amused by all the stories that were going around about the Merlin. He was the king's sorcerer according to many, who could appear and disappear at will wherever he chose. People said he had been in several places at the same time. Trustworthy people had sworn to it.

Merlin had raised the fallen monoliths of the Giant's Dance with magic, singing them into place. He smiled at that one. He had sung songs with a steady rhythm to keep the men pulling together. Even more remarkable, Merlin had made the sun stand still to honor King Ambrosius. That, of course, was an illusion during every summer solstice, but perhaps not as obvious without the stones of the Dance to mark it.

He was especially interested to see how the folk would interpret Uther's marriage to Ygerna. He learned that Merlin had used magic to change Uther into an image of Gorlois, and that no one would have ever suspected had not Gorlois been killed that same night and his body brought to Tintagel where Ygerna and Uther were bedded.

And then Merlin had appeared – magic again – to marry them on the spot, turning Uther back into himself. Whenever he heard that one, he stroked his new beard thoughtfully. Except for the magic it had pretty well happened just like they said. Then he heard the variation that Merlin made Gorlois appear in two places at once, then turned the bedded Gorlois into Uther as everyone in the castle watched.

Everyone they met had loved Ambrosius and had welcomed his return and his treatment of the Saxons. They did not resent the fortresses that he had garrisoned. It made them feel safer, and they hated the Saxons, for the Saxons had killed their kings on the Night of the Long Knives and it was a Saxon who had killed the High King with poison.

They still felt anger for Vortigern's betrayal, for he had invited the Saxons to their land and had rewarded them with a foothold in the country. Vortigern would forever be known as a traitor.

They hoped that Uther would continue the policies of Ambrosius, and drive the Saxons back to their lands across the sea. The village folk weren't as confident in Uther and his abilities, but the soldiers they met had a healthy respect for him, considering him an excellent battle leader.

In several places they heard that Ygerna was a witch who had entranced Uther with magic charms which made them afraid of her, but in the larger cities it was said that she was a great lady, a queen in her own right, who was dignified as well as beautiful. She had ruled the people of Dumnonia wisely with Gorlois, and she would rule the people of Britannia well, tempering the impetuousness of her new husband.

All in all, most of the people seemed willing to give both Uther and Ygerna a fair chance to earn their regard.

Once in a while Calisca added stories of his own to the gossip, such as the Merlin's interpretation of the dragon that streaked across the sky, heralding the death of Ambrosius, or predicting the victories of Uther and Ambrosius against the Saxons. It never hurt, he thought, to have the people of Britannia ready to believe whatever the Merlin said.

89

BLAISE

From the winding streets of Aquae Sulis to the port of Deva in Gwynedd took the two a month. Still going north, now into Rheged, Merlin picked up the pace, using the better Roman road, but in the district of Galava which was south of Luguvallium, he turned west toward the sea, stopping just below the castle of Sir Ector in the village that footed the castle.

This was mountainous country, full of lakes and in the heart of a great forest which fringed the valley. The Lake by the castle was long and narrow, with sloping meadows around it which were dotted with cattle on the lower parts and sheep on the upper.

At first look it seemed completely peaceful and pastoral, but upon closer examination – upon which Merlin tested Lleon – the castle could only be approached from the water at one end of the valley or from easily defended mountain passes, so there had probably been trouble in the past.

Merlin pointed out the old Roman Fort on the pass that led to the sea. It had probably been in ruins not long ago, but with the refortification of Ambrosius, it was newly occupied.

They didn't stay long in the village – just two days. On both evenings Merlin tucked Lleon into bed at their room in the inn and went up to the castle. The first night he politely asked the steward to deliver a message to his master and handed him a sealed parchment. He also asked if a healer was needed by anyone in the castle. The steward was happy to oblige and would inquire on both counts. Courteously, he bade him wait on a bench in the hall.

In no time at all Sir Ector, himself, came back with the steward and invited the healer to join him in the study. He sent the steward for wine, and with a long rod stirred up the flames of the fireplace himself while they waited. When they were at last alone and it seemed they would not be disturbed, Sir Ector clasped his arm and pulled him close to the light. "Merlin?" he asked. "It is you, isn't it?"

"Indeed, but it would be wise to call me Calisca at the moment, since no one but you is to know who I am."

"Of course. I will respect your every wish ... Calisca." He said the name again, slowly savoring it on his tongue - "Calisca," then gave him a shrewd look and gestured him to a seat. "But why the secrecy? Are you on an errand for the king?"

"No. It's a private matter that not even the king is to know about, but this meeting is the reason for my travels."

Sir Ector leaned forward, pushing a lock of light brown hair out of his eyes. "Now you have me truly intrigued." His blue eyes danced, seemingly delighted to be part of a conspiracy.

Merlin leaned back in his chair. "Ambrosius told me you were a man to be trusted."

"I should hope so. When I was younger my father sent me to train with him, and when I returned I helped to train and recruit others to his cause." With pride he added, "I led a thousand men to meet him, and as you well know, we fought at his side and ousted the traitor Vortigern."

"I'm sorry we had so little time with Ambrosius."

"And I," he said quickly.

"I do know that your council was appreciated as much as your soldiers. He thought you a wise and solid leader, and a kind man as well."

Sir Ector beamed at the unbidden praise. "He was a great man. I'm glad they caught and hung the Saxon scum who murdered him." Merlin nodded. "What of Uther? Will he be a man as great as his brother?"

Merlin hesitated, then answered carefully. "He will try."

Sir Ector waited for him to go on, but Merlin stayed silent, and Ector seemed content with that. He supposed it wasn't his business, and was just as happy to stay out of the intricacies of the High King's court. Subtlety and nuance were not Ector's forte, according to the previous king. Honesty and simplicity suited him, and Merlin was pleased to see that he did not ask about the latest gossip and royal intrigues. "What can I do for you, Calisca?" he asked instead. "I'm truly at your service."

"First tell me about life here in Galava."

"It's pretty quiet. No one really consults us on the affairs of state – unless, of course, there's a war. Then we'll be asked for soldiers. I keep them training. You never can tell, and I keep them fresh by switching them around on the passes and up at the fort."

The wine glass spun in his hand slowly as he turned it, but he didn't drink from it. "Once in a while someone rides through, going west to Glannaventa on the sea, or north to Luguvallium, or some-times even east clear to York, but we're not a busy crossroads.

We keep horses and cattle, but mostly sheep, and it's the wool that's traded for what we can't grow. The soil is too rocky to produce many crops. We have just enough wheat to keep bread on our tables and enough barley for a decent ale. Oh, and there's fish. The lake provides a living for a fair number of fishermen. Once a year we have a fair here. That's how we sell most of our wool."

Merlin fingered his beard. "I met your wife once. In Londinium at the coronation, I believe. How is she?"

Ector beamed. "She's a terror. Rules this house like a captain in the cavalry, she does. If it isn't all polished and gleaming to suit her, or a meal not cooked just right, the servants get a piece of her tongue."

"From that tiny woman?" Merlin laughed.

"She may be little, but Drusilla keeps a big household running to do her bidding." He couldn't help the look of pride that leaped across his face. "And she's a happy woman now that we've finally mastered the art of having a baby." A flash of darkness. "We lost two, you know, but now we have a big, strapping boy who's already trying to run at only a year and a half."

"A runner?"

"Never wants to walk anywhere. Always wants to run." He smiled broadly, "And he's fast, Cei is."

"Cei. Is that after your father?"

"My father's father - Caius."

"It seems you have everything here to make you happy."

"It's true," Ector agreed. "I'm blessed by the gods."

"You have a bard here, as I recall. Young Dafyd?"

"With a voice like silver bells ringing sweet and pure. He's doing a wedding up in the hills and should be back in a day or two."

"I remember him and his beautiful voice. He's not a bad teacher either."

"True enough. Drusilla's fond of him for both those qualities, and for his diplomacy."

"I'm glad to hear it. Do I remember correctly that your wife came from a Christian household?"

"You do. We have a priest here as well as a bard. They are quite taken with each other and have formed a friendship."

"That's good to hear," Merlin told him. "On Ynys Witrin we consider the priests our friends too, but Britannia is also the unfortunate host of a new brand of priest – one who does not want to coexist with the Druids who were kind enough to welcome their forebears to our Isle. They speak against us, calling us witches and sorcerers."

Ector folded his long sinewy arms, rocking back and forth as he thought about it. Abruptly he was still again, giving Merlin an intent look. "What does their Pope have to say about these new priests?"

Merlin's lips stretched thin and straight. "He supports them. I'm afraid there will be trouble."

"Is he sending some new Germanicus to bother us again?"

"It could be worse. He's sending many of the new breed to convert the people."

There was total resolution and conviction in Ector's expression. "Well if any come near here, I'll send them packing. I can tell them we already have an excellent priest who serves the needs of all the Christians in our fair community." With a rude noise of exasperation he continued, "And in my own castle, I don't need one of them stirring up my wife."

Merlin nodded and finished his wine before he continued. "And now we come to it," he said, his eyes not leaving Ector's. "I have a request … actually, a very great favor to ask of you. In a few months I will come again, and this time I will bring a young woman and a baby with me. I would ask you and Drusilla to foster this child once he is weaned – to raise him as a young brother to your Cei.

"He will be with you until he is a young man ready to take his place in the larger world, and at some point I will return, myself, and perhaps be useful as a tutor to both boys. It is much to ask, but I also would have you speak of his true origin to no one." For emphasis, he repeated, "No one can know where the babe comes from. We can claim the woman is kin to you, so you fostering him would raise no questions."

Ector did not look away from Merlin. For a long moment both were silent, then he said, "I have three questions. First, you seem very sure that it will be a boy. How do you know that? Second, why don't you keep him at Ynys Witrin and school him there? Finally, why me?"

Merlin smiled. "I have the sight. You know that. I have seen that the child will be male, and I have no doubt that the vision is a true one. Second, Ynys Witrin would provide a limited education for this boy. He will need to know of things the school could not teach him.

"And, why you? There are many reasons. You will train him, along with Cei, to be a soldier, and when there is a need for advanced training, you will hire the best you can find. You will teach him Roman ways, Druid ways, and Christian ways, for he will have need of all three. But also, because you have a small community, he will learn how the common people think and what they need."

Merlin leaned back and crossed one leg over the other. "I'll not deny that the remoteness and isolation of Galava are also an important factor. I want to know that he's safe, and he will be safe here." And now Merlin leaned forward, his hand reaching to clasp that of Ector. "But most of all, Sir Ector, I chose you because you are a good man and will teach him to be a good man and to value other good men."

Ector's spare hand closed on top of Merlin's. "Thank you. I will …"

"No, promise nothing tonight," Merlin told him, rising to leave. "Discuss this with Drusilla. I will come tomorrow night for your answer."

"You will come for supper as well."

Merlin declined graciously. "I think not. I'd just as soon no one in your service wonder why I looked familiar and where they had seen me before. But since the shoulder injury you took at Doward has been acting up, I'd be happy to see what I could do to ease the pain."

"Oh? Oh, I see. Yes, it's been giving me a bit of trouble lately. After supper then?"

90

BLAISE

When Merlin arrived at the castle the next night he was welcomed by the Steward and shown immediately into the Sir Ector's study. A few minutes later Sir Ector arrived, stretching and flexing his shoulder before Calisca and complaining of pain for the benefit of the servant who was bringing a tray with wine and glasses. Before the man had set the tray down on a table by the fireplace Drusilla arrived, commenting that she wanted to make sure that Ector listened to the good healer's advice and followed it.

When they were finally alone, she gave Merlin a quick hug. "It's good to see you again. We're more than honored by your trust in us, and we are extremely happy to oblige."

Sir Ector laughed. "She couldn't wait to tell you."

"I can't wait to fill this house with children," she exclaimed. She glanced shyly at her husband, "Perhaps, by the time you arrive again, we'll have another one on the way."

"Go on, Dearheart. Tell him the rest," Ector said.

"I have family in Gwynedd. The girl should be from there, and sad from the loss of her husband in a fishing accident. She's welcome to stay as long as she wants, but if and when she decides to leave, we'll have a convenient letter from her father, saying he's arranged another marriage for her." She positively twinkled with happiness. "I frequently receive letters from them, so it will be readily believed. Oh, and her name should be Caitllyn. That way I can mention the terrible loss of her husband after the next letter."

"I can see you've thought of everything," Merlin told her. "Caitllyn it shall be."

Merlin wanted to leave quickly, but when he exited the room, the Steward was waiting. "There are several people who would like your help, Sir Calisca. I have them waiting just down the hall, and a room for you to work in."

There was a stable hand whose badly bruised foot had been stepped on by a horse, a soldier who had broken a wrist while training with the sword, a cook who had a nasty burn on her forearm from soup that had bubbled and spat from the pot, a maid who had fallen on a stone stairway just after she mopped it and had gashed her cheek, and the Steward's own wife with their baby girl who had a fever. Thus, it was a good two hours before Merlin could make his way back to the inn.

He was anxious to leave now that his affairs were settled, but had to choke back his impatience. He was also amused that his own offer to help and his own guise as a healer were now serving to thwart his desire.

He did have Lleon up and saddling the horses as the sun rose the next morning. They rode north to Luguvallium, though Merlin really wanted to be riding south. He forced himself to spend two days there, showing the boy four new medical procedures.

He didn't want him to suspect that their mission had been accomplished in Galava. He wanted nothing to point to Galava as important. If anyone ever investigated their journey, Galava should seem no more important than any of the other places they had visited.

They went south via a different route – one that took them through Verterae and Lake Fort. A little south of Lake Fort they ran into their first really bad weather. This too was part of the learning experience for Lleon, and Merlin pushed them on through a driving rain that was as cold as it was wet, but when the wind picked up, making it even colder and more miserable, he found them shelter in a farmhouse.

The next morning. they journeyed on. Though the wind had died down, it was still raining and it was still cold. "Let's push the horses," Merlin told him. "I think we may be in for an early winter, and I don't relish being away from Ynys Witrin when it comes."

Three more long days of riding under sultry grey skies that kept their moisture but constantly threatened put them within sight of the Tor and they were both grateful to be near home.

They camped in the forest on both nights and the rain caught up with them again. Merlin rigged a tent from a spare cloak and the branches of the trees, which kept them fairly dry the first night, but on the second this did no good at all, for the wind whipped up and blew the rain in sideways.

They huddled together under their hooded cloaks until the sun came up, led their horses back to the old Roman road as soon as it was light enough to see, and swung up onto their saddles.

The horses looked as wet and bedraggled as they did. Merlin eased the horse into the marshes, hoping the causeway hadn't been obliterated by the rain. It was hard to see and definitely not a good place to get lost.

Then he realized that the horse had picked up the pace a bit. It knew the path better than he did, and knew that it led to the stable. He rested the reins and gave the horse its head. "Not long now," he called over his shoulder to encourage Lleon.

The boy gave him a huge smile that seemed to fill the entire face of the hood. "I know!"

Merlin smiled back, and knew exactly what the boy was thinking. A hot meal, a long soak in a hot bath, and his own bed piled high with furs would be welcome, indeed.

91

BLAISE

Merlin took several days to rest and to catch up on his work as High Druid Priest, then he sent for Ralf who had been serving with the regiment at Caerleon. "I'm sending you right back," he told him after giving him a hearty meal and hearing the news that all was quiet in the City of Legions. "Find uniforms for us with the colors of Gwynedd. We'll be soldiers, performing escort duty soon. We'll also need horses suitable for soldiers, including two pack horses, and another to pull a litter."

"Consider it done," Ralf answered cheerfully. "Then right back here?"

"Yes. Then on to Londinium sometime after Christmas."

The one thing he worried about was finding a wet nurse for the baby. Such women were to be had, he knew, in Londinium, but how to find one available at just the right time, how to find one willing to not only travel, but to stay in Galava for a year or more, and, most of all, how to find one who would keep his secrets was puzzling.

He didn't have much experience with women, but he did know that they didn't have the same expectations or the same desires that men had. What would make a woman happy? What would make her give up the life she knew and the friends she'd made and the ties with her own family?

Would a purse full of gold coins be enough? Would it buy her silence as well? His mother could have advised him, but his mother was dead.

After agonizing over it for several days he decided to consult the only woman he had ever really talked to besides his mother. He wasn't sure that Vivianne could really offer much in the way of counsel. Her world was far different from that of a Londinium wet nurse, but she did understand women, and … he finally admitted to himself … it would be a good excuse to see her again.

Merlin could have taken the hidden trail that led to the Isle of Avalon, but it was simpler to take a boat. Except for assorted hills and the Tor, which was so high it served as a beacon on the Severn Sea, the terrain consisted of a swampy wetland, occasionally dry, but usually flooded.

The three main islands were connected with narrow bands of land, sometimes visible under shallow water. One had to know these submerged trails well to use them. What looked like solid footing often turned into mud or bog, and was so confusing that getting lost was more common than finding the way.

Those small, dark people who were native to the area used flat boats, not much sturdier than a raft, which they stood in and propelled forward with a long pole. To compound the problem on both land and water the low areas were generally so foggy that it was difficult to see where you were going.

Merlin walked to the shoreline and looked out over the water. The fog was so solid this time of year that there was nothing to be seen. Lifting both arms high he said the words he been taught to summon the boat and waited.

The boat came silently out of the mist. He climbed in and sat. Just as silently, it left the shore and suddenly he was engulfed in a damp fog so thick that he couldn't even see the boatman standing in front of him. It was as if a world of grey and silence had opened to swallow him.

The journey was endless. It was quick. He didn't know which, but he was thankful, as always when the mist parted, showing him a world of water and sun and so many green apple trees on the shore that he was barely conscious of the Tor rising behind them.

He drew in a breath when he saw her waiting, and let it out slowly, noticing that both her long black hair and her blue cloak billowed out behind her in the wind. Of course, she had known he was coming and was waiting for him. Vivianne always knew.

When he had clambered out of the boat with thanks to the boatsman, she put an arm on his and walked him toward the small house she lived in, which was separate from the dormitories of the other women. Gracefully she gestured him to a seat by the fire and handed him a glass. "It's apple wine," she said, smiling.

"And you won't join me," he said, pulling her down to a seat opposite his. "You only drink water from the holy well."

She laughed easily, and he could not help but think how pleasant it would be to stay here with her and forget the troubles of the world outside the mists. "You are welcome to stay as long as you wish," she said, reading his mind – a habit she had that had quite disconcerted him when he had first met her.

"Have you seen that I will do this?" he asked, knowing he sounded hopeful.

"No. The pool of visions has shown me that you were away and that you will go away again. Soon."

"Too soon," he said, leaning forward to clasp her hand.

Her breath caught as she spoke. "Simple pleasures are not for you, Merlin. Nor for me."

She caressed his hand, then put it gently in his lap and leaned back. "Tell me," she said. "Tell me everything."

He told her all of it, watching the changing light of the fire make shadows and erase them from her face and thinking how beautiful she was. He ended with his concerns about finding a wet nurse. "Will you advise me on how I should go about it?" he asked.

Her bright laughter filled the room. "I'll do more than that, Merlin. I'll solve the problem for you." She rang a little bell on the table and a priestess appeared, bowing her head as she entered. "Will you bring Anna to us?" she asked. The priestess bowed once more and left silently.

"Now, have you never noticed that we have children here and a school for them?"

He merely looked puzzled.

"Most are children born of Beltane rites, Merlin. Loved, no cherished would be a better word, and they all start as babies. Not all of the priestesses are inclined toward motherhood, but those who are help tend them, and some of them are, indeed, wet nurses – for years if they wish it.

"The one I have sent for – Anna – is from Segontium. I think she'll do nicely if you like her. Payment isn't necessary, of course, and discretion is part of the training of a priestess. Ah, and here she is," she added, looking at the door.

Anna was tall for a woman, and very blonde though the hood on her cloak nearly hid the hair. She was almost pretty, especially when she smiled which she did after bowing her head and looking up. Merlin was pleased. She had the height and coloring to match a child that Uther and Ygerna would produce.

"This is the Merlin, Anna. Please answer any questions he might have," Vivianne said.

"Hello, Anna. I'm pleased to make your acquaintance," he said. "Please join us." He stood and pulled a chair over to the fire for her."

"I'm honored, Sire. I'm pleased to answer whatever you wish to know," she said formally. There was a nice manner about her – an easiness and confidence where another young woman might be tongue-tied.

"Tell me about your background, and about Gwynedd," he said.

"My grandfather was a Roman soldier, awarded land for his service on the outskirts of Segontium. My grandmother was a local girl who became his wife while he was still a soldier."

Good, thought Merlin. She has Roman heritage and she's actually from Gwynedd as Caitlyn is supposed to be.

"The land was split between my father and his brother when Grandfather died. My parents had twelve children, all healthy and living, thank the Goddess. I'm the ninth and last of their daughters." She smiled a smile of self-deprecation.

"I think they were quite relieved when I chose to come to Avalon for training. It was a hard job to provide dowries for my sisters and I relieved them of that chore." She shrugged her shoulders.

"I was fifteen when I came here six years ago. I haven't been back to Gwynedd since I left it, but I remember the land I traveled through. We went southeast through the mountains to Viriconium, then picked up the Roman road and came south to the isle."

She frowned in thought, but her hands were still and she seemed at ease. "I can tell you nothing about the local politics. The king was old when I left and died shortly after. His eldest son claimed his throne and there was no dispute. You probably know all that. I can say that the people were happy enough under the old king, but I can't tell you if his son earns the same loyalty. Is there anything else I can tell you?"

"You've answered me well," he said, "and I thank you." He nodded to Vivianne.

"Anna, there are many ways that we serve the Goddess," Vivianne said. "Sometimes it's necessary to take on a task that temporarily takes you away from Avalon. We have just such a task for you."

92

BLAISE

It was February when Ralf, Anna, and Merlin left for Londinium, and it was bitterly cold. At first, in deference to Anna, Merlin stopped to warm up at every inn they passed, or sometimes built a fire to thaw out fingers and toes, but this inconstant pace made him impatient, and Anna could see it, so she pressed him to continue. "Wouldn't it be better to keep going? We'd get there that much faster."

"It would do us no good to lose a finger," he snapped.

"I promise to let you know if that is imminent," she retorted, "and you did say the fewer people to mark our existence on the road, the better."

Merlin saw Ralf trying to hide a smile and understood she spoke what all three knew as truth. He regarded them both with silence, fingering the swooping dark mustache he had grown for the occasion, then drew himself tall and straight like the soldier he was pretending to be. "I apologize for my foul mood, Lady Caitlyn. We shall make haste."

When they finally arrived in Londinium two days later, the late-night sky was dark with clouds and the gate was closed and barred just after they went through it. Merlin took them to an inn not far from the gate where he settled them with rooms and food and charged Ralf with Anna's safety. "It won't be long now," he told him.

"Where are you off to?" Ralf asked, seeing that he was heavily cloaked again.

"I'm going to make sure that the king remembers his bargain with me."

Ralf gave him a level look, his head cocked at a slight angle of amusement. "It's not the king I'd be worried about - it's the queen."

"True enough. I may have to convince her myself."

Ralf had been right. "No!? She flung herself awkwardly to her feet, put a chair between them, and hugged her bulging belly protectively.

"It's not an unkind thing I do, Ygerna. There are enemies … look what happened to Ambrosius with all his soldiers around him. Babies get sick and die frequently, and who's to say if it was poison? A young boy can meet with numerous sorts of accident."

There were tears running down her face now, and she made a sound like a wounded animal, clutching the chair to keep from shaking.

"He'll be safe with me. Safe to grow and learn to be a king."

Uther was at her side now, supporting her with both arms. Unexpectedly, he came to Merlin's aid. "There will be other children, My Love - children who won't be questioned as illegitimate or as the spawn of Gorlois."

"You too?" she asked, turning to face him with tears of frustration.

"Ygerna," he pleaded. "I gave my word. Please tell me you understand."

Her shoulders straightened. "No, I don't understand, but I will believe you if you say it's for the best. You are my life – my love – my dream who stands real before me."

She turned slowly to Merlin, blinking back tears. "On the day of the birth, wait at the postern gate. My woman – Barla, who's been with me since I was a child and can be trusted – will bring him to you at midnight." Then she went into Uther's arms, and Merlin saw that she was sobbing.

The very next morning the inn was buzzing with the news that the queen was in labor. Ralf leaned across the breakfast table so that his face was just inches from Merlin's. "How did you do that?"

"Friend, I did nothing," Merlin assured him.

"It's the Goddess," Anna told them, whispering. "It's the Mother of us all who brings forth life." Realizing that this might not be a good place to give Ralf a lesson on religion, she shut her mouth firmly and pulled at the hair she had styled to cover the mark of a priestess on her forehead. It was a small blue tattoo, a crescent moon, which was the symbol of the Goddess.

Ralf persisted. "Well, if you didn't actually do something that would start the Queen's travail, how did you know to bring us here on this exact day?"

"Actually, we're a day late. I wanted to give us a day of rest, but now we'll have to run around Londinium, replenishing our supplies, while you go find us a suitable litter."

"If we could rig a harness to hold the babe firmly to my chest, I could ride a horse," Anna said softly. "It would be faster."

"That's a good idea. The two of us will work on it," Merlin answered, "but I still want Ralf to find a litter. We can break it down and rope it to one of the supply horses until we need it, but when you enter your new home, I want it to be in style, with us before and behind as a proper guard should be."

Ralf was looking back and forth between them, arms crossed, eyes narrowed. He had grown his hair much longer than it had ever been before. It was pulled back and held into a long tail by a thin scrap of leather, and he too had grown a mustache which was a popular fashion in Gwynedd. "I'd still like an answer to my question before we set off. How did you know that today would be the day?"

Merlin knew that no matter how confident he looked at asking such a question, he was still in awe of his master, and Merlin wanted to keep it that way. "I saw when to come, of course." He looked toward Anna. "And the Lady of the Lake confirmed it."

By supper, when they were gathered together again and discussing the success of their forays to the marketplace, bells rang to announce the birth, and a bit later a crier came by, calling that the kingdom had a prince.

There were cheers in the inn's common room and cheers outside on the street too, and the inn keeper gave a free round of ale in the prince's honor. The three celebrated with equal fervor to the others at board, but just when many were climbing the stairs to their beds, Merlin settled the bill and had their horses saddled and brought round.

He knew it was a strange time to be leaving an inn, but did not satisfy the curiosity of the inn keeper, other than to mutter that they had meant to leave much earlier, and would have to ride half the night now.

They rode across the city, skirting one of the walls that Merlin had helped build when they came near Tower Castle, and out the North Gate, which was the one closest to the castle. They kept riding until they reached the forest, then cut into it on a logging trail that Merlin knew of, doubling back toward the castle.

When they were near, they stopped to rest, and built a small fire. Luckily, the moon was full to aid them and the weather had shifted. It was still cold, but not bitterly so, and the next day they would hear birds announcing the coming of spring, though the land would have a few more draughts of freezing before it would burst into the cycle of new life, and there would be frequent rain, for rain was never far from falling in Britannia.

Near midnight Merlin left them, and made his way carefully on foot to the postern gate. There were guards on the wall which in this location was part of the castle, and he paced his dash to the shadowed gate when no one was looking his way. Carefully he climbed an outside staircase until he reached a locked door on the third-floor landing.

Once there he spent the longest half hour of his life. Barla was late.

There was a sudden scraping sound just above his head and Merlin shrank into the shadowed shelter of the wall, such that it was, and held very still, holding his breath and trying to slow the rapid beating of his heart.

A dim light spilled out. Merlin heard more sounds and identified them as the folding and latching of a window's shutters. The light went out – a candle, he thought. He began to breathe again, but remained perfectly still and waited, counting the seconds, adding them up to minutes.

He had just decided that the occupant of the room above had crawled into bed when the occupant spoke. He flinched. He couldn't help it. But then he realized it was a child's voice, so soft it was nearly a whisper.

Slowly he turned his head and looked up into Morgana's eyes. "Have you come for my brother?" she repeated.

Merlin considered lying to her. That would be the smart thing to do, and what he might do if it had been a different child, but he realized he wouldn't – couldn't – lie to her. "Yes," he replied, matching her quiet tone, "but it's supposed to be a secret. How did you know?"

She considered her answer carefully. "I saw it."

He understood what she meant and suppressed a shiver. "You have the sight?"

"That's what my mother calls it."

He nodded. "You can't tell anyone. If you do, it could cost your brother his life."

Her eyes grew very big as she realized the importance of his words. "I will keep the secret. I promise." She paused, regarding him with an expression he could read only as longing. "Will you do something for me?"

"In return for secrecy?" he asked.

She shook her head. "No. I'll keep the secret even if you won't grant my wish."

He liked this child. "What is your wish?"

"Will you take me with you? I would like to learn from you, and I could help you with the baby."

The request took Merlin by surprise. He knew he couldn't do it, but he pondered as if considering it. "I can't do that," he finally said. "It's because of your mother. It has hurt her very much to give up the babe. Imagine her feelings, if she were to lose you too."

Her expression changed from hopeful to sad, and Merlin quickly added, "But I have seen that there is a place you will take in a few years." He paused, surprised at the vision, savoring it and knowing that it was a true vision.

"You don't belong in a royal court, Morgana. You belong in a school that will train you as a priestess, and your role in Britannia will be even more important than a queen's. I will see that this happens, you need only wait a while. I promise," he added.

There was no time to hear her response, for Barla had finally come, and he was infinitely grateful when he heard the lock turn and saw it pushed to a narrow opening. He recognized her - he had seen her at Tintagel – and she recognized him, making a small gasping noise when she saw him emerge from the shadows.

There were tears running down her face and she moved as the very old do, slowly and carefully, knowing her bundle was precious. There were no words between them until she had seen the bundle transferred safely to his arms, then she whispered threateningly, "See that you care for him proper, Sir Merlin of Ambrosius. See that you care for him proper."

"With my very life, Grandmother," he swore. Looking up to see that no guard was watching, he concealed the babe under his cloak and darted down the stairs and across the field to the relative safety of the tree line.

There he turned back to look at the castle and to readjust his tiny bundle. It certainly would not do to smother the child.

Two guards on the roof were discussing something and he stayed long enough to see them part, knowing that had he been the subject of discussion an alarm would have been raised.

His eyes were drawn to the corner room that was shared by the king and queen. Candles were burning brightly there, and he wondered whether they would need to produce a dead infant and how they would announce the death. Though he did not trust Uther in personal matters, he did trust Uther to take care of those details. It was not his problem and he wouldn't worry about it.

He looked at the window where Morgana still stood, her white shift visible against the darkness. No, there was no betrayal there. She would keep the secret as promised.

That was when it occurred to him that Barla had called him Merlin of Ambrosius. Did she know his secret? A moment of panic overtook him until the reasoning part of his mind came to the conclusion that she meant Merlin who had served Ambrosius. Yes, that made sense.

Finally, he turned to the forest and let his eyes adjust to the darkness of the trees before he took a few steps. There was a hiccough from the babe, and then another.

Alarmed that crying might follow, he moved swiftly, one hand patting and supporting the baby while the other swept branches away. He was thankful when he saw the fire ahead and whistled softly to alert them.

Moments later the child was nestled into the carrying cradle they had rigged, and snuggled against the warm breasts of the midwife. They mounted and Merlin led the way, looking carefully for obstacles on the trail, with Anna immediately behind him. Ralf followed, leading the three packhorses.

They were all relieved to reach the road and for two hours rode swiftly to put distance behind them.

The baby's cries stopped them finally. Merlin judged them far enough from Londinium to camp at a short distance from the road in a convenient clearing. He built a fire while Ralf tended to the horses and Anna tended to the babe and they settled comfortably for a short sleep before dawn.

Merlin was the first to wake the next morning. He nudged Anna and took the baby from her outstretched arms. While she set out a simple meal and while Ralf, who leaped to his feet, knife in hand until he judged them safe, saddled and packed the horses.

Merlin heard the sound of water and walked toward it. Moving slowly, so as not to disturb the child, he walked along beside the stream, following it upstream, not down where he knew it would join the River Thames.

He considered the small bundle in his arms, wondering at the light weight and the helplessness that would someday grow into a man, straight and tall.

The land rose gradually, tempting him toward the sun, so he left the stream to climb to the top of a hillside. At the crest he watched the sun rise. He felt the baby stir and unwrapped him slightly, freeing a tiny hand.

He was quite startled when the boy latched onto one of his long fingers and clung, and he laughed out loud at himself, enjoying the surge of life from this small creature. The baby opened his eyes, which were very blue in the sunlight and regarded him sleepily. Slowly he lifted the child high.

"Do you see, Arthur? This is your land, and when you are a man you will rule it." His voice changed, taking on the tones of High

Priest. "You are the land, and the land is you, and you are blessed by the one god that is all gods. You are Arthur, Child - Arthur who will be a legend among kings and a bridge between old ways and new. In you runs the blood of Roman Emperors and Celtic Kings. You will lead your people with the courage of a soldier, with the wisdom of a sage, and with the love of a father."

As if he understood, the babe gave one lusty cry.

Merlin held him out to look him over, then settled him against his shoulder. "Arthur," he said again, patting gently. "You will be king above all kings. You are Arthur."

Robyn Lamm

ACKNOWLEDGMENTS

I would like to thank my two readers, Kendra Stevens and Jill Brinkerhoff. Their comments were invaluable in producing a final version of the book.

Josh Arklin contributed the wonderful cover illustration, working diligently through many revisions.

I also want to thank Anna Hayes for her advice on publishing and marketing.

The book would have had a much less finished look without the work of my husband, David Lamm. His frequent questions on form and polish were appreciated, and I can't thank him enough.

Finally, I want to thank the countless other people that contributed support and understanding during the time it took to prepare this manuscript. I appreciate each and every one.

A NOTE FROM THE AUTHOR

The slaughter of the Druids happened around 63CE at the order of Paulinus, the Roman Commander of Britannia, but Gwion, Gwydion and their story was from my imagination, though there was an ogham alphabet, finger spelling, and secret training of Druids.

Boudicca and her daughters lived during Nero's reign.

Joseph of Arimathea was real, but no one has definitively proved that he came to England.

Pelagius and Germanicus were adversaries, and the former was executed in 420CE by the Pope.

The Romans did leave Britannia in 410CE. Through the four centuries of occupation many of their soldiers retired in Britannia and many had native wives and children. When the Legions left, some of those with wives and families deserted and stayed. There were also desertions from those who felt that Britannia was their home, for they had known no other. In the areas that the Romans had occupied, the people considered themselves Roman (all men in Britannia were given Roman citizenship), and followed Roman ways. They felt betrayed, because they, too, were being threatened by invaders.

Those who were not near to Roman settlements retained the Celtic traditions, living in completely autonomous tribes where the leader was the strongest and best in battle, and the battles with each other were frequent. There is evidence that in the late fifth century all banded together (a first for the tribes) to fight the incursion of invaders from Northern Europe. For one hundred years they held off the invaders, which is one of the proofs that one or more strong leaders existed during that time period. It could have been Ambrosius, Uther, and Arthur. If not them, where are the tales of other leaders?

All of the places in these books were real, with the possible exception of Camelot which I will place in Cadbury due in part to excavations that prove that a hillfort existed there during the correct time period, and Avalon which has been claimed in various parts of Great Britain and even in parts of France. I have chosen Glastonbury as its location for many reasons including tradition.

I have set my books in the late fifth century to the early sixth, because this is the time period that seems to fit best in the scholarly argument.

There is evidence for the actual existence of Constantine III and his two oldest murdered sons, and for Vortigern, and the Saxons Hengist, Horsa, Eosa, and Octa.

Ambrosius Aurelianus lived, but he may not have been a son of Constantine III, and may not have been king.

Taliesin was a real person, and a handful of Merlins from several different centuries were too. To reconcile the various Merlins, I chose to use the word as a title, which I cannot claim as an original idea.

The other main characters (with the exception of Lancelot who was invented in the 14th century and comes into the story in my next book) are mentioned in many early sources, but not historically verified.

Part of this confusion as to reality comes because separating the categories of fact and fiction is a relatively new idea, so early writers often combined wildly imaginative adventures, tales of ancient ancestors who were endowed with godly characteristics, and actual history. There are also many texts of the time period that have never been translated from Welsh for the simple reason that not many Arthurian scholars speak Welsh.

When I began my research into The Matter of Britain (imagine my surprise at discovering you must look under that title, and not Arthur or Arthurian), I wondered whether Arthur and his Knights, Guinevere, Lancelot, Gawayne, Morgan, Merlin and the other main characters were real people, but after reading many arguments on both sides, I came to believe that their actual existence was unimportant.

What did seem important was the fact that this was a story that has been told and retold for over fifteen hundred years. I wanted to discover why this was true. What is it about Arthurian literature that makes it relevant century after century?

I found that many authors have changed the story, adapting it to interests of their current readers. There are books featuring battles with detailed descriptions of fighting gear and the prowess of each knight, books featuring the romance and tragedy, books with magic, books with none, books with humor, and books told from viewpoints of the different characters. These changes have made The Matter of Britain come alive for each generation.

There is also a subconscious impact in many aspects of the story, and this is, perhaps an important concept to grasp. Sometimes it's ancient poetry singing truth that strikes at the emotions, truly moving the reader. Sometimes it's the pull of sacred centers tying the earth to the spirit world. There are rites of manhood, sometimes tied to the spiritual conquest of the grail, as well as ancient rites where the king becomes so woven with the land that if he becomes sick or wounded, the land, itself, follows suit becoming a wasteland. The social upheaval of patriarchy (Roman) versus the older matriarchy (Celt) underlies a changing social structure, and the new religion (Christianity) fights for supremacy over the old (Druid).

Madness, both when soldiers go battle mad and can't control their actions, and from the insanity that self-destructs some of the characters, fights the more enlightened calm of reason. The search for the Holy Grail (which will be in my third book of this series) becomes a trial for each searcher to pass from unenlightened to enlightened.

The perfection of Arthur and his Realm, which used might for right, which protected his people from harm for many years of peace and harmony and which became the model for kings in all countries that knew the stories, is, in the end, destroyed from within. If the reader hasn't been dragged into the emotional conflict of the three who love each other, this ending of Camelot will surely move him or her, perhaps causing reflection upon the frailty of perfection. There are so many wonderful adventures, conflicts and characters from The Matter of Britain that we will always appreciate new stories about Arthur and his Realm.

I hope you will look for my next book, <u>The Making of a King.</u> It continues the story of Merlin, describing his adventures before and during his tutoring of the young Arthur, until the boy is ready to take his place as High King under the Red Dragon Banner.

MODERN IDENTITY OF PLACES

Abred – The real world – as opposed to the spiritual.

Albion – The island of Great Britain.

Annwn - The Otherworld, the realm of deities and possibly the dead.

Aquae Sulis – Bath.

Avalon – Glastonbury. During this time, it was an island in a marshy sea. The swamps were drained for farming in the 17th Century with the help of Dutch engineers.

Britannia – Roman England.

Brittany – Lesser Britain in northwestern Gaul (France).

Caerleon – A fortress in southeastern Wales, near Cardiff and the coast of the Bristol Channel.

Caledonia – Scotland.

Cambria – Wales.

Camulodonum – Colchester.

Carnates – Chartres in France. Headquarters of the Druids.

Dementia – In Southern Wales.

Deva – Chester.

Dimiliac – One of Gorlois' two castles in Dumnonia.

Dinas Bran – Vortigern's castle in Northern Wales.

Doward – A fort in North Wales where Vortigern made his last stand.

Dumnonia – Northern Cornwall.

Dyfed – Central Wales.

Galava – Ector's kingdom, Southwest of Hadrian's Wall, where Arthur is raised.

Gaul – France.

Giant's Dance – Stonehenge.

Glennaventa – Town on the Irish Sea, west of Galava.

Gwynedd – In northern Wales.

Hadrian's Wall – The Emperor Hadrian built this wall, complete with fortified watchtowers, across the island, dividing Scotland with its unruly Picts and more civilized and Romanized England.

Hibernia – Ireland.

Holyhead – A sacred island west of Ynys Mon (Anglesey).

Island of the Mighty – Great Britain.

Lake Fort – In Southern Rheged.

Lesser Britain – Brittany.

Logres – England.

Londinium – London.

Luguvallium – Carlisle.

Maridinum – Carmarthen – A town in Southern Wales where Emrys was born.

Menai Strait – the strait between Ynys Mon and the mainland.

Northumbria – In Northern England.

Ostia – Rome's port city on the mouth of the Tiber River.

Powys – In Northern Wales.

Rheged – East of Galava in England.

Segontium – A fort on the mainland near Caernarfon and Ynys Mon.

Severn Sea – The Bristol Channel.

Tintagel – A castle/fortress on the west coast of Cornwall owned by Gorlois.

Tor – A flat-topped mountain in Avalon/Glastonbury. It is so tall that it is visible from the sea. Sailors used it to navigate.

Verulanium – A city Southwest of St. Albans.

Viroconium – A Roman city in Powys, near Wroxeter.

Wroxeter – A city Southeast of Shrewsbury.

Ynys Mon – Anglesey, an island off the northwest coast of Wales where the Druids were massacred by the Romans.

Ynys Witrin – Isle of Glass. In Arthurian times the area around Glastonbury was a marsh which ran clear to Bridgewater Bay on the sea. There were islands in this marsh, including Ynys Witrin, Dragon and Avalon.

GUIDE TO CELTIC PRONUNCIATION

a – Usually 'ah'.

Final e – sounded 'uh', as in Vivianne (vih vee ah nuh).

I - 'ee' or 'ih'.

ae, ai – 'I' as in tight.

ao – 'ay' as in day.

c – always 'k', never 's'.

caer – car

ch, kh – always 'k', as in chord, never like child.

dd – "th" as in then.

g – as in garden, never as in ginger.

ll – close to 'kl' sound, but softer with one's tongue touching the teeth.

Nimue – (nihm oo ay)

Sidhe – shee

w – 'oo'

OTHER HELPFUL TERMS

Ap – Son of.

Battle of Godeu – Battle of the Trees fought between the gods Bran and Gwydion.

Beltane – Druid celebration of Spring.

Caer – Castle. Often combined with the place name where it is located.

Cor – The heart or center of a place.

Cymbrogi – Celts.

Fianna Eirinn or Fenians – Irish warriors of unmatched skills.

Night of the Long Knives – When Hengist betrayed Vortigern, slaughtering all of his men.

Ogham - Druid alphabet of 20 letters, each named for a tree.

Penbard – Chief Bard.

Pendragon – Battle Chief.

Saxons – Invaders from Germany. There were other invaders, such as Angles and Jutes, but for the sake of simplicity, the term "Saxon" is used to represent all of them.

Sidhe – The Fair Ones / Fairies.

Triad – A teaching verse consisting of a question with three answers.

CHARACTERS

Ambrosius Aurelianus – High King of Britannia who defeats
Vortigern and the Saxons. Father of Merlin with Ninianne. Son of
Roman Emperor Constantine III who was murdered.

Anna – (1) First wife of Gorlois, mother of Cador, older sister of
Ygerna. (2) A Druid priestess, wetnurse to Arthur, alias Caitlyn.
(3) Merlin's mother becomes Sister Anna as a Nunn.

Ariandell – A faerie.

Arianrhod – the god, Gwydion's sister. Later one aspect of the
goddess. Souls go to her castle, waiting to be reborn.

Arthur – High King of Logres (Britannia) after Uther. Son of Uther
and Ygerna.

Bertrano – Second Druid priest to the Merlin. Lives in Carnates in
Gaul.

Blaise – A Druid historian and Head Master of a school on Ynys
Witrin who taught Merlin.

Boudicca – A Celtic queen who led a rebellion against the Romans
during Emperor Nero's reign.

Bran – Legendary High King of the Island of the Mighty (Great
Britain).

Brigid – Llew's Sister.

Cador – Son of Gorlois and his first wife, Anna.

Caeron – Colim's wife.

Caitlyn – Alias of the priestess, Anna.

Calisca – A name Merlin used when traveling incognito.

Catas Decianus – Roman commander who had Queen Boudicca
whipped and her daughters raped

Cei – Son of Ector and Drusilla. Arthur's foster brother.

Ceridwen – One aspect of the goddess.

Colim – Llew's older brother.

Dafyd – A Druid and teacher in Ector's court.

Dierdra – The Lady of the Lake during Gwydion's life.

Dinacat – Ider's bard.

Drusilla – Wife of Sir Ector.

Dubricious – Archbishop of Canterbury.

Ector – Ruler of Galava, husband of Drusilla, father of Cei. Foster father of Arthur.

Emrys – Becomes the Merlin.

Eosa – A Saxon Leader.

Gerd – Master Singer who trained Merlin and served Gorlois.

Germanicus – Sent by the Pope to debate Pelagius.

Gorlois – Ygerna's first husband, father of Cador with Anna, his first wife, father of Morgausa and Morgana with Ygerna. King of Dumnonia.

Gwion – The sole survivor of the Druid massacre in 63 CE.

Gwydion – (1) Gwion's successor. (2) A Hero God – Pre-Druid.

Hengist – The Saxon leader rewarded with land in southern England by Vortigern for aiding a battle with the Irish and the Picts. He betrays Vortigern and opens the country to many more invaders who fight the native Celts for several hundred years.

Horsa – Hengist's brother.

Ider – Leader of Dumnovii during time of Gwydion.

Joseph of Arimathea – The follower of Christ who provided his tomb. He settled in Ynys Witrin and built the first Christian church in Great Britain.

Jostyn – The Druid who accompanies Emrys on a visit to his mother and who saves him when he is kidnapped by Vortigern's men.

Lleon – Apprentice to Merlin, training to be a Druid.

Llew – Son of Llewellen during the time of Gwydion. He's called the Path Finder.

Llewellen – Fisherman during the time of Gwydion.

Maelgwyn – King of Dementia, Merlin's grandfather and father of Ninianne.

Mariana – Cador's wife.

Merlin (the title given to the Archdruid) – Emrys.

Morgana – Daughter of Gorlois and Ygerna, half-sister of Arthur.

Morgausa – Daughter of Gorlois and Ygerna, half-sister of Arthur, wife of King Lot.

Neldda – Llew's mother.

Ninianne – Merlin's mother, daughter of King Maelgwn of Dementia, Sister Anna as a Nunn.

Nudd – King of the Faeries.

Octa – Saxon leader.

Paulinus – Roman Commander who slaughtered Druids in Ynys Mon in 63 CE.

Pelagius – Christian leader in Britannia who denied the Roman Catholic doctrine of original sin and taught freedom of will. Recalled to Rome, he was put to death by the Pope in 420 CE.

Ralf – Merlin's squire and friend, protector of Arthur, Master of Stables for Sir Ector.

Rob mac Tave – Fenian and sailor during time of Gwydion.

Timoreas – Master Builder for Ambrosius.

Ulfin – Uther's squire.

Uther – High King after his brother Ambrosius. Husband of Ygerna, father of Arthur, son of Roman Emperor Constantine III who was murdered by Vortigern.

Vivianne – The Lady of the Lake (title of the Druid High Priestess).

Vortigern – the Usurper King of Britannia. After the Romans left he murdered Constantine III and was defeated by Ambrosius and Uther. He was responsible for the Saxon invasion.

Ygerna – High Queen. Mother of Morgausa and Morgana with first husband, Gorlois. Mother of Arthur with second husband, Uther.